Friends Don't Kiss

A Small Town, Friends-To-Lovers Romance

BELLA RIVERS

v4

ebook: 978-1-962627-10-8
print couple cover: 978-1-962627-11-5
print discreet cover: 978-1-962627-12-2

Developmental editing: Angela James

Copyediting: Aimee Walker Editorial

Proofreading: Teresa Beeman, Next Chapter Editing

Cover: Echo Grayce, Wildheart Graphics

Contents

1. Kiara   1

2. Colton   13

3. Kiara   25

4. Kiara   30

5. Colton   34

6. Kiara   46

7. Colton   58

8. Kiara   62

9. Kiara   67

10. Colton   74

11. Kiara   84

12. Colton   93

13. Kiara   101

14. Colton   118

15.	Kiara	124
16.	Colton	129
17.	Kiara	135
18.	Kiara	138
19.	Colton	145
20.	Kiara/Colton	155
21.	Colton	163
22.	Kiara / Colton	170
23.	Kiara	181
24.	Colton	187
25.	Kiara	193
26.	Colton	202
27.	Kiara	213
28.	Kiara	221
29.	Colton	233
30.	Kiara	238
31.	Kiara	253
32.	Colton	261
33.	Kiara	266
34.	Colton	277
35.	Kiara	284
36.	Colton	292
37.	Kiara	298
38.	Colton	301

39. Kiara   311

40. Colton   320

41. Kiara   326

42. Colton   336

43. Colton   342

44. Kiara   347

45. Kiara   355

46. Kiara   360

47. Kiara   366

48. Colton   374

49. Kiara   380

50. Kiara   391

51. Kiara   394

52. Colton   408

53. Colton   415

54. Emerald Creek   419

55. Colton   427

56. Kiara   430

57. Colton   435

58. Kiara   439

59. Colton   443

60. Kiara   447

61. Kiara   452

Epilogue   461

About the author   471

Acknowledgements   473

CHAPTER ONE

Kiara

"Why are you so nervous?"

Willow watches as I pipe the final swirl of white chocolate ganache onto my grandmother's birthday cake. She turns the plate so I can finish, then steps back, phone in hand, snapping photos while I arrange petal-shaped curls around the white chocolate roses. Grams will appreciate the extra touch.

I take a slow breath, trying to ease the tightness in my stomach. "I'm not nervous." *Just bracing myself for the family reunion.*

"Uh-huh." Willow tilts her head. "You're biting the inside of your cheeks, and your place is serial-killer-level clean."

I grunt.

"It's super weird to see the Fearless Leader of the Bitch Brigade rattled," she says.

Willow and I became friends not long after I moved to Emerald Creek a few years ago. She works at the bakery that hired me, so we're constantly crossing paths—during shifts, at Lazy's, the town bar, or at one of the girls' nights out someone inevitably organizes. I'm the part-time pastry chef, and whenever I'm on the schedule, she gets bumped from the register to help me bake macarons and chocolate soufflés.

But today, she came to my place to help me bake for the family reunion. We've been at it since morning and through lunch, yet there's not a fleck of flour on the floor, no stray utensils, not a dish soaking in the sink. The couch is pristine, books aligned, throw pillows fluffed, candles angled just right on the white coffee table.

My private space is the only thing I can control today, and I'm hanging onto that with desperation.

"I like my place under control. It's more comfy that way." Even I can hear the sarcasm in my tone.

Willow sees through my lie. "I'm sorry it has to be that way with your folks," she says softly as she ties a ribbon around the boxes of petits fours we made together.

I shrug. "Eh, family. You know how it is."

She gives a small chuckle. We both come from homes that are broken in different ways and understand there's no fixing these things—just learning how to live with them, distance ourselves from them if we can, and build lives for ourselves that don't feel like a constant struggle.

The cake is done. I step back to admire it, satisfaction settling in my chest. It's everything I wanted for my grams' birthday. Everything *she'd* want. The seven-layer torte is cloaked in snow-white fondant, an elaborate arrangement of royal-icing roses artfully spilling down its sides, the most intricate piping I've ever done circling its base.

"Grams is going to love it," I say as much for myself as for Willow.

"It's gorgeous," Willow whispers, awe in her voice. "Let's take pictures and post it on socials. It looks like a wedding cake." She pulls out her phone again. "And wait 'til she tastes it."

The layers of dacquoise—maple, vanilla cream, and hazelnut crunch—are interspersed with dark chocolate ganache and fresh raspberries, all this on a base of Italian meringue. Just the thought of how my creation will bring her the joy she deserves is enough to chase away my family reunion-induced anxiety, at least for now.

"I was gonna say you outdid yourself, but that wouldn't be fair. Everything you make is above and beyond," Willow says as she turns the phone around the cake to capture the variations in the decor.

"Thanks." The word comes out quieter than I intend, my thoughts drifting to the one thing that keeps me going now: establishing myself as a legit pastry chef. I'm almost there. Almost. But true success keeps eluding me.

I still don't have my own shop. I still haven't made a name for myself. No matter how hard I push, how many hours I put into my craft, I can't seem to break through.

Glancing at this cake again, I can't figure it out. What bride wouldn't want something this beautiful, something that tastes as exquisite as it looks?

"How 'bout you make more of these," Willow says, switching to pictures. "Different designs, different flavors, so you have more to show?"

I thought about that. About the flavor combos, too. "M-hm. Orange blossom, pistachio, and Meyer lemon. Pear, white chocolate, and chai. Mint, dark chocolate, and walnut." I grab my notebook and write these ideas down, before something else takes over my brain and I forget. "I could make those next week. Pretend I'm swamped with orders. Fake-it-'til-you-make-it type of thing," I mumble.

That means spending hours baking cakes no one ordered with supplies I can barely afford. I could eat them. Wouldn't hurt to put on a few pounds.

"Tell me when, and I'll come help. Hey, we should post it on socials, saying we're prepping tastings for next season's brides?"

Wow. Why didn't I think about that? "That's brilliant!" I'm moved by the dimples forming on her cheeks, by the way her deep brown eyes are dancing with true happiness. Willow doesn't have an easy life, yet she finds happiness in the smallest things. *I need to be more like her.*

"Okay, let's put this baby away for now. Open the fridge for me?" she says, snapping me out of my thoughts.

Once the cake is cooling, I make us some coffee and we both plop on the kitchen chairs. For the first time today, I let myself relax.

"What did you call me earlier?" I ask.

She shrugs like she has no clue what I'm talking about.

"The fearful bitch?" I nudge her.

She laughs so hard she almost chokes on her coffee. "The Fearless Leader of the Bitch Brigade," she finally manages to say.

That gets me laughing too.

"After, you know…" she adds.

"Yeah-yeah-yeah." Last summer, when our friend Grace nearly lost her spa, we rallied the troops. The name Bitch Brigade came organically to me. Being called their fearless leader is a stretch, but it's still nice. "Thanks for today. I owe you one."

"It's nothing." She takes a long sip of her coffee, her eyes on me. "You'll have your own place one day, I promise. The world is gonna find out what a great pastry chef you are, and you'll have more work than you can handle." She smiles deviously. "Then I'll guilt-trip you into paying me an insane salary with benefits. I'll remind you how I saved your sorry ass more than once."

I tip my coffee mug toward her. "Fair enough. In that case, I need one more thing before you go. If you have time," I add.

"It's Saturday. Chris gave me the day off to help you, and I don't have a life." She shrugs. "What do you need?"

"Help me figure out an outfit."

Willow squeaks with excitement, downs her coffee, and dashes to my bedroom.

I finish my coffee to the sound of the closet door opening and closing and Willow humming to herself, then rinse our mugs and join her.

Any sense of order and control I thought I had is completely obliterated. Half my wardrobe is piled up on my bed, tops on one side and bottoms on the other. "What you got for me?" I say, faking enthusiasm as I stretch my mouth into a smile.

Willow doesn't catch onto my near state of despair. "How about this?" She thrusts a pair of black skinny jeans and a bright green tube top my way.

"Yeah, nope."

"Oh." She blinks, seeming surprised. "More conventional?" She offers a pair of gray slacks and the white blouse I only wear when I have a meeting at the bank.

I scratch my head. Willow isn't making it easier, but at least I'm not doing this alone.

She tilts her head. "With your body type, you can wear whatever you want." She flings the clothes on the bed and finds an empty spot to sit on. "Why don't you tell me what this is about?" she asks with a kindness that is worrisome.

"Just my grams' birthday party. Eighty years old."

"Yup. We just spent all day baking for her, 'member? Try again." She nudges me with her elbow in an attempt to perk me up.

"Alright. *Fine.*" I lean against the closet door, cross my arms, and try to gather my feelings into something that makes sense. "I haven't seen my mom and my sister in a long time."

Willow's facial expression shifts. "Oh. And... are we happy about seeing them?"

I let out a humorless laugh. "Well... They still think I'm a loser who tore the family apart."

After my falling out with them, we went two, maybe three years without speaking. Then Grams forced us to patch things up, and I thought all the ugliness was behind us. That we were a family again.

I was wrong.

Whenever we see each other now, it seems their only purpose is to remind me of how inadequate I am. Of how unlike them I am. Of how I don't belong. Mom calls and texts me, acting like a normal yet distant mother might, but her efforts don't fool me. There's something broken beyond repair in our relationship.

I've learned to shove my feelings down into the pit of my stomach, where no one can see them and they can hurt only me. I've learned to toughen up. I've learned to accept that I don't have a family, that it was ripped from me when I was a teenager. That any so-called family reunion is just another reminder that I fucked up in a major way that will never be forgiven. That no matter how much Mom pretends otherwise, I will never really be back in the fold.

Willow knows the gist of it, but not the details. I've also learned to pretend that I don't care about these things. It's called adapting, and I like to think I've become pretty adept at that survival skill.

She stands and wraps me in a quick hug. "Fuck them!" she whispers.

"Maybe the blouse but with black pants," I say.

She shakes her head. "You'd look like a server." Turning to the pile of clothes, she asks, "Do you want to give them a big fat Eff You or do you want to try and blend in?"

Both.

Since the events that got me banned from the family, I've come a long way. I moved out of my car and into a legit apartment. I made friends that feel more like family than the one I was born into. And I've become a pastry chef—at least, in my mind I am.

But today isn't about me. It's about making Grams happy. Removing any point of friction between us would be the first step. "Blend in," I concede.

"Okay, so traditional, bordering on uppity," Willow says as she extracts a plaid skirt I didn't even remember owning, and pairs it with a black sweater that might be cashmere.

Ditching my yoga pants, I slip into the skirt. "How d'you figure that?"

She shrugs. "The stuff you had when you got here wasn't exactly homeless gear. You had designer jeans and brand-name handbags."

I look at her in surprise as I zip up the skirt, which hangs a little loose on my hips. I always viewed myself as the broke, messed-up black sheep. Did Willow see me as a bougie runaway?

"You were cool though," she says, handing me the sweater.

She totally saw me as a bougie runaway. Which, to be fair, I kind of was.

"Tuck it in, she instructs. Her eyes widen as I do. "Oh wow—that looks great on you."

I turn to examine my reflection in the mirror. "I look like a sixth-grader entering boarding school."

"No you don't." Willow says, tossing a pair of fishnet stockings in my direction. "Where are your booties? The ones with the mile-high spike heels and the gold buckle?"

Once I'm all decked to Willow's instructions and standing six inches taller, I bite my lip. I look like a K-drama heroine. "I think that'll work. Thanks!"

Willow gives an exaggerated sigh. "You look hot, Boss. You forgot the feeling. Tits out!"

"What tits?" I smirk.

She pinches my left boob. "Shoulders back, chin high, ass out. You remember how to walk in those?"

I nod. "Like riding a bike." I lean over to give her a hug. "You're a lifesaver."

"That's me." She smirks. "Now go kick ass and have fun with your grams."

"I will," I lie.

After the door shuts on her, I turn to the mess on my bed and smile. Then, as I start hanging and folding my clothes, I belt out Bejeweled at full volume.

The last step is to style my short blonde hair in its usual spiky, edgy look, which has the distinct advantage of adding another half inch or so to my height. *Perfect.* Just to be on the safe side, I give it one more spritz of hairspray.

Good.

I go back to the kitchen, take the cake out of the fridge, and check my list.

~~Cake.~~

~~Petits fours.~~

~~Candles.~~

Shit. Candles. Where did I put them? There's a strike through the word, so I must have packed them, but now I can't remember where. And just because I checked them off the list doesn't mean I actually did what I was supposed to do with them.

Wouldn't be the first time.

I look around. *Eighty candles.* Can't really misplace eighty fucking candles. Did I even buy them? Yeah, yeah, I did. I remember buying them. I remember deciding they would ruin the aesthetic of the cake—so seventy-nine would go on the petits fours and only one on the cake itself.

Petits fours! Yes. There they are. And inside one of the pastry boxes—candles.

Found them! Crisis averted.

I exhale and let my shoulders drop. I can relax now.

Then my phone dings, and the name on the display makes me think the relaxing might not happen after all.

Mother

Are you still bringing someone?

Fuck. I forgot about that.

No, Mother, I'm not bringing anyone. Who the fuck would I bring?

That's the plan.

Is that a yes or a no?

Does it really matter? Of course not.

It's 90% yes. He had a last-minute thing at work and is trying to get out of it.

What's his name again?

Ugh. I better not answer that, because I'm guaranteed to forget what I told her and then I won't be able to keep my story straight when I'm interrogated—at this point, it's fair to say that I will be.

I exit the chat.

Sighing, I glance out the window, my tension easing incrementally as I let my gaze wander past the small apartment complex where I live—Sunrise Farms—down toward Emerald Creek. The village sits nestled in a bend of the river, huddled around a green. The golden numbers on the church clock gleam in the setting sun, its white steeple sharp against the winter sky. Thick snow blankets the roofs, and plumes of smoke billow softly from chimneys—maybe from Ms. Angela's bed-and-breakfast, or my friends Chris and Alex's Victorian house-slash-bakery.

I could say I made my home in Emerald Creek, and it'd be true.

But it's more than that.

Emerald Creek took me in when I was at my lowest and built me up. This place and the people that live here are my true family.

Taking a deep breath, I count to three. It's only one evening. And it's for Grams.

My gaze drops to the small parking lot below, and I grimace. There are many advantages to living at Sunrise Farms. Lockers for skis, snowboards, and bikes. Management clears the access for us.

But the downside? No covered parking. And winters in Northern Vermont can last six months.

Luckily, my first friend in Emerald Creek—and incidentally responsible for me moving here in the first place—Colton, the town mechanic, installed a remote starter for my Corolla.

Which isn't working this morning. I stab the fucker again. Open my window, bracing against the cold.

Nope.

Great. I'll tell Colton—eventually. Not now for sure, or even this weekend. Knowing him, he'd want to fix it immediately. And since he also lives at Sunrise Farms, it would literally be a right now situation. He already does so much for me, no way am I asking him for anything on a weekend.

The falling snow already added a fresh layer on my car, even though I cleared it before Willow got here. I shove my heeled booties in my bag, swap them for my snow boots, and haul my cakes and pastries outside. After securing all the boxes so they don't slide around in my trunk, I climb into the driver's seat and recheck my list.

~~One cake~~

~~Petits fours~~ 9 boxes

~~Candles~~ 1 box

All good.

I turn the ignition.

Click. Nothing.

"Fuck."

Turn. Click. Click. Nothing.

"Come on, you little shit."

Turn. Click.

Fuck me.

I glance around the parking lot. Good. Colton's truck is here. He's home. I guess I'm asking for his help. *Again.* This really needs to stop.

> Yo Colton

Colt

> **Wassup**

> Can you jump-start my car

Now?

<Thumbs up emoji>

Now?

Duh.

<Thumbs up emoji>

Is that a yes?

<Thumbs up emoji>

CHAPTER TWO

Colton

I glance at the profile on the dating app and immediately regret my life choices. Why did I agree to that first date again? I'd much rather be at Lazy's, kicking back with a beer and unwinding with my friends, than dressing up and making small talk with someone I don't know.

I get that meeting someone new is the whole point of the first date. The whole point of a dating app. But it's not what I want anymore.

Maybe I'm getting old, even if I'm not yet thirty. My finger hovers over the screen. I should just cancel.

Oh come on, man. The woman is probably getting all pretty for her date. Don't do this to her.

Fuck. Okay. I'm picking her up at her place, then meeting her friends at this upscale lounge, so I made an effort.

Suit: Check. (white shirt, no tie)

Nails scrubbed free of grease at my sister's spa: Check. (Not done done, just cleaned up)

Shaved: Unfortunately, check.

In a nutshell? I'm already pissed off, but I have no one to blame but myself.

So when my phone dings—or rather, chimes—with the sound I've programmed for my friend and neighbor, my mood instantly improves.

Sweetness

Yo

Wassup

Can you jump-start my car?

Now?

<Thumbs up emoji>

What is that supposed to mean?

Now?

<Thumbs up emoji>

Is that a yes?

<Thumbs up emoji>

Jesus, Kiara, use your words.

Glancing out the window, I spot her below, looking up at me with two thumbs up and a big, shit-eating grin from behind her quickly fogging-up windshield.

Of course she's smiling.

Stifling my own grin, I grab the keys to my truck so I can get my cables, my coat because it's snowing, and my phone and wallet in case I'm running short on time and need to leave right away.

It's funny how fast we became friends once she moved into Sunrise Farms, shortly after we met. Proximity helped, for sure, but it's more than that—there's just something about Kiara that's easy to like.

It doesn't hurt that she's a pastry chef and uses me as a guinea pig on the regular. And it certainly doesn't hurt that she likes video games and is only one flight of stairs away from me. Online gaming is fine, but I like the company.

Not that there's anything between us. She made sure to shut that down real quick, real tight, at the very beginning. We're just friends. Always will be.

She pops the hood as soon as she sees me step outside, then opens her door and climbs out

"Your ceiling light is on," I point out. It's glaringly obvious in the darkening afternoon—the plague of Northern Vermont winters. Four o'clock, and it's already dark out.

Kiara's arms are wrapped around herself, her breath curling in the cold. I can't help but notice that under her coat, her bare legs are decked out in something sexy bordering on provocative. "Yeah?" she says, shivering.

I snap my gaze back to her face. "Yeah."

She frowns, then understanding dawns. "Oh."

Yeah, it's not the battery.

"Start it." I lean over the engine, watching as she gets behind the wheel.

Click.

Not even a sputter.

I shut the hood, round the car, and lean on her open door. "It's probably the starter motor. You going somewhere?" Her coat is now open on the sides, revealing that she's all dressed up.

"My gram's birthday party. Shiiiit." She glances at her phone and swiftly turns it upside down. "I'm so fucked." She closes her eyes briefly, then rubs her forehead and sets her light gray eyes on me. "You have a car I can borrow? Like, a loaner?"

Yeah, I do have that. But... "Where you going?"

"Granby. Thereabouts. Why?"

"I'm going that way too. I'll drive you."

She shakes her head. "That's... far, and I need to stay at the party and then come back. I'll—can I just borrow your loaner?"

"Someone else has it," I lie. Am I trying to get out of my date? Maybe.

She narrows her eyes on me. "Where are *you* going?" She does a quick eye-sweep of my clothes.

I push off the car. "Come on, let's go."

"Wait! I have a cake and stuff."

I shrug. "Kay. I'll get the truck started." I pull out my phone to check the address for my date. Huh. It's actually not too far from Granby. Perfect. This will work itself out.

I hop in the truck, start the engine, crank the heat up, rub my hands. Where the hell is Kiara?

Glancing toward her car, I see a huge, pink box wobbling its way through the snow, seemingly balanced on a pair of sexy legs, teetering as accumulated snow gets in her way.

I jump out of the truck to grab the cake, but she tightens her grip.

"Open the door for me," she snaps.

Then, huffing, she adds. "Please."

I dart to the truck's side door, yank it open, and clear a space on the back seat. Once she's set the box down, she rushes back to her car, emerging with another stack of boxes.

"How many you got in there?" I call out.

"Just five more. And my bag."

Holy shit. I jog over to her car to grab the rest.

It takes us a solid minute to get the cakes secure in the back seat. When I slide behind the wheel, I lower the heat and take off carefully.

After a couple of turns (and a quick check that the boxes aren't shifting), Kiara turns her attention to me.

"Whatup, penguin?" she asks.

"Goin' on a date," I grunt.

She makes a sound somewhere between interest and amusement. "I can tell. She a keeper?"

"Nope."

"What's wrong with her?"

"I dunno yet, never met her, but I'm not keeping anyone around."

"She the country club type?"

I turn my head to look at Kiara. She's been on my case about being single for a while now. Sometimes she even bakes cupcakes for my dates--like that somehow seals the deal.

"No idea. Why d'you ask?"

"There's flowers in the back."

I smirk. "See, what you *should* have noticed are my nails." I spread my fingers, and she frowns as she leans over to examine my cuticles.

"And?"

"I went to Cheyenne for this"—this gets me an appreciative whistle—"and I had to explain why I was there." Cheyenne is the nail artist at my sister's spa, A Touch Of Grace. She wasn't as pissed as I thought she'd be when I told her what I needed: a scrub and as many chemicals she needed to get rid of the grease.

"And?"

"And Randy was there delivering one of those crazy bouquets."

"And?"

"I forget you're the slow kind."

Kiara punches my bicep. "Ow," she mutters to herself.

"Randy decided I should have a flower to give the girl. Can you believe it?"

Kiara beams at me. "Look at you, you followed advice! You got the girl a flower! What's her name again?"

What *is* her name? Shit. "I didn't get her a flower. You crazy? Randy took a flower from the bouquet, wrapped it up, and shoved it at me as I was leaving. I wasn't gonna say no and... hurt his feelings."

She frowns. "You shaved," she declares as she leans into me. "Cut yourself, too."

What does that have anything to do with—

"Ooh, and you're wearing cologne."

"I'm not."

She leans closer to sniff me, the smell of her freshly shampooed hair hitting me in a sweet whiff. "Are you sure?"

"Are you saying I smell good, grasshopper?"

She ignores me, preferring her own line of questioning. "You sure you're not proposing?"

I laugh. "Nope."

"Meeting the parents?"

"No! What makes you think that?"

She gestures at me like it's obvious. "You're wearing your suit."

"Um. I'm wearing *a* suit, and no tie."

"You're wearing *your* suit. And *no tie* is 'cause you don't own one."

I'm not going to argue that. She's right. "I could have borrowed one from a friend."

She seems to think on that. "That would have meant answering questions from said friend."

We have pretty much the same circle of friends in Emerald Creek. And yeah, we tend to be in each other's business a little too much. "I wouldn't want to wear a tie." The truth is, I don't want to talk about my date with Kiara. It's... uncomfortable.

"How come you're all dressed up for your grams' birthday?" I've met her grandmother once. She came to Sunrise Farms a few years back. I remember her as a laid-back, no-nonsense type. Hard to picture her hosting a fancy party.

"Ugh." She presses the back of her head against the seat. "Peer pressure and shit."

"Peer pressure? You?"

She waves dismissively at me. "You don't wanna know."

I kinda do want to hear why one of my best friends, a badass who doesn't take shit from anyone, is suddenly feeling peer pressure over her grandmother's birthday party.

Now again, I haven't met her family. All I know is, when Kiara came into my life, some bad shit had happened to her. But we'd only met recently, so I never asked for specifics. "What's your family like?"

"They're nothing like me. Except Grams. She gets me."

"That's too bad," I say. I'm not a big talker, so I can't blame her for not opening up.

She chuckles bitterly.

"What's it going to be like? That party."

She takes a deep breath. "Mostly nice people who'll be happy to see me. A couple who won't and will make my evening a nightmare."

My blood boils. "And who are these assholes?"

She looks out the passenger window. "My mother and my sister."

Oh shit. Didn't expect that. Although, thinking about it... All I can come up with for an answer is a sympathetic grunt.

"Why did you become a pastry chef again?"

"I thought I told you."

She did. She totally did. But it's a story I like to hear over and over.

"I don't think so. I'd remember."

"Yeah. Maybe get your memory checked. Or better, check yourself into an Alzheimer's unit already."

I smirk and come up with something that'll rile her. "You said you liked the colors."

"See?" She jolts back to look at me. "You remember."

"There was something about working night shifts," I say, pushing her a little. When I came across Kiara, she was homeless, working nights so she was safer sleeping in her car during the day.

She turns her face to me, forcing a tight smile. "I'm gonna be alright, Colt. Scout's honor. Just bummed I'm also missing opening day at Red Mountain."

"If you say so, grasshopper."

We stay silent for a while. She plugs her phone in, and the directions to her grams' house pop on the oversized console screen.

Her silence is making me nervous. I'm not used to her being quiet. "You sure it's not too hot in here? For the pastries?"

"It'll be fine. They're not meant to be eaten straight from the fridge anyway," she states, matter-of-fact. The soft swoosh of an incoming text on her phone sounds through the cab. She jumps when the text displays on the truck's screen and scrambles to exit it. Not fast enough.

Mother

What's his name??

What's going on? Why is Kiara trying to hide something from me? "Whose name?"

She crosses her arms. "No one's."

I lift my foot from the gas pedal and motion to the screen. "What was that?"

Kiara never hides anything from me. She might not share everything about her family, but that's the past. When it comes to her present, she tells me everything—when she's late on rent, when she lands a new contract, a catering gig, or the competitions she enters, win or lose.

She's even introduced me to a couple of her dates, not that I particularly cared for it. But she did it, she said, to "get my take on them". Point is, she doesn't hide stuff from me.

"Kiara, what the fuck?" I say when she doesn't answer.

She looks at me, her eyebrows shooting to her hairline. "Oh no. It's like, *literally*, no one. I told my mom I'd bring a boyfriend, and she's asking for his name."

"Why'd you tell her that?"

"Because..." She blinks a little too fast. I've never seen her like that.

"Because what?" I focus my gaze back on the road and try to loosen my grip on the wheel.

"It's stupid."

"Even better."

"She and my sister... God it sounds *so stupid* when I say it out loud!" She actually snorts, making me feel better.

"You haven't said anything yet. I can't wait."

She waves across the cab and raises her voice. "They're always giving me shit because I can't keep a man! Why the hell do they care?"

Yeah, why? "And so you...?"

"And so I said I'd bring my boyfriend. So now they want a name."

"Imagine that." Despite my best effort, a smile spreads on my face and I struggle to keep my laughter in. "How you getting out of this?"

She giggles. "I said there was a ten percent chance he'd be stuck at work."

"That doesn't solve your problem. You need to come up with a name. They're gonna grill you."

"I know."

"So—what's his name? And what does he do for a living, that he's "stuck at work" on a Saturday night?"

She shuts her eyes. "I'll just tell 'em I dumped him."

"That'll take care of it. Tell 'em you don't date guys who can't make time for your grandmother's birthday."

"Un-huh." She fidgets with her stockings, poking her thin fingers in the holes between the threads.

"Careful," I say, dragging my gaze away from her legs and back to the road. *Fuck. Get a grip, man. She's your friend.*

"What?"

"You're gonna break 'em... or whatever that's called."

I feel her turn toward me, but resist the urge to look. "You concerned about a run in my stockings, Colt?"

I don't like to see you nervous. Or miserable. "I'm not concerned, I'm... never mind." *I hate that you feel like you have to wear something that makes you uncomfortable just to please your family.*

She laughs, the sound cascading through me, warm and effortless. "What do you think?"

"'Bout what?"

She kicks up a foot. "The fishnet stockings. Am I rocking it or what?"

I risk a glance. "Can't say it's not sexy." *Eyes on the road, Colton. Eyes on the road.*

She fist-pumps. "I'm sexy as hell, is what I am!"

Jesus! How does she manage to be sexy *and* hilarious at the same time? "Are you okay?" I chuckle, feeling better about her state of mind.

"Yeah, yeah. Just practicing affirmations. Oops—here we are." She scratches her neck nervously and glances at the cakes as we dip down her grandmother's steep driveway.

Several cars are lined up in the carefully plowed area in front of the entrance. I make a U-turn and park at the front of the line, ready to take off after I drop Kiara—and her cakes—off.

Kiara grabs the big box from the car, which she's told me is the birthday cake. I follow with half the smaller boxes, set them on the covered porch that wraps the house, then jog back to the truck for her bag and the rest of the cakes.

She waits by the door, swapping her snow boots for high heels.

On an impulse, I grab the flower. I'm not giving it to my date (I really should check her name), and I don't want her to see it in the car. As I join Kiara on the porch, she pushes the door open, light and warmth spilling out in the cold.

And voices deeper inside the house.

I sense them before I hear them, probably because I'm attuned to Kiara's mood. I feel her tense. I see her brace herself. And when it comes, I feel the blow almost as deeply as she does.

"So who's the boyfriend?" an elderly voice asks. You can tell there's a smile in her voice. Kindness. Genuine interest. *Her grams.*

A huff. "She wouldn't even say. That girl is a disaster." *A mature female voice—her mother?*

"It's no one! She has no one! Don't you get it?" This comes from a younger voice. "She's making stuff up, as usual. Just trying to get attention—oh hey, Kiara."

"Well look what the cat dragged in." The words slap like the gavel on a final judgment.

I stand back, trying to calm my growing anger as Kiara says, "Hey, guys." It's her voice that settles it. The defeat in her tone. The utter sadness. The feeling of *whatever* that emanates from these two words.

She worked her ass off baking for them. She drove from an hour away, all dressed up, looking great. And no one even holds the door for her, offers to carry the cake, or asks how she's doing.

And all that because—what? She doesn't have a boyfriend? What kind of bullshit is that?

"Sweetness, where do you want this?" I ask Kiara loud enough for everyone to hear and with a big smile that's only for her. Then I shove the bright pink boxes on the first free countertop I find without awaiting her answer, dash back to the porch, grab the rest of the boxes and the flower, and set the boxes next to the cake.

I tackle her mother first, taking her hand in mine as I say, "Colton Harper, ma'am. Kiara's boyfriend. Such a pleasure to finally meet you."

I give the sister a curt smile. She doesn't deserve a second of my time. Grandma? I remember her. "Happy birthday, Eloise," I say, taking her in a quick but warm hug, then give her the flower.

Chapter Three

Kiara

How does he remember Grams' name? That's what my brain is hung up on. Better that than thinking about what he's doing right now. While Grams inhales the flower and grabs a vase, and Mom watches with pursed lips but curiosity, he wraps me under his arm and looks at me, then drops a kiss on my temple. "You okay, Sweetness?"

But my eyes are narrowing on the next person to enter the kitchen. *David*. My pulse quickens. Not from seeing him.

From the fact that no one thought to warn me he'd be here.

He was my boyfriend in high school. Or so I thought, until I caught him with his tongue down my twin's throat. It's been a long time, but the memory of the double betrayal took a while to wash away.

I'm surprised she's still with him, though. I didn't think they'd last.

"You remember David, right, Kai?" Maya asks, wrapping herself under David's arm the way I'm under Colton's. This is so childish. What, are we playing who's got the best boyfriend? Mine is fake and hers is a cheat.

"Uh... lemme think." I squint.

"We recently reconnected," she adds like I need a hint as to how far back in time I should go. "Right, David?"

"I... yeah, the name is familiar, but I can't quite place you. Are you from St Johns? Or—wait. Don't tell me." Pretending to think hard, I pinch the bridge of my nose with my free hand, the one that's not wrapped around Colton's waist—where it landed naturally when he pulled me in. Right now, it's a tether I really need.

Excitement hits me when the story unfurls in my twisted brain. Pointing at David, I exclaim, "I remember! Claire Mansfield's graduation party! You popped her cherry—"

Mom gasps. "Kiara!"

"She thought she was doing it with Bert Lawlor—the quarterback?" I continue, ignoring Mom and drinking in David's paling complexion, the telling clench of his jaw. "But she insisted on keeping the lights off and then she was so upset when she turned the lamp on *after* and found out it was you!"

Mom talks over me, "Stop this right away!"

But I just keep going. "She came screaming out she was so disappointed, and then you followed in your baggy white—"

"That's enough," Maya hisses, her cheeks flushed.

I turn my gaze to her. *Get a taste of your medicine.* "Oh, honey, that was ages ago." *See, I can be catty too.* Fuck but I hate this. Five minutes with them and I'm already a monster, just like them.

"Yeah, I don't remember a Claire Mansfield," the asshole thinks smart to inject at this point in the disaster, and I have to bite the insides of my cheeks to refrain from laughing.

Colton squeezes my shoulder and cuts through the tension. "Anything I can do to help, Eloise?"

Grams brightens, latching onto the change of topic. "Nope! Why don't you join the party?" She points to the living room where the hubbub of polite conversation rolls, punctuated by the occasional laughter.

Maya, David, and Mom storm out of the kitchen.

"I need to make a quick phone call," Colton says.

"I'll plate the cakes, Grams. Be right there!" I need a minute to calm down, and taking care of my pastries will do that. Always.

Once alone in the kitchen, I let out a deep sigh. "Thanks for the save, Colt. I owe you. You should get going, you're gonna be late." I start on the birthday cake, loving how awesome it looks, while Colton takes his phone out and presses a few keys. "I'm not going anywhere," he says. Looking straight at me, he talks into the phone. "Hey, Colton here. Listen, I'm really sorry, but I can't make it tonight. A… friend needed me and I'm going to be tied up all night." He waits a few beats, the tinny voice on the phone coming unintelligibly out.

My head spins a little while I plate the mini chocolate and mint eclairs.

"Oh good, okay… That's great… Yeah… I'll make it up to you… Alright, bye." He pockets his phone and rubs his hands. "How can I help?"

By now I've moved onto the coffee mousses. My gaze fixed on my task, I snap, "What did you do?"

He shrugs like he didn't just make the biggest mistake of his life. "Changed my plans. Why?" He opens the box of bite-sized harvest pies and plates them, our elbows touching.

"You don't cancel at the last minute on Miss Country Club. That will not go well."

"Nah, she didn't care." He moves onto the maple meringues and slides them all at once on a serving dish, then gathers the empty boxes and stacks them neatly in a corner.

I put my fists on my hips. "What did she say?"

"What do you care?"

"I hate seeing you alone, Colt. We've talked about this." I even baked cupcakes for some of his dates to show what good friends he has! "Go get her. Get the girl."

He closes the distance between us. "Shh, sweetness, people are gonna hear you," he whispers, his molten gaze drilling softly from my eyes down to my core.

"Why are you calling me sweetness?" I whisper back.

The shadow of a smile plays on his lips. "That's what I'd call you if you were my girlfriend. That, or sometimes sweets, maybe honey, possibly sugar. Definitely not grasshopper."

He's making me all kinds of mushy right now. I don't know this Colton. "What's wrong with Kiara?"

"Nothin' wrong with Kiara. It's a beautiful name." He takes my chin in his fingers. "But no one else calls you sweetness."

Between his words and his touch and his gaze, I'm losing sense of reality here. My body is reacting to him in a not-friend way. "What are you doing?" I whisper-hiss. "Method acting?"

He narrows his eyes on me and speaks even softer. "Your sister is watching from across the living room. I'd like to give her a little show, yeah?"

I start shaking my head. "That's not—"

He shuts me up with his lips on mine, one hand behind my nape pulling me to him, the other cupping the side of my face in a way that makes me feel *wanted*, even though this is all fake.

My eyes close on their own, while my hands find their natural place on his arms and slide up to his neck. His body vibrates with an energy that feels both safe and exhilarating. His lips are soft yet demanding, and when he lets out a little groan that goes straight to my core, my mouth opens before I even realize what I'm doing.

Embarrassed, I clamp my jaw shut, biting on his tongue.

He lets out a small growl, and I jerk back, trying to apologize, but he simply presses his forehead onto mine and says, "We shoulda practiced." Then he lets the smile on his lips morph into full-on laughter, pinches my waist, and drags me into the living room.

Chapter Four

Kiara

"Hey, I'm sorry about the kiss, okay?" Colton says as soon as we're in the car, driving back to Emerald Creek.

I glance at him and lick my lips, the taste of him still there, haunting me. *Oh no.* I have to stop that right now. I can't be fantasizing about my best friend. That's all kinds of wrong.

"Hey, I said I'm sorry," he insists when I don't say anything.

Well, I'm not. Best kiss ever. "Yeah-yeah-yeah, don't worry about it."

"Your sister has a way of getting under my skin... I don't know what it is with her."

I huff. "Tell me about it."

He chuckles. "Not that you needed to share the story about her boyfriend. That was brutal. Even if it was a long time ago."

"What sto—oh that? No, I totally made that up." I pick at my cuticle, tearing off the piece that's been nagging me since dinner with my teeth.

He glances at me, frowning. "Why would you do that?"

I take a deep breath. "Just some high school drama. Nothing that matters now, but it felt good for a minute to get back at them."

"Alright..." he says, clearly expecting more. Yep, there it is. The raised eyebrow.

I cross my arms, forcing myself to stop picking at my nails. "The usual. We were dating, and then he started fooling around with my sister."

"Wait-what?"

"I mean, she was—still is—way prettier than me, more feminine, more everything—"

"What the fuck?"

"And clearly more interesting. The pretty twin. The outgoing one. Turns out, he was using me to get to her. Smart, I guess."

"What?" he says, trying to interrupt me.

I shrug, ignoring his protestations. "I get it. But fuck! Someone should have told me he'd be there tonight." Although, honestly, who would have told me? Not Maya. Not my mother. And apart from them, no one would remember that David and I were ever a thing. At the time, there was so much more drama, that little heartbreak never registered. "If she'd told me, I wouldn't have felt cornered."

"Sweets, she provoked you with her question."

Sweets? My heart takes a little break to ponder this, then resumes normal operations. "I guess."

"I'm sorry," he says softly. "On the other hand, your uncle Bill rocks."

"Right?" I uncross my arms. My mother's brother is her exact opposite. Warm, cheerful, always in my corner. Watching him and Colton talk cars, races, and all that gearhead stuff—it almost felt like having a normal family. "I feel real bad."

"'Bout what?"

"That he thinks we're in a relationship. I could tell how happy he was for me."

Colton grunts.

"I'll call him and tell him the truth," I decide.

"Maybe wait a little?" Colton suggests.

Why should I wait? Lies are insidious. Destructive. The longer they sit, the deeper they hurt. "No, I'll call him tonight. He won't say anything. He'll get why I did it."

"What if… what if there's another family reunion and you need your favorite boyfriend for support?" He flashes a devilish smile at me, whatever defenses I still had quickly falling apart.

"Nah, I'll handle them." If I'm being honest with myself, I'm a little embarrassed that Colton felt the need to pull a knight-in-shining-armor move. "Are you going to tell Country Club that you kissed me at the time you were supposed to be out with her?"

"I didn't kiss you."

"Yeah you did."

He slants his dark eyes at me. "Honey, that was not a kiss. That was barely a peck."

I re-cross my arms. I'm not going to try and make my point by re-living this moment. By describing to him that the way he'd drawn my nape, the way his body tensed under my touch, the way he growled—I heard him growl, okay?—the way his lips didn't feel placed on mine like for a mock kiss only for show, but instead encapsulated mine, and especially—*especially*—the way his tongue found its way into my briefly opened mouth, felt like a real kiss.

Like something he should think about in the scope of potentially dating someone that wasn't the person he kissed. But then again, look at David. Are all guys like that? No wonder I can't find a shoe that fits.

"If you think that was a kiss, you have never been properly kissed."

I roll my eyes. "I'm not talking about French kissing, Colt. But there was…" *Nope. Nope. I'm not going there.*

"There was what?"

I shake my head. "Never mind." I squeeze my thighs together to shut down the hot tickle. "So you're saying, you're not gonna tell her."

"Sweets, I've yet to meet the girl. And honestly, the way you talk about it, makes it sound like a lot of work."

"What sounds like work?"

"This relationship thing."

My mouth goes dry. He wants a *relationship?* Not a casual thing? Is that new? Was I not paying attention? "What are you saying?"

"Don't think I'm gonna see her."

My traitorous stomach does a little happy dance, and what's up with that?

"I get it. You had a taste of a toxic family, why would you bother with the nice and proper type?"

"Aw, come on. Overall, it wasn't that bad, was it?"

Yeah, you don't know the half of it.

CHAPTER FIVE

Colton

I clench the wheel tight because what I want to do is take her hand, hold it firm, maybe pull her into me. Make her feel better without saying a damn word. There's things a hug can do that words can't, and right now that's what she needs.

There's always something about being together in the small space of a car or the cab of a truck. You share the view, the conversation, the destination, the music. You feel the other person without—most of the time—looking at them. It's like your senses are heightened, sharpened.

At least that's the way it is for me right now with Kiara. Sharing a car ride has never felt so intimate.

She shuts down again when I try and make light of her family. Make her see the good side of it. There's clearly more going on than just douchebag cheating on her with her stuck-up sister. I wonder what's up with her father? I've never heard her mention him.

I'm definitely not asking her now. I did enough damage today. Instead, I retreat to a safer topic. "So, when are you getting a proper vehicle for your business?"

"Soon as my favorite mechanic repairs it?" she says, and the way she does—with a smile my way that lights up the night—the way she says I'm her favorite even though I'm the only game in town, makes my brain a little foggy.

I messed things up between us with that kiss, and our friendship will need to come back from it. But damn, those lips. Soft and plump and welcoming. And the way she held herself to me, as if she was losing her balance. The way her eyes closed on instinct, and fuck me, how she opened her mouth?

"So... when's that gonna be? You have the part?" Kiara asks.

My dick strains against the seam of my pants. "Huh? Uh, probably." What was—oh yeah, the starter motor. "If I have it, I'll fix it tomorrow for you."

"You don't have to. Tomorrow's Sunday." Her words are stilted. I really fucked things up, didn't I? I need to get us back to normal.

"I'll get the loaner back tomorrow in case I can't fix your car."

She narrows her eyes on me. "Why would you get the loaner back if you're not open and giving someone their car back?"

Excellent point. Did not think that through. "Long story." I shrug. "Seriously though," I add, needing a semi-change of topic but going back to my primary concern, "when are you going to trade in the Corolla? It's not what you need to deliver pastries."

She sighs and shakes her head like I'm a little dense. "After I get my own space to bake." She starts picking at her cuticles again, a sure sign she's stressed.

"Why does it need to happen after?" Once Kiara started working part-time for my cousin Chris, who owns the bakery in town, word quickly got out what a great pastry chef she is. She started fulfilling catering orders out of her kitchen in the rental apartment. Then she got more business from a few hotels and restaurants.

For those accounts, she bakes on-site. It keeps her afloat, but it won't allow her to grow.

"It doesn't. It's... a lot to think about, and an investment."

"But it'd help you grow your business, yeah? A nice little refrigerated truck with your logo painted on it. I can see it..."

She stops biting her nails and crosses her arms. Or maybe she crosses her arms *to* stop the biting. "Yeah, don't worry, Picasso. The day I have my own van, you'll get to paint it." She's looking out the window, so I can't tell if she really means it, but a smile tugs at my lips anyway. Kiara giving me nicknames means we're back to normal.

"What kinda truck you thinking?"

She whips her head to me. "I'm not thinking anything. Jesus, Colt, you're so literal."

I am literal, she's right. "Okay, then. If you were to have a truck, what would it be? Just say the first thing that comes—"

"A VW van."

"What? The Volkswagen Type 2?"

She shrugs. "Sure." Her tone's uncertain.

"The microbus?"

She crosses her arms tightly. "Yup."

"You mean the rear-wheel drive, tiny little hippie van that can't handle a snowflake and has shit for heat?"

She rolls her eyes. "You said the first thing that came to my mind."

"You didn't let me say that part, actually."

"But that's what you meant."

Yes, that's exactly what I meant. *Of course* it's what I meant. We're close enough to finish each other's thoughts. "Nope. I meant to say, before you rudely interrupted me," and she snorts at this, "the first thing that comes with an all-wheel drive or four-wheel drive, good ground clearance, good cargo space, good fuel efficiency. These are non-negotiable."

"You're so full of shit." Finally the tension leaves her as she laughs.

"Am not," I pretend to be serious.

"You would never, ever, call a car a thing."

Well, that settles it. "Seriously though, a VW?"

"Seriously, I am not getting a new *vehicle*." She spits the word like it's dirty. Then she perks up and adds, "but if I *could* get a vehicle, it would totally be a souped-up VW Camper."

"Souped-up, huh? I don't think anyone can do that for you."

"Why not?" Her arms are crossed again, but in a challenge. We both know she's never getting a VW bus for her business, souped-up or not.

"Well, for starters, you'd need a new engine. New transmission. The wheels are ridiculous, especially for the winter season. The inside is..." I glance at her, then smirk when she returns the gaze, "I guess it's to size."

She punches my bicep. "Jerk."

"Why?" *Small is beautiful.* I snap my eyes back to the road and think better than to add that last part. We're finally back to normal, and honestly, why do I feel the need to give her compliments now? It was never like that.

I take the last curve before my garage and instantly notice my loaner sitting on the side of the bay under a foot of snow. Kiara doesn't notice it, or if she does, she could think it's any random car. But her mind is elsewhere. It's almost like I can feel the tension radiating from her.

The fork where I'd take a left to go back to Sunrise Farms is coming up, but I don't want to go home yet. I need to unwind from this weird evening by hanging out with friends. And I don't feel like going home with Kiara just one floor away from me. I just need to get back to norm—

"I could use a beer," Kiara interrupts my thoughts. "At Lazy's?" she adds quickly, in case I thought she wanted a beer with me, the two of us alone at my place or hers. Like we've done a hundred times. *Bad idea.* At least we're still on the same page.

I keep going straight, toward the center of Emerald Creek, toward The Green and Lazy's. It's one of those moments when it's clear to me how damn lucky I am to live here. When driving into Emerald Creek gives me that feeling of *home.*

Not just the fact that to my left, down Timberline Way, is where my parents live; that to my right, up Hardscrabble Road, is the Arena where I spent so much time playing hockey. Or that my third-grade teacher, Ms. Angela, now owns the bed-and-breakfast on Winooski, on top of working occasionally at the general store and the bookshop, and overall being in everyone's business in the most endearing way.

Or that my cousin's bakery is now famous and sits right on The Green.

It's all of it. The knowledge that in a minute, I'll walk into Lazy's, grab a beer, sit with my friends, and just *be.* No expectations.

We glide down the empty streets, freshly plowed and bathed in the warm glow of streetlights. The bright gleam of storefront windows showcases cute displays—most of it overpriced stuff tourists lose their minds over. But what do I care? It's good for business, and no one's complaining. Most of the town lives off tourism and if—

"Holy fuck!" Kiara screeches as she sits tall, looking out the passenger window.

On instinct, I hit the brakes, though lightly enough to keep control in the snow. A furtive shadow darts across the sidewalk, sliding into the narrow alley between two buildings.

"What happened?" I say.

"Whoever that was just threw eggs at the Shy Rabit!"

"It's Shy Rabit," I say, and we both chuckle as I stop the truck and get in reverse. The relatively new name of the bookshop is a topic of gossip, and sometimes heated discussion, at Town Hall meetings. A few years ago the store was bought anonymously through shell corporations, so we don't know who the owner is. The name was changed to Shy Rabit and the manager, who'd worked for the previous owner, repeatedly assured there should only be one B and no The. *"It's not a rabbit,"* she'd say and roll her eyes.

I squint at the storefront. "Fuck, you're right." Two bright yellow streaks drip down the window, frozen solid before they could hit the ground. Kiara steps out of the truck and picks something up from the sidewalk. I lower the passenger window and cold air quickly fills the cabin. "What are you doing? Come back in."

"We interrupted them," she says, showing me a carton of eggs.

"Good! Now get back in here, it's freezing." I start closing her window, but she raises her voice above the rumble of the engine.

"We need to report this!" Her eyes are widening like I'm missing how bad this is

Seriously? "Sweets," I say, the nickname escaping me, "it's just eggs. Come on."

She stays on the sidewalk, holding the eggs up. "Declan needs to know about this!"

"You're reading too much into this!"

The minute the words leave my mouth, I know I'm in trouble.

Her eyes bug out. "Excuse me?"

I take out my phone. "I'm calling Declan," I say, referring to our chief of police. "Come on, get in the truck."

She stays put on the sidewalk. "I can't believe you said that!"

"Said what? It's cold." I hold my phone up. "I won't call him till you're inside. Don't be ridiculous."

She stomps to the truck and slams the door. "I'm sorry," she mumbles. "I can't stand when people say I'm reading too much into stuff. It's a lazy cop-out."

"Noted," I say, trying not to chuckle as I call Declan.

He picks up on the second ring, and I fill him in quickly.

"You have the eggs?" he asks.

"Yup." Kiara, now next to me in the truck, is holding them on her lap.

"I'll need them as evidence."

"The weapon," I add with a smile.

"Right," he adds. Declan isn't exactly the joking kind, but it's because he's always looking out for us. Anticipating what could go wrong.

"We'll be at Lazy's," I tell him, then hang up.

"You're holding evidence, it seems," I say to Kiara.

"Oooh. Cool. Can you lift fingerprints from a carton?" she says, lifting her hands from the eggs.

"Probably. And DNA."

"Shit. How 'bout from eggs? I didn't open the box."

"You'll have to ask Dec. You're his only witness."

"Ugh. Is he gonna want to interview me? The day just gets better," she mutters.

"Matter-of-fact, it does," I say as we pull up in front of Lazy's. "Come on." I hop out and grab the leftover cake Eloise insisted we take. The other leftovers—neatly packed in plastic containers—are coming home with me if Kiara doesn't want them. Especially Uncle Bill's meatloaf.

Inside, the pub is full of familiar faces. And as we walk in, every single one of them falls silent.

"Where you guys coming from?" my sister, Grace, asks. Her gaze goes between Kiara and me, sliding up and down to appreciate how overdressed we are.

"Ugh, you don't wanna know," Kiara says as she hoists herself on a barstool between Willow and Haley, two of our friends.

I drop the cake on the bar and flip open the box, revealing a section of the masterpiece Kiara brought to her grandmother's. Willow claps her hands, hops off her stool, and starts slicing the cake, loading small plates that Haley passes out.

Alex, my cousin's pregnant fiancée, laughs. "Did you guys secretly get married, and this is your way to tell us?"

Kiara rolls her eyes. "Ugh. Even *that* sounds better than what happened." She doesn't look at me. I don't know if she said it to kill the rumor mill—which, if so, *mission accomplished*—or if she's genuinely disgusted by the idea of being married to me. I'm vaguely offended that it may be the latter.

"Oh no," Alex says, leaning in. "What happened?"

"Are you *that* bad?" Grace calls out to me from across the bar, chuckling, then listens to Kiara recounting our evening. I pay close attention so we keep our stories straight.

I'm hoping she leaves the kiss out, but with Kiara, you never know.

"Man, this is so good," Haley says, pointing to her plate. "So he pretended to be your boyfriend? Way to go, man!" she adds, flashing me a grin.

"You took one for the team," Justin, the owner of the pub and Haley's brother, says to me.

"Hey! Fuck off!" Kiara shoots back playfully.

"My point exactly," he says, pouring us each a beer. He takes a bite of cake Haley shoves in his direction. "Mmm, darn it. *That's* the shit."

Kiara ignores the compliment. "He did great," she doubles down. "He even..." she pauses for dramatic effect, takes a sip of beer, then licks the foam off her upper lip. I can't help but watch, tasting my beer on my own lips, wishing it was my tongue on hers—fuck it. *Got to stop.*

"He even what?" Grace asks, holding her fork up mid air.

Kiara glances at me, mischief flashing in her eyes. *Don't say it.* "He even promised my uncle Bill to take him to his next car race."

"Aww man, that's sweet! Colton! I didn't know you could be such a *good* boyfriend," Alex says.

"That's because he's fake," Kiara chimes in.

Ouch.

"How long you planning on pretending like that?" Grace asks, a frown marring her forehead.

"I'm telling Uncle Bill tomorrow that it was fake. And I don't give a shit about the rest of the family. I'm not planning on seeing them for at least a year. Plenty of time for a fake breakup."

"Oh, good," Alex says like that's the best thing ever. Looking at me, she blushes slightly, then adds, "You don't want to play those charades too long. It's gotta be exhausting."

"It was fun, actually," I say. "I could always be an actor if the garage thing fails," I add, stealing a line Mom always uses when she sees us do something moderately well. "Fooled everyone over there."

Kiara twitches on her chair, the reference to acting surely stirring up a memory. She lifts the beer to her plump lips again, but sets it down immediately as Declan comes into the pub.

I'd already forgotten about that.

The conversations die. Declan might have grown up here but when he shows up in his uniform, we know there's potential trouble. When he's in plainclothes? He's one of us.

But tonight, he's in uniform.

He gestures for Kiara to step aside, takes his notebook out, and gets her testimony. This does two things. One, everybody's up to speed with the same, accurate information. Two, I get to look at her with no interruption for the full two minutes that Declan's interview lasts.

Really *look* at her. Not just get a glimpse of the little ball of fury that she can be in the evenings when her day went to shit and she stops by my place to blow off steam and we end up watching MMA or playing video games. Not the grumpy, half-awake persona that comes out of the building in the mornings. Not the swearing, don't-give-a-fuck Kiara that terrifies town newbies with her quick judgments and eerily accurate nicknames.

No, I get to look at a collected, young yet seasoned woman who's had a long, mostly shitty day (though I like to think I made it better). By the way her soft gray irises reflect the light in a changing pattern of little fireworks, I can tell she's holding her smile for now, respectful of Dec's police business that we called in.

She stands as straight and tall as her five foot one (she insists on the one) allows her, which pushes her perky tits up. She has them molded in a ridiculously soft sweater that's kind of a tease in itself because even if it shows no skin at all, it begs to be touched. With that, she chose a tight skirt in a pattern that gives stuck-up vibes that are totally not Kiara. Wild guess, it was to blend in with her mother and her sister. It molds her ass nicely though, and it does stop way above her knees, which is a blessing given she's wearing what she calls fishing stockings, which are the dress-up version of torn jeans, I guess, except sexier.

Her tiny little feet are—

"You done?" Chris's voice jolts me. *Shit*. I didn't even see him come up to me.

I jerk my head. "Done with what?"

Chris has a small smile, but his gaze on me is stern. "Eye-fucking her," he growls under his breath.

"Get your mind out of the gutter. I was...wondering why she's wearing these weird clothes."

Chris raises an eyebrow. "Didn't she say something about her family being a pain in the ass?"

"That's what you wear when your family's a pain?"

He ignores my perfectly valid point. "You sure this was fake? You're not keeping something from the rest of us for whatever reason, right?"

"Not everyone's like you," I respond under my breath. Chris and his then apprentice Alex were sleeping together way before any of us clued in on that. Or most of us. I'm usually the last one to catch up on these types of developments.

"If you say so," Chris says.

"Where's Skye?" I ask to change the topic.

"Asleep upstairs, at Justin's." He produces an earpiece that I hadn't noticed. "We're testing the baby monitor."

I chuckle. "Cute. You look like a bodyguard."

"Wait 'til you have a kid. World doesn't look so cute anymore."

I shrug. Although in the past I might have expressed my views on what kind of father I'd be, I don't see myself becoming a dad. The more I try to date, the less that whole domestic life getup holds appeal.

Declan pockets his notebook, then scratches his head. "I don't like it," he declares, looking at all of us. Really, two eggs on a window has our chief of police rattled? This town needs real problems.

"I'm sure you can handle it," Chloe says with a frown. Justin's wife owns the restaurant next door to his pub, and last summer some nasty business erupted with her chef that required police intervention.

Declan bares his teeth in a grimace and tilts his head. "Yeah, there's more," he says. But instead of filling us in on the more, he makes for the door.

"Seriously, Dec, you're gonna leave us hanging?" Kiara spits, her fists on her hips. "What more is there?"

"You'll figure it out soon enough, Nancy Drew," he says over his shoulder.

CHAPTER SIX

Kiara

When I wake up the next morning, the left side of my head is a fogged-out mess, and I can only see the right side of the room.

Shit.

Incoming migraine.

Might not be too late to kill it, though.

I drag myself to the kitchen, take a double dose of painkillers, a tall glass of water, and get some coffee going. Although I feel like crawling back under the covers, I force myself to stretch my arms above my head, then gently turn my neck and massage my temples, although my skin is already a little sensitive.

I'm over what happened with Colton yesterday. Really, I am. In the most rational way. Colton and I didn't share a moment. I was just... *in the moment*, I suppose, and his obvious boyfriend skills caught me off guard. My reaction to him was only that—a physical reaction. But my brain and my heart understand what my body doesn't: that nothing can, or will ever happen romantically with Colton, because that would kill our friendship.

And I value our friendship more than anything.

I weigh the pros and cons of both situations. Girlfriend or good friend? Assuming he was even attracted to me—which he's not—the answer is obvious. Dating Colton would inevitably lead to a breakup (I have nothing to offer him), while remaining his lifelong friend would be immensely satisfying and enriching on a personal level.

Satisfied with my decision, I tackle the one thing still looming and causing me to tense up. One thing I need to fix about yesterday.

"Really," Uncle Bill says when I expose our charade. I'm curled on the couch, the phone on speaker so I can sip my coffee and drink my water and massage the back of my neck.

"I'm sorry," I say.

"Didn't look fake to me," he counters.

Yeah, Colton pulled all the tricks. His arm curled on the back of my chair, his fingers absently twirled my hair. His hand rested on my shoulder, thumb tracing agonizingly slow strokes on my neck. Sometimes he'd lean into me, taking my hand, squeezing it gently, a slight caress. I've never had a man do things like that to me before. Tender things, signs of mindless attention. If that's what it's like to have a boyfriend, I should work harder at getting one.

Because that was *awesome*.

And that was all fake. Imagine if it hadn't been! Although not sure it could get any better than that. But then again, it was Colton. Shit, he really should get a girlfriend. So much wasted potential there.

"I'm sorry we fooled you." I suppose our private jokes, the way we finish each other's sentences, all that didn't exactly point to a fake relationship.

"Nothin' to be sorry about, kiddo. You did what you had to do. Your mother, ah..." He lets his sentence hang, a growl summarizing his thoughts.

I let out a short, bitter laugh. "Yeah, you'd think of all people, she'd have seen it."

"Aw, sweetheart, people only see what they want to see. Deep down, your mom, she wants to see you happy with a man. You bring her a man, she's not gonna wanna look beyond that. 'Specially with how happy you both looked." He stays silent for a while, and I ponder his words, the migraine threatening to come back as the pain from the past stabs me.

My dad had been leading a double life. A family here, another one elsewhere. We were his other family. I might have had older half-siblings. When I found out, my life—all our lives—exploded. Since we never should have existed anyway, he chose them over us. We were only his dirty secret. His mistake.

Uncle Bill clears his throat. "You gonna be okay, Spitfire?" He must be thinking about the same thing I am.

"Yeah, been a long time."

"Oh, I wasn't talking about the asshole. I was talking about Colt."

Colton? "Sure! Why?"

His only answer is a half-formed groan. "Say, you don't mind if I keep seeing him, right?"

I smile, happiness spreading through me. "He's my friend, Uncle Bill. Not my ex. I'd love for you guys to hang out." It's the best thing that's come out of Grams' birthday party, this new friendship between Uncle Bill and Colton.

After I hang up, I feel lighter. I couldn't stand it if I had to lie to Uncle Bill. Or worse, tell him Colton and I broke up. He'd be sad, and he'd lose a friend. None of this needs to happen now. Being truthful is always the best course of action.

Well, most of the time. No way am I telling Mom and Maya it was fake. The look on their faces when Colton introduced himself as my boyfriend? Priceless. He did good. I was, like, *"Eat this, bitches!"* Yeah, yeah. Not how you're supposed to talk about your family, or anyone, really, but that's what they are. Bitches.

Speaking of bitches—the good kind. I reach for my phone.

To: Bitch Brigade [Grace, Alex, Emma, Willow, + 5 more]

> Gonna need a ride

Willow

> Already on my way

Nice.

Recently, the Bitch Brigade started hanging out on Sunday mornings at Easy Monday, the best coffee shop in town, owned by Millie, a sort of hippie dreamer who also opened a weed shop called 420 on the other side of her coffee shop. Her coffee is my one luxury expense of the week, and I make it count. All my friends are there. We plop on Millie's super comfy couches, read the dirty books she has on display, and talk. Some would call it gossip. Whatever, it's fun. My favorite part is the reading.

There's also a game night going on every Thursday. We also go there, but so do a lot of other women in Emerald Creek. It's a different vibe. Real gossip. And we drink wine, not coffee. But there are no books.

I pull my hoodie on and slip into my boots and coat. As I get out of my apartment—backward so I can lock the door after me—I slam into a hard mass of muscle.

"You going to church, grasshopper?" Colton's deep voice seeps into the deepest confines of my body. It never was that way. God that's annoying!

"Yeah. I'll say a lil' prayer for ya." I step to the side to get to the staircase, but he slides sideways, blocking my way. "Move."

"You forgetting something."

"Yeah?" I tilt my head back to look him in the eye, but my gaze stops at his lips. Without my heels on, Colton's mouth is more out of reach. I wonder how low he'd have to stoop to kiss me now, if—

"You done?" That possessive mouth of his morphs into a smile.

I snap my eyes higher, trying to fight the blush I feel creeping up my cheeks for having been caught in the act of staring at his mouth. "What'd I forget?" Certainly not the kiss. Godohgod please make him not mention the kiss.

He wiggles his fingers at me. "Car keys."

Oh. Right. My car. I unlock my front door and grab them off the kitchen counter, then pass them to him. He closes his fingers around mine. "You okay?" he says, a frown marring his forehead.

I'll be okay once you stop touching me. "Yeah, course I'm okay." I slip from his grip and turn to lock my front door. *Take slow breaths.* It's a trick Chloe taught us. And surprisingly, it works. "Thanks, by the way," I say, my voice coming out a little funny. He is going to work on my car, and as usual, he won't make me pay for labor.

"It's just, you have your migraine face," he says.

He can tell? I tense. "I do?" I say as I take the staircase. "I think it's under control." I hope it's not coming back. It doesn't feel like it will.

Colton falls into step behind me. "You got a ride?"

I nod. "Willow."

"Oh." He seems disappointed.

"You need me for something?" I suddenly feel guilty I'm going to spend some time with my friends while he'll be working—for free—on my car.

"Nah. Just gonna tow it into the shop now, have her ready for tomorrow, first thing." He holds the door open for me, making me feel both special and weird. Did he use to do that before? Before yesterday.

I can't remember. He probably did, and I didn't notice, or I'd tease him for practicing his good manners on me. That sounds about right.

I should do this. Tease him.

But I can't think of something sassy that only he would totally appreciate. My brain freezes as much as my body warms up. I am so fucked. I roll my eyes at myself, then catch myself before Colton can see me.

"You gonna be okay?" he asks as Willow turns into the parking lot.

I walk with him toward his truck and Willow. "Sure," I say, rubbing the back of my neck to ease the tension.

"You talk to Bill yet?"

His change of topic catches me off guard, his question inexplicably making me sad. "Yeah."

"What'd he say?" he asks, stopping at his truck.

I tilt my head to look at Colton's gentle eyes, and I can't get a read on him. "He was hoping you guys could still go to the races together. I said yes. Hope that was okay?"

Colton squints, looking away. "Cool," is his only answer. Then he climbs into his truck, and I get into Willow's car, feeling weirdly lonely.

"You don't look too good," Willow says.

"Migraine," is all I can think to answer as we follow Colton's truck outside the parking lot. My gaze stays on him as he takes a right, toward his shop.

Willow makes the left toward town. "Oh, no. Let me know if you need to get home all of a sudden, okay?"

"I'll be okay." Coffee with my friends is what I really need right now.

As we drive through The Green, I glance at my friends' businesses. To the right, the large Victorian house where Alex was an apprentice not so long ago, until she and Chris, Emerald Creek's baker, fell in love. The house is decorated for Christmas with string lights outlining all the windows and trim, and a gorgeous wreath on the door.

To the left, across The Green, Lazy's is still closed, but Clover's Nook is lit, looking totally cozy with holiday greens and lights in their window boxes, and crimson bows hanging on each window. "Chloe's Nook is busy already," I say, pointing to patrons walking down from the church at the top of The Green.

"Chloe's killing it with her brunch. What pastries are you making for her this week? I heard Emma saying she bases her dinners there on their dessert menu," Willows says with a playful wink.

"Really?" It's probably not true, or not entirely, but it's a nice thing to say. "Carrot cake, tiramisu, and a chestnut mousse with maple crisps and whipped cream." It's nothing fancy or even creative, but it fits the expectations for Chloe's guests this season, and it pays my bills—or part of them.

"You had me at chestnut mousse," Willow says as she pulls up to Easy Monday. "You should bribe Emma with it and have her help you with your business plan." Emma is a CPA, and I use her services—along with everyone else in town. Willow has been on my case to look at my numbers and make a plan, and she has a point. It's time for me to step up my game.

"You're right." I sigh. "Now would be a good time. Before the rush of the holidays." Thinking about looking at rows of numbers threatens to bring back my migraine, but as I step out of the car, the cold November air hits my lungs in a good way.

I take a few steps toward the large stone building. Behind it, the grounds slope down to the river. In the summer, it's a garden where Millie puts tables and chairs for people to sit and watch the river flow. Right now, it's a serene white expanse, leading to the river freezing up on the sides. In its center, the water still rushes in a loud, bubbly stream, as if in a hurry to get somewhere before the deep cold of January stops it entirely in its tracks.

"You coming?" Willow says, taking me out of my contemplation as she holds the bright yellow front door open for me, the sweet and rich aroma of coffee calling to me.

Easy Monday is large, which allows for it to be way more than just a coffee shop. With its deep, comfy couches, it's a place to stay a while and admire the art from local creators—paintings and some sculptures.

But my favorite thing about Easy's is all the kissing books Millie has there. I'm talking rows and rows on wobbly bookshelves, and when the bookshelves overflow, stacks of romance novels spill onto the floor in haphazard towers. You can take a book or two home, as long as you bring it back.

"Kiara? Kiara?"

I focus my eyes to where the sweet voice is coming from. Millie is smiling at me, holding a paper cup. Somehow we made it to the front of the line and I'm supposed to place my order. "How can I make your day awesome, sweetheart?" she asks me. I frown at her. She *never* calls me sweetheart. I must really look like shit.

While my muddy brain tries to come up with an answer, she suggests a Mystified Mocha.

"Yeah. That sounds right," I answer.

She turns around to do whatever she needs to do that makes her coffee machine hiss like the sirens from hell. If that doesn't bring the migraine back, I should be good for today. I flinch, waiting for the banging inside my head to resume.

It doesn't.

"Heard you had quite an adventure yesterday?" Millie says over her shoulder.

I narrow my eyes on her. What is she talking about? Colton's tongue sliding inside my mouth in the most delicious way is the only adventure my overloaded memory can produce right now. There's no way in hell Millie already heard about that, is there?

She turns, grabs some stuff on the counter, pours it in my coffee, all the while glancing at me with a smile. "The egg bombing?" she says to jolt my memory to where her mind is.

The what now?

"It was all over Echoes last night," she explains, referring to Emerald Creek's social media platform.

Egg bombing? Is that what we're calling it?

I suppose the "egg bombing" is a worthy concern, and it belongs alongside information about potholes that appeared overnight, Daisy the cow seen wandering again in the vicinity of Ms. Angela's flower baskets, and Chris running a special on his croissants. Who am I to say it isn't? I'm the only witness. And I did have a what-the-fuck reaction when I saw it happen.

"Yeah, it was... pretty shocking to see, if you ask me." I grab my coffee and hand her my rumpled bills.

"On the house today," she singsongs. "On account of being the only witness of the *crime*," she adds with dramatic effect. "Figured you'd need some comfort."

"Hey, thanks." I'm not going to say no to free coffee, especially one that's more of a mystical experience than a hot drink to wake me up. I drop a dollar bill in her tip jar and follow Willow like a zombie, then plop on the couch nearest a stack of books. I start sifting through the pile for something I haven't read already.

His Willing Captive. Read that one.

Stay With Me. That one too.

A Very Handsome Neighbor. That one was gooood.

His Secret Virgin. Oooh, haven't read this one. I settle next to Willow on the couch we favor, kick my snow boots off, and tuck my feet under my butt. Then I take a long sip of coffee and start reading.

Before too long, Grace, Colton's sister, comes and sits next to me. "Hey," she says with a smile.

I look up from my book. "Hey."

She nudges closer to me. "So back to Colton and your little... deception."

I feel Willow perk up. "M-hm?" I say.

"Funny story. Dad is disappointed it isn't true and Mom agrees with him, which is rare enough. Seems like there's a Team Kiara within the Harper household." With a chuckle she adds, "I swear I tried to tell them you want nothing to do with their son, but you know how they are."

"*Team Kiara* suggests there's another team," Willow interjects.

Grace blushes slightly. "Well, Valerie's back in town."

"Oh, she was cute!" Willow says, and then the rest of the conversation gets lost as my ears woosh with blood.

Valerie is a great woman...but not for Colton. There was something about the two of them...every time I saw them together... it felt *wrong*. I have to admit, I was surprised when she moved in with him. Well, and also a little pissed, to be honest. No more late-night gaming sessions with Colt for me.

I tried, and failed, to feel sorry when she left. The day I found out, I showed up at Colt's with a pack of beer and a pizza, like a good ol' buddy. We went back to how it always was. And it felt great. At least to me it did.

And now she's back? Suddenly my coffee doesn't sit well in my stomach. I set my book on my lap, but I don't think I can add anything kind to this conversation.

Grace rattles off about how her brother is too difficult and although I wholeheartedly agree with her, there's nothing I want to say. If I did, she might enlist me to get him back together with Valerie. Since Grace has been back with her long-lost love, she wants everyone to get their happily ever after. Problem is, Valerie can't be Colton's happily ever after. And this isn't me being jealous or possessive or having any illusions of my own with Colton. Like I said, I value my friendship with him far more than anything else.

It's just... she's not *right* for him. He seemed off when they were together.

It wrecks me to know she's back. To know he might fall for her again.

And be miserable.

As I pretend to have no interest in Colton's love life by losing myself again within the pages of the book, reading and rereading the same page over and over again, I force myself to analyze why I'm feeling what I'm feeling about Colton insisting on driving me last night. About him posing as my boyfriend. And about his kiss. His *fake* kiss. Despite this morning's resolve, it's clear I'm not solidly in the friend zone yet. And that's okay. I'm allowed a wobbly journey back to normalcy, as long as I don't ruin anything.

From the dim confines of my brain, two things are clear.

Being in Colton's arms, being *kissed* by Colton, made me feel incredibly safe for the few, fake seconds that it lasted. Colton saved me once before, a long time ago, and he did again yesterday. Not from my sister or my mother or even David and their snarky remarks. He saved me from myself, from my self-loathing. He made me feel valuable and-and-and... *necessary*. As if the party would have been nothing close to what it was without my presence. He reminded everyone how long I worked on the cake— not in front of Grams. He took a family photo with Grams blowing all eighty candles, making sure I was seated next to her, smack in the middle. He told everyone who would hear how proud he was that I was "a self-made woman, and not many people can say that. Soon she'll be more famous than our baker, you watch." I punched him playfully, *"Oh stop,"* but I blushed under the compliment. Everyone in the room still remembered, and probably had watched, Chris winning the TV baking competition. Now my whole family was looking at me with a different eye.

"What do you think, Kiara?" Willow says.

"About Valerie? Nothing," I snap.

"Ooh." She leans toward me and whispers, "We moved on from that topic a while ago. Good to know where your mind was. Speaking of which," she adds, elbowing me.

I look up and see Colton push the door open.

My cheeks warm. Damn it. "My mind was on my book," I answer, bringing it up to my face to make a point.

Just then, my phone rings. *Grams.* I set my book down and step away to take the call.

CHAPTER SEVEN

Colton

Thank fuck Kiara's piece-of-shit car (on account of its age) is a Corolla. And that I had the part.

Once on the lift, hood popped open, and battery disconnected, it was a breeze to get to the starter—right there under the intake manifold with nothing in the way. I pulled off the wiring harness, removed the couple of bolts holding the starter in, slapped the new one in, torqued the bolts to spec, reconnected the wires, hooked the battery. She fired right back up.

Could I have done this yesterday? Ah. Not if I wanted to stay nice and clean and dressed up for my date.

The date I didn't want to go to.

The date I ended up canceling anyway.

So the answer would be no. No, I couldn't have done it yesterday. Because I wouldn't have wanted to.

At least I'm not lying to myself. I needed a little bit of Kiara in my day before going on my date, and what's wrong with that?

And yeah, as things progressed, as she started telling me about her family, I wanted to be by her side as she walked in. Moral support and all that. That was before the fake dating idea even remotely appeared in the back of my brain. Waaay before her lips were under mine. Because that's what friends do, right?

I push the door to Easy Monday, looking forward to the scent of coffee. To seeing my sister and her friends, even for just a quick hello. To maybe sitting down in an armchair and reading the newspaper like a proper old man. After all, I'm going on thirty.

This morning, though, my gaze searches and stops on Kiara like a heat-seeking missile. Her petite shape curled on the couch moves me. She's deep in her book, biting her bottom lip, her cheeks slightly flushed. I notice her delicate neck, the way her eyes dance as they scan the page, the—

"Hey, Colt," Grace calls out.

Just then, Kiara's phone rings and she stands to take the call.

I lift a few fingers in a half-assed wave, but instead of going to place my order at the counter, I find myself walking up to the group of women. I try to avoid looking at Kiara, so I'm not too obvious.

It's near impossible.

There's like a radiation coming from her, a heat only I can feel, and fuck it.

I don't care that yesterday was fake. I don't care that she thinks I kissed her only to annoy her sister. I know what she felt because I felt it too.

In this crowded coffee shop, with my hands reeking of automobile grease, my coveralls under a thick flannel jacket, and my work boots leaving snow marks on the floor, I take one long look at Kiara. Delicate. Fragile. An artist in the making.

I take in the gorgeous gray eyes she hides under too much makeup.

Her beautiful blonde locks of hair she cuts short and covers in gel so they spike up.

Her delicate neck that gets blotchy when she's nervous.

The way she looks when she's reading and thinks no one is watching. The way her breaths accelerate, her eyes dance with mirth, her lips tilt up. The way she comes alive in her world of fantasy, much like she does when we play video games.

I want to give her that. I want to make her come alive under my touch, my kiss, my body. Show her that the real world is not just bitches and dipshit exes.

She already has most of that, here in Emerald Creek. She has her girlfriends. They have her back.

But I want to be closer than them. So much closer. More than her helpful neighbor. More than her favorite mechanic. More than her best friend.

It's decided.

I'm gonna make her mine.

Then, as if I hadn't just altered the course of both our lives, I put my hands on my hips and declare, "Your car is fixed."

She whips around, her cheeks a little flush, her eyes shiny. Covering her phone, she breathes, "It's Grams."

I nod. "Tell her I said hi."

Half a beat goes by, and she passes me the phone. "She wants to talk to you." Putting her hand on the phone again, she whispers, "Just go with it, I'll fix it later."

My eyes on Kiara, I put the phone to my ear and engage in friendly banter with Eloise. Turns out, the asshole proposed to Kiara's sister, and now Eloise is throwing them a party—and she wants us there. Something warm spreads through my body as I hum my agreement to whatever she wants and sear the date and place in my mind. I give the phone back to Kiara. Cheeks crimson, she wraps up with Eloise, then clears her throat.

"Thanks... I, uh... obviously haven't told her anything yet, so yeah... nice uh... nice improv." She tucks her phone away. "Obviously, we—you're—you're off the hook. G-Goes without saying," she stammers.

I smirk. "We'll see about that."

She chuckles. "No, really. I got this." Then her eyes light up. "Did I hear you say my car was ready? You really shouldn't have worked on it on a Sunday. Thanks so much." She gives me a big friendly smile that's nothing like the way doe-eyed Kiara looked at me last night at dinner, shivering under my touch.

It bothers me a little that she's more excited about her car being repaired than having me as a plus-one to her sister's engagement party. Maybe we shouldn't have been friends this long. Maybe that's what the problem is. She doesn't see me as boyfriend material.

I can change her mind.

"Lemme grab a cuppa, and I'll drive you back." Then we can have a nice little talk in the car, and I can show her how nothing was fake in that kiss, despite what I said yesterday. I can show her how sweet a second kiss would feel, when I'm not taking her by surprise. And a third.

The way her cheeks tint, she knows what's up. She wants it. "Your coffee's on me," she says, leading the way to the counter.

See? Easy. We're meant to be. Nothing weird about it.

CHAPTER EIGHT

Kiara

"L emme grab a cuppa, and I'll drive you back," Colton says.

That's sweet. That's *really* sweet. Except I'm still too unsure of myself to spend even a few minutes in the intimate isolation of Colton's car. I mean, the way he spoke to Eloise? Total internal melt.

"Your coffee's on me," I say and walk away from him. That's okay, right? Least I can do to thank him for working on a Sunday.

I make a beeline for the counter. With a few long strides, Colton is behind me, the warmth in my lower back registering as *maybe* his touch? I'm too embarrassed to check. Millie gives me a wide smile, her eyes darting between the two of us. She doesn't say anything, just waits, as if there was some confusion she was not going to point out or attempt to clarify.

I turn to Colton, the movement bringing my body closer to his and his hand briefly on my hip, before he removes it and shoves it in his pocket. "What are you having?"

"Road to Heaven, extra shot," he says without missing a beat, talking to me, our gazes briefly locking.

"Two, please," I say to Millie. Judging by how my cheeks are burning, I must be crimson.

I take a step away from Colton and register him crossing his arms on his chest. I resist looking at him and instead get lost in admiration of the new refillable mugs Millie's selling. They're conveniently placed opposite from Colton, in different sizes, colors, and even designs. Grace's fiancé even started her a collection—that's how pretty they are.

When we get our orders, I let Colton take his, mumble "thanks again," pay Millie, and grab my cup. Then I bravely declare, "I'm gonna hang with the girls a little more." He did offer to drive me back.

He looks disappointed. How weird is that? I'm about to tell him he should hang with us, but I don't trust my motives yet. Am I being a good friend extending a natural invitation or am I still confused? Better to keep a little distance for now, until my physical reaction to Colton is back to normal.

He brushes my upper arm, a gentle goodbye. "I'll leave your car keys in your mailbox."

I go to answer—to thank him again—but he's already leaving, stopped on his way to the door by Cassandra who tells him something that makes him frown and scratch his head, then answer something I can't hear.

I go back to my friends and slip onto the couch, feeling a little off-kilter, watching him rub his stubble and finally leave with a thin smile for Cass, his long steps taking him into the cold.

How am I going to heal from the burn Colton's barely there hand left on my lower back? Then on my hip. And just now on my arm when he grazed it for a casual goodbye.

Now I'm torturing myself. Should I have gone back with him? But for what? Was he expecting that, and that's why he didn't bring the keys to Easy Monday? Did he not want me to stop by his place later to pick them up?

Is he doing something today? If yes, what?

Ohgodohgod. Kiara. Full stop. We are not going stalker mode on Colton. You are going to get yourself home with your book boyfriend, who is everything you need and nothing you can't have, and let the real people in your real life be.

"You sure you're okay?" Grace says as she drops me off, much later, at Sunrise Farms. She has her brother's complexion and the shape of his eyes, and it stuns me that I'd never noticed that. "Kiara?" she asks, calling me back to reality. "I heard Colton on the phone with your grams." She seems to hesitate, then says, "He can be annoyingly nice sometimes. He finds it hard to say no to people. But you can tell him to back off—he won't break."

"Yeah-yeah-yeah. Absolutely. No, he knows," I assure her. "He *knows*. He's just—like you said, too good. I'm—the plan is to tell them we broke up."

"Oh good," Grace says.

"Of course. Just giving it a few days."

She squints at me but says nothing.

"Umm. Okay." I go to open the door.

"So what's wrong?" she asks, totally clueless.

"I think that migraine is coming back," I lie.

"Oh, I see." Something tells me she's not buying it. Still, she adds, "Can I do anything?"

On impulse, I lean over the console to give her a quick hug, taking comfort in her friendship. "I'm good," I say, blinking away stupid tears. I leave the car before she has time to notice anything.

Later that evening, I'm on book three and the topic of Colton is safely tucked away somewhere I can't reach, when a soft rap I'd recognize anywhere startles me out of my fantasy of handsome, wholesome billionaires. Three quick, two slow.

I startle and freeze, in no state to interact with who's behind that door. Maybe he'll think I'm still out with the girls. For once, the presence of my car in the parking lot doesn't mean anything.

Other than he fixed it and brought it back to me. On a Sunday.

The rapping repeats, louder. Then, "Hey, Kiara?" Colton's deep voice makes me feel guilty with how it's touched with concern. "You there?"

I can't decently ignore him. We always keep tabs on each other. I pull myself upright and get to the door, making no effort to look alert. "What's up?" I say, my voice neutral as I open the door.

He's shuffling on his feet, uncertain.

I open wider, not really inviting him, but not leaving him out either. If he wanted, he could come in.

"Grace said your migraine came back." He speaks low, so as not to hurt my head further. "Need anything?"

I feel crappy for seemingly avoiding him. At least that's how it feels to me. I don't know if I'm trying too hard to not be more with him, or if the idea of being with him makes me feel bad because I haven't gotten rid of the kiss effect yet. It's all very confusing. "All good, captain," I say, forcing a smile. "Migraine under control."

He huffs, pushes a smirk. "Okay, uh... Wanna hang? This week?"

"Sure!" We never make plans. Why does he need to make plans? "Day after tomorrow?" I ask a little too quickly. Maybe too eagerly? When am I going to stop overanalyzing everything I do around Colton? It's exhausting. "I'm testing a cream puff Christmas tree."

His eyes brighten. "Cool. I'll have pizza."

"Great," I say, giving him a mock salute with two fingers to my head as I push the door softly closed. We don't agree on a time. We don't need to. It'll be like always. Whenever I'm ready, I'll head over.

CHAPTER NINE

Kiara

I'm a little nervous about going to Colton's tonight. I'm telling myself it's because I'm testing a new holiday dessert on him that I'll be making for Chloe's Nook. It's a tower of cream puffs filled with an orange spice cream, dipped in white chocolate, sprinkled with crushed candied ginger and pistachio, and arranged on a spiced gingerbread base to look like a Christmas tree.

I made a tiny one just for the two of us.

Colton is a discerning taster. Over the years, I've taught him to appreciate the balance of flavors and textures. Sweet and sour, soft and crunchy. Then I introduced unexpected ingredients without telling him—like a vegan chocolate mousse that uses avocado instead of eggs.

It's been fun to see him open up his culinary expectations and horizons. I credit him for helping me perfect my almond biscotti by pointing out they missed a hint of bitterness, which prompted me to add a touch of espresso powder.

But who am I kidding?

The real reason I'm nervous today is not my Noel Puff Tree.

It's Colton. More specifically, it's me in regard to Colton and everything that in an alternate universe he could be, but in this life, shouldn't.

I knock on the door and let myself into his apartment. He's not sitting on the couch like he usually is, so I set my towering dessert on his kitchen counter. "Yo," I call out. The smell of pizza heating in the oven hits me just right, like old times (those being last week and before), and I relax. This will be a normal evening.

A shuffling sound comes from behind me. "Hey," he says.

I turn right in time to see him coming from the general vicinity of the bathroom, pulling on a T-shirt, his bare midsection showing. I glance away, pretending to check on the pizza. By the time I turn back he's in my space, the scent of shampoo and clean laundry like a warm blanket around me.

He clears his throat like he's a little tense. "Beer?" he asks as he reaches behind me to open the fridge.

Although I'm attuned enough to him to feel something's bothering him, I'm also acutely aware of how good he smells right now.

I put some security space between us. "Sure," I answer.

He passes me a bottle, pops his open, and takes a long gulp. Then he wipes his mouth with the back of his hand, and I'm pretty sure at this point he's making a conscious effort not to look me in the eye.

"Pizza seems ready," I say.

He doesn't answer, just takes another swish of his beer.

Something's not right.

I take the pizza out of the oven, set it on the range, and grab two dinner plates from the cupboard right above. What's up with Colt? He's lost in his thoughts. I put three slices on one plate that I hand him and one slice on the other.

"Couch or kitchen?" I ask him.

He sets the plate on the countertop and takes another swig of beer.

"What's going on?" I ask.

"There's something I need to talk to you about first. *Ask* you." He takes a deep breath and I can tell he's hesitating.

Finally he looks at me, his gaze flinching a little. I fight the attraction I still feel, the lingering memory of the kiss and the fake dating and how good it all felt. I focus on him instead of me, trying to assess what's got him tongue-tied.

And then I get it.

He probably realized he can't stand the idea of going to the engagement party with me, but he's too nice to simply tell me. He wants to ask me if it's okay. And how sweet is that?

I crack a big smile at him, resisting the urge to give him a side hug. "Of course you're off the hook for the engagement! Goes without saying. I'll tell Grams—"

"I think we should date," he blurts out.

I frown. Like fake dating but every day, here in Emerald Creek? Why? "I'll tell Grams we broke up," I finish my sentence.

"I think we should date for real," he repeats, clarifying.

My mouth goes dry, and something sharp hits me right below the ribcage. Panic and disbelief. A touch of hope, quickly killed off. I huff. "Yeah, right. Very funny." I step away from him to the other side of the kitchen island and try to laugh, to show him how comical he is, but my efforts stay strangled in my throat.

"I'm serious," he says, his eyebrows shooting up.

He's kidding, right? The reason *I'm* not laughing is that, some time Saturday night, I lost my sense of humor when it comes to Colton. "You don't date," I counter, my eyes dropping to the logo on his

T-shirt. I tear a bite off my pizza to show him how unmoved I am. That I really take this for what it is—a joke. Even if I'm not laughing.

He narrows his eyes on me. "With you I would."

It's like a rock hits the bottom of my stomach. Dinners and movies and stuff with Colton? And cuddling and kissing and... all the rest? "Yeah, right," is all I seem to be able to say, again. I set the pizza down and grab the countertop for purchase.

He rounds the island and takes both my hands in his. Paralyzed for a moment, I try to pull away from his grasp but only succeed in having him tighten his grip. "I like you. I like spending time with you." His mouth morphs into a delicious smile. "I liked kissing you. I think we should give this a try."

And that's the problem. Giving it a try, knowing it could go either way. I can't take that risk.

"Nu-huh. Nope. Not a chance."

He frowns, looking completely confused. "Why not?"

"Because we're friends."

"Exactly! We're... great together."

Desperation bubbles to the surface of my brain. If I can't shut this down right away, I'm in for a world of pain. It's written all over Colton's strong features, in the depths of his irises, in the tilt of his mouth. I will never get over him. "It would ruin our friendship."

"Um. No. It would make our relationship stronger."

Oh, Colton. You don't want a relationship with me. I'm just convenient because I'm right there. No work involved. "Not in a million years." He's probably only moderately attracted to me, physically—and who can blame him. Otherwise, why wouldn't he have made a move earlier?

Without dropping my hands entirely, he releases his grip on me, but I stay in his warmth, in his touch. Because when will this happen again? Never. And he's that good. Feels that good. Looks that good.

"Why?" he asks again, the defeat in his tone nearly undoing me. "I-the other night I-I know I said I was sorry I kissed you, but I wasn't. Maybe that makes me a pig and I'm sorry if it does. But I think... I thought there was something there, and I—"

"We'd lose each other as friends," I stop him before he says something that might convince me. Dating Colton would be a terrible, terrible idea. He's way too... too everything for me. Too good. Too kind. Too strong.

I almost died when he pretended to kiss me—even if now he's suggesting he wasn't really pretending.

The truth is, I could never live up to his expectations. Sooner or later, he'd grow tired of me. He'd say something like, *"Hey, Kiara, this was fun, but I like us better as friends."* And I wouldn't survive that. I would lose myself and be a zombie inside for the rest of my days.

"I disagree," he states but steps away from me, hands on his hips.

"You're just being lazy." I push him, hoping this will settle it.

"Excuse me?" He grabs his empty beer bottle and throws it in the recycling trash can, where it lands with a crash.

I got him angry. That's good. Should send us right where we belong: in the friend zone. "You only want to date me because that would require no effort on your part," I explain. "I'm right here, we're already friends, there would be no *courting* needed," I say like that's a disgusting thing. "No getting to know each—"

"Are you saying I just want to fuck?"

The word in his mouth doesn't sound as offensive as he's trying to make it. It's actually... arousing. Despite the armor I've built to get people to believe I'm tough and shit, I'm shocked that Colton would want any level of intimate involvement with me.

The heat seeping from his gaze almost convinces me to give in. To say *"Hey, yeah, let's jump each other's bones. Get it out of our system so we can get back to normal."*

But that's the problem. For Colton, it might be a matter of scratching an itch the maybe-not-so-fake kiss created. Of exploring options, making sure no stone is left unturned in this difficult dating landscape we're in. And it makes sense. I get it. For someone like Colton, who's solid in his self-acceptance, it's even pretty smart.

For me? It's the opposite. I know myself enough to realize that I have major abandonment issues. In other words, my daddy problems are more acute than for others. I follow this relationship specialist on social media and this is all she talks about, and every time I hear her, it's like she's talking specifically to me although she has tens of thousands of followers. It's hard for me to trust, and it's hard for me to love myself, and it's hard for me to let people in.

But I'm proud of myself for knowing this about me—many people don't.

And this is why I can't be the kind of person who'd leap at the suggestion of giving dating Colton a try. If I were wired differently, I'd already have my hands around his neck, his mouth would be on mine, and in three seconds or less I'd have my legs wrapped around his hips as he carried me to his bedroom.

The thought increases my arousal, so my brain tries to course-correct by wondering if he has the dark blue or gray sheets on this week. (I notice his unmade bed on the way to his bathroom, and I know he rotates his sheets weekly.) Unfortunately, the thought of Colton's bed (especially the particular way in which it's rumpled—Colton never makes his bed) does nothing to calm me down.

Neither does the way he glowers at me, fists on his hips, jaw tense, chest heaving.

The way his jeans and T-shirt strand on his muscles, calling my attention to all the deliciousness barely hidden there, right within my reach.

The way his last words hang between us, *"Are you saying I just want to fuck?"*

Suddenly I'm terrified, and I don't know what to say to make it right. I don't know how to act around Colton to keep him as my friend. Snapshots of the past flash before my eyes like emotional scars—catching my dad lying, catching David cheating. It's a terrifying déjà vu of the times I messed up with the men who meant the most to me.

Although I recognize Colton is not betraying me, I can't escape the fear that every man who matters to me ends up leaving me, no matter what I do. Maybe if I can dial back time, this time I can fix it.

Desperate times require desperate measures.

My answer snaps through the air. "Isn't that what you want?"

He huffs, pain registering in his eyes.

"See? It's already messing with our friendship," I say, my gaze unable to hold his. "Can we pretend none of this ever happened?" I say as I walk to the door. "I'm just gonna go home."

I leave without waiting for his answer, hoping he understands I'm not rejecting him. I'm only trying to preserve our friendship. *And selfishly, my heart.*

CHAPTER TEN

Colton

"*Pretend none of this happened.*" Yeah, right. And how am I supposed to do that? How am I supposed to forget the look of panic on her face, the blotches on her neck? How am I supposed to forget I did this to her?

I scared her away. I shouldn't have come onto her like that.

She's better than that.

But how was I supposed to do it? We've always been open with each other. I wanted to date her, so I told her. How did she jump to the conclusion that I just wanted us to be fuck buddies?

Does she think so little of me?

I guess she doesn't feel for me what I feel for her. That's the only answer I can think of. I could have sworn though, during that kiss... and the way she looked at me in the days that followed... I really thought there was something way more than friendship building between us. I thought wrong. I *assumed*, based on what I was feeling.

Another mistake.

Will our friendship ever recover from what I did? Me forcing myself as her fake boyfriend was bad enough—not to mention the kiss. But this?

See, this is why people should take better care of their cars. None of this would have happened if Kiara'd let me do regular checkups of her Corolla. Changed what needed to be changed before she was stranded. The Corolla would have started without a hiccup, she'd have gone alone to Eloise's birthday party, she'd have survived it just fine without my intervention, and we'd still be friends—no awkwardness.

But no. She pretends she can't afford the regular maintenance, or doesn't want me to work for free, and look where we are now.

I stare at her dessert, feeling guilty I didn't memorize its name. I thought we were going to have a long evening of kissing and cuddling, and more if she was up for it, and we'd get to this little work of art later at night, maybe spoon-feeding each other. She'd ask me what I thought of it, and of course I'd be wowed because everything Kiara makes is perfection, but she'd push and push until I came up with something that could use improvement, and she'd take notes on her phone and finally be content.

It was going to be perfect.

Instead, the little edible Christmas tree sits on my countertop untouched, like a silent reproach—the memory of what should have been. I place it in the fridge, then plop on the couch with the plan to play video games until Kiara comes back (you never know) or I fall asleep.

Neither happens. Once 4:00 a.m. comes around I get into the shower in hopes of washing away last night's bitter taste, then get ready for work.

Opening the fridge to take a slug of orange juice, I'm jolted by Kiara's dessert staring at me. I'm not coming back to this reminder tonight, so I take it with me to the garage.

The guys will be happy.

I pull into Harper's Body Works at five, the moon still bright, early workers driving by me on the main road in and out of Emerald Creek.

Merritt, who owned the garage before me and taught me pretty much everything I know, used to say that we mechanics provide one of the most essential services to this world. Sure, a couple professions—he called them trades— were more important. Like doctors and teachers. But try getting to the doctor's or to school by foot or on a horse. Doable? Sure. Just a helluva pain in the neck.

We're the lubricant that keeps the cogs of society turning, and Merritt taught me to take pride in my work here for my community. Again, according to Merritt, there's a reason beyond mere convenience that we're located a mile and a half outside the center of town, before the first houses.

We're the first and last stop people make going in and out of their hometown. Filling up their gas tanks, checking their tires, their levels of fluids. Really, they're checking in with themselves as they go about their lives.

I like to think of us as the beacon on these first shift workers' route.

The light is on in the reception area and in the bays, and fresh snow tracks lead to the back of the garage, where my staff and I park our cars. My lead mechanic Orson's truck is there, ticking softly off.

"Hey, boss," Orson greets me as I step into the reception area. He glances up from the computer, steaming coffee mug in hand. "Just made a fresh batch. Ooh, what's that you got?" he says, looking at the dessert.

I grunt, "Kiara made this."

"Inn't she precious, always spoiling us. How come she's not coming by today?"

I shrug. Kiara's been bringing muffins every Monday morning "because it's the start of the week" and cupcakes every Wednesday "because it's hump day." She's become like most people in Emerald Creek—in everyone's business in the kindest sort of way. The way that made the garden club offer to add window boxes and planters to the garage "to cheer up the entrance of Emerald Creek" the moment Merritt sold the business to me. He and his wife took to the RV life, and it was clear I didn't have a green thumb.

"She wasn't sure she could make it," I answer. Maybe it's a lie, and maybe it isn't. I guess I'll find out.

"Everythin' okay?" Orson asks. Kiara never misses one of her self-appointed deliveries.

"Uh, sure. Far's I know."

"That's some fancy shmancy thing she made," he says. "Inn't she something?"

I pour coffee in my cup, forcing myself to act normal, and over-all be a good boss. It's not my fault I made a shit decision that's making me cranky. "You're here early," I say to make conversation without talking about Kiara. "Your old lady finally kick you out?"

His body shakes with soft laughter. Orson is living his fifties with a "fuck it" philosophy that's resulted in an ever-growing beer belly, high cholesterol, and a couple of heart scares. But he and his wife of thirty years are still madly in love, and she's entirely devoted to him and their family.

"Nah, she wants us to go pick the grandkids up from daycare and take them for pictures with Santa. Figured I'd get an early start and scoot outta here by one."

"Sure! What do we got today?" I ask, pointing at the computer where today's appointments are listed.

"Parker's beamer. Regular maintenance."

I grunt. Owen Parker is not my favorite person. "What else?"

"Eh, there's the Corvette with the faulty exhaust pipe. Wanna take that?" he asks me.

Hell yeah, I want to work on that. Who wouldn't? We have a reputation for our work on vintage cars, but we don't get to work on a 1966 Stingray that often, if ever. "You should take it," I say. Orson is more experienced than me in that area.

He tilts his head and ticks his tongue. "Might not have time to finish it. And you could use the practice."

All good points. "Okay." The client dropped her off last night, so I down my coffee to get right to work. Anything to keep my mind off Kiara. "I'll call if I need you," I say before stepping into the bay. Orson follows me to get started on a couple of oil changes and filter replacements.

I slide under the car and try to shut off the outside world to focus on the task at hand. The old exhaust is showing lots of rust spots, the bolts fused to the connections—mainly the exhaust manifold and the flanges. I grab the penetrating oil and hit each connection. Then I take my ratchet and get to work.

We work in relative silence for the next hour or so, until the rest of my crew shows up. First Linwood, the other old timer who, like Orson, came with the shop. Then Patrick, the tire specialist I hired a couple of years ago. Then, finally, two apprentices, the names of which I may not bother to remember if they keep showing up late every day.

I roll out from under the Corvette to get them squared away with their tasks for the day, then focus back on my work rather than obsess over how I seem to fuck up with women, not understand them one way or another.

This work I created for myself, it's good. Familiar. Controllable. Down to the smell of grease, the whooshing of a hydraulic pumping up in the next bay, the clanking of a dropped tool, the occasional swearing. It's something I know and understand and control.

Kiara said, "Pretend none of this ever happened", and this is the only way I can try and do that. Focusing on the stuff I understand. The stuff that makes me feel good. Fixing cars. Taking something that's not working and making it work. This is my world.

I fix things.

As far as fixing relationships, different story.

My ex, Valerie, used to insist she didn't dislike the smell of grease on me when I came home at night and tried to scrub off the nastiness in the shower. She said it gave me an edge. She had fun naming my garage, Harper's Body Works, even designed a logo for it. It only took me the few months we lived together to understand she got off on being with a guy from what she considered to be the wrong side of the tracks. Someone who worked getting his hands dirty.

I was a little slow on the uptake, but to be honest when she packed her bags it didn't hurt. Even when she said, "you're gonna miss me," and for a little while I sort of did. I missed having company. I didn't really miss *her*.

When Kiara said, "Can we pretend none of this ever happened?" it hurt like hell. Like I'd done something disgusting to her. I can't even blame her. Or be angry at her. I wasn't smooth at all. I was blunt, and Kiara is anything but blunt.

Not to draw comparisons, but with Valerie, it went very differently. Her parents owned a vacation home around here. We hooked up—at my place, obviously. Repeatedly.

Took me three months to realize her parents had sold their house. At the time, I was working super hard building up the garage with not enough staff, so I think I get a pass for not figuring that out sooner.

That wasn't why we broke up. She wanted me to move with her "out West", where she was convinced her artistic talent would be better rewarded, and so would my skills in repairing vintage cars.

That's when I understood she thought we were together. So I suppose it was a breakup for her. Not for me. For me, it was just the end of a long hookup that was beginning to wear off, if I'm honest.

With Kiara, it's entirely different. Opposite. I want to build something with her, and the error I made was to not give it enough time and thought. I took for granted that she was of the same mindset. Mistake.

I wiggle the old exhaust pipe free from its hangers, surprised, like always, by the weight of it. I roll out from under the car, ready for a quick coffee before I tackle attaching the new exhaust. This is going to be tricky, what with the Stingray having a fiberglass body, and this model having a side-exit exhaust.

Exactly what I need to keep my mind off Kiara.

"Hey, sweetheart," Orson calls out. Happiness seeps into his rocky voice. It can only mean one thing.

"Hey, guys! Got your favorites today—lemon, poppy seed, and chocolate." Just the sound of her voice makes me all soft. I roll from under the Corvette and wipe my hands.

"You didn't need to do that!" Orson exclaims. "We got that little beauty here."

I step into the reception area right in time to see Kiara's gaze on her Christmas dessert, flinching for half a second. "Oh! That was a little surprise for you guys," she says, her voice cheery. "I know you're partial to your cupcakes. But someone's gonna have to go destroy that little beauty. Colton, you should do the honors," she says, turning to me, looking at me as if nothing had happened at all last night. Is it really that easy for her?

"Uh—I don't know. It's really pretty," I say. "I'd hate to break up something that looks so good."

She shrugs. "Nothing lasts forever." She's still pissed at me, that's for sure. *So much for pretending nothing happened.* Our little word-sparring weighs heavy on my chest; I'm not going down this route with her, so I don't answer. Producing a knife, she stabs through the tree, detaching the top and handing it to me. "The star goes to Colton though, I wouldn't have it any other way." Her voice breaks a little in a way only I can perceive.

And the way she looks at me right now? Her words in front of the guys?

I might have heard her right last night, but I read her wrong. She's more complex than I thought, and that's on me.

I said I'd make her mine, and dammit, one way or another—I will.

But for now, I set the star on a small paper plate next to the computer and mumble thank you.

I duck back into the bay right as Owen Parker appears, dangling the keys to his BMW, and slide back under the Corvette

"Owen," I hear Orson say. "Why don't you relax and have a muffin, yeah?"

I roll to the side in time to see Owen ignore the baked goods, his gaze instead trailing Kiara up and down with a gleam I can't stand.

I roll from under the car, wipe my hands, and stomp back to the waiting room. By the time I get there, he's chatting Kiara up, and she's telling him about the hard time she's having finding a commercial space within her budget.

"Full service, yeah?" I interrupt him, getting on the computer. "We'll have her ready by tonight. D'you want the loaner?"

"Just a ride into town," he says, looking at Kiara. "You going that way?"

"I'll give you a ride," I say. "Or you can have the loaner. Kiara isn't going that way." I grab my keys and open the door for him.

Ignoring Orson's belly laugh behind me, I take a deep breath, step out, tilt my head up to the wide expanse of bluebird sky, my gaze following a cardinal until it lands within the cottony arms of a bush covered in snow. *It's gonna be alright.*

"How's business?" Owen asks once we're in my truck. I expected him to rib me about being territorial about Kiara. I guess he's matured and I haven't.

"Pretty good. Better'n expected, actually. How 'bout you?"

"Good, good. Can't complain." Owen is the only lawyer in town, and everyone knows him. I stop at the intersection of Maple and Elm. Ms. Angela takes her sweet time crossing, then stops right in the middle of the crosswalk to wave at us, beaming.

We wave back.

As she trots to the other side—not because she's holding traffic but because her friend Cheryl calls her from the steps of Shy Rabit—Owen says, "Tell me, how would you feel about joining the Select Board?" Only the largest cities in Vermont have mayors. The rest of us are governed by Select Boards, and their meetings are public. A good way to make sure all topics are discussed in the open, and no single person has the monopoly of decision-making. Cassandra is on the Select Board, as well as my mother's friend Lynn, my friend Noah, and Owen.

Owen and I have history, and it's not a pretty one. But it's old history. Still, the fact he's asking piques my interest.

I clear my throat and make a right into Morgan Way. "I don't know, Owen. I'm not good at all this... debating stuff. I just like things to get done. No offense but you guys spend too much time talking. I don't think I'd be good at—"

He turns in his seat to face me. "Well and that's why you'd be the right person! No nonsense. Straight shooter. Get the stuff done. We need someone like you. Can you believe Stan moved away and despite posting the vacancy on Echoes several times now, only that old witch Louise came forward? People have no sense of civic duty. And I don't mean you," he adds quickly.

I give him my non-committal answer. "I'll think about it."

"Really?" He sounds genuinely pleased. Almost impressed. "We'd need to have your application in soon, so we can review it before the selection meeting."

I nod. "Cassandra told me." She asked me at Millie's, the morning I fixed Kiara's car, and again another time. I kept telling her I'd *think about it*.

I pull up to Owen's office, a brick federal building on a tree-lined street right off The Green.

He beams. "Ca-Cassandra? See? If you can make Cassandra and me see eye to eye... you're really the person we need." He gets out of the truck, then leans back in. "I hope you join us," he says, and for once I believe he's being honest. *Why* he wants me to join is another story.

By the time I'm back at the garage Kiara is gone, and I get back to work with a low-level frustration that doesn't let up until the end of the day.

But that evening at Lazy's, sitting alone at the bar in front of my beer while Kiara and her girlfriends are laughing at a booth, the plan takes perfect shape in my brain.

There's no rush. There's a perfect place and a perfect time and a perfect way this is going to happen. I didn't see it until now.

So for the next few weeks, I just let her be.

Chapter Eleven

Kiara

Why am I going to this engagement party again? I promised myself—*promised*—I wouldn't deal with them for at least another year.

Yet here I am.

Stressing out over what I'm going to wear. How I am going to spend a whole weekend with them?

"Pouvez-vous m'indiquer la poste, s'il vous plait?" the melodic voice on my language learning app sounds. Somehow this calms me down, and I strive to answer the question correctly. Since the whole debacle with my family and with Colton, I've been focusing on ways to make strides in my career, and I came across a scholarship at one of France's most prestigious pastry schools.

You never know until you try, so I applied, and that's why I'm learning French now.

There's a knock on the door, and from the sound of it, it's Colton. Three quick, two slow, assured, not too loud, not too soft either.

My heart does a little skip and a jump, and I take a breath.

He could have been my boyfriend.

But I'd rather have him as a friend.

I scold my features into *mildly unwelcoming, I've got shit to do.* Then I crack the door open, hoping Colton doesn't catch onto the fact I'm getting ready to go somewhere.

But he has a bag at his feet, a carton tray with two coffees, and his charming smile on. I retreat inside my apartment, leaving the door open for him.

"Thought you might need a friend," Colton says, handing me the carton tray. Two cups, each with a name. *Colton. Kiara.*

Ignoring the temptation of Millie's coffee—a clear bribe if I've ever seen one—I set them on my kitchen counter and cross my arms. *Please tell me this is not what I think it is.*

"Going somewhere?" I ask, my chin pointing at his duffel.

Closing the door after him, he leans his hip on the other side of the kitchen counter, crossing his arms too. "Maine," he answers, dragging the word.

My palms moisten. "M-Maine?"

"*Prenez la première à droite, puis la seconde à gauche. La poste...*" I click my app shut.

"You all packed?" he adds.

Shit. I shut my eyes. "You don't need to—I didn't think you'd..." *I didn't think you'd remember.* But of course he did. Of course.

"Bill reminded me," he says, and my heart drops a little. Smirking, he adds, "Disappointed I didn't remember?"

Annoyed he can read me so well, I cross and uncross my arms.

"You're an open book to me, grasshopper," he says, then after a pause adds, "for the most part."

Pushing himself from the counter, he pops the coffees out of their carrier and hands me one. "This party is important to Eloise." He looks me top to bottom. "And I thought you could use a friend."

I feel sorry for him. Colton is always coming through for me—hell, that's how we met—and he always seems to be giving way more than I have to offer back. There's only so many cupcakes a guy can eat, even if you add his staff. That'll never compensate for the many ways he's always there for me. But this is reaching whole new levels.

I set my coffee on the counter. "Colt, you don't need to get roped into my family's dysfunctions." I sigh. "I don't understand why Uncle Bill reminded you. He knows... I mean I *told him* we're not together. What is he...?" I raise my hands, giving up. "Why did you even engage with him on that?"

Something hot passes in his gaze, something that brings back the memory of us standing in his kitchen and him declaring, "We should date." But there's no way Colton could *genuinely* be interested in me that way. He was just being lazy that day—and I get the feeling. The dating scene is tough. But I know his type. And it is not me.

"Grasshopper, get ready. We're gonna make the most of it. That's what friends are for, right?" He takes a long draw from his coffee.

I swallow with difficulty. "It's an overnight thing."

"I know." He gestures to his luggage.

I narrow my eyes on it. The bulky thing on top of his duffel bag? It's his dressy jacket on a hanger. "I mean, I booked a room. One room. If we're pretending to be—"

"I'll take the floor," he interrupts, understanding what I mean: If we're to continue with this charade, we'll need to share a room. "Or the couch, if there's one."

"I can't ask that of you," I say, embarrassed that he's willing to sleep on the floor for me.

He takes another long sip of coffee. "Fine then, we'll share the bed," he answers with a smile, not missing a beat.

That makes me laugh—kind of. It's more like a bitter chuckle. I'm such a mess of confused feelings right now. "Colt, you can't spend the weekend with these nutjobs. Trust me. It's not going to be fun."

"Friends aren't only for the fun parts of life."

I can't really argue with that, and the little flutter at the bottom of my belly confirms what I'm dreading: Colton is successfully breaking my barriers. "Don't you have better things to do this weekend?"

His eyes dance a little at my question. Bringing his cup to his mouth again, he tilts his head back then darts his tongue to lick the foam off his lips. "Can't think of anything better than to keep you company."

I force my expression to betray none of what my body's feeling. "Colt, we're not dating." He really needs to stop the act. Has no one ever told him that when you're a ten, you don't pretend to be with a four, even to come to their rescue?

"Don't think I haven't noticed." His gaze falters a bit, and I feel like crap. Maybe he doesn't consider himself a ten. Maybe he doesn't think in numbers or grades.

Regardless, I can't take the risk. "Look, I'm sorry I've been avoiding you lately."

"Apology accepted. I've missed you. As a *friend*," he adds quickly.

"But we can't keep doing this."

"Doing what?"

"Pretending we're dating."

"And miss out on riling up those assholes? You're no fun these days," he answers with a chuckle and a genuine smile. "Come on, even Bill loves the idea."

Uncle Bill loves Colton, and he wants him there. He might even think throwing Colton and me together like that will lead to something.

"You're early," I say, effectively conceding defeat. I guess we *are* going to my sister's engagement party together.

He smiles in a way that makes me lose a little of my composure, with his gaze doing something close to a caress. "Wanted to make sure you didn't leave without me." Rubbing his hands, he adds, "Where's your bag?"

"I'm not packed yet." The procrastination has been brutal this morning. "I need breakfast first," I declare, planting my ass on one of the two kitchen chairs as I resume my coffee-drinking activity.

Colton opens the fridge and takes eggs out, making me instantly uncomfortable. "That's not what I meant, Colt. Jesus, I don't want you to cook me breakfast." I was stealing some time. Hoping we could simply be together without our minds on this stupid weekend ahead of us. Meanwhile, Colton sets a pan on the range, then drops English muffins in the toaster. "I just wanted to enjoy the delicious Road to Heaven you brought me." I take a sip. "Thanks, by the way." I need to stop the bitch act. It got me nowhere anyway.

"Nice to see you've had time to go grocery shopping," he mumbles as he cracks eggs in the pan.

Then he reaches for his coffee cup and as he brings it to his mouth, I can't help but stare again, remembering the feel of his lips, the taste of his tongue, and his possessive grasp on my nape as he brought me closer and I got lost in him.

The toaster snaps, making me jump, the smell of toast not nearly as arousing as the memory of him, but something familiar to hold onto. Colton calmingly puts the coffee down, takes two plates out, slides two eggs on each, butters the English muffins and sets them on each plate. Then he puts one in front of me, one across from it, sets cutlery and napkins, and finally sits down and starts eating like it's the most natural thing ever.

Like we do this every day. Which we used to—though not at breakfast. So this has to be good, right? I take a sip of coffee.

"You learning French?" Colton asks out of the blue.

I takes me a second to understand where his question is coming from. "Yeah. Nudging the universe, like Cassandra would say."

"What?"

I've totally confused him. "I applied to this pastry training in Paris. I don't stand a chance, but I decided to act as if I'm going. See if that makes a difference."

"What's Cassandra have to do with that?"

"Nothing. She just has these theories." I wave between us. "Never mind."

"How long is the training? And when?" he asks, squinting his eyes at me.

"You realize I haven't been accepted, right?"

"You will be. How long is it?"

I take a beat, Colton's faith in me hitting me hard. "Three months."

He looks at me intently, making me almost squirm. "Okay." His voice comes out low, yet strong.

I don't know what *"okay"* means right now, so I stand up, collect our dishes, and take them to the kitchen area.

I hear his chair scrape the floor behind me. "I'll take care of this, you go pack."

Not five minutes later, his footsteps sound in the short hallway. "What are you wearing tonight?" he asks once in my bedroom. From the corner of my eye, I can tell he's just as lost as I am, looking at all the clothes accumulated on my bed.

"Hell if I know." What do you wear to your evil twin's engagement party?

"Where's your red dress?"

"My what?"

He produces something from the very back of my closet. An old memory jumps at me, from a time that seems to be slipping away—real fast.

"I can't wear that."

"Why not?" Colton asks.

This is the dress I wore to the prom-like party the community college organized after our little graduation. I'd never been to a prom, and I was so full of hope for the future. I can't say that my life turned out bad—it didn't—but at that time, I still had some pretty unrealistic expectations. I thought by now I'd have my own legit business with employees, a storefront, and a state-wide reputation. Turns out having seed money can be crucial to getting a start in life, and seed money doesn't grow under the foot of a runaway teenager. Others in our class had their lucky breaks. I'm still waiting for mine. I'm hoping the all-expenses-paid training in Paris might be that.

"D'you think I could Airbnb my apartment?" Now *that's* an idea to make some extra cash while I'm gone.

"Don't change the topic, grasshopper. Why can't you wear that dress?"

"My body changed," I declare.

"Not that much," he answers straight away, making me blush slightly.

I huff but don't move. I am not trying this clingy dress on, and certainly not for Colton.

"Come on." He holds the dress at arm's length, toward me. "There's gonna be dancing. This dress moves real nice on you." He gives it a little shake as if to prove his point.

"How would you know?" I'm not looking for trouble with my question—just for answers.

He frowns at me. "That's the dress you wore at the party the community college organized for us. Don't think I didn't notice. Don't think *anyone* failed to notice."

Heat flushes my face. "You spent the night with whats-her-face."

He quirks an eyebrow. "I wasn't sleeping with anyone at the time."

I cross my arms. "That's not what I said."

He frowns, his mouth setting in a thin line. "I asked you to come with me to that thing, and you said something about not shitting where you ate."

This isn't going well. "See, this is why we shouldn't be doing this."

"This what?"

"This blurring the lines. We're great as friends."

"The only person blurring the lines is you. You go all jealous on me because years ago I danced with some chick I don't even remember but clearly you do. Wouldn't have happened if you'd gone with me. We would have danced together, had a good time. Instead you turned me down. Rudely. Hurt my feelings a little," he adds with a smile that belies his words.

"And we wouldn't be friends anymore."

He rolls his eyes. "Not this again. You made your point. We're just friends. Not crossing the line. Now try the fucking dress on."

"How do you even remember the dress?"

"Trust me, grasshopper, any dude with half a dick has that dress seared in their memory for decades."

I gasp at his words. Then blush harder. Then snap it from him and duck in the bathroom to try it on.

When I come back out, he's sitting on my bed, looking down at his phone. He glances up at me, does a quick body scan, and his eyes widen for a fraction of a second before he looks away and stands. "'Kay, I'll be waiting for you out there while you pack the rest of your stuff," he says and walks out of the bedroom.

I look down at myself, not sure what's going on. I was pretty happy. I was going to concede he was right: I thought the dress looked fine after all. "What's wrong with the dress?" I semi-shout so he can hear me.

He clears his throat. "Who said there was anything wrong with it?"

CHAPTER TWELVE

Colton

"I need to pick your brains on something," I say to break the silence after an hour of driving. We're almost on the other side of New Hampshire, Weather is treating us right, traffic is scarce, and our coffee refills from Easy Monday are finished.

Kiara glances up from the book she snatched on our way out of Millie's. "Sure." This is something I've been mulling over for a while, and I don't know why I'm not able to make a decision one way or another. "Cassandra asked me to join the Select Board. And Owen."

She purses her mouth appreciatively. "Okay. What's the question?"

I frown. *That's* the question. "What do you think? Should I join?"

"Yeah! You'd be great at it." Funny how she has no reservations whatsoever. "What's the holdup?" She frowns and adds, "Who would you be running against?"

I shrug. "No one. Stan Monroe had to resign because they moved away. The board is looking to appoint an interim until the next election. I mean, other people might apply, but there wouldn't be an election. They just hold a meeting to select the replacement."

Kiara tucks her foot under her and turns to me. "You gonna be butt-hurt if they choose someone else over you? Huh. I didn't think you'd care."

"Hell no. That's the best that can happen. Give me my nights back." Members of the Select Board do a lot of work on their own in the evenings. Even if the meetings are spaced out, the workload is nothing to look down on. "Nah, the thing is, I think Cassandra wants me there because I wouldn't make waves. She said they need a peacemaker like me." I really don't know what to make of this, and I need Kiara's input. She's guaranteed to give it to me straight.

A smile spreads on her lips. "She's right. You *are* a peacemaker. That doesn't mean you're a pushover."

I grunt. "Owen's on the board. Not sure how long I can stand him and still remain a *peacemaker*."

"What if that's the point? The town needs someone like you, Colt, to tip the scales back and make them even."

That's what I can't put my finger on. "What can I do that Cass and Noah can't?" Lynn, Mom's best friend who owns the King farm, is also on the board, but with her gentle nature, I can see her get totally overcome by someone like Owen.

"Maybe they need more support," Kiara answers. "Maybe they need someone who's not involved in anything else and can't be accused of conflict of interest. Cassandra runs the events, and Noah chairs the chamber, owns the general store, and god knows what else his family is involved in. Him also being on the board has to be dicey sometimes."

She's right. "Yeah, knowing Owen, he's probably holding the tip of a knife to their back, threatening to push the blade in at any time."

"Is he really that bad?"

He used to be worse. "I guess I'll find out if he's changed any."

She sits up taller. "So you'll say yes? You'll join?"

To make you this happy, yes. A thousand times yes. "I'll give it a go. What's the worst that can happen?"

She laughs. "You get into a fistfight with Owen?"

"That could be fun." I chuckle. "Although I don't believe that's how these things are run."

"Bummer," she says, flipping her book back open.

The deep rumble of the engine takes over, my thoughts drifting to Kiara.

"You never really told me about your father." I want to get to the bottom of her rift with her family. I feel there's an important piece I'm missing here, and since I'm set on making her mine in all the right ways, I need to know which wounds she needs mending.

Though we're not touching, I feel her stiffen at my question. "There's not much to say," she mumbles, her gaze still on her book.

"My dad was an alcoholic," I volunteer, to get her started. "I told you, right?" I did tell her—several times.

"Mine was a cheat," she answers. Then, with a sigh, she shuts her book, picks up the empty mug on her side of the middle console, then tips it over to drink the last drops. If she were a smoker, this would be the part where she'd light a cigarette.

"I didn't mean to bring up the past." I glance at her. "I mean I *meant* to, but..."

Her gaze is locked ahead of her, but it's clear her mind isn't on the white expanse glimmering under the cold sun. It's lost somewhere in the past, or maybe way inside of her.

Her fists are bunched on her lap, and I bet if I looked right now I'd see her nails digging in her palms.

I wish I could hug her. "We're not responsible for our parents' mistakes."

She lets out a chuckle, then a sigh.

"What?" That was boilerplate comfort speak. Not sure who could argue with that. Well, except Kiara. I glance at her, expecting to see sarcasm painted all over her features. Instead, there's a tear spilling over her eye. Easing my foot off the gas, I reach to wipe it with my thumb, and her hand bumps into mine. I fold my fingers around hers and give her a squeeze.

I expect her to shy away. Instead, she leans onto my shoulder. "You're a good friend," she whispers, so softly I barely hear her over the roar of the engine. "The best. That's why I can't ever lose you."

"You're not gonna lose me," I say, wrapping my arm around her to give her a side hug. I want to be the shoulder she can lean on, metaphorically or for real.

After about thirty too-short seconds of her scooped under my arm, she sits up and takes a short breath. "My father had a double life. Another family. When..." She hesitates, then continues, "when it came out, he disappeared from our lives."

"Shit, I'm sorry, Sweets," is all I can think to say. I always knew something wasn't right where her family was concerned; I didn't realize how bad it was.

'Yeah," she says, and fiddles with the playlist on her phone. "Now you know."

There's still a lot I don't know. Like, why she isn't speaking to her mom and sister? Why do they treat her so poorly?

"Life is shitty," she mumbles. "You have to fight for every little thing you want and you never, ever, get anywhere close to what you dreamed of having."

I'm about to ask her what her dreams are now, but I think better of it. She's not in a good place. I just need to get her through this weekend with minimal damage. Then we can talk about her dreams.

I'd like to help her make them come true.

For the rest of the trip, her playlists fill my truck. And it turns out, all the hype about Taylor Swift is totally deserved. Add to that Kiara's off-key singing, and her sweet scent, and her bouncing up and down in her seat to the beat of the music when she forgets to check herself.

Driving to Maine isn't the drag I thought it would be.

Quite the opposite.

"All good?" Kiara asks me once we're in the room, as she checks her reflection in the mirror. It gives me a little pang of want, the way she asks. Like she's insecure. I've rarely seen this side of her. I suppose being surrounded by her family brings it out. I do like that she's leaning on me for comfort, even if it's only metaphorical.

"Yup," I answer between clenched jaws.

The way she looks in that dress? Holy fuck. I thought I remembered from that make-shift prom they threw us way back then. I was wrong. My memory obliterated all the good parts, leaving only a general impression that was hot enough to fuel many late-night fantasies.

My fingers are still tingling from helping her zip it up a few minutes ago, my dick still straining hard against my own pant zipper. I'm going to have to spend the evening with her by my side.

And the night.

I'm so fucked.

Now she's sifting through her carry-on, then looking around the room. "Shit," she says under her breath.

"What?"

She shrugs. "Nothing," she says, stepping to the door.

I set my hand on the doorknob, keeping us inside. "Kiara. What is it?"

"I forgot my phone charger." She shrugs again. "It's fine. Let's go."

I open the door, liking the way her body brushes against mine as she steps into the hallway. "You had it in the car. You probably left it plugged in."

"Oh, right. Taylor Swift," she says with a smile. "Thanks for putting up with me," she adds as we exit to join the dinner party.

I stop in my tracks, keeping us right outside the room. "What do you mean?"

"I wasn't in a great mood."

"Understandable."

"We only listened to my music."

"Nothin' wrong with Taylor Swift."

She sighs and gives me a half smile. "When are you going to stop being perfect?"

I like the sound of that. She takes a quick inhale that usually precedes some kind of tirade, so I turn her to me with one hand on her hip and shush her with a finger on her lips. Then I lower my mouth to her ear, and whisper, "Just being a good boyfriend," right as someone walks by.

She clears her throat, then takes my hand as we make our way downstairs.

The inn overlooks the ocean, which at this time of day is a dark mass outside the bay windows lining one side of the dining room and two living rooms. Inside, it's comfy and simple. Wooden floors, thick carpets showing some wear, comfortable furniture. A roaring fireplace in each room. Books and paintings of ships. Small lamps on side tables.

"How do you like this place?" Eloise asks as I'm considering whether to line up for the dessert buffet. Kiara went to the bathroom, so I walked away from the table with her. I don't want to offend the hosts, but nothing here looks even remotely enticing compared to Kiara's pastries

"It's really nice. Your friend really came through. How long has she owned it?"

Eloise leans closer to me as if to tell me a secret. "She doesn't actually own it. Her daughter manages it. And she had the idea for this little shindig, to keep her staff busy during slow season."

She nudges me toward the dessert table, cackling. "You can't go wrong with their wild blueberry pie. It's really good, but not Kiara levels of good. Take your girlfriend a slice too, so she has something else to bitch about than her family."

I try to shake myself out of my thoughts about Kiara's complicated relationship with her family when she joins us back at the table. It isn't hard. Kiara's dress cups her curves just the right way and the glass or two of wine she's had put a tint in her cheeks and a spark in her eye. She even smiles when I stand to pull her chair out and leans into my hand when I let it trail on her shoulders.

She's good at faking this stuff. She could fool even me, if I didn't know better. This playing pretend is both highly entertaining and downright infuriating, when I consider the fact that we'll be sharing a room tonight.

I see a very cold shower in my near future.

Conversation at the table we share with Bill, Eloise, and two other cool couples turns to pastries right as Kiara's mother decides to join us. Bill refills the glass of champagne she brought along.

"So what is it that you do, Colton," Kiara's mother asks, in fact terminating the pastry discussion.

It'd be insulting to tell her that Kiara was explaining something about pie dough that half the table seemed interested in hearing, so I simply answer her, "I'm a mechanic."

She pouts. "Oh," she says, taking a quick drink from her bubbly.

"Colton specializes in classic American cars and rally cars. Old rally cars. From the seventies. In addition to all the normal stuff garages do," Kiara says, and is it just my imagination or is that pride in her voice?

Her mom narrows her eyes on her, something cruel glinting in her gaze.

"Racing cars are fun to work on, but I take more pride in being there for my regular, hard-working, local clients. The work on the race cars helps us stay afloat and keep our prices down for the rest of the business," I say, partly to change the topic.

"What type of rally cars?" her mom asks.

I open my mouth to answer, but Kiara beats me to it. "He's done a bunch of Mini Coops."

The Mini Coop. That would be a cool car for Kiara. And since she's noticed them, that probably means she likes them. I make a mental note to be on the lookout for a good secondhand Mini I could entirely refurbish for her. In addition to something appropriate for her business.

"That's interesting," her mother is saying. "Kiara's father was a big fan of the Lancia Stratos. He used to be a racer too. Might still be."

Kiara stiffens. "Goes to prove, not all racers are dickheads."

Chapter Thirteen

Kiara

There. That should shut her up. What was she thinking, drawing a comparison between my father and Colton? They're nothing alike.

Nothing.

Mom takes a deep breath and says, "I really don't understand why you need to be a pastry chef. I mean, you work all sorts of crazy hours. I'm surprised to see you keeping a man. Be careful not to go and lose *that*."

The words slice through me. She has a point. Who wants to date someone who's always working when it's time for everyone else to have fun? She can't know what Colton and I have is fake, but the words still sting. So many echoes to the past. To my faults. To what I supposedly broke.

Colton's protective touch lands lightly between my shoulders, its warmth instantly relaxing me. "You honor me, Mrs. Smith."

Mom tightens her lips. This is not the answer she expected.

"Every day with Kiara is a blessing," Colton adds, leaning to drop a feather kiss on my temple, where it burns straight down to my soul. "I don't take any for granted."

Mom clears her throat. "What I meant to say was, the line of work she chose… it's not conducive to a stable relationship."

I open my mouth to answer, but Colton gives me a gentle squeeze on the nape, effectively shutting me up, all while saying, "I hear you, Mrs. Smith. I do." His hand creeps up into my hair as he adds, "Lucky for my girl, I'm fine with her crazy hours. I'm fine with all her crazy."

Eloise gasps, suddenly catching onto the conversation. "Are you going to propose?"

His breath catches and he looks at me weirdly. *He can't be serious. Come. On.* He gives another squeeze, like he's talking to me with his fingers, tenderly.

"Now, Eloise, this is Maya and David's day. I would hate to steal the show. Come on, babe, this is our song," he adds, taking me to the dance floor.

One arm wraps around my waist, drawing me in, while his other hand captures mine and presses it to his heart. We sway to the music, his chin caressing my temple. "I'm sorry you had to go through that," he says.

"Thank you," is all I can answer. If I look up at him now, I might add something stupid like *I love you*, so I keep my head down and lay my forehead against his chest.

"Kiara, look at me," he rumbles.

I tuck tighter into his embrace.

"Please," he adds.

I look up, his gaze on me setting off the wildest fire. I never thought I could feel something this strong.

His eyes drop to my mouth. "I'd kiss you right now, but with the way I want to do it, we might create a commotion."

I shut my eyes. "That's the alcohol talking," I say and dip my head back down into the comfort of his chest.

"Right. You keep telling yourself that, Sweetness."

"Don't," I answer, my voice harsher than I want it to be. I'm up-tight, and angry, and I'm not dealing well with Colton's assault of gentleness.

Mom's barely veiled attacks brought back so many feelings, it's like she low-key triggered some PTSD. *Life isn't a bed of roses. You have to make concessions. You had to go and break everything we had.* And the best one: *If only you didn't read so much into things.*

I shut my eyes and dismiss the thoughts. I don't regret being who I was. Who I am. And what I did and said: the truth.

The music changes to something fast-paced, something that doesn't require Colton's arms, and I breathe a little better when he begins to let me go. But he's always there, touching my hand, my lower back, looking at me like I'm the only person in the room. His jacket is long gone, his sleeves are rolled up on his corded forearms. His shoulders strain the shirt, the muscles testing the seams in a provocative way.

At some point he leaves the dance floor to get us some water, and I end up between a cousin I haven't seen in forever and Uncle Bill. But without Colton, I feel lonesome. This is my family, and I shouldn't feel this way, but I do.

When he comes back, Eloise has gone to bed. "I think we can go now," I say in his ear.

"Whatever you want, Sweets," he answers, then pats Uncle Bill on the back and leads me upstairs.

Once in our room, he shuts the door softly and says, "You okay, Babe?"

I flinch at his term of endearment but choose to ignore it. "Tired," I lie. I'm wound up, and horny, and angry. I could use a good orgasm right now, but I'm not going to tell Colton that.

Reaching inside his pocket, he says, "Got you your phone charger." He plugs the cable in an outlet he fishes from his bag and looks around for my phone, but I'm too stunned at the moment to make a move for it. Colton didn't need to do this, and I almost say the words. But of course he didn't need to. He wanted to.

As Colton snatches my dead phone from the bed, it hits me. This is Colton's love language. Fixing my car. Getting my charger from the cold. Keeping me from my family.

How long has this been going on?

My voice comes a little strained when I say, "Thank you," but he doesn't seem to notice, or if he does, it doesn't show.

"Take the bathroom first," he says, sitting on the one armchair in our room. "I'm gonna get comfortable here for the night." He wiggles into the chair as if to find the right angle for his lower back. If he thinks he's settling for the night, he's thinking wrong.

I search through my bag for my pajamas and toiletries. "Colt, it's a king bed. We'll share. I'll put a pillow between us or something."

He shrugs. "I don't mind the ch—"

"I mind. You're not sleeping in this chair. Or the floor." Not with everything he's doing for me.

Friends can share a bed, right?

He doesn't answer, and I take his silence as a yes. Standing at the bathroom door, my gaze stays on him a beat too long. He's playing with the TV remote, his attention off me, so I steal a last look at his profile. The set of his jaw, the bump of his Adam's apple, the planes of his face, his high cheekbones and strong nose stir something inside me that they didn't use to. The way his mouth dips slightly down at the side, twitching up as he finds something to watch that he might like makes my stomach flutter as I witness an emotion—any emotion—pass through him.

"Did you want to tell me something?" he asks, making me jump. His gaze is still firmly fixed on the TV, and he mutes it while still flipping through channels.

"Um... no." I take a shaky breath. He's still not looking at me, yet his presence alone fills the whole room, makes me lose my breath and my train of thought. I could fall for him, in fact I might already have, and I strengthen my resolve to remain just friends. The one thing I value in my life is the friendships I forged, and Colton's is at the top. I'm not risking it to satisfy a physical attraction.

He plops the remote on the couch where it lands with a soft bump, stands, and in two strides is in front of me, lightly touching on my shoulder. "Turn around," he says under his breath before I have time to retreat into the bathroom.

Clasping my stuff against my belly, I do as I'm told. In that split second, my resolve does a one-eighty. Whatever it is he has in mind, I'm not saying no this time. Giving into Colton this evening might not have been the plan, but it ended up being so good. What if I let him take the lead the rest of the weekend... the rest of the way? Any regrets I'll inevitably have will be for later. It'd be nice to live in the present for now.

It's decided. I'll say yes to anything Colton asks of me.

His fingers gently flutter against my back as he fumbles with the zipper of my dress. When he's done with the clasp, he unzips it slowly, the sound agonizingly arousing as I imagine his gaze on my naked skin, lowering to my bottom. His voice catches when he says, "All set," and gently pushes me inside the bathroom.

Once in the shower, I forgo the self-care I had sort of planned in my head at some point in the evening, then brace myself for the confession I'll have to make before we go any further.

But when I come back out he's created the Great Wall of China down the center of the bed, using the couch throw pillows in a line that runs the whole length of the bed. He's turned the side lamps on and the main lamp off, in effect creating a romantic atmosphere at odds with the sleeping setup.

"That was fast," he says, unfolding his stature from where he was crouched next to his duffel bag. My eyes lock onto the tattoo on his muscled back and I find it hard to swallow. He's wearing nothing except a pair of dark briefs that mold his perfect ass. I stay frozen in place, clutching my dress in front of me.

I'm both mortified and relieved that I packed the ugliest pair of pajamas I could find as a shield to this particular situation. At least the contrast between us is evident. Mom is right. I could never keep a man like Colton. No way.

The twinkle in his eye tells me that his mind is right back where it should have been all along. Securely in friend territory. "Is that what you wear to bed, grasshopper?"

I step inside the bedroom and drop my dress on top of my bag. Looking down at my tattered, baggy pajamas, I answer, "When I'm sharing a room, yes."

His mouth twitches. "Do you own any other pajamas?"

"Do you own *any* pajamas?" I ask back.

He shakes his head. "I sleep naked," he answers, then quickly adds, "but for you I'll make an exception."

Good to know.

My feet are stuck on the floor right now, so much so that I'm unable to move as he brushes past me on his way to the bathroom.

Embarrassed by the way I look, I scamper to the far side of the bed, get under the covers, turn my night light off, and pretend to be asleep when the bed dips slightly under his weight and he clicks his light off.

I can feel him awake next to me but don't dare move. I try to force my breath to a slower rhythm. Eventually, he clears his throat, the bed moves, and his breathing slows. After a few minutes, his leg jerks, then he turns. I risk a glance over the wall of pillows. His back faces me, rising and falling in a slow, even rhythm. Asleep.

Settling on my back, I stare at the ceiling. Colton's manly presence isn't helping me relax. I should've taken care of business in the bathroom. Now I'm on the edge. Forcing myself to close my eyes, I relive the evening's events in flashes of light, stills of emotions and situations. Colton's strong profile at the table, talking about me like I'm really his soon-to-be fiancée. Colton at the bar, telling my sister something that makes her pale. Colton on the dance floor, exuding sexual tension and directing it at me.

Despite my protestations, he made me feel safe. Beautiful. *Wanted*. None of this felt fake. And yet— it was, wasn't it?

Lying silently next to him, the sound of his deep breathing slowing my heartbeat, I take a calming inhale, drinking in his scent—coconut shampoo and the sweet musk of his skin. Then I silently creep my head up the pillows again, and with my eyes now adjusted to darkness, let my gaze roam his shape.

How would it feel to run my hands in his hair, to caress his strong shoulders, to draw the outline of his tattoo? How would it feel to be tucked inside his embrace, wrapped in his strong arms, sleeping the night off knowing that come morning, he'd have my back again?

His black hair is splayed on the pillow, and I don't even know if it's soft or coarse. Does he always sleep on his side or is it only to avoid me? And that line about sleeping naked—was it just to rile me up?

I could reach out to him. Extend my fingers and touch his ridiculously defined bicep and tell him I'm fucking scared. That I want him, but I'm scared to lose him.

But what good would that do? He'd say the right thing in the moment, and I'd live to regret what would happen next. Present me might be itching to take the risk, but future me will be thankful in the end that I took the reasonable course of action.

"Something bothering you, grasshopper?"

Stifling a yelp, I duck back to my side of the bed. "Thought I heard some noise," I lie, my voice muffled by the pillow I'm smothering myself with in an effort to kill my embarrassment.

"No other noise than the sound of your overthinking," Colton says in a sexy-as-hell sleepy voice. The bed moves under his shifting weight. Keeping my head under my pillow, I turn my back to him and hug the edge of the bed, one foot sticking out of the covers.

I wake up startled by sharp rasps on the door, the kind made by a metallic object. "What the fuck time is it?" Colton asks.

Rubbing my eyes, I swing my legs over the edge of the bed and draw the curtains open, ignoring whatever's going on on the other side of the door. It's a gray morning, the sun losing its battle against the clouds, bathing everything in a milky light with no sparkle.

"Kiara!" Maya's voice hisses outside the door. Is that really her? What does she want now?

"Want me to get it?" Colton asks, his voice thick with sleep.

I glance at him. He's on his back on the bed, one arm folded under his head, the other pulling the sheets over his midsection. His gaze is on all of me at once, it seems. With his torso splayed out, his morning stubble, his hair disheveled as if I did manage to play with it, he looks like a cover model for one of the books Millie liberally dispenses at Easy Monday to keep us coming back.

As my glance turns into more, the gleam in his eye sharpens, the corners of his mouth turn up, his head settles into the pillow, turned toward me to get comfortable.

He's tempting and he knows it.

"I got it," I answer.

I nervously run a hand through my hair then down the front of my pajamas, like that's going to help make me look prim and proper to my sister.

I look like shit; what else is new? Taking a deep breath, I crack the door open.

She lets an airy laugh out when she sees me. I don't need her to tell me what she finds so funny, but she spells it out for me anyway (because why would she pass on that kind of fun?). "No wonder you can't keep a guy." She giggles.

I open the door a tad more so I can lean on it for emotional support without slamming it in her face. "What do you want?"

"Just checking—oh, hey," she says, her gaze moving somewhere behind my shoulder.

Colton fits himself right behind me, clasping his naked arm around my midsection. With a deep, contented sigh, he reaches under my pajama top and palms my belly. Then he leans into me, kissing the top of my head, trailing down the side of my face, nudging me to give him access to my neck.

Which I do. I tilt my head so he can full-on kiss, nibble, and lick.

Maya's eyes round a bit, but she keeps control. She always seems to have control.

She takes us in, the image of a couple in love caught in a moment of intimacy, and envy colors her features. This is her engagement, yet still she wants what she thinks I have.

We must play our part really well, because her nostrils flare as she narrows her gaze on the shape of Colton's hand under my pajamas.

His thumb splays out, reaching the lower swell of my breast. "Hey, Maya. Whassup?"

As she bites the inside of her lip, I straighten to break the contact, but he growls and fully cups my breast. "You coming back to bed, baby?" he says to me, not waiting for an answer.

Maya clears her throat but still can't seem to bring her eyes up to mine.

I grip the door harder, because my knees are becoming less and less dependable. "What's up?" I repeat Colton's question, trying to keep the quiver off my voice. As if Colton fondling me in public is perfectly normal. As if his calloused hands gently stroking my most sensitive parts was something so ordinary I don't even notice it anymore.

Her gaze lifts to my face but never quite makes it to my eyes. "Brunch is in thirty minutes," she answers crisply. "You never RSVP'd to it, but since you're here…" she trails off, her gaze dropping back to the outline of Colton's knuckles.

I'm really not in a position to make any decisions right now. I'm fighting an orgasm by nipple stroke—not something I knew could occur. I'm wondering what's going to happen when this door closes, brunch or no brunch. "Um…" Taking a page from Colton's book, I improvise. "You wanna go to brunch, Romeolicious?" I turn my face to him. Seizing the opportunity, I stroke his forehead, scooping the hair out of the way, getting a good feel for it in the process.

I expect a chuckle at the nickname, a lift of the lips, maybe even a what-the-fuck that will expose our charade. I get none of that. Instead,

I'm thrown off-kilter by the look he gives me. By the way our gazes lock for a split second.

Maya sighs. "It's not really optional," she clips. Her tone hits something deep in me, something primal. It's the tone she uses to lecture me. Judge me. Put me down. I know that tone. I don't need to hear whatever's coming next from her to feel defeated already—not good enough.

I turn back to tell her we're coming—anything to make her go away, really—but Colton beats me to it. "Tell you what," he says, still possessively cupping my breast, his front intimately pressed against my back.

There's no way I can ignore the hard beating against my upper hip. I lay the hand that's not gripping the door on Colton's arm, maybe in an attempt to stop him fondling me, or maybe to say this is totally cool. In all honesty, I don't know what I'm thinking anymore, much less what I'm doing.

"I never heard of an engagement party to begin with," he says. "I'm ready to puke just thinking about you guys's wedding. Your sister called out of work to be here, looking fucking gorgeous which in turn makes you look good. This is the first we hear about your fucking brunch, so you're going to give her all the time she needs to get ready, and if that includes me giving her an orgasm to undo all the stress you're giving her, then so be it. We clear?"

Maya swallows visibly, the red on her cheeks almost as deep as the dress I wore last night. Without a word, she dips her head down and scampers away.

My head falls back against Colton's chest as I stroke his arm still wrapped around me.

He shuts the door softly, pulling me closer into him as he does so, his erection beating against me. We stay like that a few moments that feel like forever, then he says, "You okay?" while the hand he still has under my jammies starts making slow circles on my breast.

I clear my throat, but no sound comes out and no coherent thought forms in my mind. All I can focus on is how good he smells and how warm he is and how strongly he's holding me up, when in normal circumstances all I'd want to do would be to pack my stuff and run away and regret coming here.

I don't regret coming here with Colton.

I don't regret sharing a room with Colton.

I do, however, regret having to tell him what follows.

Letting my head fall forward, I run my fingers down his veined forearm. "You can let go, now, Colt." My voice comes out husky—not the intended effect. It seems even my vocal chords are affected by what Colton's doing to me.

He whispers in my ear, "Do you want me to let go?" My whole spine shivers as he punctuates his words with his lips trailing down to where my neck meets my shoulder.

"I think you should."

"You're so tense, though." He brings the hand that was on the door to my hip, then teases the pants' waistband open with the tip of his fingers. "I wasn't kidding. You need an orgasm."

Fuck yeah. I do.

"Colt..." My voice comes out a low rasp. Nothing in it indicates I'm not agreeing. I clutch his arm closer to me while my head rolls back on his torso again.

His dick beats against my back, and reality hits me. I can't let this happen. "We can't."

"Who says anything about me?" he murmurs. "I'm just a friend doing you a favor. Let yourself go. Come on my fingers, grasshopper. You know you need it. Ignore my morning wood."

My hips move forward and he takes it for what it is—yes.

"You're not coming in front of the door," he says, scooping me up and setting me on the bed.

I make quick work of my pajamas. Colton's hard-on, even if he called it morning wood, boosts my confidence a little. I can't look that bad to him, especially if the way he's looking at me is anything to go by.

Swallowing hard, he licks his lips and rakes his gaze over me. Is he going to change his mind? I trail my fingers between my thighs. I do need this orgasm. His eyelids get heavy, and he drops to his knees, hooking my legs to pull me to him. Then he gently removes my hand from my center and dips his mouth to my folds.

In the milky light bathing the room, I wonder if maybe I'm dreaming. I run my fingers in his hair (it's thick and soft) and cling to it as he runs his tongue around my clit. The tease is unbearable. "A little more to the right," I finally whisper.

He lifts his head and looks at me, a smile lifting his mouth to one side. Brushing up the insides of my thighs, he says, "You think I don't know where your clit is, Sweetness?" at the same time the pad of his thumb rubs me right in the center, making me arch and cry out. The sensation is more than electric, the orgasm building up but not quite there.

"There," I sigh.

But he removes his hand, bringing it back to my thigh. "Not yet," he growls as he lowers his face between my legs.

"The fingers... the fingers were fine," I say.

"I thought you wanted an orgasm." He peppers kisses on the insides of my thighs.

"I do. Please. You said-you said..."

"I said I'd give you an orgasm."

"But you said I'd come on your fingers," I whine. This teasing is really torture.

He looks up again, smiling like I've never seen him smile. He's soft yet arrogant, dominant yet on his knees. His dark hands on my body are strong enough to snap me in half, yet he's taking all my strength away just by the power of his tongue. "I changed my mind," he says as he dips back down between my legs.

His tongue draws lazy circles on the outside of my labia now.

"This is not... this is not..." I sigh in exasperation, trying to bring his head back where I want it.

"Beggars can't be choosers," he says, the rumbling of his voice making my center clench. He breathes softly into my folds, an exhale that's both admiration and want.

Ohgodohgod, he's going to want to go all the way with me. Panic seizes me, then relief. Then worry. This is exactly what I didn't want.

"Get out of your own head, Sweetness," he says.

I snap my gaze down to him. His hair is covering part of his eyes, his hands are cupped around my hips, thumbs stroking me gently. The strong ridge of his nose is a stark contrast to his full lips hovering over me. "Never tasted anything so good. Now show me how you sound when you come on my face." He dips back down, sucking and teasing and growling, then narrows down on my clit, getting what he wants.

The sensation is like nothing I've ever had, from my curling toes, to the electricity coursing through my entire body, and the shock waves that shake me. I hold his head down, committing everything to memory—the sight of him, his shoulders rolling as he strokes my thighs, the smell of my sex mixed with his fresh sweat, his palms cradling me as if to worship me.

When I come down from my high, I spread my legs wider to welcome him and open my mouth to say something.

But then he stands, his dick straining his briefs, takes quick strides to the bathroom and locks himself in.

The shower starts running, and I'm left wondering. My body is spent in the most delicious way. I try to sit up, but my legs barely cooperate, so I plop back flat on my back, one hand on my belly, listening to his sounds behind the closed door, feeling the deep relaxation that's spread to every one of my bones.

When he comes back out, wrapped in a towel, he doesn't look at me right away. His hair is a mess I'd like to untangle now, but I'm not sure where this leaves us.

There's no going back, though.

His lips tilt up. "Feel better?" he asks with humor in his voice.

"What just happened?"

"I gave you what you needed." He drops the towel, giving me a first-row view to his muscled ass as he steps into a fresh pair of briefs. "Ready to tackle Cruella and the gang?"

I sit up, and suddenly self-conscious of my nudity, cover myself with the sheet. "I mean," I start, then hesitate, lick my lips, and add, "where does that leave us?"

He grabs a dark green Henley and pulls it on, then fixes his hair by running his fingers through it. "Whaddaya mean?"

"Well…"

"I did you a favor. That's what friends are for. No?"

I blink several times. An idea forms in my hazy brain. "So are we like, friends with benefits?"

He pauses to think about that. Or maybe it's just that the jeans he's attempting to put on have a sock stuck somewhere in one of the legs, and he seems utterly puzzled by this. He doesn't answer.

"Colton?"

"Huh?"

"Are we, like, f—"

"Not sure about labels, grasshopper," he interrupts, seeming suddenly upset. "Are you gonna get ready or what?"

Why the mood change? This is not like him. "Ready for what?"

His features soften as he puts his hands on his hips and tilts his head to me, a small smile forming on his lips. "The brunch. We don't have to go. Your call."

Oh shit. I forgot. I jump off the bed, trying to hide my intimate parts as I look for my jammies.

Colton rolls his eyes, shakes his head with a smile, and plops on the couch, grabbing the remote, his gaze away from me.

I gather some clothes, get in the shower, and think this through.

Despite how physically attracted I am to Colton, how my body craves his and a part of me is obsessed with how he feels and makes me feel, I can't let myself fall for him. I won't let another man I care deeply about come into my life only to disappear from it.

While for me, giving fully into my attraction for Colton would mean forever, it wouldn't for him and that's okay. It's understandable. His sudden mood change after... *what he did* proves my point.

I can rationalize that. Colton is a very masculine, sensual, *sexual* guy. He never was attracted to me physically, until he made the mistake of fake-kissing me. For a guy like him, that would have awakened the desire for more. It's a mechanical chain-reaction. Guy kisses girl, guy wants more, guy pursues girl until he gets what he wants, then guy moves on to next girl. It's the way of the world, and what happened earlier is proof of that. Colton won't stop until he gets what he wants from me, and I can't in all consciousness fault him for that. It's how men are wired.

But what if I could control the outcome to our mutual benefit? He wants me. I'll admit, I want him too. It's the heartbreak I can't deal with. We both want to remain friends after.

The solution to our predicament presents itself to me in its beautiful simplicity. One time is all we need to both get what we want. Well, to be fair, Colton will be on the winning end of that bargain. Because I'm certain I could have an infinite number of other times with him. It's the breaking up that I'm not okay with, and I understand it's unreasonable of me. Going in knowing it's just one time guarantees I never have a breakup with Colton.

I'll let him scratch the itch he has with me, and I'll get to be entirely with him without any further expectation to shatter. One time with me is all Colton will need to move on. And since I'll go in knowing this is what I get, I'll be perfectly fine with it. I'm actually looking forward to imprinting every last detail of him in my memory forever. It will be our mutual little gift.

It really is a win-win situation.

Now all I need is to get Colton on board. I'm expecting some resistance if I open with the assumption that he'll be done with me after one time. He'll think I see him as superficial. Truth is, I'm being realistic. But I don't want to hurt his feelings.

So instead, I'll use Colton's passion for fixing things. I can be his little project.

I think it'll work. Hell, he might think it's genius.

CHAPTER FOURTEEN

Colton

I'm proud of myself. She needed an orgasm—badly—and I gave her one.

She doesn't want to be my girlfriend, so I didn't try to take advantage.

God knows I could have. It wouldn't have been taking advantage at this point. It would have been giving her what her body was screaming for.

I'd never really understood the meaning of the expression "hungry eyes". I do now, having seen how she looked at my cock that was threatening to break free of my briefs.

Thinking back to what happened minutes ago, I grip the remote so hard I might break it. Spending four hours in the truck with her is going to be pure torture. I tried to scrub her scent off me in the shower, but the memory is stronger. It won't let go. I knew it wouldn't, but I'm a glutton for punishment, so I dove right into her sweetness and fed on it, drank from it, inhaled it, studied it. I can map her from memory if I need to, from her perfect perky tits to her hipbones to her center. From the way she shivered when I kissed her earlobe and the way the shake went straight to her spine when I licked my way down the side of her neck. From the way her fingers clasped on my head when she finally let go—let all her troubles disappear and gave in to me.

It's going to be hard not to beg her to give into us. We would be so good together. I could make her so... happy. I know I would. For the first time in my life, I feel like I can make someone's life better. Fuller. I'd worship her. She'd never have to call these people family again. I'd be her family. *We'd* be a family.

Maybe she'll change her mind.

I rub my face in my hands. I can't go down that path. It's not what she wants, or she would have said so.

None of this *friends with benefits* bullshit.

The bathroom door opens, and I feel her stop inside the room. I give her three seconds to say whatever's on her mind. Then three more.

When she doesn't speak but still I feel no movement, I mute the TV. "Ready?" I say.

"So..." she starts.

This is a good start. She's shy. It rips me apart, but in a good way. I always knew Kiara's bravado was a front. A wall. A protection.

I'd just never really seen Kiara shy. Uncertain. Vulnerable.

I turn the TV off to show her she has my full attention. Then I stand to face her. She's a little flush, but that could be from the shower. Her towel-dried hair falls in free curls around her face, something I'd never seen before. It gives her an angelic air that I'm sure she'd hate if she only knew.

Kiara works so hard on being a devil.

"Yeah?" I ask, trying hard not to stare at her nipples pebbling under her tight sweater. Instead, I check my phone, pretending to look at the time.

"I was thinking…"

Oh this is good. This is very good. I pocket my phone back and look at her. I don't know what to do with my hands. It's too soon to draw her to me and kiss her and tell her how long I've been waiting for this moment. So I shove them in my jeans pockets and tilt my head to the side. "Yeah?" I can't help the smile that spreads to my whole face. She's so fucking adorable.

It's pretty simple, really. I love her. I'm not going to tell her—I'm not an idiot. But I'm going to savor every moment of her coming slowly into herself as she sees how good I am for her.

This is the story I'll be telling our grandchildren. The way she shyly lifts her eyes to me, ready to ask me to take the next step, will be seared in my memory until I take my last breath. So yeah, when I'm old and wrinkly, I'll be telling our grandkids how stubborn their grandma was, and the merits of my patience.

It's going to be a fun story, one I'll perfect over the decades.

For now, I watch it unfold, remembering how upset she was when I wanted to be her boyfriend. How she avoided me for weeks. How she didn't even want me to come here with her. We know how that went.

"You were thinking?" I prompt her. I'm patient, but come on.

She sits on the bed, one leg folded under her. "Here's the deal." She licks her lips and frowns. "We're friends, right?"

I nod.

"And well… you just proved what a *good* friend you are."

I'm not sure where she is going with that, or that I like the usage of the word friend back-to-back, but I can't help but smile at the memory of how I proved my *friendship*.

"You're welcome," I say, maybe a little too smugly.

She doesn't acknowledge me. She picks at something on her lap, probably nothing at all. "I'm in a pickle," she finally says.

"Okay."

"And I think you can help me."

I shrug. "Sure, anything."

She takes a deep, shaky breath, then lifts her gaze at me. "I'm a virgin."

Holy shit, that explains a lot. Thank god I held it together, earlier. For a moment there, when I went down on her, I thought she was going to pull me to her, and I wouldn't have resisted if she asked me to fuck her.

I sit on the bed and lift my fingers to her curls. Their texture astounds me. Without the product she puts on to make her hair stick up like shards, they're soft as silk. "I'm glad you're telling me," I say, not recognizing my own voice. Kiara's vulnerability is hitting me hard, in the best way.

And then I realize: she's had no other men. Although none of this will make it in the story I'll tell the grandkids, my heart swells. If she's ready to give herself to me (which I think is what she's getting at), it confirms that she wants to build something with me.

I take her hand in mine and rub my thumb on her palm. A little bit of pink tints her cheeks. "There's nothing to be ashamed of," I tell her.

"I'm not ashamed," she answers a little defensively, slipping from my grasp to pick at her cuticle. "I just... thought I could ask for your help."

I'm not sure what help she's talking about. Does she need explanations? She knew exactly where her relevant body parts were, and how they factored into the whole experience, earlier. "Sure... what-what do you mean? What kind of help?"

She takes a deep breath. "I thought maybe, with us being friends... like... intimate friends..."

I'm getting irritated at her usage of the word *friends*, but I give her the space she needs to tell me what it is that's bothering her so much. "Yeah?" I say softly to encourage her.

Another deep breath and she lifts her beautiful eyes to me. "I thought we could, like, you know..." She takes a deep breath and the rest comes out super fast, "sleep together just once so you could get it out of your system and I could get it over with."

Years ago, Owen Parker dared me to jump into the Emerald Creek right after the ice had broken. It must have been March. The edges of the river were still frozen, the ice hanging onto the banks. The middle was raging with spring melt. I was at that age when my brain wasn't fully formed—far from it. When I hit the water, I didn't feel anything other than a huge weight constricting my chest, and a force so powerful I could barely move my limbs.

Today, sitting on that bed with Kiara asking me to *get it out of my system—so she could get it over with*—I feel worse.

Way more stupid. Way more blind. And maybe really this time, dying.

I bolt from the bed and go to the window. Big fat snowflakes are twirling to the ground. Maybe we should skip brunch and make it home before it gets worse.

"Colt?" Kiara asks, her voice small.

I can't bring myself to be angry at her. Staring at the window, I say, "You should be in love with the man who takes your virginity."

I hear her huff behind my back.

Turning to look at her, I add, "It's... it's too intimate for a friend to do, Kiara."

She stands, runs her hand in her hair, and goes into the bathroom, leaving the door open. "And what you did earlier wasn't intimate?" she shouts.

The whole place doesn't need to know what's happening here. I leave the window to stand at the bathroom door. She tilts a bottle of hair product, fills her palm with foam, then spreads it all over her soft curls. "What's the difference?" she asks, her voice lower now that our gazes are meeting in the mirror.

The difference is I thought something was happening, earlier. When she took comfort in my embrace when her sister was being bitchy. The way her body relaxed into mine, like I was all she needed. The way she didn't swat my hand away once Maya was gone but instead leaned on me.

The difference is from the tender and passionate way she played with my hair when I made her come, I thought we were really going somewhere, the two of us, without saying the words.

The difference is I didn't think I was being used—not to that extent. Just a tool to pop her cherry.

The difference is I hadn't fully admitted to myself the depth of my feelings for her.

"It's just not the same," I end up saying.

"They say you never forget your first time," she says with a playful smile. "This way I'll never forget you."

At least the river wasn't twisting a dagger in my heart.

CHAPTER FIFTEEN

Kiara

The vibe between us shifts dramatically, but for the life of me I can't point my finger on what happened. One minute he insists on giving me an orgasm, the next he's all offended about taking my virginity.

"Well, I'd never forget you anyway, Kiara," he bites at my attempt to make light of my apparently offensive request. "What, are you planning on leaving? Going somewhere, that you're talking about forgetting people?" There's a harshness to his tone that sets me off. What's up with him suddenly? I thought guys had a thing for virgins. I thought... I don't know what to think anymore.

I shrug. This training in Paris might pan out and lead to something bigger. Who's to say? I might end up staying there. Or I might have an offer in...maybe Italy. Or Australia. You only live once.

But Colton seems a little upset, so I direct my thoughts back to him. "I wouldn't forget you either," I say. My voice shakes a little. "As for leaving..."

He crosses his arms. "Yeah?"

"I'm not sure Emerald Creek was the right move for me."

Frustration, maybe even anger, radiates from him. He was the one who convinced me to come to Emerald Creek. I add quickly, "I mean, at the time, it was. Definitely. And I'll always be grateful to you for that." Our eyes meet in the mirror, emotion threatening to creep up. Five minutes into meeting me, and he already believed in me. Introduced me to Chris, who took a chance on me. "But now..." I focus my attention back on my hair. God, I look like an old doll who got a haircut from her bratty owner armed with dull scissors. My hair hangs in limp strands that don't even have a proper bounce. It's like everything's giving up on me. Thank god for mousse.

And for vibrators, since Colton is not on board with this V-card thing. Looks like he has his limits, and sleeping with me is a hard one.

"Now?" he prompts me.

My hair finally looking good and strong, I grab my makeup. "I'm stuck," I answer. "Not in Emerald Creek," I add quickly. I love that small town—it's the best that's happened to me in my life. "In my career. I'm just adding small jobs and it's..."

He looks a little hurt, and I get it. He feels responsible for what I'm feeling now: disappointment in myself. What he should feel, is proud of the way he helped me when I was down. "Colt, it's not like that." I look at him through the mirror, sensing rather than really seeing his tension. I set my makeup pouch down, but don't quite get the courage to turn and face him. I'm disappointing him, I can tell. First the virgin thing, now the fact I didn't make it the way I should have. "I thought by now I'd have my pastry shop. Or at least if I was going to cater to restaurants and bakeries, a legit space. Something professional to call my own. A *business*."

From the group we formed at the incubator, I'm the only one still working for others. I'm the only failure. It's no one's fault but my own. I know what I need to do: I need to have a big name on my resume. When I go see a banker for a loan, I need to be able to say I won some famous award or worked three years with a star pastry chef. I wouldn't mind a partnership with one of these guys who made it big. I'm not so infatuated with myself that I need my own name on my storefront. Owning a high-end franchise would suit me just fine.

"And you think leaving Emerald Creek is gonna do that for you?"

"Remember this pastry training in France I told you about? The sort of accelerator for pastry chefs I applied to?"

His face doesn't move, if you exclude a nerve twitching at the edge of his right eyelid.

"What?" I say.

"And who's gonna bake pastries when you're gone?"

I blink several times. I hadn't thought of that. "They'll be fine without me."

He doesn't answer, just stares me down. *What?* It's true. Chris initially gave me a job because Colton asked him, not because he was hiring. Now I'm training Willow, who was his shopkeeper, and I bet she could do just as well alone as she does when I supervise her.

Then there's the restaurant, Clover's Nook. They bring me in once or twice a week to bake for them. I'm not sure how much they depend on me—I'm going to say they wouldn't really feel the difference if I were gone. They might have to resort to simpler desserts that their chef could totally do on her own.

Emerald Lake Resort, the third place I work at, might be in a little bit of a bind, given that they think they're high-end and need stuff that only I can make in the area, but I don't give a shit. I don't like management there. Money is the only reason I keep working for them.

"We'll be fine without you, huh?" Colton asks.

It doesn't escape me that he includes himself in the generic *they* I used. I suppose no one but me would bring the guys pastries twice a week, and *that* thought depresses me a bit. "Totally."

"Okay, then," he says, the bitter set of his chin telling a different story. And what's up with that? I'm about to ask what the fuck he's upset about, but in the last few hours I've asked enough of Colton for a whole month—make that a whole *year*. I'm not starting a fight with him because he thinks I should "think positive".

I know I don't amount to much. His positivity might aim at making me feel better, but right now it'll do the exact opposite: expose again what a failure I am.

Turning back to the bathroom mirror, I do my eyes extra smoky so the dark circles look like they fit right into the vibe I'm going for. Colton pushes himself off the doorjamb and the TV starts again. His scent floats, leaving me wanting and wishing he'd said yes to the V-card thing

I don't really get his point. Was he in love with the first girl he was with? We've never had those conversations, and I wonder why. But now that I think about it, he never brings up his ex-girlfriend, Valerie. Maybe he's still in love with her, and that's why...

The thought twists cruelly in my belly. Maybe that's it. Yeah, that's totally it. His commitment issues come from a bad breakup. It would have to be with Valerie. I think she was the only serious girlfriend of his I heard mentioned. And she's back in town. That has to mean something.

Colton's previous relationship occupies my brain all through brunch. I summon threads of conversations and mentions of his ex I've heard over the years and filed away as unpleasant but necessary. Now it appears vital to me that to understand Colton, I need to understand where he stands with his ex. They lived together for a few months; that much I know. Since Valerie, he hasn't had a steady relationship. I should have paid more attention to the circumstances. Asked more questions.

Chapter Sixteen

Colton

"Why did you and Valerie break up?" Kiara asks out of the blue on our way home. During brunch I played the part of the loving boyfriend, but the way she felt under my touch tore at me. I don't know if I'm more upset at her for wanting me to help her *get it over with*—I hated how it sounded like something to cross off her to-do list—or if it's because she thinks she wouldn't be missed if she left Emerald Creek.

How did we fuck up so majorly that she doesn't feel at home there? Does she really think her asshole family (except Bill and Eloise) comes anywhere close to us in the way we feel about her?

"Colt?"

"Huh?" Oh, yeah. Valerie. Why the fuck is she talking about my ex? "What?" I snap.

She turns the dial of the radio down, and I feel like taking her hand in mine and keeping it there. Squeezing it to show her how much we all love her.

"Why'd you and Valerie break up?"

I frown. "What's that gotta do with anything?"

She tucks her left foot under her, so her body is twisted toward me, like when she's about to start a long conversation. "What happened?"

"Been years, grasshopper. Who cares?"

"Maybe I do."

I'm not going to ask why. Despite the poor way she's been treating me, she still has best friend privileges. "It just ran its course."

"Ha!" she says softly.

I raise an eyebrow. "What's that supposed to mean?"

She spreads her hands like I just made her point. "Relationships run their course, and then people are over each other. Friendships don't." If there's anything I know about Kiara, it's that she likes to examine all aspects of a problem in a scientific way. I can see where her thoughts took her from me refusing to *get it over with,* back to me asking her to date me. She's trying to understand my logic.

The thing is, there is no logic.

"We were never friends, Val and I." If Kiara thinks she can convince me we can be friends with benefits, like she says, she's got the wrong angle with Valerie. "And she was nothing like you," I add to drive my point home.

Kiara untucks her foot and looks straight ahead. With a bitterness in her voice that sounds a lot like jealousy, she snaps, "Didn't she move in with you?"

Yeah, she did. Kiara got that right. It was Valerie's decision, not mine. But I'm not getting into that with Kiara. Somehow I don't think bringing my past relationships into the conversation is going to help my case at this juncture. "She moved in, and then she moved out," I answer Kiara's question.

"What happened?"

"She didn't like hanging out with me, I guess. You'd have to ask her." I don't share with Kiara the part about Valerie wanting us to move away. It's irrelevant. Kiara is the one person I'd follow anywhere.

"Didn't she *tell* you?"

There had been some shouting, but honestly, at that point, I was done listening. I'd stopped listening to whatever she said right around the time she decided I spent too much time playing video games and we should take up backgammon, and when I came back from work that day my gaming stuff was stashed in a box next to the trash. It might have been that week that she moved out. "I don't think we really gelled," I tell Kiara.

"What about Country Club?"

From a live-in girlfriend to someone I've never met, she's giving me whiplash. "What's with all the questions?"

"I'm trying to figure out why you won't... help me out. What's wrong with me? I'm not asking for anything more than... you know..."

Her hands move around each other in little tumbles. Is this her representation of people sleeping together? Despite me, a smile forms in my belly. I pinch my lips to keep it from spreading to my face. "Than *sex*?" I ask, letting the word pop out like a mini BB gun.

"Yeah! Sex," she repeats, drawing out the *x*. "You have a lot of experience, and you don't seem to need to loooooove the people you sleep with. So..."

"Nope."

She sighs. "So let me recap. I won't date you so we don't ruin our friendship and you won't... sleep with me... because...?"

Because I already feel more for you than friendship. And when we sleep together—if we sleep together—it's gonna have to mean pretty much the same for both of us.

It'll mean the beginning of forever. Or at least, an intention toward that.

I make the mistake of glancing at her. Her eyes are watery when she says, "You don't find me attractive."

I huff, upset that she's placing this on the purely physical plane, but I do need to set the record straight. "That thing in your lower back wasn't a gun, sweetheart."

"You said it was just morning wood," she hisses.

"I was lying." Her sister's voice alone would kill anyone's boner. But Kiara's body giving into my strokes, her nipples pebbling, her thighs tightening, her nails digging into my forearm, and most of all her head falling against me when she needed my support: That did me in.

"Then why won't you sleep with me?!" Her hands spread out in disbelief, her tone is exasperated.

"Because I don't want to just *sleep* with you." There. I've said it. I want more with Kiara. And I'm done being her tool. It was stupid of me to initiate the fake dating. I know why I did it: to be closer to her.

All I got was a raging hard-on, some information I wish I never knew, and the confirmation that Kiara sees nothing more in me than a good friend with a functioning dick.

"Fine," she snaps.

I stupidly hold my breath, thinking she's going to agree to be my not-fake girlfriend.

I'm honestly ready to beg for Kiara. She'd be worth it.

We'd be good for each other.

She crosses her arms and looks out the passenger window. "We'll stay friends."

My stomach plummets and I clench my jaw. Pressing on the accelerator, I move us to the left lane to pass a line of trucks, then stay there for a while just for the heck of it. After three miles, the silence in the truck gets to me and I start looking for a radio station that's not playing stupid breakup shit.

Turns out, heartache is favored by songwriters. I turn the radio off.

"When I was seventeen," Kiara says, her gaze straight ahead, "I thought I was in love with David. I thought I was going to spend my life with him. I had planned on sleeping with him after prom. *We* had planned it." She turns her face to the passenger window. Is she crying? Is she not over him?

Shit.

She turns back and looks at her hands. "After I found him cheating on me with Maya, I took the car I'd bought with my dad's help for my sixteenth birthday. I drove, aimlessly at first. Found myself in Burlington, where my dad had an office. He'd said that morning he was going to work from there before catching a plane for a business trip. I'd never been, but knew the address. It was in a building close to the lake, right next to the ferry. I'd memorized that somehow. I don't know how or when and I wish I never had." She shakes her head as if to clear the rabbit hole of memories and continues with her story.

"I just needed to... I guess go cry to him. Not sure what I was thinking. Point is..." She takes a deep, shaky breath. "That's the day I found out he had another family. I was walking up to the building, totally focused on my little sob story, when he came out the door. He was on his phone, didn't see me. He had a big smile and was talking to someone he called *son*. And then he said, 'Tell your mother I love her.' And then, 'I'll see you in a couple of hours.' For a minute I thought he had a clone or a doppelgänger or something. A twin he'd never told us about. But he was wearing the same shirt he'd put on that morning. I remembered—it was a Father's Day gift. I didn't think. I just called out to him. And he turned around. And the look on his face...

"He tried to deny it. Said I was '*reading too much into things*'. Kept repeating that, like what I heard could mean something different." Her mouth purses and she takes a shaky breath. "'Reading too much into things'? Fuck that... Yeah, it all went downhill from there."

CHAPTER SEVENTEEN

Kiara

After confronting my dad, I went home and told Mom, as gently as I could. Sat her down and told her what I'd seen and that I knew she wouldn't believe me, but she had to, it was the truth, and that I loved her.

"She got so angry at me," I whisper to the window, so low I feel Colton lean over to listen. I turn my head and make a painful effort to speak out. "She knew. All along she knew. And now she was accusing *me* of destroying everything. Because I'd opened my big fat mouth, is what she said."

"I-I'm still not following," Colton says.

"I know." I take a deep breath. It took me a while too—to process this. "Turns out, my mom was having an affair with a married man. When she got pregnant with us—listen to this—Mom said he was so good as to not leave her. Even promised to take care of us. Made up some work excuse with his other wife to spend half his time with us." I snort at how Mom had put it. "She said he'd sacrificed himself for us.

Bent over backward to give us a normal family. That I should have been grateful. But instead, I had ruined everything. Because I had opened my big fat mouth. Made a *scene*, apparently."

I'm angry that tears are forming in my eyes again, just telling the story. This isn't how it was supposed to go. I'm only trying to let Colton know why I ended up having trust issues with men. It has to be because I saw my mother again. It reopened old wounds.

"My dad never came back. So of course I took the blame."

Colton's voice is coarse when he asks, "What happened then?"

"I left home the morning of my eighteenth birthday. Didn't see any of 'em until Gramps died. Saw them at the funeral. Eloise asked us to make up. So we pretended. For her."

He reaches for my hand and I let him take it. "I'm sorry." He gives it a squeeze.

"Now you know why they hate me. I burst their ugly little bubble." Shifting in my seat, I connect my music app to the truck's radio. "The worst part is, the older I get, the more I can understand her side. Life isn't always black and white. I get it, but I'm not her. I'm never compromising."

I force a chuckle. "Just thought you should know why..." My stomach feels knotted as I try to push the words out my mouth. I free my hand from Colton's and stare out the window. Without physical contact with him, if feels easier to express myself. "...why I'm broken in a lot of ways." *Why I'm still a virgin at twenty-six years old.* "And why having you as a friend is more important than anything else to me."

He laces his arm around my neck and brings me softly to him. Eyes still on the road, he kisses the crown of my head. "I'll always be your friend, no matter what." Then he releases me, and I'm left wondering what this *what* could possibly be.

"When you break a bone," he says after a while, "it grows back stronger. To protect you from another break. I never thought you were broken..." he starts with a glance my way, the shadow of a smile playing on his lips, "but I always wondered why you were trying to protect yourself so hard." Eyes back on the road, he adds, "Now I know."

And his smile spreads out, warming my own core, making me feel incredibly light and carefree.

I should have told him all this so much earlier.

Chapter Eighteen

Kiara

After last weekend's debacle, I'm ready for some quality time with the Bitch Brigade. Thankfully, it's already Thursday, which means Game Night in Emerald Creek. It should really be called Girls' Night In, but nobody asked me. They started it way before my time, so there's that.

All the women get together in the back of Cassandra's lingerie boutique, supposedly to play games. In reality, we chat, drink, and eat. Basically, we have a good time—without any men around. The whole Bitch Brigade is in attendance.

"Hey, boss," Willow greets me as I leave my boots in the mudroom. "Haley made some sumac wine. Wanna taste?"

Sumac wine? "Just a drop." I glance inside the large room, decorated in tones of white and gold and pink, with bean bags and couches and a few tables to play games. Haley is busy behind the mirror-paneled bar that reflects the glimmer of the fireplace. Thick throw rugs and flickering candles add an extra touch of comfort to a space that's exactly what women need, especially now the long winter season is upon us.

I place my contribution on the bar—almond tuiles with a pistachio dip. "Hey, rebel," I say to Haley as I arrange my dish. "Any chance of us getting grape wine anytime soon?"

"Try this," is her answer.

The tart, citrus flavor hits my tastebuds in a surprisingly good way. I take a moment to smell the small glass she's poured me. "Nice herbal notes," I compliment her.

Willow wraps her arm around my shoulders. "Told ya, this is great. You should sell that through the general store, Haley! Kiara sells her chocolates there. Right?"

"Yeah, I might," Haley answers.

"I could talk to Noah for you!" Willow offers, her cheeks coloring at the mention of the owner of the general store.

"Yeah, next time you take his refill order for us?" I suggest.

"Or like, tomorrow," Willow counters.

"I should go myself," Haley says. "I should talk to him, bring him a sample bottle."

"Or I can go," Willow repeats with a bright smile.

Haley narrows her eyes on Willow. "Still holding a torch for Noah, huh?" she says. "You go, girl. I'll set a couple of bottles aside for you to bring to him. But don't hold your hopes up, okay? I don't want to be responsible for your broken heart."

Willow does a small fist bump that makes me chuckle. She's been trying to get the moody guy's attention for years now, but he's clearly not interested. I'd have given up a long time ago.

"Bonne chance!" I tell her in a vague attempt to practice my fledgling French on actual people.

"Oooh fancy," Grace says. "Are you trying to attract the French Canadian clientele? You should start a partnership with Cassandra. 'Buy a bra, get a macaron!'"

Cassandra lifts her glass to me with a side smile. "Now there's an idea. And get a massage," she adds for Grace.

"How d'you say massage in French?" Grace asks me.

I shrug. "I don't know. The course didn't get to that point yet."

"Isn't massage a French word already?" Willow asks.

"Wait—you're taking a class?" Grace asks. "That's awesome!"

Willow grunts. "Wait til she tells you why."

All eyes zoom in on me. "Why?" is the collective question.

"I need to expand my horizons," I answer.

Willow tilts her head at me. "Be more specific."

I stifle a sigh. "I'm hoping to be accepted in a pastry school in France. It's a short program."

Grace frowns, genuinely puzzled. "But why?"

With all my friends narrowing their eyes on me, my motivation wanes. Mostly, I don't want to hurt their feelings. They've always done everything they could to make me feel welcomed here. "I think I need something more to make progress in my business."

"You need a storefront," Ms. Angela declares as if that wasn't the crux of my problem.

"She can't get one," Willow answers her, turning to me with an apologetic look. "Right?"

I freeze, ashamed to admit my failure. "It's complicated," I say in a voice way more assured than I'm feeling.

Before anyone can ask more, or maybe feeling my discomfort, Grace says, "Speaking of complicated, I hear Colton went to Maine with you this weekend?" Her eyes dance with unconcealed mischief. "He came back in some mood. Mom had to threaten to take away his serving of lasagna, just like when we were kids, if he was only going to grunt instead of speaking to us."

Ms. Angela's face lights up. "Is there some progress I missed?" Turning to me, she adds, "Did the fake dating finally turn into something more?"

I feel myself turn crimson. *Yes, Ms. Angela, the fake dating turned into real petting and a real orgasm.* "No, that's—we shot that down. We had our fun messing with my family, but nope. No more."

A series of disappointed *awws* echo through the room.

I try to laugh it off. "Guys, really? It was fake!"

Ms. Angela pets my arm. "We were hoping it would turn into not-fake. You two look so cute together, you know. We were hoping..." She sighs and looks at Cassandra, who gives her an enigmatic smile.

Cassandra is rumored to have witchy gifts when it comes to matchmaking. I think she's just perceptive and makes her move when she knows the relationship is going somewhere.

"Hey, the good news is, I decided it's time for me to date for real," I drop.

Grace, Willow, and my other friends clasp their hands. "Ethan just hired a couple of very handsome single men," Grace says. "I can set up a dinner, make it look caj."

Yeah, I don't think so. Being introduced by a friend is too much pressure. Then there's the question of the V-card. I'd rather keep that to myself and get it over and done with with a perfect stranger who won't have anyone to open his mouth to.

Colton, I could trust. But Ethan's new employees? Who the hell knows them? I don't want to be the Monday morning topic around their watercooler at work. "I think I'm gonna get on the apps," I drop.

Several gasps sound through the room, especially from the older generation. "I totally get it," Cassandra, of all people, says. "See what's out there. Just stay safe, okay? Drive yourself, meet in a public space, don't agree to be at their place until you've met their friends and they're... normal people."

I should roll my eyes and come back with a snarky retort, but Cassandra's motherly concern touches me. I've never gotten dating advice from someone older than me, but not *that* old that they were out of touch with my generation.

"Oh and send someone a screenshot of the date's profile to at least one of us," Grace adds.

Willow is tapping on her phone. "What app do you want to get on? Can I make your profile?"

I unlock my phone and hand it to her. "Have at it."

Another fist bump from Willow, then she points my phone at me and tells me to smile. "This one's a good one," she says. "Let me edit it."

"Don't make me look too cute. I don't want them to have high expectations."

Grace sighs. "Wow... Well, I hope this goes well. Or maybe it'll make Colton see what he's missing and wake him up."

"What do you mean?"

She throws up her hands. "You're perfect for him! How could he mess it up so much?"

I can already tell she's ready to go to bat for me and have a talk with her brother. That's the last thing I want. "Maybe it wasn't him. Maybe *I* don't want to date *him*!"

"What's wrong with Colton?" Grace asks, offended.

"There's nothing wrong with your brother. It's ..." How am I getting out of this one? Lying seems like the only viable option, one where no one gets hurt. "I don't want anything serious. I just want to have fun and be able to... you know, move on once the fun has worn out."

Grace considers me as if this were a totally new idea. "Oh. Oh, sure."

"That's why I can't date Colton. Or anyone I know, really. Including Ethan's new guys."

She frowns. "Right. Makes sense. And so... apps, huh?"

Willow waves my phone at me. "There! All set!"

"Lemme see?" The picture she took is cute enough without being staged or over-promising. It looks like me. For interests, she wrote *Running experiments on my friends, Exploring how to make the world a sweeter place, one bite at a time.*

"Good enough," I say. I'll play with it later, maybe change a few things around.

Ms. Angela takes out a stack of Christmas cards from her canvas bag. "Welp, these aren't going to write themselves!" She takes a comfortable seat next to the fire, uncaps her pen, and gets to work.

Meanwhile Sophie, the town librarian, pulls out a tarot deck and sits cross-legged on the floor. "Anyone need a little wisdom?" she asks.

What's the harm? I sit in front of her.

Half an hour later, slightly unsettled, I sit back as she reads cards for Alex's unborn child, hearing without really listening.

"Honey, why don't you follow me," Cassandra says, holding her hand out. She pulls me up and leads me out of the room and into her boutique, flicking lights on as she goes.

Oh, this is good. Cassandra is known for giving single women lingerie that she claims has magic powers—like making them meet the man of their life. I always laughed about this, but I've been supposedly proven wrong recently. I maintain Cassandra is intuitive, and she was only giving them the extra nudge of self-assurance they needed in their new relationship.

Cass rummages through her drawers, lifting folded garments. "There," she says. She unfolds a thin black fabric, holding it out in front of her, then sets it aside on her high counter, takes out silk paper, and wraps the garment. "The most beautiful gems are best left to shine on their own," she says while she ties the small package with twine. "You know I've given your friends lingerie that gave them the confidence they needed at the right time." *Ha! I knew it.* No witchcraft involved in Alex's bodice, Chloe's negligee, or Grace's swimsuit.

She slips the mysterious black garment I didn't even try into a purple bag adorned with an owl. "Turns out, you just need to warm up to the idea," she adds with a smile. "Hence, this thermal. Oh and—you'll want to make sure to wear this cami with it, because of the zipper," she says as she adds a rolled-up black garment to the bag.

A *thermal*? I mean, these things are expensive as shit, and Cass only sells top quality. I should thank her before she thinks I'm disappointed. "I don't know what to say, Cass. Thanks so much, this will... this will be super useful." And it will. It really will. Layers make all the difference here.

And I get the message. I really do: Sexy lingerie isn't for me.

"Make sure to wear the cami underneath it."

Thermal. Cami. Got it.

"You heard what I said earlier, right?" she says, not letting go of the bag just yet.

"I need to keep warm?" I thought she'd said something about warming up to an idea, but I must have heard wrong.

She rolls her eyes in a cute way. "The most beautiful gems are best left to shine on their own. Just remember that."

Chapter Nineteen

Colton

"So that whole thing with Kiara is over, huh?" Willow asks me when she picks up her CRV that I've been servicing at the garage.

"What'cha mean?" I hand her the paperwork. "Keys are on the dashboard." I walk her to the car, wanting to know what she's talking about.

She has a playful smile. "No more dating? Fake or otherwise?"

"What makes you say that?" Despite everything Kiara said in the car, I know how she felt in my arms. It's only a matter of time before she gets off her high horse and agrees we should be... together. But the decision needs to come from her.

She lifts her shoulders. "She's on the apps," she says as she opens her car door.

That dagger she planted in my heart last weekend twists a little deeper. "She's what now?"

She throws her handbag on the passenger seat and turns back to face me. "On the apps. The dating apps?"

Yeah, I got that part. "What the fuck?"

"She didn't tell you?" She frowns and looks at me with sympathy bordering on pity. "It happened last night. I'm sure she will. Grace told her to send screenshots of her dates to a friend. I kinda assumed she'd tell you..."

The harder my heart beats in my ribcage, the more her words trail off until she stops talking completely.

"Yeah-yeah, I'm sure she will." I force a smile and knock on the roof of her car as a goodbye. "Take care," I say and turn around.

"Colt!" Willow calls out.

I turn around reluctantly. Being the object of someone's pity isn't exactly something I like. I school my features to seem professional and absent of emotion. "Yeah?"

She shuts her door and walks toward me hesitantly. "Maybe... maybe I could help you."

"Help me with what?" Willow grew up here, like me. I've known her all my life. She's a great girl, for sure. She works for my cousin Chris—started as a shopkeeper in his bakery and is now doing the pastries with... *Kiara.*

Her eyebrows shoot to her hairline as if I'm being a little slow on the uptake. "Kiara!"

I try to hide the punch to the stomach I feel at the sound of her name. Stroking my chin's three-day stubble, I answer, "Not sure what you mean."

Hands on her hips, she tilts her head. "You're fooling yourself. That sad puppy look would give it away if I didn't already know you two need to give this a real shot."

I tilt my head to the sky, take a deep breath, and turn around, raising my hand in a goodbye gesture.

"Are you really okay with her going out with strangers?" she calls out, raising her voice so I can hear her. "Cos I'm not."

Me neither, but I don't say that. I don't say anything; I'm sensing a trap. Willow might not be a cop, but anything I say can and will still be held against me.

"Colt?" she insists.

Glancing at her over my shoulder, I say, "She'll be a'right. Won't do anything stupid." Apart from letting another man set his hands on her.

Willow catches up to me. "Are you okay with her going out with someone else?" she asks again, disgust on her face.

"Kiara is entitled to date whoever she wants." I just need to get her out of my system.

"She's scared of commitment, Colt," Willow continues. "That sound familiar?"

I stop in my tracks. "No, it doesn't."

Willow sighs. "Does the name Valerie sound familiar?"

"The hell does she have anythin' to do with Kiara?"

"You let her get away, for starters. That's something they have in common."

Seems to me I dodged a bullet when it comes to Valerie. "What makes you think I wasn't the one who broke it off?"

Willow plants her fists on her hips. "Well, were you?"

One thing I'm not doing, is going over my relationship history with Willow. "Is there a point you're trying to make? I'm kinda busy."

"Yes, there is a point. Kiara is perfect for you. She's your best friend. You have stars in your eyes when you think about her."

I don't know about having stars in my eyes, but I'm not going to argue that I have feelings for Kiara. More than vague feelings. The idea of her on a date with a stranger revolts me.

Willow reads my mood. "Let me help you."

"And how are you going to do that?"

She smiles like she's won Ms. Angela's spelling bee a-fuck-ing-gain. "I'll put you on the same dating app as Kiara. It's slim pickings, so I'm sure she'll be interested in you."

"Why would she click on my profile?"

"Oh, she won't know it's you. I'll put a fake picture."

That doesn't sound right. "Isn't that, like, illegal or something?"

"Well, you're not trying to go out with other women, right?"

This makes me pause. But how would trapping Kiara on a date with me make things better? I don't like this scheming. "I don't know, Willow. I don't like it."

"Oh, come on. What's the worst that can happen? She doesn't swipe on your profile? She leaves your date when she sees it's you?"

I chuckle. "She'd be pissed, for sure."

"Pissed is her baseline attitude. You got nothing to lose."

If it works, it could be fun. I already know where our first date will be. She'll absolutely love it. Even if nothing comes out of it, we'll have a fun night. Willow's right: what is there to lose? "I'll think about it."

"Good. Don't think too long. I put her profile up last night, and she already has a lot of... interest."

Fuck. I check the time. "I have to head to the Select Board meeting in half an hour." I finally put my name down, and tonight the board is interviewing the candidates and making their selection. The meeting is in an hour, and I'm not showing up late. Not with how Kiara encouraged me to join.

Willow lets out a little shriek, runs to her car to grab her bag, and drags me to my office in the back.

Five minutes later I'm revising my opinion on Willow not being a cop at heart. "Alright, interests. Tell me everything you like, and we'll keep only what'll tickle Kiara."

"Pepperoni pizza, Allagash IPA, dark grade syrup on Noah's bratwursts, Chris's brioche, napoleons, chocolate cheesecake, Mom's lasagna... You're not taking notes?"

She purses her lips. "Let's maybe elevate this out of the food arena."

She making fun of me right now? "You asked what I liked."

She sighs, then sits up, realizing her patronizing attitude isn't the way to go with me. "Okay." She spreads her fingers out, counting. "Snowboarding. Video games. Fixing cars. What else? What do you do for fun?"

"I race cars."

She tilts her head again. "How did I not know that?"

"Keep that to myself. Mostly."

"That's pretty cool. Does Kiara know?"

"Yeah."

"Okay then, let's muddy the waters. We won't mention racing or she'll see right through it. Give me a few minutes. I'll come up with something."

As I walk into Town Hall that evening, I know it was the right call. It's time I not only give back to my hometown but also put my mark on it. Kiara said something to that effect too.

The meeting goes as planned. I'm asked a few questions, the other applicant as well, then Lynn, Cassandra, Owen, and Noah retreat to a small office, followed by Ms. Angela who serves as secretary. They come back minutes later and announce they chose me to replace Stan for the remainder of his term. The meeting is adjourned, and the few people in attendance start leaving.

"Colton, dear," Ms. Angela says. "Stay a minute. We have things to discuss with you." She produces a thick three-ring binder with my name on the cover. "Why don't you take this home, look through it, and let us know your questions."

The binder has several tabs, including procedures, minutes, and upcoming meetings. *Fuck.* This is gonna be real work—not that I didn't know.

"Appreciate it," I say, tucking the binder under my arm and zipping up my jacket. Then I make it to Lazy's, right around the corner from Town Hall.

"Yo, Colt. They rope you in?" Justin asks, drawing my favorite IPA.

"They sure did."

"Thanks for stepping in, man. And congratulations," he says as he sets a beer in front of me. "On the house."

"Thanks, man," I say, lifting the pint glass to my lips.

Cold seeps into the pub as the door opens on Grace, her husband, Ethan, Chris and Alex, then Kiara and Willow, and finally Noah. Justin's dog Moose greets them, sniffs the outside air, then lies back down next to the bar.

Instead of congratulations, my friends and sister thank me. "I was hoping you'd step up," Grace says, looking at the three-ring binder I set on an empty stool. Kiara gives me a friendly back slap. "Proud o'ya," she says, her gaze averting mine.

"You're exactly what the town needs," Justin confirms. Then, to everyone, he asks, "You guys gonna eat something?"

Several "hell yeahs" echo, and we move to the far end of the room, pushing two tables together so we can all fit, the guys naturally gravitating to one end while the women take the other.

"You're gonna get even more popular than you already are, you watch," Justin tells me once we're all squeezed in and eating. He sat on the board for a while, after his accident.

"I'm plenty popular," I joke, struggling to not let my gaze slide to Kiara.

But the rest of the group falls silent as Justin dispels pieces of advice.

"People are gonna ask you to vote for this or that," he explains. "Try to make you see their point. It can get... a lot. Give 'em some standard answers like, 'We're looking into it.' Or: 'You have a strong case. You should come to the next meeting and make your point.' Now, any questions about rules and regulations, just go straight to Ms. Angela. She knows everything and everyone. She'll tell you why things are done a certain way—there's always a reason. Sometimes it makes sense, sometimes not." Then Justin turns to the rest of the group. "Just—you guys, leave him be. Don't ask him for favors or shit. We wanna make sure he stays on the board and doesn't give up. Got it?"

Everyone nods and hums.

"He's right," Noah says. Then, after a quick glance around the room, he adds in a low voice, "You guys should listen to Justin, or else we'll only be left with people like Owen who actually enjoy giving favors."

I lean over to Noah. "Is he that bad?"

Noah shrugs. "You'll find out. Don't want to spoil all the fun," he adds with a smile.

I'm about to ask for more details, but my attention shifts to the other end of the table when I hear Willow say, "What do you mean, he looks too good to be true?"

"What's 'at?" Grace asks, leaning across the table.

"Nothing," Kiara says, while Willow leans over and whispers, "Dating app".

My blood freezes.

My sister pushes her chair back, eyeing me. "Time for a bathroom break!" she says, effectively summoning the other women to follow her.

"Sure got quiet here," Justin says as his wife, Chloe, leaves the room to follow along. "I wonder what they're up to."

Chris looks at me. "Are we still supposed to pretend you guys are dating or what? I heard a rumor."

"What rumor?"

He shrugs. "Breakup? Fake breakup? Fuck if I know. Be nice to be notified, though. I'm kinda losing the plot."

My phone dings with a sound I don't recognize. Grateful for the distraction, I pull it out.

Pixie802 hearted your profile. I frown.

"Everything okay?" Ethan asks.

"You good?" Noah echoes.

I rub my stubble. "Uh... not sure. I guess?"

Noah adjusts his glasses. "Anything you wanna share?" He's not nosy, just being a good friend. On top of running the family general store, Noah is our resident geek along with Ethan, who recently moved back. Noah glances at my phone, but more out of concern. His gaze quickly settles on Justin. "When's the next community dinner? I want to advertise it at the store. Get more people who need it to come."

My thumb hovers over the app's logo while Justin, Noah, and Chris discuss the next community dinner at Lazy's—a get-together where food is free and the more fragile in our community have a chance at receiving help, through friendship and donations.

Kiara's pretty face is staring at me in a neat little circle, with a heart next to her screen name: Pixie802.

I have no fucking clue what to do with that. Do I answer? If yes, how? This is when I need Willow, but of course, she's locked up with the girls in the bathroom.

"What's up, man?" Justin asks.

"I don't even know where to start."

"At the beginning," Ethan suggests.

I give them the down-low of what Willow set up. Set the phone on the table so they can see for themselves. They all huddle over it once they catch the gist of what I've gotten myself into.

"Wouldn't touch that shit with a six-foot pole," Chris mutters, looking at the phone like it might bite.

"Willow set you up with that?" Noah asks. "That's fucking catfishing."

"That's what I said. Didn't know the word, but it didn't seem right to me."

"Delete your profile," Noah instructs, looking anxiously toward the bathroom door, from where the girls are bound to reappear at any time.

What's taking them so long?

"Wow-wow-wow," Justin intercedes. He hovers his hand over my phone like he wants to protect it, while looking at it like it's a bomb ready to detonate. "What's the harm? Just say hi."

"It's wrong," Noah says.

"Eh," Chris argues. "It's Kiara. What's the worst that can happen?"

"I'm with Chris," Justin says. "Go for it. This could be fun."

Noah shakes his head but has no counter-argument.

"I don't want to have fun at the expense of Kiara. That was never the goal." I glance nervously toward the women's bathroom, but there's no activity.

"What's your goal?" Ethan asks.

Taking a deep breath, and at the risk of losing my man card, I concede. "I... want to date her. I..." Fuck but these words are hard to say. "I care for her. And honestly, knowing she wants to date other guys, I just..."

"D'you try asking her out?" Justin says like I'm an idiot.

"Yeah—she won't."

"But she's fine being on a *dating app*?" Noah nearly screeches and pushes his glasses up his nose. "This woman is *nuts*. You sure you want to date her?"

My glower shuts him up, and the energy radiating from me must carry over because all four look at each other and nod in agreement. "Go for it," Chris agrees. "Just don't you hurt her. She's the best. You know that, right?"

Yeah, asshole, I know that, I want to answer my cousin, but I don't because my finger taps on the screen and now I'm staring at a chat box.

CHAPTER TWENTY

Kiara/Colton

Kiara

"Eeep! He's on."

A collective gasp emanates from my group of friends. Chloe and Grace are sitting on the vanity, while Willow leans over my phone, crowding me.

"He's like... surreal gorgeous," Willow points out.

I look at the dreamy yet rugged face with soulful eyes. If I had to describe everyone's fantasy man, this would be it. Although to be honest, Colton's features superimpose in my mind's eye when the words *fantasy boyfriend* form in my brain. "Yeah, that's kinda sketchy," I answer Willow.

"What? He's perfect!" Willow gasps, like she has a vested interest in this guy.

"Getting cold feet?" Grace asks.

"More like, lukewarm," I answer.

"Why?" Chloe asks.

"He's just... too perfect."

"It's only a picture," Chloe says. "He probably chose a good one. Let's hope he did."

"He *is* surreally gorgeous," Grace admits. "Let me text Ethan to run a reverse search on him." She points her phone at mine and snaps a photo of the guy's profile pic. "You can never be too careful."

Colton

Noah places his hand on my wrist. "Before you type anything stupid, let's do a little research on how to approach this. Have any of you losers ever been on a dating app?"

"Sort of," I admit while my friends shake their heads. Then Justin adds, "Only for hookups." At the looks we throw him, he adds, "What? I never led them on. Can't help you with building a connection on an app, though."

"The girls are onto something," Ethan mumbles. "Dude, where'd you get that picture?"

Noah interrupts him. "Alright, here we go," he says, reading from his phone. "First, compliment her profile, but nothing relating to her physical aspect."

"What does her profile say?" Justin asks.

I didn't even look. But I do now. "Says she's looking for a casual but fun connection."

"That's not her profile," Noah says. "What does she like to do? Says here the next thing to do is ask her questions about herself."

"That's pretty basic," Justin mumbles. "People don't know that?"

"We know what she likes to do," Chris jokes. "Boss people around, give nicknames, invent ways to put maple syrup in everything she makes."

Trying to focus, I look at Kiara's profile again. I've memorized it. For the life of me, I still don't understand why she wrote, *When life hands you lemonade, question the lemons.*

Does she think she's going to attract guys with that? I'm not complaining, just—

"That's hilarious," Chris says, now looking at her profile over my shoulder. "She's a real funny girl."

"What's yours say?" Noah asks.

I huff. "I don't remember," I mumble.

"Come on, dude. Just click back to your profile."

I do, and show him the screen, the words grating so bad I don't want to read them out loud.

Ethan interrupts us. "Guys, we got a problem. The girls are onto something," he repeats. "Grace asked me to do a reverse-image search on your—"

"Did you find something?" Grace asks, sneaking up on us. I shut down my app. "Awww you guys are cute! Everyone's researching the guy. So, what's the verdict?" she asks Ethan.

He frowns at his phone. "Guy is legit. Lessee... LinkedIn, over five hundred connections." He makes a face and Grace swats him playfully. "That's good! That's all we need."

"What are you guys up to?" I ask Grace with a scowl. She'll sense something's up if I don't show interest.

"Just... helping Kiara with something," she says as she leaves.

Kiara

"He's legit," Grace says as she comes back. "What's up? You look like someone killed your cat."

"He went offline," I explain, looking at my phone. Next to the profile picture, the heart that symbolizes whether the person is online or not is now barely visible instead of red.

Grace hoists herself back on the vanity. "The guys were so cute. They were all looking at their phones, searching for this guy. Lemme tell ya, you don't need brothers with a group like that."

"What did they say?" I ask, curious what Colton's reaction was. I'm kind of dreading it, to be honest. I used to ask him for feedback on my dates, but with everything's that's gone down between the two of us now, it doesn't feel right this time.

Grace blushes slightly. "I kept it vague. I think my brother has a thing for you—didn't want to rub it in his face. I texted Ethan the basics, so he'd know it was serious. He might have shared."

Guilt with a side of almost-shame settles in my ribs. Colton didn't need to know this. Not yet. He'll find out eventually—the perks of living in a small town, amply demonstrated by the Bitch Brigade convening in the bathroom. But this is early stages after a roller-coaster weekend for the two of us. Emotionally and otherwise.

"Oops!" Willow says, pointing to my phone. "He's back on!"

Sure enough, the heart next to his name is no longer grayed out.

Colton

Once Grace is safely back in the bathroom, Noah gestures for my phone and pushes his glasses up his nose as he resumes the study of my profile. "'*I've been told forever might never come, and I'm good either way.*' Okay, that's... cute and... girly." He frowns at me, a what-the-hell look on his face. "'*Foodie. Cars. Sports.*' That's more like it."

Clicking my phone back to the chat function, I explain, "Willow thought it would work on Kiara. Clearly she was right. Means I'm serious but also open to casual. Since Kiara doesn't know what she wants, we're covering our bases," I add, hoping the guys don't ask me follow-up questions on Kiara's wishes in terms of romantic involvement. There is no world in which I tell them she's a virgin, and no alternate reality where they discover what she asked of me. "Kay, question. Um... so something about lemons, maybe?"

Chris and Justin both grunt their disapproval.

"What? How 'bout, 'Hi there, totally dig the lemon thing—'"

"*Dig*? Nobody says that!" Ethan looks horrified.

Kiara

"He messaged!" Willow screeches. You'd think she's the one potentially dating too-hot-to-be-real. "Read it!"

"Shouldn't we go back to the table? It's kinda rude, disappearing like that," I say. Who knows how long a chat with this guy is going to take?

"Are you getting cold feet?" Grace asks. "It's totally normal. Just see what he has to say."

I take a deep breath. "Okay. Here goes. *'Totally dig the—'*"

"Eww," Grace says. "Who even says 'dig' anymore? How old is this guy? Ask him how old he is."

Willow tuts. "It's on his profile. Don't be rude. He's probably nervous."

This whole dating app thing was a mistake. I don't want nervous. I don't want to *be* nervous. Yet here I am huddled in a public toilet so I can plot with my besties how to get a guy. I'm just going to get this over with and go back to dinner with my friends. All my friends. I'll read the whole message, shoot an answer, and forget about it until tomorrow. "*'Hi there, totally dig the lemon thing, and I want to know more. I'm not sure where to start, though. How about thank you for hearting my profile?'*"

"Awww," Willow coos. "That's so sweet. Right?"

It *is* sweet. I guess? I type an answer.

"Guys, we should go back there," Grace says. "We've been gone a while. The men are gonna wonder what we're doing."

I raise my eyebrows. "I don't hear anyone knocking on the door. They don't seem worried."

"Why don't we continue this at the table? Ask the guys what they think? It could be fun," Chloe says.

Colton

The answer flies right onto my screen.

That's a very sweet thing to say. The lemon story is a long one.

Shit. Is she planning on spending the evening in the bathroom? I look up, but the group of women is filing back to the table, Grace in front, Kiara with her gaze glued to her phone, then Chloe, and finally Willow, who's making the cut sign over her throat, her eyes rounded at me.

I stand to go to the bathroom and pass the girls. Kiara's scent and her total ignorance of my presence drive me wild in too many different ways. I don't like what I'm doing, but it's too late to back out now.

Once safely in the men's room, I type my answer.

⚬⚬⚬

Kiara

His message is polite, even kind. But it feels a little like he's giving me the brush off. "*I'd love to hear a long story, but I'm out with my friends. Can we continue this conversation at another time?*"

The heart is still red. I type, Sure, and the heart grays out.

Grace is leaning over my shoulder, reading my phone. "What a dick," she says. "He hearts your profile, asks you a question, and then he says he doesn't have time for a long conversation?"

"He's with friends," I explain, feeling defensive.

"So are you," Grace counters.

"Who's a dick?" Colton asks, pulling a chair out and seating himself. I'm relieved he wasn't there just now, when my girlfriends told the guys that I was on a dating app and a cute guy was interested in me. I expected more overreaction from my male friends, to be honest.

Granted, Grace had given them the down-low and they'd already re-searched him.

"No one," I answer Colton.

He grabs my phone—why am I still staring at it? And stares right at the profile of the guy. "Yeah well, you get on a dating app, you gotta expect dicks," he says as he gives me my phone back.

"That's very funny." I smirk at him. Something passes between us when our eyes lock. He's not as resentful as I expected. And I'm more mortified than I care to admit. But when a shadow plays in his irises, I avert my gaze.

CHAPTER TWENTY-ONE

Colton

The next morning I'm standing outside my garage, looking to the bluebird sky for inspiration to get me out of this mess, when a 1965 Ford Mustang slows down and pulls up.

The car's a real beauty. Bottle green that looks almost black in places. She's buffed, gleaming under the cold sky. That kind of shine doesn't last a day in the winter here. Her owner must be buffing her daily. I'm surprised she's out at all in the winter. Although it's not looking like fresh powder is coming our way today, there are patches of packed snow in front of driveways that wouldn't do well with the way this car sits low to the ground.

My thoughts are interrupted by the sound it makes. Within the familiar rumble of the engine, there's a rat-tat-tat I don't like one bit. The owner drives up to the pump, turns the engine off, then comes out.

I walk up to the guy my age coming out of the car. "Hi there," I say.

"Hi." He waves and starts filling her up.

"Nice ride," I say. "You had it long?"

He smiles proudly. "About six months."

Six months. Damn. "You have someone look at that noise?" I ask, suspecting the answer will be no.

The guy frowns suspiciously at me. "What noise?"

"Like little firecrackers. Rat-tat-tat."

He tilts his head. "'Ts'an old car, it's bound to make some noise." I know what he's thinking: that I'm after making a quick buck. Too many people in my line of work take advantage of the ignorance of their clients. In the end, it's not good for business. But I'm not going to change the mentality of half my industry.

I'm worried about the guy, though. I step back, feeling his wariness, as I say, "Get it checked soon as you get home. Tell them to look for a leaky exhaust." As I turn to get back inside, I can tell I have the guy's attention. I add over my shoulder, "And just to be on the safe side... I know it's cold, but leave a window cracked open when the engine's on."

By that point I'm back in the warmth of my office.

The door opens two minutes later. "Can you tell me what noise you're talking about?"

Back outside, he starts the car and stands next to me. "You hear that?" I ask him, tilting my head to the engine. "Like a machine gun in the distance. You hear it?"

"Yeah," he says, "like drumsticks calling a beat?"

I nod. "It's exhaust gases coming out from where they shouldn't."

"Is that dangerous? You said to leave a window open."

"It can be, if the exhaust gases make it into the cabin. You won't know until you get it checked."

"Can you check it for me?"

"Sure can. But depending on what I find, the repairs can take a couple days. More if I need parts. Let's check to see what we're dealing with, then we'll decide on your best course of action."

I get the car on the lift, then pull out my smoke machine and attach it to the tailpipe. "I'm going to turn this on. It'll fill the exhaust system with smoke, and we'll see it coming out where the leaks are."

Within a few minutes, just like I thought, smoke comes out from the exhaust manifold. "See here?" I show the guy. "That's one leak. There might be more." Straightening, I take a peek inside the cabin. "That doesn't mean you'll have gas in the cabin, though. Might need another minute or so to be sure... Hell no. Here it is. See here?" Smoke is slowly seeping in from the cabin floor.

"Shit," the guy mumbles. "Fuck, man. I been driving this?"

I tilt my head. "You got lucky."

"No one ever told me. So what now? Can you fix it?"

I leave the car on the lift. Looks like the owner is reasonable and I'll be doing repairs. I'll need to take my time identifying all the leaks. "How long are you in town for?"

He spreads his arms out and grins, his eyes dancing under his Patriots cap. "I just moved here. I have all the time in the world."

I eye him top to bottom. I like this guy. "Oh well, welcome to Emerald Creek." He looks vaguely familiar too. He might have come on vacation, rented a house. That must be it. It's how a lot of people who move here started out. "Do I know you from somewhere?" I ask as we walk to the office.

He tilts his head. "Nah, I just have that kind of face." I think I see a twinkle in his eye, but it's gone in an instant. When I look up from our scheduler, he pulls his cap tighter down over his eyes. "D'you want to leave her now? I can get you a loaner."

"Loaner would be great, if it doesn't put you out. Or else just a ride home."

"I can arrange a loaner. It's free, by the way."

He smiles and says, "Appreciate it."

"You sure you've never been here before? On vacation, maybe?" I ask again as I give him the keys to the Subaru.

"I'm sure, mate." He turns around and sets his hand on my shoulder. "Hey, I owe you one. Really." His eyes mist a little but he catches himself and flashes me a big grin. "It's a nice change to be with good people. Let me know if there's anything I can do for you. I mean it."

Inspiration strikes me after he's rounded the corner and is out of my sight. I have something he can do for me, sooner rather than later, so I get on his car right away.

I end up finding three leaks, and one of them requires welding. Thankfully, I have the parts to replace, so the only time I need to put in is my own. No waiting for a shipment that may or may not arrive in the next week.

When I'm done repairing the leaks, I patch the cabin. I end up putting ten hours on the Mustang, but when I test her at the end of the day, there's no leak and no sound.

I take her for a spin downtown for good measure, appreciating how she purrs nicely. It being Saturday, I half expect to see the Subaru on The Green or whereabouts, with the guy having dinner somewhere, but I don't. When I get back to the garage, I call to let him know his car is ready.

Fifteen minutes later, he's here. "D'you work on it all day?" he half-jokes as I print out his invoice.

"Matter-of-fact, I did," I admit. "Figured you'd want her back soon. And I wanted to make sure there were no parts I needed to order. Once I got started, I was just as well getting it done."

"Makes sense," he says, sliding his credit card through the terminal. "All the same, I really appreciate what you did. And I meant what I said earlier—if you need anything, let me know."

I take a deep breath. *Nothing ventured, nothing gained.* "Well, actually, there is something you could help me with."

I'm expecting some hesitation, some weariness. But I get a big grin. "What is it?"

I take him to the back room and tell him my idea. "I need someone whose voice she won't recognize," I summarize to drive the point home that I really need him.

"Uh-huh. That sounds illegal, but whatever. I trust you. You don't strike me as a serial killer."

It should give me pause that this stranger points out he's asked to do something illegal, but he's fine as long as no *killing* is involved. Holy shit, what kind of a world is this? I could take this as a sign that what I'm about to do is seriously messed up, but I don't. Because it's a sign that I'm saving Kiara from people who only stop at serial killing. Like there isn't a whole range of nasty stuff that could happen to her in between.

He scratches his stubble pensively. "Okay," he says, moving on. "So I'm to impersonate this fake person you created on the app. When's the phone call? What does this guy do in life? Supposedly."

"I didn't mention his job."

"Good, gives us options."

"Right. For hobbies, I said he's a foodie and—"

"Foodie, that's gonna be tough, man." He chuckles. "I guess I'll spin it." Then he full-on laughs, a deep, stomach laugh that makes me wonder for a split second if I'm making a monumental mistake. But it's not like I have any other options. Kiara and I know all the same people, and I'm not about to ask one of my racing friends for that favor. They'd screw it up massively. For some reason, I trust this guy is up to the task. And he's giving me good vibes. "What else?" he asks.

"The outdoors." The profile says *Outdoorsy*. What the hell does that even mean?

"M'kay. Music? D'you mention your musical tastes?"

Shit. That would have been a good one. "I didn't think about it."

The guy makes a face, then sighs. "Well, what else would make her agree to a date?"

I open my mouth, then shut it.

"Mate, you want this woman or what?"

"I do."

"Then you better know what she likes, or... sorry to say, but you're not the right person for her."

"Safety. She needs safety. She needs to feel loved and cared for and she needs to understand she's already the center of my universe, and if she's mine, she'll feel it to her bones, so much so she won't even need me anymore. I'll build her back up. I know I will."

"You really love her, don't you?"

"I do."

"Then why the hell can't you tell me what would make her go on a date with a dude she picked on an app?"

Because that's not her. Because she's scared shitless to open up. "Friends. She'll need her friends around. Tell her you want to meet her friends, and just have a beer or something at-at-at... Lazy's!"

"The pub in town?"

"Yeah. It's her turf. She'll feel safe."

The guy shakes his head. "Let's say she agrees. Then what? She walks in, sees you, sits somewhere else so she can meet her date, then you sit and tell her it was you all along?"

Put like that, this plan sucks. Why the hell did Willow think this was going to be a great idea?

"Where would you want to take her to make her see... everything you said before?"

I don't know that that will happen right away. But I do know where I want to take Kiara on our first date. And our second. And our third. After that, I'll let my inspiration take over. "Tell her you'd like to go snowboarding together."

He lifts an eyebrow. "Are you sure?"

"Positive."

CHAPTER TWENTY-TWO

Kiara / Colton

Kiara

"So... were you ever married or-or in a serious relationship?" I say into the phone, then tuck my feet under my butt and try to relax in my couch. Willow is sitting cross-legged on the floor, eating popcorn. This is the night the guy on the app and me are having our first phone call. I asked for back up, and she seemed excited to help.

When the guy—Nigel is his name—answered the phone, she kneeled up to listen briefly, but after a few seconds she gave me privacy and now she's back on the floor, her glances alternating between me and her phone.

"Y—not really serious," he answers. "You know how it is. Trying to find the right shoe."

"Lotsa fitting sessions?" I blurt out, then catch myself. "Sorry, that was... huh... Forget I asked. Can we rewind the conversation?"

He chuckles. "Sure, how far back?"

Until I ruined it just now, this conversation was going well. First off, the guy has a sexy-as-hell voice, with a hint of an accent I can't quite place. When I asked him about it, he answered, "I don't have an accent. Where's yours from?" and you could tell he was joking. I liked it. Humor? Check.

When I said I was a pastry chef (which, it was already on my profile, but whatever) and I pointed out his profile mentioned *Foodie*, he simply said he liked to eat. And then he laughed again.

Objectively, he has a good, hearty laugh. Honest. The fact that it doesn't affect me doesn't mean anything at this point.

And he doesn't seem taken aback by my nosiness. Now that's a plus.

"Your answer to whether you were married or in a serious relationship. I sensed hesitation."

"Oh, I see. Depends what you define as serious. At some point, I'm going to want to settle down, but right now, I'm in Prattsville for only a month or so. I'm not looking to plant my roots here."

Prattsville? Perfect. Close enough to get together, far enough not to run into each other.

He clears his throat, and there's some background sound, like he's with someone else. Is it weird or not? I mean, *I'm* with someone else. But that's different. "What-what were you looking for?" he asks.

I frown. "Like my profile says, casual. Same as you, except I get to stay here."

"Ouch, sorry about that."

"Nothing to be sorry about. I love it here." The answer comes out defensive, and without any thought. I can't help but have a flashback of what I'd told Colton about needing to maybe leave, and how he seemed hurt, and how I'm sort of in his camp now.

"Are you from around here, then?" he asks, the inflection in his tone really cute.

"Not originally, but I call Emerald Creek home."

"Emerald Creek?! Love that place."

I perk up in surprise. "You know it?"

"Been through it once. Actually had an oil change at this garage... What's it called again?"

"Wait! You went to Harper's? Colton's my best friend. He's the reason this is home to me now." I sit up, excited to be talking about Colton.

"Really? Colton Harper is the reason Emerald Creek is home?" He chuckles lightly. "Is he your ex?"

Colton

What the hell is this guy talking about? This conversation was supposed to be short and to the point and lead to a first date on the slopes. Period. Nothing else. I don't want to know what Kiara's answer is. I stand from the stool and pace toward the window.

But her voice fills the room as he switches to speakerphone. "Oh, no-no-no. Just a really, really good friend. The best. Salt of the earth. The kindest soul there is."

My jaw clenches. I resist scowling at him. The guy is a new customer doing me a favor. But the fact remains, he shouldn't be making her talk about me.

He glances at me, seeming happy with his scheming. "Huh. You sound like... you really like him."

Her voices catches when she says, "I do."

And I nearly lose it.

Because I see what he's doing. And that was not the plan.

Kiara

I do care for Colton. I'm not gonna lie. But talking about him feels both right and wrong, as if by bringing him into the conversation I'm not really doing what this feels like: cheating on him.

"But he's with someone else," the guy states with finality in his tone.

Why would he say that? "Um. I'm not sure. It's hard to tell, with Colt. Different woman each time." The taste of bile invades my mouth. I have nothing to support that theory, but it's like... *I know.*

"Are you jealous?" he asks, surprising me.

My heartbeat picks up. "No! Not at all. Why would I be?"

"You say you really like him. You say he's not an ex. I'm... look. I've been burned before. So far I'm getting a good vibe with you. I just don't want to be led on. If you're holding a torch for someone else, then..."

I get the guy's point, and I would feel sorry for him... except: "I thought you were looking for casual?"

He clears his throat. "And I am. I'm just a bit territorial. That okay?"

M-hm. Territorial in a casual relationship? That could be fun. From what I've read, it can only make the sex hotter. "Sure. Yeah. It's—I was a little confused, is all."

"Tell me more about Emerald Creek. How is it home to you?"

"Oh, that's... that's a long story but..." I glance at Willow. I've never shared the details of my life before Emerald Creek to anyone, except briefly to Colton, and that was just the other day. And under emotional pressure to explain my weirdness. "Bottom line, I was down on my luck and they... they took me in. Treated me like one of their own. I found a job and a place to stay, and basically... you know."

There's some ruffling on the other end of the line, then he says, "No, I don't know what you mean."

"Well, this is my home now." Hell if I'm going to open up to a perfect stranger. "How 'bout you? Why are you in the NEK for what—a month?"

He seems to hesitate. "Uh, just needed to get away from it all. Recharge."

"You hiding from something?" I ask, laughing a bit to make him at ease. Suddenly the idea of going out with a perfect stranger isn't so appealing anymore. I know nothing about this guy. I glance at Willow, and she gets closer to my phone, trying to listen in.

"N-no. Why would you say that?"

"I dunno. The NEK, the casual but territorial, the hesitation over being married or not, the foodie who just likes to eat. Just trying to get a picture here."

"Ah! I didn't know this was going to be a phone interview," he says, releasing that infectious laugh again, making me relax. "Nah. You're reading too much into all this."

Colton

My heart stomps. Shit. She's gonna hang up on him. There's no way. *Fuck.* Why didn't I remember to tell him not to say that? That's the one thing that drives her crazy. Well, among other things. But that, I should have thought of.

I make the universal sign for cut and grab a piece of paper off the stack of invoices on my desk. The guy gets the idea that he messed up, maybe because he sees me panicking, or maybe because Kiara is chopping his ear off. I don't know. I can't tell. The blood wooshing in my ears is too loud to hear her voice.

"What I meant to say," he says slowly, "is... how can I put it?" He looks at me, a little panicked.

I turn the paper over and scribble, *I'm here to do some reading.* That should work, right? Pretend he got his words mixed up or something. He came to the NEK to do some reading. Not much else to do around here in the winter except snow shoe and ice-fish. The dude doesn't look like he'd be able to hold a conversation about either of these very common Vermont activities.

He glances at the paper and rolls his eyes. "You read too much!" he blurts.

Kiara

My jaw drops open. Is this guy for real? I put my hand on the phone's mic and stare at Willow, trying to come up with a summary for her.

She throws a popcorn in her mouth. "What?" she asks, her eyes dancing.

"I can't believe him!"

She scoots closer. "What'd he say?"

I move the phone further from her. "First he says I'm reading too much into his story." I pause for dramatic effect, rolling my eyes.

"Ouch," Willow says. "In his defense, he doesn't know your aversion for the expr—"

"And then," I add, not wanting to hear her defense of the douchebag I've already decided I'm not interested in, "he says I read too much."

She tilts her head like a curious puppy. "Hm? Ask him what he means."

"Dude, I'm just gonna hang up."

She shoots her hand out toward me. "No-you're-not," she replies instantly.

What does she care? "I'm not interested!"

"You can't make a decision like that on a-a-a—"

A hunch? I abso-fucking-lutely can. I bring the phone down and aim my index at the red button.

"Wait!" she yells, then adds in a regular tone. "Just tell him *he* doesn't read enough." Whispering, she adds, "let's have some fun. See how bad he really is."

"And maybe you don't read enough," I say, looking at Willow and smiling. Excitement courses through my veins. I feel like a teenager again and am vaguely ashamed yet outrageously entertained by the whole thing. I put the phone on speaker.

Colton

"And maybe you don't read enough," she says. I can hear Willow giggling and whispering in the background. This is a shit show of epic proportions. It's going to blow up on the proverbial fan and Kiara will be pissed. Majorly pissed. Does Willow even realize her job is on the line if Kiara finds out?

With the desperation of a man who has nothing to lose, I grab an invoice from the top of the pile, turn it over, and start scribbling as legibly as I can.

This is my last chance at saving not only this disaster of a scheme, but, this time, my friendship with Kiara.

Kiara

"Or maybe I read between the lines," he says in a suave voice.

Willow jerks back into the couch, clasping her hands on her mouth, giggling excitedly. "HOT!" she mouths silently.

I have to say, he got me there.

He continues, talking super slow. "Maybe I'm only here for a month... to get away from it all... and I'm ready... I'm ready to meet someone who's not... not like anyone else I've been with... before. Someone real... and honest... and no bullshit. Maybe... maybe that's what your profile said to me... between the lines... and... and your voice... between the words... and your answers... between my questions. Are you that person, Kiara?"

Colton

I sense her hesitation on the line. Did I go too strong? I scribble another line.

Kiara

When I don't say anything, he adds, "I just want to connect with... with someone real, and for a short time." He takes a deep breath, like a man who fucked up and knows it. "Is it too much to ask?"

I'm not sure what to answer, so I stay silent, listening to the ruffling of papers on his side of the phone call. I'm waffling between the feeling that something is off, and the attraction I feel from his words alone.

"Tell you what," he finally says. "Do you like snowboarding?"

I roll my eyes and press my palm on the phone so I can talk to Willow. "He wants to go snowboarding," I whisper.

Colton

I can't believe I let him go so long before bringing up a first date. Snowboarding. Safe. Public. There's no reason for her not to go for it. I've finally reached the end of this disaster. My nerves are so shot that at this point I don't care if she hangs up or not.

I'll find another way to make her see we belong together.

But with Willow clearly in the room with her, there's no reason she won't encourage her to go for it.

Kiara

Willow stifles a giggle and motions me to keep talking.

"Why'd you want to go snowboarding?" I mean, I'm all for it. Little to no conversation. I'd avoid chairlifts—these could lead to long conversations and awkward physical proximity—and opt for gondolas, pretending I needed to warm up a little. It's rare to be alone in a gondola. The presence of other people would drastically reduce the awkwardness of having to get to know each other. No dressing up and trying to look pretty. So, for me? Perfect.

But why would a guy want that? Is he some kind of loner who's awkward around women? I'm looking for a man, a real man, with experience. Someone who can, you know, pop my cherry in an expert manner. I'm willing to go through all the crap if it leads to that.

I know I'm not experienced, but I don't think snowboarding—the baggy clothes, smelly socks, matted hair, not to mention the physical exertion that generally leads to me falling asleep before dinner—ever led to one losing their virginity.

"I just thought we'd... do something fun, have lunch together. Don't you like snowboarding?"

"Yeah, I do."

"Scared you can't keep up with me? I'll wait for you."

The guy is lucky he's got a sexy voice. I hate that I don't find the strength to tell him off. To be honest, I'm curious what kind of person he is. Sometimes he can say the most outrageous things. Other times, he's spot on. Covering my phone with my hand again, I whisper for Willow's benefit, "I think he might have a split personality." Then I ask him, "D'you know where Red Mountain is?" and stick my tongue out at Willow, who's rolling her eyes. She firmly believes the research the guys did on this dude is solid and I have nothing to worry about.

"I'll figure it out," he answers, a smile in his voice. "Saturday?"

Inspiration hits me. "Can't do Saturdays. I can't do days, really. How 'bout tomorrow night?"

There's a slight pause, and for a few seconds I'm both hoping and dreading he's going to bail on me. Tell me he has poor night vision or some shit. "Tomorrow's perfect. Four o'clock at the main lodge?"

"Six." That'll give me time to get ready. And then we'll get into the later hours of the day, which will be more conducive to warming up with... a drink at the bar. And more if we gel. Screw smelly socks and such. Night skiing shouldn't make me too gross. It's too fucking cold to break into a sweat.

"Six it is. I'll be wearing a... a light blue ski jacket."

With the weather we have coming, there won't be many people in the main lodge at six. Just the die-hards, and they won't be standing around. "I'll find you from your picture. I'll be the—"

"You'll be the most beautiful woman in the room," he cuts, getting me another eye roll. "See you tomorrow."

He hangs up before I can answer, and I have to say, I kind of like it. I'm jittery from the phone call and confused by the different things he said. I can't get a read on the guy, but overall I got a good feel.

CHAPTER TWENTY-THREE

Kiara

Not gonna lie, I'm nervous as hell. Not about meeting a stranger and the whole safety aspect of it. I got that part covered. Willow has a screenshot of my date's profile, plus I'm sharing my location with her in case he shoves me in a snowmobile and smuggles me to Canada. At the last minute, I also texted Colton to let him know where I would be and to "send dogs and the snow patrol if I'm not back by midnight."

His answer? *Have fun, Cinderella.*

Not even jealous, not even a *Who is this guy?* It makes me a little sad that he's already given up on me (I know, right? What am I thinking?) but mostly confirms I was right not wanting to date him.

I want fun and temporary. Just not with Colton. But clearly, he's already moved on, and that's okay.

I set my snowboard in the outdoor rack and walk into the lodge, helmet under my arm. There's a massive fire roaring in the stone fireplace to my left. Across from me, the back of the lodge is all glass, opening the view to the slopes, yellowish under the night lights.

I get a tingle of anticipation at the idea of the first run of the season, but a quick scan of the place and my temper rises.

Standing between the near-empty bar area and the ticketing booth? Colton.

Colton!

Seriously?

I take another quick sweep of the place under his hot gaze. No sign of Nigel—the guy from the app. Did Colton actually meet him and pack him off? That is so... I don't even have the words.

I march to him. He's standing, arms crossed, a small smile on his lips, his gaze up and down my body in a way he has no business making so hot. I'm on a date with someone else. My lady parts shouldn't be allowed to react to him, but they clearly didn't get the memo.

"The fuck did you do?" I ask. I know what he did—I *know*. He came here before me, found Nigel, and scared him away. *Fuck that.* "You had no right. What did you tell him?"

"Who? Nigel?" His mouth twitches like he's making fun of him.

"I sent you his information as an extra precaution. As a *friend*. Not as—"

"Sweets, relax. There is no Nigel."

"What do you mean?" I look around, like Nigel is going to show up at any moment, prove him wrong. But something heavy settles in the pit of my stomach.

Colton's eyes shut for a bit, and he groans. "Shit. I knew this was a bad idea," he mutters to himself, like I'm not even standing in front of him, fuming. "Look. I did a thing, and I'm not proud of it, but I... Please don't hate me." His gaze is pleading, and for a bit I feel sorry for him.

If only I knew what he was talking about. "D'you kill him?" I semi-joke.

He nods. "Worse."

I tilt my head. Worse?

"I made him up. There is no Nigel. It was me all along."

Nice try. "I spoke with him. What did you do, Colton?"

While he pulls his phone out, he says, "You spoke with Luke, who just moved into town." He shows me the dating app on his phone, with his profile, and the damn picture. Next to it, the edit button proves Colton controls the profile.

Understanding washes over me like a cold and hot shower. I feel stupid, played, useless. Tears prickle my eyes. "Why would you do that?"

He shuts his eyes briefly, seeming as hurt as I am. "I wanted... this. You and me. Give me a chance, Kiara. Please."

I don't want *a chance*. I don't do tryouts, not with Colton. I want Colton in my life, for sure and forever. There's a statistically much, much better chance to have him in my life as a friend than as a... romantic partner.

I want this whole situation to not be true. "I spoke with him," I say, denying what I know the truth to be. "We had like, a whole conversation."

"Shit, I'm sorry."

Doubt seeps into my brain. Does Colton not know that? What is he doing? I frown at him.

"It... I was telling him what to say," Colton explains.

"Who? Nigel?"

"Not Nigel. There is no Nigel. Luke.'

"Who the hell is Luke?"

"New guy in town. The guy who pretended to be Nigel. So you wouldn't recognize my voice."

I swallow, tears still threatening to spill but the feeling teetering between disbelieving and bitter.

Eyes to the ceiling, he sighs deeply. "I knew this was a bad idea," he mutters.

This is so crazy. "Prove it," I say. "Prove it was your friend with the sexy voice talking and not Nigel."

"He said he was staying in Prattsville for a month or so. He didn't really want to answer the question about his previous relationship. He said something about not having an accent. And then he messed up and said you were reading too much into stuff." Colton's jaw tenses. "I thought I'd lost you then, but I tried anyway. He kept laughing because he didn't know what to say and he needed time to read what I was scribbling."

The whole time he's talking, his eyes are scanning my face. Colton is scared that he messed up, that I'm going to ream into him.

Should I? He did play me. Made me believe he was someone else. I told him already I don't want to date him. *Can't take the risk.*

Then why am I so jealous when he mentions Country Club messaging him? Why do I feel so threatened knowing Valerie is back in town, even for a visit?

Is this the person I want to be? Scared to commit because a long time ago, my trust in men was shattered by my piece-of-shit dad? (And my boyfriend. That makes two.) But Colton? Colton is *nothing* like these men. Colton has always made me feel safe. He has always been there for me. Hell, he's the one who gave me my life back.

I pretend-huff and take a step to the side. "Lemme get my ticket."

He produces two night passes and a million-dollar smile. "You're not paying for anything when you're on a date with me."

My heart ba-booms but I try to conceal it.

"And don't you give me an eye roll," he adds just as I'm ready to... yup, roll my eyes at him.

"He has a nice voice."

"So you've said."

"Sexier than yours," I add to rile him up—to see if he'll be jealous. If he's really that into me, or if this is just a lazy move, like I've told him before.

"Didn't factor that in, but I'm sure glad it worked." He leans over to attach the pass on my jacket like I'm some kid, the brush of his fingers against me warming me up. "Anything to get you here, Kiara," he says, the deep timbre of his voice rumbling through my chest.

Special. He's making me feel special, and my heart threatens to explode already, as if it knew it was in for a world of pain. "What's this guy's name again? I might want to catch a beer with him."

He straightens, chuckles, and attaches his own pass. "You mean the guy who thinks you read too much into things? Who thinks being a foodie means you like to eat?"

"You were really writing down what to tell me?"

He tilts my chin up to look me in the eyes, and dammit if his fingers don't burn my skin in the best possible way. "This is how this date is gonna go," he says, and it doesn't escape me that he's not answering my question.

I want to know what Colton told Nigel—or whatever his name was. I want to know which parts were Colton and which were not, but Colton has moved onto his topic of choice.

"We're going to freeze our asses on the slopes," he's saying, "but have a lot of fun."

I suppose, if I let Colton take things further, I'll get to know if he's also a sweet talker, or if that was all Nig—what's-his-name. Though

I have to say, what's-his-face's voice might have been objectively sexy, but it did nothing for me. Not the way Colton's does. Not even close.

"We'll take the gondola," he's saying, "so I won't be tempted to put my arm around you on the chairlift." The traitor manages to smirk at that. "When you're done having fun you let me know, we'll come back in and get a hot chocolate. Then we'll drive our separate ways. Sound good to you?"

My shoulders relax, yet I feel a tinge of disappointment. This is just going to be snowboarding, after all.

His lip tips up at the corner. "Don't worry, there'll be other dates." He lets my chin go, but not without tracing my jawline with his knuckle, then adds, "Taking it slow."

My knees buckle slightly at his words, spoken under his breath, his gaze showing all he's not saying in case I needed captions.

I don't know how to feel about the fact that Colton went through all the trouble of creating a fake profile and getting some guy to stand in for him on the phone. Basically catfished me. I should be angry, maybe even concerned over his state of mind.

But I'm not. Even if he played me, I know where he's coming from. I haven't been playing hard to catch with him. I've effectively shut him off, when he's been so good to me. I'll chalk his little deception under desperate times calling for desperate measures. And I can't say that I'm immune to Colton going to all this effort... just for a date with me.

"'Kay, let's go," I say a little too briskly. If I can't get the tingling under control, I'm going to make a fool of myself on the slopes. Rubber legs won't be my friend.

CHAPTER TWENTY-FOUR

Colton

Kiara glides effortlessly on the snow, carving her path like a pro. Our first run, I let her go in front of me, enjoying riding behind her, where I can keep my eyes and thoughts on her without having any explaining to do. She takes the easy route, down on Avalanche, the main slope leading back to the lodge, staying straight ahead where a fork leads to a more challenging trail. She's giving us time to get into our riding legs but doesn't stop once for a breather or a quick chat.

The second run, I pass her and stop mid-slope at a natural outlook. During the day, the view is spectacular here, and I can almost fill it in from memory. But now, it's even more compelling. Contrasting with the yellowish hue of the snow we're on, flattened by artificial floodlights, the dark expanse at our feet seems endless, punctuated only by the flickering lights of cars on roads and the occasional farm on a hill.

Balancing on my board, I wait for Kiara to join me. "Tired, old man?" she calls out as she comes to a stop two feet downhill from me.

"Just looking at the view," I say. I tilt my head up, hoping for a sky full of stars, but the cloud cover is thick.

"Much nicer during the day."

"Yeah," I drawl, "my date wasn't available to come during the day."

She smiles and shrugs. "Makes for better après-ski."

I grind my molars. Is that why Kiara suggested night riding, when she didn't know who she was talking to? So the guy would what—take her home afterward? Jesus.

"Après-ski is only as good as the skiing was," I answer. Now's not the time to have a semi-argument with Kiara about online safety. This is a date. The *first* date, where you want to make the best impression. The one that may or may not lead to a second date. *Don't screw this up, Colton.*

She lifts her goggles and lays her gray eyes on me. "Is it good so far?" she asks.

She's not talking about the skiing. She's talking about our date, and it affects me deeply. I should be asking her that question, but it's too soon. I got her to not rip me apart when she found out why I was here. I don't want to appear like I'm trying to make her admit I was right all along—that we belong together.

But what really catches me off guard and sends me spinning is how she's asking *me* how the dating is going *for me*. Like she's unsure I'm having a good time. Doesn't she know what she means to me?

"Just warming up," I say to answer her question. I push off and hop to skirt around her. "Let's go!" I take the lead, shredding through the snow so my thoughts take a back seat for a minute.

Before we reach the fork off Avalanche, I switch and ride fakie to make sure she's still following. Lifting my goggles for an instant, I slow down as my heart quickens at the sight of her smiling at me. "Afraid I can't...?" The second part of her sentence is lost in the sound of the snow crushed under our boards, but the trill of her laughter rings in my ears. I switch back and at the fork make the turn to the narrower, trickier trail.

The joke's on me because the moguls are bigger than I'd anticipated. With my longer board, I'm at a disadvantage. While Kiara bobs up and down, using the terrain to switch and curve and jib over the moguls, I stay to the side of the trail, doing kick turns to avoid this mess altogether. She glances at me over her shoulder, and of course her laughter rings through the mountain. She can make fun of me all she wants, if this is the sound I get out of it. It warms my core before lodging itself in my dick.

Count on Kiara to make me snowboard at night with a hard-on.

We take a few more runs, using the gondola rides to warm up. Kiara insists on the moguls again, so I follow her, trying not to break a leg. "Let's take Devil's Pass," she says. "Last run."

"Gotta be the last. They're about to close."

"Look at us! Closing down the mountain."

Her use of the word *us* makes my lips tilt up and my dick twitch again. "Real party animals," I say without thinking. As the words tumble out, the image of Kiara naked under me suggests itself to my lizard brain.

Devil's Pass is an ungroomed, narrow trail. It's not as bad as its name suggests—the hardest trails aren't open to night skiing anyway, and this one is. "Go ahead," I tell her, relishing the sound of her heaving breathing as she passes me.

Yes, I do like looking at her. Even in baggy snowboarding gear, with her black helmet on, her glow-in-the-dark stickers shining under the less-than-flattering artificial light spilling from the lamps, she's the only person I want to look at.

She almost loses her balance and shrieks lightly, then laughs as she catches herself. I love seeing her so happy, so carefree.

We're almost at the bottom, where Devil's Pass joins Avalanche, when a cloud of snow builds from the ground up as Kiara tumbles, limbs rolling over limbs, the glitter of her stickers the only indication of where her head is.

Panic seizes me as I slow down and force myself to stay calm. Bending low, I manage to grab her snowboard that she lost in the fall without stopping entirely—a massive pain in the neck in ungroomed snow. But when I reach Kiara, I stop downhill from her and lift my goggles. "You alright?" I ask, my voice shaky.

She's spread on the snow like a starfish. "Ohmygod I can't believe I fell."

Thank god. She's talking. She's breathing. She doesn't seem to be hurting. *Yet.* "But are you alright?" I ask again.

She tries to prop herself on her elbows, but the snow collapses under her and she ends up flat on her back again. "Colt! Why did you stop?"

Why did I stop? *Why did I stop?* Because for a freak second I thought you might be hurt. Because you're going to need help getting back up. Because... because... "Thought you might need this," I end up saying, placing her snowboard gently at her feet.

She lifts her head. "Ugh," she says, then dramatically lets her head fall back into the snow. "I would have gotten it. You never, ever, stop in ungroomed snow. How are we gonna get back there? And they're about to close!"

"We're real close to Avalanche. Maybe two hundred feet. Come on, give me your hands. You're gonna get cold." I struggle to maintain my balance, and to stay relaxed as the freezing temperatures seep into my clothes. "You sure you're not hurt?" We'll find out when she gets on her board again.

She grabs onto me, her hands feeling tiny even through our two layers of gloves, and gets to a seated position. Dropping to my knees, my board digging into my butt, I scrub the packed snow from her boots as best I can and help her fasten her board. Cold makes our movements slower. "Here's what we're gonna do," I say. "I'm gonna tilt back on my board, you're gonna lift with me, and we're gonna try and keep our balance so we can slide down. Worse comes to worst..." I pull on my neckie to unfog my goggles, the cold making me lose all feeling around my nose and mouth.

"Yeah?" she says, her eyes hopeful on me.

Hell if I know. We'll walk down, snow up to our waist. We'll hold onto our snowboards like surfboards and belly down the rest of the trail. "We'll figure something out."

Her eyes widen, then she starts laughing uncontrollably, her hands sliding off my grip as she clutches her helmeted head.

"What?" I'm torn between laughing with her for no reason and getting a move on to get out of the cold—not to mention the closing mountain.

"Your plan! 'We'll figure something out'," she repeats, taking a low voice and bobbing her head in what I'm assuming is her imitation of me.

"What's wrong with that?"

"Is that supposed to make me feel safe?" She laughs again, then takes a breath. In the silence that follows, my world comes apart. Is she for real? Does she really think I'll let her be in any kind of danger? Is she testing me? She's as seasoned a rider as I am. She could get out of here on her own. *Maybe.* She clears her throat, a low hum, then sticks her hands out. "Sorry, let's try this again."

I pull her up, then bend my knees suddenly and take her in a firefighter hold. Her yelp only makes my dick twitch again. She's so light on my shoulder that I barely feel her when I jump to get some momentum. "Colton, you're gonna kill us both!" she half laughs, half yells as we gain speed. "Put me down! I'm peeing myself! You're pressing on my bladder!"

"Only thing dying on this mountain tonight is your pride."

CHAPTER TWENTY-FIVE

Kiara

"Please, Colt, I'm begging you."

His hold on my butt tightens. "Careful, Kiara. I kinda like it when you beg me."

I swallow hard at his words. "We're on Avalanche. You can put me down, now."

"Nah, I kind of like you there." He gives my butt a squeeze, and I have to focus not to writhe under his touch. Man, I can't wait for the après-ski part. And I'm not talking about the hot chocolate.

We pick up speed, and he slides right up to the lodge. He sets me gently on the packed snow right in front of the racks lining the outdoor patio.

Several bonfires are roaring with Adirondack chairs in tight clusters around them. "Go to the ladies' room, I'll meet you right here," he says, setting his helmet and gloves on two chairs before I can say anything. I follow him inside, admiring his broad shoulders, brushing lightly against him as he holds the door for me.

In the bathroom, I look at myself in the mirror, wondering what he sees in me that he went through all that trouble for a date. My nose is as red as Rudolph's, my hair looks like a mop, and my body, bundled as it is, looks like a stuffed sleeping bag. Yet he set up a fake account, chatted with me online, and found a guy whose voice I don't know to pose as him.

All this for a date with me.

Go figure.

When I come back, he has us set up with two hot chocolates and churros on the flat boulder separating our chairs from the fire. He pulls my chair out to help me sit and I can't help but think how very *date* this feels.

I have to admit, this is nice.

"Mmm, it's good," he says, dipping the churro in the hot chocolate. "Here, try it," he adds, presenting me with a dripping churro.

I lean forward, barely catching the overly sugared, overly delicious treat. I smile at Colton. "I had a great time, Colt. Thank you."

He smiles back. "I did too." His gaze lingers on my lip, then he says, "you have sugar right there," pointing at the corner of my mouth.

I wish he'd lick it off. Or at least wipe it with his own finger. He's done way more than that to me, and not so long ago. Why is he so skittish all of a sudden? Is it something I did? Something I said? But it's not like I can ask him, right? *Hey, why aren't you turning this into something more?* That'd be... weird.

Instead, I wipe my own lips, then shamelessly admire how the hues of the fire dancing on his features soften the planes of his face. His hair is a mess, one I adore. He must have tried to fix it by running careless fingers through it, because it has this tamed wildness that is presently doing something very concerning to my middle. His stubble is at about 3.5 days, which means he might consider shaving it tomorrow.

I don't know if I will be mourning the bad boy look or craving the clean-shaven, polished version of him.

"So... what got you into being a pastry chef?" he asks, breaking my dreamy train of thought.

"I told you already," I answer. I get this is date number one, and we're supposed to get to know each other, but this is Colt. He knows me.

He shrugs. "You told Grace you sort of fell into it because you got night shifts at some hotels, and that allowed you to sleep in your car during the day. Which we both know led you to trouble," he adds, with a half smile that makes me all giddy. The trouble he's talking about is him finding me asleep and dragging me to Emerald Creek to start the rest of my life. "But at the incubator, you said you wanted to create sweetness in the world. That true?"

"Did I say that?" It sounds like something I would say.

"You didn't really say it-say it." He blushes slightly in the most adorable way. "I kind of... I... Is... is that why? I mean, I *think* that's why you do it. I just kinda... it made sense to me, after you told me about your father. What he did to you, and what the rest of your family did to you. Must have been awful lonely and brutal out there."

I shove a huge piece of churro in my mouth so I don't have to answer.

"I mean, I knew you were brave from the moment I met you," he says, his voice turning gravelly the way it does when he's talking about something that means a lot to him. "But I guess... I guess until the other day, until you told me about your dad..." His words are a little strangled now, as if he's taking my pain and making it his. "I kinda thought someone with your backbone... you know... would be... I don't know a-a-a super cutthroat businesswoman, or a Special Ops—"

I giggle at that, because what he's saying is too deep and heavy for me to process—on so many levels that I can't even begin to imagine what comes next in the conversation. "Special Ops? Did you look at me?" I ask from the side of my mouth, then shove the last piece of churro in my mouth.

He smiles, his gaze doing an extra-sweet sweep of my body. "I'm sure they could use a super ninja to slide through enemy lines undetected. You could have done anything you set your mind to. Had enough pain in you to turn it into wanting to fight. Instead you're just wanting to spread sweetness, and that's the ultimate sign of strength right there."

The last bit of churro stays stuck as my throat closes in on the emotion. I've never phrased it that way, but he's spot on. Working on creations with foods that never disappoint, never leave a bitter taste, always look pretty, always bring a smile to everyone, has been my refuge since I left my family.

I've never realized it. But Colton did. Colton sees me. He gets me.

I'm beyond elated that I let him take the lead on our relationship. I'm too much of a mess, but he definitely knows what he's doing.

Churro finally swallowed, I ask the mirror question, a pitiful attempt at returning the favor. "What made you want to become a mechanic?" Any good friend would know the answer. What does it say about me that I don't?

He takes a deep breath. "You know, I just... just feel good in my garage. With my guys. I like to take things that aren't working the way they're supposed to, and fix 'em. My boss, Merritt—I told you about him, right—he used to say things like, 'let's go fix what we can in this world.'

"And he'd show me how to change a belt or weld something. And then when I was done he'd say, 'You fixed something that didn't work before, and that's more than most people can say today.'"

Merritt ended up selling his business to Colt, and he's now living his retirement in an RV, traveling the continent with his wife. "Sounds like he was a really good man."

Colton takes a long gulp of his hot cocoa and nods.

"How does he like his new life?"

"Seems to love it. I think they spent the summer in Alaska, and last I heard they were going down the PCH—the Pacific Coast Highway."

I down the last of my hot chocolate, feeling the warmth spread inside. Cruising down the Pacific sounds idyllic. Deep blue sea. Palm trees. Warmth.

It's what a lot of Vermonters dream about this time of year. And yet, the melted snow in my back from my earlier fall, the darkness enshrouding us in a deepening cold, the flames of the bonfire reflecting in Colton's irises, are memories I will hold dear for a long time.

There's no place I'd rather be than at the bottom of Red Mountain right now. "I like it here," I say.

"Good," he answers, his mouth tilting up.

"Growing up here," he continues after a prolonged silence, "it was the best. And not only this—having the mountains and rivers as a playground—but the *people*. When my folks were going through rough times, I'd go with Chris to the King's farm on the weekends. And after school, I started apprenticing with Merritt and Orson. They didn't just teach me how to fix cars." He glances at me, seems to hesitate, then continues. "When my parents were considering separating, they made sure to show me that relationships required... mutual understanding and respect. They made sure I understood that with love, every couple could be saved—just like my parents eventually were." He stays silent, and I'm too scared to say anything.

I know where he's going with this. But I'm caught like a deer in the headlights, having spent so much time resisting what's happening now.

His mouth twitches as he adds, "The point I'm trying to make, is that a good mechanic doesn't throw away an engine just because it stopped firing up. Just like with people, it's about understanding what went wrong and giving it the love it needs. Then it runs like new."

My heart is beating hard in my ribcage. I should say something, but there's so much I need to process that I don't even know where to start. I know he's right. I just need time to process what this means for me.

"I think they're trying to tell us something," Colton says as the lights inside the lodge are being turned off. We're the last people outside at the bonfires, too... He stands and pulls me out of the Adirondack, and I stiffen, hating myself a little for it, but unable to fight the reflex.

But as soon as I'm up, he lets go of my hand and clears our tray. Then he insists on carrying my snowboard with his and walks me to my car, loading it inside for me.

When he's done and I've shoved my helmet and gloves in the car, I stand tall, waiting for what's next.

He bores his gaze into my eyes and says, "Thanks for the date, Kiara. I hope you liked it as much as I did."

Okay. I was expecting more, but at the same time—maybe not? I'm so confused right now. Why isn't he asking me if I want to go somewhere next? If only for a nightcap at his place.

But no, he simply leans over and kisses my cheek. "Drive safe."

The feel of his lips burns like bitter disappointment as I start the ice-cold car. I don't even feel like starting a playlist. The silence is loud enough for my thoughts, filled with the words he said at the bonfire.

On the drive home, I don't see his lights following me. Could he have left before me and already be at Sunrise Farms? But when I pull up to our parking lot, his truck isn't there.

And his locker dangles partly open and mostly empty when I store my equipment. I feel... suspended. As if for this situation I'm in, I need instructions.

After I shower, I glance outside to the parking lot. Still no sign of Colton's truck.

My heartbeat accelerates, and I pick up my phone. Could something have happened to him on the way back? Instead of texting Colton directly, I open up the app, more as a joke.

ME: ARE YOU OKAY?

NIGEL: GREAT!

ME: ...

ME: ~~WHERE ARE YOU?~~

ME: ...

NIGEL: EVERYTHING OK WITH YOU?

ME: ...

ME: WHERE ARE YOU?

NIGEL: GOODNIGHT

The next day, I'm already up and working on new creations for Valentine's Day when the intercom rings. It's barely seven in the morning. Peering down through the blinds, I see Randy's delivery van, lights on and engine running.

I don't remember an order we might have worked on. We often collaborate on decorating cakes, especially for weddings, or fill orders of chocolates and flowers together. Wondering what he could possibly want that couldn't be handled over the phone, I let him in.

He hands me a bouquet of chamomiles, lavender, and violas tied with twine and plucked in a mason jar.

There's a note that says: *Would love to do this again—Colton.*

Randy is still standing in the entrance of my flat when I fold the note back into its envelope, my cheeks warming at Colton's written words. "They're all edibles," Randy thinks necessary to point out. "He had me order them specially."

I can't help the smile building inside me. "Thanks, Randy. That's really sweet of you."

"I-I'm just following orders. But I've never seen Colton so specific in his orders."

My smile sours a bit, but I fight to hide it. "He orders a lot of flowers?" I ask, taking the bouquet to my coffee table so my back is temporarily to Randy's. I can't have him see the jealousy slowly building inside me.

"For his ma, yes. He gets her a bouquet each month. It's his Christmas gift. He gives her like a pretend fancy voucher at Christmas that says 'Twelve Bouquets' or something like that."

"That's sweet!" The word is weak, far from what I'm feeling.

"It's the first time he orders flowers from me for anyone else than his ma," Randy says. He blushes a bit, then backs out of the apartment and closes the door behind him.

It takes me a minute to collect myself. Last night, after Colton's non-answer by text, I was vaguely pissed. Where was he? I had the intention of staying up to check when he came back, but in the end, that night riding got the best of me and I fell asleep on the couch.

When I woke up at four, his truck was here. I went to bed, tossed and turned, sleep out of reach as a growing mental discomfort took a hold of me. In the end, at five I got up and started working.

I take a picture of the bouquet and send it to "*Nigel*" with a simple *Thank You*.

An hour later I hear his footsteps on the staircase. My palms moisten like a silly teenager's, and I wipe my hands, ready to answer his knock on the door. But the footsteps hasten, then there's the distinct muffled bang of the front door, then the soft rumbling of Colton's truck starting.

Not gonna lie, I'm feeling a little off-kilter. The firefighter hold. The hot chocolate near the bonfire. The kiss on the cheek. The flowers.

The whole talk about how relationships are supposed to work.

All this is so sweet and unexpected but also a little... distant? Even his speech—I haven't been able to process it yet. He was talking about us, but he wasn't. I could have used a whole night of hashing it out, except he just vanished. It feels like eating cotton candy when you're craving pecan pie.

I need pecan pie, so I go to the window and peer out.

Colton's face is looking straight at me, flashing his white teeth in a devious smile that goes straight to my heart.

And he actually winks at me as he peels off the parking lot.

He's teasing me, taunting me. Taking control of whatever it is that's happening between us. I should be panicked, but I'm not. I just feel crazy happy, and that's the scariest thing. I don't want to lose that.

Chapter Twenty-Six

Colton

I have to say, I'm pretty satisfied with how my plan is going so far. Even if it's a real challenge to stay away from her. It'll all be worth it.

The memory of her gazing at me down from her window plays as a softening background to the bleak day I have ahead of me. I've never thought of Kiara in the role of housewife, waiting for her husband to come home, but I have to admit, knowing she was in the warmth and comfort of her home, probably in light clothing (something easily removable), looking down at me with—what was that in her gaze?—desire, longing, affection, any or all of these—made something stir inside me that I never thought I harbored.

I wanted that. I could picture this as our future. Sharing an apartment, or maybe a small house if we could afford it. Her being warm and comfy as I braved the elements—fuck, this is so clichéd and outdated. But why do I like it so much?

Just as I liked carrying her in a fireman hold yesterday.

After she left the mountain, I stayed in the truck a bit, so she'd have a head start. If I'd pulled up behind her at Sunrise Farms, there was no way I wasn't following her into her apartment. And she would have wanted that for reasons I don't like.

I'm going to show her there's so much more I could be to her.

So after ten minutes had passed, I pulled out and went to Lazy's instead of going straight home, even if there was a good chance Kiara was already tucked in bed by that time.

Yeah, just that thought made me hard again.

This morning, I bypass Easy Monday and Millie's coffee (ah-ma-zing coffee, as the sign says). I'm not in the mood for the curious glances and whispers behind my back. The downside of living in Emerald Creek is that your private moments aren't private. Which can be an upside, depending on what's going on in your life. But this morning, I'm not sharing the details of my date with Kiara. Because of course everyone will know we went on a date. A real one, this time. It wouldn't be Emerald Creek if they didn't.

I'll settle for the mediocre coffee I offer at Harper's Body Works.

I even go as far as sipping it in the garage, in the company of cars, amidst the smell of oil, looking at the heart of the business I've created for myself over the past few years, with the help of Merritt.

The first bay is empty, as that's where we do the oil changes and quick fixes that don't require an overnight stay. In the second bay is Chris's truck that was damaged when a deer jumped across the road. Luckily, his pregnant wife, Alex, who was driving, didn't swerve to try to avoid it. That's when people get *really* hurt, or worse. Hitting a tree to avoid a deer is not something you want to do. Unfortunately, swinging the wheel is a reflex, and it takes a little training and a lot of nerves to be able to stay the course when collision with the animal is inevitable. Keeping straight and honking are the two things you need to do when a deer is rushing to you. Alex had enough self-control to do that, and the only damage was to the truck.

In the third bay, an Airstream is gleaming softly in the dark. Wendy and Todd, who own the smaller hotel in town, brought it to us so we could retrofit air conditioning units for the cross-country trip they want to take once they retire. Linwood has been working on it, and he's convinced them to let him source parts to renovate the kitchenette. He's bringing in a friend to work on the upholstery.

I'm a little envious of him working on that project. There's something about breathing new life into a vintage work of art that makes all the sweat and elbow grease so worth it. Not to mention the satisfaction of making the owners over-the-top happy, as I know Wendy and Todd will be.

I sit on the steps leading to my office and sift through the print-out of orders for the day. Three oil changes, including one for Ms. Angela. An inspection. And a tune-up for... Owen Parker's bimmer? He was here a few weeks ago. Owen is a major pain in the ass. I sure hope we didn't miss something last time.

It should be a standard day, with the two projects we have ongoing, and the inevitable calls early morning when the cold makes people's cars uncooperative. If I'm lucky, I'll be able to leave at five tonight, get in a shower, and be at Lazy's by six. Maybe Kiara will be there. Tension zings through my veins.

How long should I wait to invite her out again? I know where I'm taking her. Is this upcoming weekend too early? Should I wait a little longer?

Nah. She's going to think I'm not interested after all. And she's still on the app. Who knows what she's doing on it now? I grab my phone and pull it up, hoping her profile will have disappeared.

It's still there. She could be chatting with someone right now. Making plans for the weekend.

Screw it. I start typing.

Me

> ~~Are you free this S~~

> ~~Clear your Sat~~

Shit. She might have some catering to do this Saturday.

> ~~Are you free this Saturday during the day?~~
> ~~Or the next?~~

Better: *I'd love to take you on a second date. What Saturday are you available during the day?*

I look at the message. Look at the time. 7:30 a.m. *That's way too eager, Harper. Give the woman some time to breathe. You wanted to show her how good dating you would be. Don't smother her.*

With that pep talk clear in my mind, I delete my message, pocket my phone, finish my coffee, then stand right as the shop's phone starts ringing. I've made the choice to not have a receptionist for now. I can't afford it, and the clients love to talk to the person who's actually doing the work.

When I hang up, two of my guys are in the bays, working.

"I'm going to check on a guest at the hotel," I tell them. "I'll be back as soon as I can. Can someone take the phone?"

"Yup," Patrick, my youngest mechanic, answers. I set the handheld next to his workstation before getting in my truck.

As I pull out, I see Owen Parker going the opposite way, signaling that he's about to turn into the garage. I wave at him, and he waves back. I should have checked his file before leaving.

It's over an hour before I return from the hotel—frozen fuel lines are tricky—and Owen is still there. He made himself comfortable in the waiting room, sitting squarely in the middle of the only two-seat sofa. Under the fluorescent lights, the top of his head shines a pinkish hue where his hair is prematurely thinning. He's reading the paper, sipping reheated drip coffee from a Harper's Body Works mug.

"Hey, man, what's up?" I ask him. "What's going on with your BMW?" I get behind the computer at the reception desk to pull up the detail of his most recent service. His car is still parked outside. He wasn't due until ten this morning, I notice, which makes me wonder why he came in so early.

"Talk to you for a sec?" he asks me, his chin pointing to my office door in the back.

What the heck is going on? "Sure, come on over."

He takes his coffee mug with him as he precedes me to the back. His suit is strained at the seams, barely containing the soft roundness of his body. It's wrinkled, large streaks across the back of the jacket, and messy crisscrosses on his pants. His shoes try to look fancy but can't do anything against the snow and the salt and the mud that prevail here eight months a year. As always, Owen is trying to look important.

I show him the stool while I take my seat behind my desk.

He sits without flinching and looks around my office, seeming to look for something to compliment me on. Coming up empty, he says, "We're really fortunate to have you on the Select Board."

Growing up, Owen Parker was my bully. My personal hell, my everyday battle. Not everyone who's been bullied has the pleasure of giving not a fuck when they see their former tormentor. Of not even thinking that the tables have changed, or in my case, that there aren't tables anymore. He has no hold on me. And I do not wish to have any type of hold on him.

This is thanks to my friend and soon-to-be brother-in-law, Ethan. He was older than me, and he looked out for me. He looked out for everyone. He straightened Owen out using fists and words in equal measure, just as he straightened me out by giving me the confidence I so bitterly lacked. Taught me how to fight back. Taught me I didn't need to care what Owen thought of me.

So when Owen is clearly trying to make an overture by complimenting my space but can't find anything because, let's face it, the place does look like shit—the furniture has to be fifty years old and not in a good way, the visitor chair is a wooden stool, and the decor on the wall consists of yearly cardboard planners, staff schedules, a list of supplier's phone numbers strategically placed to hide the smattering of brown spots that pay a testament to the previous owner's weapon a choice: the fly swatter—when what Owen says is *"we're really fortunate to have you on the Select Board,"* I measure all the progress made since our youthful years.

I nod. "Happy to help." Owen is a lawyer, and he bravely decided to hang his shingle right here in Emerald Creek. And I applaud him for that. The thing is, his bread and butter, due to him being in Emerald Creek, is property disputes, maybe some small labor conflicts, trusts and wills, and real estate transactions. The concept of conflict of interest drastically reduces his pool of clients, and he's stuck with who gave him their business first. His potential for growth is, at this juncture, extremely limited. And he's only a few years out of law school.

But Owen loves the idea of being important. Being on the Select Board is a status thing for him, not a service thing like it is for me.

And that's okay.

He shifts on the stool, choosing to cross one ankle over his knee, leaning his elbows on his thighs, and stapling his fingers. Owen should do yoga. He'd be great at it. Maybe he does? "So, we have an application coming up, for a variance," he says softly.

"Uh-huh?" Select Board topics shouldn't be discussed privately, but let's hear him out.

"I'm not sure if you know how this works?" he asks, lifting his eyebrows to confirm this is a serious question.

Ah, there we are. Condescending Owen, taking newbie Colton under his wing. That's a new one. I sit back in my chair (which has a back *and* armrests) and staple my fingers—not just to mimic his pose, but more so to hide my grin. "Tell me," I say.

He goes into the details of the zoning regulations in Emerald Creek, which I'm pretty familiar with, but whatever. When he starts explaining to me under which conditions we can say fuck it to said regulations, I ostensibly pull out my phone, check the time, and place it face up on the army-green metal desk. Then I resume my stance, looking him in the eye.

He shifts his gaze to a spot on my shoulder. "George Richardson—you know him, right?"

I was born here, dickhead, just like you. Of course I know Georgie. I nod.

"He's—"

We're interrupted by a quick knock on the back door—the one leading to the bay—and the door flies open. My guys aren't specially trained in privacy matters. I like it that way. I have nothing to hide. "Boss!" Linwood's voice sounds in my back. "Oh, sorry."

"Just a sec," I answer without looking back. I nod to Owen to continue as the door shuts.

"Richardson's applying for a variance."

Yup, saw that on the agenda. Got the email from the town offices. Planned on looking at it tonight to prepare for our next meeting. I raise an eyebrow. "Is he?" Owen loves to feel like he has the upper hand.

And there he is, straightening his posture, puffing out his chest. He nods. "And that's where you come in." He clears his throat. I strive to show no emotion. Just glance at my phone. It *is* getting late. "He and I... we do business together." Course they do. Georgie is the largest land and building owner in Emerald Creek; Owen is the only lawyer in town. Georgie uses Owen. Nothing wrong with that. "Which means, I don't want to vote in favor of the variance. I-I-I-don't want to be seen as doing him a favor, you see—but!" he adds with a finger raised, "I wouldn't—if I did. I would be doing *the town* a favor. But no one's gonna understand that. I mean, *you* know it. You know how people are around here. They just stop at appearances. They don't see the bigger picture."

"But you do," I say, wondering if he'll catch the irony in my tone.

"I do! Thank you. Thank you for noticing." He leans back, then catches himself when he remembers he's on a stool. "You know, you've come a long way."

I take a deep breath so I don't roll my eyes. I really do want to know why he's here, why all this flattery, and then it hits me just as he says it.

"We'll need your vote in favor of the variance—the *town* will need your vote."

I raise an eyebrow. "I was going to look at it tonight," I say right as another knock sounds on my door. "Be right there!" I shout.

Owen stands slowly. "It's important." He extends his hand to shake mine, and I don't really see a reason not to. "You'll do what's right."

I free my hand and stop myself from wiping it against my jeans. "I said I'll look at it. That's all I said."

He looks down at me pointedly while I pull up his file on my desktop. "Tell me, what did we miss in your car last time? Didn't we have it in a few weeks ago?"

He frowns. "My car?" Then he breaks into a small chuckle. "Nah, that's just for... purposes of, ya know, why I was here. You got me?"

Seriously? He needs to build an alibi for talking to me? This guy is nuts. "Totally got it." I force a smile as I stand, round my desk, slap his shoulder, and open the door. "Glad you're happy with our services," I say as he walks through the now crowded waiting room.

He waves goodbye, not looking back at me.

Scanning the waiting room, I meet Chris's gaze. "Patrick's got me," he says. "Almost done."

I nod, Owen's words still ringing in my ears. *You'll do what's right.* The bitter taste in my mouth has nothing to do with my subpar coffee. "Who's next?" I ask. All the faces are familiar, and that's no surprise. But there are a lot of people here this morning. Way more than had an appointment.

"Ms. Angela can go first," Willow says.

I frown, looking down at the computer. "Ms. Angela?" She's not on the schedule. Neither is Willow, but I can guess why she's here. "What's the problem?"

"Oh, you know. Oil change," Ms. Angela answers.

"Already?" We had her during foliage, three months ago. "Got the warning light on?" I convinced her to upgrade to a newer model. She shouldn't be having problems. That was the whole point. I look out the lot where she parked her SUV. "Gimme your keys," I say, wiggling my fingers at her.

"I was here last," she says. "Lynn was here before me and she said she has an appointment for her oil change, and Sophie needs to get back to the library, but she booked her inspection today. Maybe you can get started on them while we all just... chitchat." She sits deeper in her armchair, crosses her hands in front of her belly, and smiles at me.

I can't believe her. She didn't see me this morning at Millie's, so this is what happens? She holds her gossip court right here? "Need a refill on the coffee?" I ask, my hands on my hips, narrowing my eyes on her.

"Oh, don't you worry over that. I made a fresh batch," she answers with a sweet smile, meeting my gaze. "Also cleaned the dirties. Tidied up the cupboard. You know."

At that moment my accountant, Emma, comes in. She catches the last of Ms. Angela's words. "I keep telling him he could use a female touch around here," she says. "Hi, everyone. I got yogurts and fresh eggs for you, Colton. I'll put them in the mini fridge, don't forget to take them home."

Willow sighs audibly. Chris rolls his eyes. Grace told me all about the drama with Emma a while back. I don't want to get into it. But I don't want drama either. "I wasn't expecting you today," I tell her.

She stiffens as she places an egg carton and little glass jars of yogurt in the fridge. "You're welcome anyway. And you're right, I'll see you next week." She turns to the audience as she walks back out. "Just trying to be nice," she snaps.

Luke—who doesn't have an appointment either—holds the door for her, giving her the once-over.

"She's a good accountant," Chris offers once Emma's gone.

Ms. Angela tut-tuts. "How were the trails last night?" she asks. The room falls silent. Luke perks up, Chris chuckles, Willow and the rest pretend to be fascinated by their phones or their cuticles.

If Emerald Creek ever needs a motto, it should be: *Hide from the gossip and the gossip will find you*. "I'll get started on your oil change, Lynn," I say as I grab her keys, then take refuge in the bay.

Around lunchtime, everyone who was there this morning is finally gone without having gotten a word out of me about how I spent last evening. And I send Kiara the text message I've been mulling over for hours.

Chapter Twenty-Seven

Kiara

I t's the first time someone has given me flowers, and I'm not sure how to describe what I'm feeling. It's like a warm blanket, but inside. Something that radiates to my outer shell and pulls my lips up slightly. This feels deeper than a simple smile. Time has stopped still and it's only me and the flowers in the bubble of my cozy home.

I smell them again and turn them just so, until they capture the morning sun in the best possible way. Adjusting the focus of my phone's camera, I snap a picture. It doesn't even need filters. Golden motes give the flowers a dreamy halo. I could spend all day looking at them, lost in their beautiful, complex, almost messy perfection.

I need to refocus. This whole evening with Colton, this whole fake dating turned into real dating, which could in turn become losing my best friend, emphasizes how life is constantly changing.

I should know this. Things turn on a dime. One day you're part of an okay family, the next you're homeless. One day you have a solid friend, the next you have a messy situation that only gets messier as deeper emotions and lust invite themselves to the party.

I know what he's doing. He thinks he's showing me the right way to do things—the respectful way to have a relationship—and I get it. In his mind, this is what's happening. But for me, it's a slow reeling into Colton's fold that will leave me with nowhere to land once it's over. Nowhere to go to but inside the deep layers of my loneliness.

Just once with Colton would have been perfect for me. An infinite moment outside time, not to be repeated, not to build unrealistic expectations upon. A one-time to treasure for the rest of my life, without any heartbreak to go with it.

I could have walked away, at the lodge. Staying felt like facing down a double black diamond, the exhilaration growing as you anticipate the thrill of carving on ice, the dance with the mountain as you sometimes let it carry you and sometimes make your own decisions, using gravity to your advantage, letting it pull you down or slow you down. You might not be totally prepared for it. You never are. You might take a bad fall, one you can't get back from, and meanwhile the blue slope was right there in all its boring safety. Or it might be the best run of your life. You'll never know unless you try.

I didn't know what to expect last night, and it was one of the best evenings of my life. Seriously.

I wasn't prepared for being carried out of deep powder in a fireman hold. For hot chocolate under the stars, next to a roaring bonfire.

I wasn't prepared for flowers and stolen glances outside the window. And sexy smiles just for me and... winks! He winked at me, and I swear, my center reacted in a very pleasant way.

And certainly, I wasn't prepared for a speech on how to have a successful, lifelong relationship that sounded like a confession. Like something that Colton had thought about in the context of being with me and deemed important to share on our first date. He knew my fears and he attacked them head-on. Showed me he understood where I was coming from, but that didn't mean I shouldn't trust him.

And now here I am, and I feel a little lost, and a little eager, and a lot scared. Facing down the double black diamond.

What if the answer is to seize the moment, and keep tomorrow's heartbreaks for tomorrow? I've never been so uncertain about the next step in my life. What if—

My phone dings with an incoming message on the dating app. *Nigel.*

Nigel: What day are you available?

Me: For what?

Nigel: ...

Nigel: For another date

My heart skips a beat. *This is it.* This is the point of no return.

I want to say yes. I know I do. The more I look at his message, the less doubt in my mind. It's in the palms of my hands, in the tightening of my heart, in the tingle spreading through my whole body.

My gaze skims higher on our text messages and stops where I asked him where he was last night. Jesus, does he realize what a needy bitch I'll be if we get deeper into this dating thing? I can't even help myself.

Nigel: If that's okay with you

One taste of Colton, one evening as his date, and I'm totally gone. I want more.

I want his company as my friend, his attention as my date, his
affection as my lover. It's time I admit it. Even if heartbreak still feels
inevitable, I'll brace for the fall and that's okay. He'll be worth the pain.

Me: Sure, when?
Nigel: Any day that suits you
Me: Is this a whole day thing?
Nigel: Yup

A whole day? Are we going snowboarding again? That was fun,
but... I have a shit ton of work to do. With the holidays—

Nigel: Can you?
Nigel: ...
Me: My weekends are tied up with catering and shit
Nigel: I know. A Monday work for you?

A Monday? He wants to take a whole day off to spend time with
me without impacting my business.

Me: What about the garage?

His answer comes right away, no hesitation:

Nigel: You come first

The words send a jolt through my whole body, a realization of
how deep Colton's feelings go, and how they're wrapping themselves
around me and pulling me in.

ME: Next Monday works

Nigel: I'll pick you up at 10

I'm buzzing with anticipation.

ME: Where are we going?

Nigel: Surprise

Hmm. No snowboarding? What else could take a whole day?

ME: How should I dress?

Nigel: Like any day

Nigel: gtg. See you Monday

I heart his last message and look at the screen, rereading our messages, a silly smile taking residence on my lips, my cheeks hurting, my heartbeat accelerating.

My palms tingle with excitement. I need to tell someone, anyone. Willow? She'll rub in my face how right she was. Grace? She's Colton's sister.

A thought seeps through my mind. Opening my text messages, I pull up Colton's name.

Wanna hang out tonight?

Colton

I can't

Why not?

I'm seeing a girl

What?

...

I went on one date with her last night, and I really like her. I think she might be the one. So I don't want to ruin it.

What the actual...?

She just said yes to another date next Monday, all day.

WTF

I'm taking it slow with her, like I said. But I don't want to ruin it by hanging out with a friend.

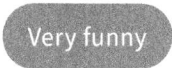

Very funny

Yeah, I'm funny like that.

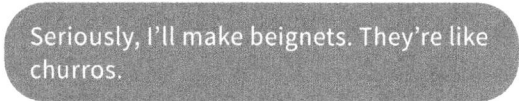

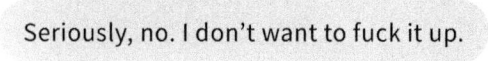

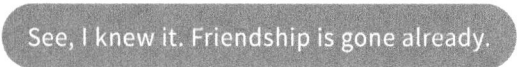

Seriously, I'll make beignets. They're like churros.

Seriously, no. I don't want to fuck it up.

See, I knew it. Friendship is gone already.

...

Friendship is being put respectfully to the side while I explore a more meaningful connection

You're very confusing. Why can't you take me on a date

Typing these words make me all sort of hot and bothered. I pause, thinking this through, then resume my typing.

while still hanging out casually with me?

I don't cheat on sweetness with grasshopper. That's a rule.

I'm the same person

It's not really the same thing, though

Also, you never had a problem hanging out with me when you were dating other girls. This is bullshit.

This is true, with the notable exception of Valerie. There was no hanging out with Colton (or the both of them) when she had moved in with him.

I wasn't dating any of them.

You think if I ever got serious with another girl I'd be hanging out with you over pizza and video games in the middle of the night?

But he did. He always used to. And he wasn't celibate...

What does he mean? I reread his message and see how right he is. What girlfriend would be okay with him hanging out with me? But then why did he...? All these times, when I'd bring him cupcakes for whoever he was seeing. When he'd drop a name, or a place they'd been. Was this all nothing to him?

> Make no mistake

> You always came first

> But now I want it all with you

My fingers are too weak to type anything back. I read his last lines over and over, and the more I do, the more my stomach feels queasy—but in a good way. I end up clutching my phone, wishing it was Colton, wishing I knew what to answer to that.

Make no mistake
You always came first
But now I want it all with you

> See you Monday at ten

Frustrated that I he won't see me *now*, I turn to the app. Maybe there I can ask him to hang out with me tonight. Maybe that's what he wants. A role play of sorts.

But when I bring it up, Nigel's profile has disappeared. Colton is no longer on the dating app.

He just wants to be with me, and that's all that matters.

I hit the trash can button at the bottom of my profile.

CHAPTER TWENTY-EIGHT

Kiara

I t's now Monday and we're driving in central Vermont through a maze of backroads. The Northeast Kingdom, where we live, is rugged and strikingly beautiful. Here, the landscape could serve as a model for the naïve prints found in nurseries: it's absolutely adorable.

The hills are lower, softer. Snow-covered pastures are lined with deep-green woods and the occasional split-rail fence. Dirt driveways draw straight lines from our two-lane road to white farmhouses and red barns.

Colton makes a turn onto a gravel road, and I barely have time to catch the name on the sign posted at the entrance in simple gold cursive against a white backdrop.

Is he for real? It can't be. My pulse accelerates and my eyes widen.

"Are you... are we... are you taking me to... *Sweet Grove Bakehouse*?" I ask in a strangled voice. As the words form in my mouth, the driveway curves and the familiar shape of the house featured on the logo of the iconic pastry school emerges against a backdrop of evergreens.

I'm more excited than the proverbial kid in a candy store. I want to shriek my excitement but instead ask in a whisper, "How did you manage to get us in?"

Sweet Grove Bakehouse—SGB—is the refuge of iconic pastry chef Annabel Plum. She left the craziness of working for the best restaurants on the planet to run a very profitable online channel and occasional in-person teaching. She writes beautiful pastry books with pictures from the best photographers in the world that hit the bestseller lists every time. She refuses to go on television. Or to bake for restaurants—or anyone.

As far as I'm concerned, she's the most famous hermit in the world. Her semi-private courses sell for thousands of dollars within minutes of being posted on her website.

So, yeah. My question for Colton stands as it goes unanswered, and we pull to a stop. He rounds the car, opens my door, and extends his hand to help me out.

My legs are jelly. "Colt, what are we doing here? We can't possibly…" I don't want to be rude, but a session at SGB is too expensive. Colton doesn't need to do this for me to make me understand how much he cares about me.

Annabel Plum herself appears on her covered porch. I'd recognize her face anywhere. She's wearing her signature chef jacket and, on her head, the pink bandana she adopted when she left "the life" to tackle baking in her own way. "Colton Harper! You made it!" she exclaims. "Where is she? Come on in! It's cold!"

Her smile is infectious. She's warm and welcoming and my initial shyness at meeting one of the legends in my industry dissipates to leave intense curiosity, excitement, and a bit of overwhelm.

All of a sudden a slight panic gets a hold of me, fighting with the elation of being here. I wish I'd known we were coming. I could have mentally prepared.

Somehow I'm out of the car, and Colton has my hand in a warm grip. "Relax, sweetness. It's cool," he tells me, amusement in his voice.

The legendary pastry chef crosses her arms and looks at us with kind interest, her light blue eyes dancing on her round, freckled face.

"So you kept the secret, huh?" she says as we join her at the front door. "Good for you, Colt." She extends her hand and turns her gaze to me. "Hi, I'm Annabel Plum. Call me Annabel, and welcome to Sweet Grove Bakehouse."

I stick my hand out nervously, trying to temper my urge to jump up and down. "Kiara Smith, and yes, I know who you are."

"I've heard of you too," she answers casually as she leads us inside.

I lock eyes with Colton. "What did you tell her?" I whisper, embarrassment flushing my cheeks as I imagine him gushing over my pastries to the GOAT. And why is she calling him Colt? Does he *know* her?

After we take our coats off, Annabel leads us into a large open space with a post and beam vaulted ceiling two stories high. The white landscape illuminates an immaculate space mainly dedicated to baking and cooking. Four ovens, induction and gas ranges, professional-grade equipment, three islands. Everything is of professional quality, but at the same time, an elevated decor of chandeliers, fresh flowers in mason jars, and a large live-edge table laden with Farmhouse Pottery dinnerware and Simon Pearce handmade glasses turns the space into a haven of welcoming luxury.

The white and chrome of the kitchen is softened by the wooden accents of the central dining area. Beyond that, the living room area is defined by an off-white sprawling sectional covered with pastel throw pillows, two leather chairs, and a coffee table covered with Annabel's books.

Annabel pulls three small glasses and an unmarked bottle of liquor from a cabinet. "Sit down," she says, gesturing to the stools lined at the kitchen counter. She pours three glasses and sits across from us. "To friends," she says, cheering.

"To friends," Colton answers.

I take a small sip, letting the sweet wine warm my insides. *Mmm. Interesting. A basic, classic orange wine macerated with cloves. I'll have to tell Haley to try that.* Then I decide it's time I come out of my starstruck shell and ask the first of many questions that have been assailing me in the last minutes. "So... how do you know each other?" My eyes go between Colton and Annabel. I can't believe he kept such a secret from me.

"From the garage," Annabel answers. "My husband loves vintage cars, and we've been to Emerald Creek a few times to get some work done."

"That's it?" I ask, incredulous. Colton doesn't make friends with his clients. He's friendly enough. But that's not what gets you an in with a celebrity.

"Pretty much," Annabel says. Then with a small smile, to which Colton responds with an actual blush, she adds, "He might have personally delivered a car once, and I might have invited him over for a pear and almond tart, and he might have said he had a friend who could share her recipe with me because mine lacked..." She turns her gaze to Colton, while I feel my insides shrink in horror. "What did it lack again?"

"A touch of bitterness. The types of almonds you used, if I remember correctly."

She opens her mouth in an Ah shape, and says, "Right. A touch of bitterness, just on the first bite, almost—"

Almost erased by the sweetness of the pear but still there as a memory that makes you better appreciate the sweetness of the fruit and the softness of the crust.

I'd explained this to Colton, two or three years ago. I was rambling on about how certain flavors hit certain taste buds and that it was important to consider this when creating a pastry—or any dish, really. You didn't throw ingredients together just because you liked them on their own. Pairing them so they completed each other was a step in the right direction. But analyzing the experience it would provide nanosecond by nanosecond as each layer of flavor built on each other? Now that was the foundation of a successful creation.

"—Almost erased by the pear but still there to make you better appreciate the sweetness and softness of the fruit and the crust," Colton completes. *He remembers?*

They both exchange a chuckle. "Lemme tell you, Roger thought it was the funniest thing ever." She looks at me. "Roger's my husband."

My cheeks are burning, but I don't dare ask for confirmation. Did Colton actually...? Just thinking about it, I'm dry heaving.

"And he was right," she tells me. "*You* were right. I quickly asked him who'd given him such knowledge of pastry, and he happily gave me all your information. Told me where I could buy your 'stuff.' That's what he called it. 'Stuff.'" She rolls her eyes.

Did Annabel Plum ever eat my *stuff*? And if so, what did she think?

Colton shrugs like none of this is a big deal. His eyes are on me, and he looks... proud. He's quiet, soaking it all in. He knows this is a big deal for me. Meeting Annabel Plum.

"The next time he came here to fix something or another on Roger's car, he brought a whole sampling of your 'stuff.' He said it was to thank me for the tart the previous time."

Colton lifts his shoulders. "I didn't know you were a big deal," he says as a matter of apology.

I hide my face in my hands in mock acknowledgment of low-key shame and groan.

Annabel laughs. "It was so sweet! And he was right, your *stuff* was... quite the stuff. I'm glad he brought you over, and I finally get to meet the woman that has this mechanic so wrapped around her finger that he knows the difference between a macaroon and a macaron."

I smile at the memory of how this piece of trivia came to Colton's attention. It was nothing notable, just a quiet evening playing video games. I'd told him how I'd maybe overreacted when Alex—who was at the time Chris's new apprentice—had knocked down a whole platter of macarons that took me a while to make, and he thought it was no big deal. Still high from my day's frustrations, I tore him a new one until I realized he thought I was talking about macaroons—something I'd taught Willow to do a while back.

Willing to move the conversation away from me, I twirl the deep gold wine in my glass. "This is really good," I observe.

"My grandmother was French," Annabel says. "That was her go-to aperitif. Vin d'orange. I modified it a bit." She takes a quick intake of breath. "Colton tells me you're thinking of going to the ICPV?"

The Institut Culinaire Pierre de Varanges is where I'm hoping against all odds that I'll be accepted. I didn't realize that Colton had memorized the name. I glance at him, surprised, though not upset that he shared this with her. "That's right. I'm hoping they'll accept me with a full scholarship."

"And what do you hope to get from it?" She takes another sip of her vin d'orange, looking at me over the rim of her glass, her gaze on me with kindness. I've still not fully come down from my high of sitting casually with her at what's pretty much her kitchen table, drinking aperitif—and with Colton, of all people.

"Skills, and name recognition," I answer.

She looks out the window and squints her eyes. "It's funny how women tend to seek external approval way more than men. We always think we're not good enough. Or we're a fraud. I know I was that way."

I don't respond. She doesn't realize it, but it's easy for her to say that. She's had the top chefs as teachers. She climbed the ranks among the best, making her connections along the way. Of course she doesn't see what she got from it: the ability to move to the middle of nowhere and still be a celebrity.

Not so for me. Or maybe it will be, once I go through some high-level training that leads to a career like Annabel Plum's.

"I thought we could play around with genoise and pâte à bombe today. Plan for a layer cake and see where that leads us?" Annabel asks, standing up.

"Sounds like a plan I like," Colton interjects with a huge smile, rubbing his hands. He picks up the glasses and brings them to the kitchen, rinsing them. "I'll be on dishes duty. Wouldn't mind licking the bowl and what not, if that's okay," he says from afar.

"Unless you had something else in mind?" Annabel asks me.

"To be honest," I say, still struggling to steady my voice when talking to her, "I haven't given this any thought. Colton totally surprised me by bringing me here." I'm pretty comfortable with my genoise skills, and I wouldn't mind impressing Annabel. I'm sure she'll have something to teach me anyway. "Genoise and pâte à bombe sounds great."

We wash our hands, don large, white aprons, then take the ingredients out of the refrigerator. I'm still so starstruck I barely talk, instead taking in the setting and observing every one of Annabel's gestures, the relaxed yet mindful way she handles food. "When you go to France," she says as I start a bain-marie, "you'll have eggs at room temperature all the time. Did you know that?"

I'm lightly rapping the eggs one by one on the side of the large mixing bowl that will go above the hot water, focusing on giving each shell a clean break. It'd be just my luck to start this session with shattered eggshells, like a newbie. But my hands don't betray me, and my self-confidence returns. "How so?"

"Their food safety practices focus on the source, at the farms. Europe has mandatory vaccinations that are only recommended here, and animal welfare practices and regulations that also contribute to lowering risks."

I set the eggs on top of the hot water and measure the sugar while listening to her.

"Because of that, they don't wash the eggs at the farms. The cuticle of the egg remains, which is a natural barrier against bacterial contamination. Here, we strip the egg of its natural protection. That's why we need to refrigerate them here, but not in France."

"Aren't the eggs... dirty?"

"Nope. They have strict hygiene regulations for nesting areas, and if an egg is dirty, it's discarded."

I monitor the temperature of the bain-marie so the eggs don't cook. I just need them to be at room temperature.

"There are so many different things in different countries. French butter, for example, has more fat content than US butter, and the flour is radically different too. Luckily, you won't have to worry about making your own recipes at the Institut."

"If I'm accepted," I interject while vigorously whipping the eggs and sugar together.

"I don't see why you wouldn't. They love a self-made pastry chef story."

The eggs and sugar beaten to a perfect ribbon consistency, I remove the mixing bowl from the bain-marie. Annabel discards the water while I start measuring the flour.

"I think I'll just join Colt and watch you," Annabel says, which makes me instantly blush. "Just kidding. I don't want to miss out on the fun. Here's something you can try. Fold the flour in threes instead of half, then half."

"Got it."

"You have such perfect gestures," she murmurs. "No wonder your 'stuff' is so good. It's all in the energy you project into your creations."

"Should we add melted butter?"

"What do you think?"

"Well, if we're going to layer it with a pâte à bombe, then yes. It won't be as light, but it'll be richer. And since we're likely not incorporating any syrups, then..."

"I say go for richer," Colt says. He's been looking at us, seemingly fascinated.

Annabel chuckles and pulls the butter out of the refrigerator. We quickly melt it, then incorporate it delicately so it doesn't weigh down the flour. As we put the genoise in the oven, Colt says, "That's it?"

"Now, the fun starts," I answer him.

"What she said," Annabel echoes. "Chocolate—"

"Obviously."

"What else are you thinking?"

"What you got?"

She tilts her head. "Challenge me."

"Candied ginger?"

"I make my own."

"Cardamom, star anise, saffron?'

"I said challenge me!"

I smile at that.

"Pink peppercorn? Smoked salt? Cocoa nibs? Black garlic?"

"Y-yes. Yes I do have that."

Wanting to find her limits, I add, "Black truffles?"

She crosses her arms and smirks. "Had them for breakfast, just ran out."

"Ha!"

She gives me a high five. "Alright, how we doin' this?"

Her energy is contagious and makes me want to try everything. "Let's go a little wild."

"I like it."

"On a base of dark chocolate, let's add Thai basil, a balsamic vinegar reduction to balance the richness of the cocoa, a drop of Chartreuse—"

"Or I have a liquor reduction of the vin d'orange," Annabel suggests.

"Nice. But what if we served it with the cake, instead of incorporating it in the recipe? The orange and spice chocolate would be magnificent together."

"You guys are making me salivate," Colton groans.

"I like that," Annabel says. "I especially love it when restaurants serve the right wine with the dessert. It's... it's bringing the dessert to where it deserves to be." She takes a notebook and scribbles down what we just decided. "What else?" she asks me.

"Pink peppercorn for spice."

She adds that to the list and says, "I have tonka bean." Then looks up at me and wiggles her eyebrows.

Tonka beans aren't legal in the United States. *You little criminal*. I beam at her. "Get outta here."

"You ever used'em?"

"Uh. No ma'am. Only heard of them."

"Tonka beans it is, but this stays between us."

This time I'm the one high-fiving her.

I'm excited about the tonka beans but want to refocus on our project. "How about for texture? Toasted puffed quinoa for extra crunch? In general, I love candied ginger—but here I don't want it to overpower the other flavors we have going. How about we keep it for the garnish?"

"Yes, I like that. Now, how do you feel about a drop of olive oil for extra smoothness?" she suggests.

"Oh, I've never tried that!"

"You'll love it," she answers, scribbling on her notepad. "Ok. What do you think?"

"I think we have enough to work with."

"Agreed. Oh!" She turns to the oven. "Little challenge here for you. Just checking you don't need a timer. Is this ready yet?"

I open the oven and glance at the genoise. The scent of butter and sugar wafts through the air, a good sign. But its color is uneven. "I don't think so," I answer. Just to be sure, I press lightly on its surface. The indentation stays, the cake not bouncing back. "I'd say ten more minutes."

"Let's keep an eye on it," Annabel says, visibly satisfied with my answer. We spend the rest of the afternoon into the early evening chatting and baking. I'm out of my starstruck freeze, and I find myself discussing baking techniques and product sourcing as if Annabel were an old friend of mine. The pâte à bombe turns out spectacular, and Colton is blown away. And I get to taste and bake with tonka beans for the first time in my life, an experience I won't forget.

"Isn't she the best?" I ask Colton the moment we turn off her driveway, making our way home. "So cool and sweet. Who would have thought?"

Colton's lips curve up. "She's a baker, of course she's cool and sweet. It's a requirement. Didn't you know?"

Over the course of that afternoon, I learned that Annabel's husband, Roger the vintage car enthusiast, wasn't there that day, which meant Colton spent several hours half participating in something he has a moderate interest in but I'm passionate about. It was a dream come true for me and, at best, a boring time for him.

And he did it all for me. As a date!

I slowly come down from my high to focus on the most important thing that happened today: Colton gave me a date that was entirely focused on me.

Overtaken by a wave of tenderness, I place my hand on his arm, then run it up to his neck, relishing the feel of his hair under my hand.

His mouth twitches as he glances at me.

"Thank you," I say as I lean over the center console to kiss his cheek. "Best date ever." I'm hit by the coconut scent of his shampoo in a way that moves me deeply.

The tenderness I felt a moment ago is fast turning into something way more intense, so I quickly retreat into my seat and let Colton drive us safely home.

Chapter Twenty-Nine

Colton

Her kiss on my cheek burns like an ember. I want to stop the truck, bring her on my lap, and claim her lips.

But I don't.

We're not at the point where Kiara wants me in the I'm-crazy-about-you way, but I'll get her there. I'll get her to stop seeing me as a good friend. As her favorite mechanic. As a gaming buddy.

I'll get her to see me as a man who could be *her* man and would be epically great at it.

The kind of man who knows exactly what kind of date his woman gets off on. I'd say in that respect I scored pretty high today.

How I pulled off the afternoon with Annabel, I'm not sure. It's one of those things where Mom and Grace would say the universe is at work, and for once I wouldn't roll my eyes.

The pear tart story about how we became friends was freaky enough, but the fact that when I called Annabel out of the blue a few days ago to find out her prices and book a session with Kiara if I could afford it, she'd said, "I've been wanting to meet her. Bring her in as a friend. I don't work Mondays."

After Kiara's kiss, I stay focused on the road. As much as I want her to be mine, today was eye-opening for me.

I'd looked up Annabel and found out what a big deal she was. Seeing her interact with Kiara, I started measuring what Kiara had tried to explain to me: that Emerald Creek might be holding her back. That despite all the goodness that was there, it just wasn't going to give her what she needed, wanted, and deserved.

The opportunity to develop new techniques, explore new tastes, and discover new traditions that would enrich her already vast knowledge.

A career that would expose her talent to the world.

I'd taken offense at the time, not seeing her point, but Kiara was right. Emerald Creek couldn't give her that.

And then there was what Annabel had said to me, when Kiara was in the bathroom.

"The Institut Culinaire is tough, but with her personality, I'm gonna take a wild bet and say that she'll thrive. She's satisfied at nothing but excellence. Doesn't compromise. She gives it her all and doesn't *lie*." She'd emphasized the word, and I wasn't sure what she meant. Being around Kiara so much, I'd heard expressions like *honest food*, but a pastry chef *not lying* was a new one.

"I'm not really making sense to you, am I?" Annabel had frowned kindly, looking at me like the lost man I felt. "In baking, as in cooking to a degree, the gesture is almost as important as the ingredients. It's not enough to have a recipe. You can follow it to a T and still your end result will be disappointing. Your passion and your love for the art goes from your heart straight to your hands. The gesture is what makes the difference. Without passion or love, whatever you make will be forgettable. Edible, but forgettable.

"Kiara has that passion and respect for the art. She makes pastries for the sake of bringing something beautiful into the world."

I'd seen that passion in Kiara. "You hit the nail right on the head as far as Kiara is concerned."

"How does that make you feel, Colton?"

What did she mean? "I'm proud of her," was my obvious response.

"You do realize that in Paris, at the Institut, she'll be among peers. People who have that same passion and understanding."

My heart clenched. What was she getting at?

"The question is, are you ready for her to leave you? Because that's what'll happen. When Paris, Dubai, Tokyo roll out the red carpet, you don't say no. You go."

I knew this all along, yet I was fighting it. "Isn't that what you did?"

She nodded. "It is what I did."

"But you're here now," I countered.

She raised her eyebrows. "I *am* here. Thirty years later."

Shit. Maybe that was why Kiara was so reluctant to being mine. Because she couldn't. Because there were bigger things than me awaiting her. As much as it hurt me, as much as I wanted to fight it, I wasn't going to. Kiara deserved better.

Then Annabel added, "But then again, I didn't have a Colton waiting for me in Emerald Creek."

But as Kiara made her way back to us, my chest tightened. She was looking at me differently now, I could tell. My courting hadn't been for nothing after all. She was dating me, and ready to be my girlfriend. But I had to accept that she'd probably never be more.

"I'm ready to lose her if that means she finds herself," I told Annabel under my breath.

Now, in the car, with Kiara's kiss burning my cheek all the way down to my heart, I don't feel so assured. I know it's the right thing to do. It doesn't mean I like it.

Safely tucked back in her seat, she says, "That was an awesome date, Colton. I'm not even sure what to say. If there's a next date, it needs to be all about you."

I almost swerve the truck off its lane. "Why wouldn't there be a next date? I thought I told you I'm serious about us." Just saying the words makes my heart beat harder. Despite what Annabel hinted rather heavily at—that I'd have to watch Kiara go—I do want to have whatever I can with her. And who knows? Maybe we can make long-distance work. Why does Kiara suddenly think there shouldn't be a next date? Did she overhear what Annabel said, and this is going to be yet another excuse to be just friends? Well—screw that.

At my words, I feel Kiara's gaze on me. Glancing at her to confirm she's looking at me, I'm struck by how soft her eyes are, how intense her gaze on me. I can't help it—I reach over to give her hand a squeeze.

She twines our fingers together.

I nearly lose it again. The least I want to do is bring her hand to my mouth, but I don't. Instead I let her small, talented fingers get lost in my larger, calloused paw, trying to make myself as soft and warm as I can. I rub my thumb on the inside of her wrist until she clears her throat and pulls softly away, tucking both hands under her thighs.

"Did you hear what I said?" she asks.

Nope. I have no fucking clue what happened before she linked our hands. The world didn't exist before. My brain is wiped clear. I am born again in a world where Kiara has feelings for me beyond friendship and is finally beginning to express them. "What did you say?" I ask, my voice raw with emotion. *It was just her fucking hand, Colton. You had your face between her legs not so long ago and that didn't move you as much.* Yeah, but that time, it was just sex. This right now was pure feelings, and I'd take feelings over sex any day with Kiara.

"The next date needs to be all about you," Kiara says. I start to protest, but she interrupts me. "If we're doing this, I need to know who I'm really dealing with." A mischievous smile lifts the corner of her mouth.

If we're doing this are the words that ring on repeat in my head. Hell yeah we're doing this. And since she wants the next date to be about me, I know exactly where to take her.

Chapter Thirty

Kiara

I'm still on a high from my visit with Annabel. She was the epitome of generous, and fun, and knowledgeable. I want to be her when I grow up.

How do I do that?

I already applied to the training in France, and I don't know of any other opportunities that would offer me this level of education without having to pay a cent; I only need to sit tight and wait on their answer. "The only reason they might not accept you is if they have a lot of stellar applications this time around, and it turns into eeny meeny miny moe," Annabel had said during our time together. "They're going to love everything you have to offer. Especially once I tell them all about you!"

I protested about her putting in a good word for me, but honestly? I was thrilled, and so was Colton. He winked at me when she said that, and I could have kissed him right then and there for being so happy for me. This date turned into way more than I ever thought any date could ever be.

Despite Annabel's apparent sense of certainty over my prospects, the visit with her triggered something else. Something more primal, more essential, something I've been trying to have but never achieved. Maybe I didn't try hard enough. Maybe I didn't believe in it hard enough to have it; my own space

I would make it as welcoming as Annabel's. Not as big and luxurious, of course—I couldn't afford it and wouldn't need or know what to do with it. But something *mine*. With my personality. Where people would want to come and taste confections and discuss something truly unique that I would make for them.

At the incubator I attended with Colton and others from Emerald Creek, they asked us our *why*. I don't remember what I said, but I do remember the question. It's been quietly growing around me, taunting me: *Why?* Sometimes: *Why bother?* Sometimes: *Why not?*

I'm sure what Colton remembers from my answer (*and by the way, he remembers?!*) is an accurate representation of my thoughts, then and now: Creating sweetness in the world. But that's not specific enough.

Since I came back from Annabel's, these thoughts are becoming less abstract. Less of a pun and more of a reality that's almost tangible. If I could stay in Emerald Creek, I would give my community nourishment that is sweet and beautiful. I would continue partnerships with restaurants and the bakery, but the heart of my contribution would be a space that would feel precious and beautiful, a delicate cocoon in the hills of Vermont.

Numbers collide in my brain, as my thoughts stray from big-picture vision to granular implementation. I'm suddenly excited by the possibilities, surprising myself as I open a realtor app and scroll through listings.

It's as if taking the risk of dating Colton has given me the energy and faith I needed to go after my dreams and take ownership of my future.

As I make a mental note of the different options I'm seeing and the rents posted, I decide to also book an appointment with Emma. Willow is right, I need her help to figure things out.

A listing catches my eye. The barn at Dewey's Hollow, that was supposed to be sold to Californians who wanted to move it piece by piece to the West Coast.

I know where it's located. Off a dirt road, but close enough to the village, it's in an idyllic, bucolic setting. There's even a small brook nearby, but with the barn uphill from it, the risk of flooding in case of heavy rain seems remote.

I click on the listing, and immediately fall in love with the interior, which I'd never seen. It seems renovated with what looks like a commercial kitchen, and exposed post and beam in the main room. The price is too low to be true. I go to close the app and make a note of it in my notebook when a chat box opens, asking me if I want to book a visit with Maddie Parker—the listing agent.

I'm not ready to buy anything, but what's the harm in looking around, being informed, and knowing the market for when I'm ready?

I click yes and add a note. *Can we talk first?*

Minutes later, I'm on the phone with Maddie.

I open my conversation with her by telling her I'm not ready to buy yet.

"Look, you're doing the smart thing. And no, don't worry about wasting my time," she says, answering my apology. "It's super slow right now, and I'm going stir crazy. I'd love to show you the barn. Are you free around lunchtime?"

The barn is even cuter than I remember. In traditional red, it stands out against the snow. Fairy lights are strung around the windows, giving it a festive air. The walkway from the parking lot has been cleared of snow, and large flagstones curve elegantly to the entrance.

The inside is smaller than the pictures led me to believe—which is perfect. I don't need a huge space. Don't want to have to pay for it and heat it.

Maddie greets me in a whiff of apples and cinnamon—a trick from any realtor's book, I'm sure, but still, it works. I immediately feel at home here. And when I start baking, the smells will be even more enticing.

Dammit. I'm already thinking as if I had the place.

"So—what do you think?" Maddie asks me ten minutes later, as I run my hand on the prep table.

I take a deep breath. "It's so nice. It would be perfect for me, but as I told you on the phone, it's too early for me to buy anything. But I appreciate you giving me a tour."

She sits on one of the two barstools at the kitchen counter. "Well, let's look at some numbers. The owners are open to considering a lease. They really want someone to breathe life back into the barn."

A lease? That could work. If they're motivated, their price might be workable. I might even be able to change the overhead lighting for lantern-style pendants, or even something dreamy like Chloe did at her restaurant. I could paint one of the walls in chalkboard paint and write quotes from famous bakers. And on the large window ledge facing south, I'd add an herb garden for mood and scent and atmosphere. None of this needs to be expensive. This is totally doable. Still, something nags at me. Why isn't this place occupied?

"What was it until now?" I don't remember Dewey's barn ever being a restaurant, but then again, I don't go out much. I could have missed it. What I can tell though, is that it's set up to be one.

"The owners first renovated it as a place to sell the produce from their farm. Over time they added refrigerators, and a little space for tasting. It grew into a sort of country café showcasing all their farm's products. For whatever reason, they stopped doing that, and someone leased it to turn it into a full-on restaurant, but it never panned out. That's why it's in such pristine condition. They never opened it."

I perch on the barstool next to hers and narrow my eyes, trying to understand. "Why would someone throw all this money in and never operate it? It sounds crazy." I think back at how pissed I was over my wasted elbow grease and the money spent on one antique mirror for the space I lost last summer. I can't imagine pouring tens of thousands of dollars, all for nothing.

Who would do that?

Maddie lifts her shoulders. "One person's loss is another's gain."

But all this spend? "I'm assuming it wouldn't come equipped, would it?" Surely whoever leased it is going to move their equipment out before long.

"It comes as is." She smiles at me. "Look, I know it sounds too good to be true, and you're probably wondering what's the catch. The reality is, the dining space is on the small side. Probably not large enough to turn enough of a profit on a restaurant. Now, if you're looking to use it as a catering space up to regulations, and make extra money from on-site tastings, this could be perfect for you."

"But what about the previous... well, the people who set it up as a restaurant?"

"It's my understanding they left the appliances as payment for past due rent. I didn't get into the specifics, but you would have a precise description of the equipment it will come with when signing the lease. No surprises. Actually, here's a provisional list. You can take a look," she says, sliding a printed page my way.

I'm so excited I can hardly think straight. I already noticed the type of ovens they have—a Moffat and a Revent, both with steam injection. More than I ever dreamed of having this early on.

I glance outside at the sun setting over the hill. The snow glitters, traces of a deer the only disturbance, like ellipses on a white sheet of paper—an invitation to follow into the unknown. Then my gaze turns back inside, and I can picture it in even more detail, my mind completing the decor, narrowing on the experience itself. Vintage pastry cases. An interactive tasting station. A coffee nook.

"And it's zoned commercial, right?" It's close enough to the village to assume that it is, but the absence of any other building in the immediate surrounding begs the question.

"You would run this as an Agricultural Accessory Use," Maddie answers, making it sound like it's a given. "People do it all the time. Especially as a tenant, you can benefit from their farm use. You'd just need to file a special permit with the town. I can help you with that."

I nod, not sure what she means by all that.

"That's what the restaurant people were going to do. Shame that they weren't as savvy as you are. You know, I tasted your blueberry buckle at Emerald Lake resort over the summer, and it was absolutely superb."

I blush slightly. The resort never gives me feedback on my creations, so it's good to know some people notice. "Oh, thank you." I hope I can trust her about the special permit. I don't want her taking me for a ride. People tend to do that when they see you at a disadvantage. This woman is local, and friendly. I have no reason not to trust her. But her primary goal is to get her commission. Maybe I'll ask Colton for advice, although Justin's words about people being bound to ask him for favors are etched in my memory.

"Do you also make the gingerbread house they have over the holidays?" Maddie asks me.

"I do." How do I ask her about the special permit without looking totally clueless?

She swats my arm playfully. "Stop! I was kidding. I thought for sure they ordered it from... I don't know where."

"Yeah, those things don't travel too well."

"It must have taken you ages!"

I nod. "You could say that." The gingerbread house is a statement piece they place in their grand dining room. It's great for their social media, but for me, it isn't exactly creative from a culinary perspective. But it's good money that comes when my other gigs die down for a couple of weeks while restaurants take a break early November, after foliage craziness.

"You would do so well with your own shop!" Maddie exclaims. "Imagine all the second-home owners. I mean, I heard people asking to order the desserts as takeout at the resort."

I'm stunned. That's the first I've heard of that. "Really?" I ask.

She continues with her train of thought. "At the price they're selling them on the menu, you would make a killing!"

I'd never thought of it that way. I'd never realized people who lived here dined at the resort. But with the quantities they're having me make, that makes sense now.

"How much do they pay you per dessert—don't tell me. Just think about it. And then there's your costs, of course, but… girl, you could really be successful. You know who you should talk to? Emma. You know her, right?"

Yeah, and I'm texting her right after this. "Yes, I use her services." Her talk about Emma gets drowned in what she said first. *How much are they paying me per dessert?* They're paying me by the hour. And sure, they provide the equipment and the ingredients, but…

Excitement zings through my veins as I take a last look around, projecting myself thriving here.

"So what do you think?" Maddie asks.

Do one thing that scares you every day. Can I trust myself to succeed here? Or do I still believe I need the stamp of approval of a French pastry school?

"I think this is very tempting.

> Yo Ems, how much of your time will a dozen chocolate eclairs buy me?

Emma

Ten minutes

Holy mother. She's expensive.

> Bringing six dozen. You're at the office or WFH today?

Please don't

...

Berry tartlets?

What do you need?

Help figuring out my numbers.

So I can rock it like the rest of you.

Caroline wants a birthday cake with a clown jumping out of it. Can you do that?

When's her birthday?

May.

How many hours does that get me?

Emma:For real, you can do that?

Who do you think you're talking to?

Get over here.

How many hours does that get me?

Unlimited, until the next birthday. Then we can renegotiate

Did you mean a real clown or a toy clown?

Very funny

Ok, real, I thought so.

None of my business, but you're spoiling her.

It's not like you

Do you want your business plan or what? And yes, a toy clown!

Good, cos I draw a line at human trafficking.

?

Just sayin'.

When she turns thirteen she'll want a real human boy band jumping out of her cake

...

When I get to Emma's office, on the second floor of a brick building in town dating back over a century, I bump into Noah coming out of her suite, carrying a heavy file under his arm. "Hey, how's it going?" I ask him, catching the door he is definitely not holding for me.

His head down, he darts to the staircase. *I wonder what's wrong with him.*

"Are you going to need chocolates for the holidays?" Although pastries are my forte, I've enjoyed making chocolates out of my kitchen to sell through the general store. I still haven't gotten their order, and the longer they wait, the harder it will be for me to fulfill it. But Noah is already at the end of the hallway. "Hey, boss!" I call out.

"Hey!" He turns around, seeming to only see me now. "Gimme a couple days."

"What's up with him?" I ask Emma as I make my way through her small wait room and into her office.

Emma is stacking papers together and slides them in a drawer as I come in. "Who?"

"Noah."

She shifts in her chair. "How are you doing?" she asks as she stands. "Coffee? Water?" She looks out the window and stretches her neck.

"Hey, sorry." I know better than to ask questions about her clients. "I'm good, thanks. And forget my question." She looks tense, though. "Everything okay... with you?"

She turns around, her features composed. "Better now that you're here."

"Aww, thanks." I drop a pink box with a green-gold bow on a side table.

She eyes it and her smile deepens. "You didn't have to do this, but thanks." She crosses her feet at the ankle, calling my attention to her legs, her pumps, her pencil skirt. She's so put together. Most women around here wear outdoor gear even for work. "Do you know why you're my favorite client?" she asks.

"Cos I pay you in sweets?"

She chuckles. "Apart from that." She narrows her eyes on me. "Because you're a diamond in the rough. The perfect project. The seed in the ground. I can't wait to see you blossom. It's going to be so fun." She pushes herself from the window, sits behind her desk, and rests her chin on her hands. "So. Tell me everything."

I tell her about my visit to the barn, and everything Maddie disclosed. About the fact that I don't think in terms of profit, when my discussion with Maddie made it clear I should. "I have major impostor syndrome. I know I'm good, but I can hardly apply for a loan and bring my cakes as proof of concept."

"But with some recommendations, it could be a different conversation. Let's start working on that."

"You can't tell anyone I'm actually considering the barn, Ems. It's too early. I just came from visiting it."

"I won't say anything. But it wouldn't hurt if you talked about it to a few friends. At least test the waters with how likely it is you'll get the variance."

By friends, she means Colton, who will be voting on it now that he's on the Select Board. But I heard Justin loud and clear the night that Colton was appointed: people are going to start annoying him with their requests. I don't want to be these people. "I'm not too worried about that. Maddie said it's a formality."

Emma simply nods.

"But thanks," I add quickly. "If I decide to go for it, I'll ask around."

I torture my fingernails, then add, "I applied for a scholarship to attend this school in Paris. They have three-month intensive training. I feel that if I get accepted, I'd have something that proves my worth when I return."

Emma smiles and swivels the screen of her computer. "Show me the school," she says.

I pull up the Institut Culinaire Pierre de Varanges. The first page is an impressive array of where their graduates have gone on to work. It might as well be a jetsetter's ritzy catalog of destinations.

Emma clicks through a few tabs. Her smile is dreamy, stars in her eyes. I can see why my friends who are business owners say she has their best interests at heart.

"So, tell me something," she says as she shuts down the browser and turns her attention back to me. "Where do you see yourself in five years? Because you're after two very different things. On the one hand, you're asking me to help you work on a business plan that would be for you to establish your business here—at least, that's what I can help you with. On the other, you're applying to a school that's a springboard for an international career—as an employee, if I understand this right."

I shut my eyes tight. "I'd come back," I say.

"Would you, though? What's here for you, that you wouldn't have elsewhere?"

"I have you guys." *Colton.*

She nods. "But with your talent, you know you could do better than Emerald Creek? Hence the school in Paris." She states this as a question, one I can't answer. When the silence between us stretches, she tilts her head and asks, "And... how does Colton figure into all that?"

"He's on board, totally."

She nods softly. "I just thought, maybe..."

"What?"

"It's not my place," she says.

Emma might not be my number one choice to discuss Colton, but she's definitely a model in terms of being professionally successful. "I'm giving you permission. Tell me."

"I was wondering if... and I mean, power to you. It's hard enough being a woman, and a businesswoman, without having to deal with all this relationship crap."

"You were wondering what?"

"If it was a way for you to... to soften the blow of a breakup."

What the fuck is she talking about?

She must be reading my face like an open book, because she adds, "You know, let him down softly. Tell him you can't do long-distance, you want to keep your options open in terms of your career. And I totally applaud you for that. I just want to say, you can also walk up to the guy and tell him it was fun but it's over."

I blink at her. I'm out of words.

"Clearly, that is not the case, and I apologize," she says. She does look mortified. "I thought maybe you wanted to go to Paris to flee something or someone. But I get it now. It's a once-in-a-lifetime opportunity. It has nothing to do with tall, dark, and handsome. And thank god for that. I'm so sorry I even suggested that. I won't bring it up anymore." She pulls herself together—big breath, shoulders back. "Look, whatever you do professionally, you'll be successful. You need to believe a little more in yourself. And know that I'm here to support you and advise you on all things *business* since clearly, I'm totally unqualified for the personal stuff. And my life is proof of that."

"You'll find your person, Ems," I say, suddenly realizing my own issues are highlighting the fact that she's a single mom. A gorgeous, available woman still going home alone with her six-year-old.

"Oh—I made my peace with that. I don't need a person. I have myself. I have Caroline. I kind of like it like that. Let's face it: I'm boring. I'm a CPA. I have a kid. I'm not a good deal. At all."

My heart clenches at the way my friend sees herself. "Relationships shouldn't be evaluated like a business transaction. You're gorgeous, and—"

"I appreciate you, Kiara, but really, I'm good." She turns her attention to the computer, typing at high speed, hits a button, then hands me a printout. "Here's your homework, my friend. I'll need some numbers from you, but mainly, some thinking."

I look over her sheet and thank her as I fold it.

But as I leave her office, the thing that bears most on my mind is this lingering question: Is hoping for Paris a cop-out from my found family here, a way to avoid the uncertainty of this relationship I'm building with Colton? If I could have the barn, or something like it, am I ready to take the chance?

CHAPTER THIRTY-ONE

Kiara

On Sunday, Colton brings a Road to Heaven to my place and announces he's taking me to the racetrack for our third date. "I know you gotta be tired to the bone," he says—and I am—"but you said you wanted the date to be all about me. So it's gotta be today."

We don't take his truck, but one of the low cars he tinkers with endlessly at his garage. "I need to show some guys there a couple of things with this car," he says. At least we're not in his truck towing a race car. I don't think I could watch Colton risk his life in what's pretty much a tin can and be okay. And I want to be okay.

I fight the urge to run my hand in his hair. After we came back from Annabel's, he dropped me off at Sunrise Farms, saying he had something to do at the garage before turning in for the night. The way he said it, I knew he was lying, and that's okay. He doesn't want to become physical yet—it's an endless tease he's drawing out. I know it. And I know he knows I know.

It's part of the game we're both playing, having agreed to the un-spoken rule that Colton holds the key to our physical progression after my massive fuck-up of asking him to pop my cherry. We don't need to have a conversation about it for me to understand this is what's going on. I've had time to process what I did, and I have to say, I've put Colton through a pretty messed-up ringer. First the V-card thing, then preferring a dating app to him. It's time I concede defeat and let him take the lead.

My physical attraction to him is reaching unbearable limits, and if he doesn't do something about it soon, I can't answer for myself.

How does he do it? He wants me, yet he kissed my cheek when he dropped me off. Okay, there was a little hand action on my lower back, but that's it.

Maybe I need to take some initiative. I'm already wearing skintight jeans and the super soft sweater I wore at Eloise's birthday party. Maybe that helped the kiss.

But maybe I need to do a little more. Jumpstart this action.

"Thanks," I tell him softly, then lean toward him to kiss his cheek. I trail my fingers behind his nape, run them lightly under the collar of his leather jacket, the others playing briefly with his hair.

He clenches his jaw, shifts gears, and I sit back into my seat.

"For what?" he asks gruffly. The way he moves in his seat, there's a good chance he wasn't immune to that chaste kiss. Just like I wasn't to his, the past two dates.

"For taking me to the races. Showing me a part of you I didn't know."

He shrugs and glances at me, a smile tilting his mouth. "You asked for it."

That's the best. He is, genuinely, doing this for me because I asked for it, not because he wanted to go to a race and decided to drag me along. This isn't a two-for-one kind of situation for him. "Thanks for indulging me," I say.

On impulse, I decide this is good time to listen to music, but this car has the bare minimum equipment. No entertainment center in sight. I'm going to take a wild guess and say that whatever Colton wants to show his friends is underneath the hood.

"Tell me about this race we're going to see," I say.

"Ice racing," Colton offers. "I started going before this track was legal. Made some solid friends there. It was a way to blow steam."

"Is this a race car?" I ask, suddenly worried. "Please tell me I'm not going to be in a race."

He gives me a lopsided grin and says, "You're not gonna be in a race, sweets."

I ask Colton a few questions about the technicality of ice racing, and to my surprise time passes quickly when I'm listening to him talk about something he's passionate about. And I get to learn a few things about driving on ice, which might come in handy one of these days. Like driving on the edge and listening to your tires—knowing that when they whisper, they're about to lose traction and it's time to ease on the gas or adjust steering. Or how left-foot breaking can prevent swinging out during a turn.

"Would you show me?" I ask.

"Absolutely. We can do it after the race, on the frozen lake. Much better than on the road—best way to not get hurt."

My heart is pumping with stupid excitement as Colton pulls up to a random gathering of people tailgating on the side of a lake. There are barbecues smoking up the air, country music blaring from pickup trucks, and a festive atmosphere that's plain awesome.

Colton parks next to a line of trucks, then he helps me out the low seat, and I'm reminded this is a *date-date*. An opening-doors-for-me kind of date.

When he lets go of my hand, he slides his arm around my waist, pulling me close to him as he walks to a group of people huddled around a seriously souped-up pickup truck.

A man with a beard and a backward cap detaches himself from the group. As he calls out, "Colt!" smiling faces turn to us, curiosity tinting their features as they take me in. There are maybe eight to ten people, women mainly on one side and men on the other, save for two couples holding hands. Jeans tucked in lined boots, faded ski jackets, and beanies are the uniform attire—one where I fit right in.

Colt introduces me as his girlfriend, and when conversations resume after they all greet us, he turns his attention back on me. He lowers his mouth to me but kisses me in the tender space right at the angle of my mouth. Before I can turn my head to meet him entirely, he's moved onto inhaling deeply into my hair. With a squeeze of his hand on my nape, he asks, "You good?"

"I'm good."

He gives my waist another squeeze—a thank-you—then without warning, plops me on the truck's tailgate, giving me a seat and a better view.

As the first race starts, he brings me a hot cider from someone's gigantic insulated dispenser, then talks me through the different stages of the race we're watching and each racer's merits. His energy and enthusiasm, his knowledge of all the cars and their drivers, is contagious, and I'm quickly almost as excited as Colton.

But as we both watch the race, him standing at my feet, me sitting on the truck bed, he leans against the truck, curls his arm around my butt, and places his hand on my thigh, talking all along like he's not submitting me to the most excruciating tease right in front of everyone.

Like we do this all the time and I don't even notice it anymore.

I could never stop noticing Colton's hand on my hip. Not if he did this every day for the next fifty years. Even if he's talking about something not sexy at all, like ice car racing.

He sits close to me, his warmth seeping into my own body. The roar of the cars is muffled by the snow and rings tinny in the cold air. At some point he leaves and brings me a hotdog and a beer.

"You're not having anything?"

"Later," he says, smiling quickly at me, then focusing back on the track. A few minutes pass, then he leans over me and kisses the crown of my head. "Be right back," he whispers. "Stay right here."

"You excited?" a female voice says next to me. She sits up on the truck next to me, her inquisitive glare briefly on me, then fleets back to the frozen lake.

"Yeah," I answer, looking at her pretty profile. She's tall, with jet-black hair that falls in lush waves from her knitted hat onto her shoulders. She doesn't wear makeup—she's beautiful enough not to need any. A tiny stud shines on her upturned nose.

"It's my first time here," I inform her, hoping that'll start some small talk.

She glances at me. "Yeah, I noticed," she says, then directs her attention back on the track. "You'll be fine. He knows what he's doing."

I don't have time to process what she said. My slow understanding is sped up by the announcer calling Colton's name for the fourth race, and my blood freezes as I watch the car we drove in roar onto the icy expanse under the cheering and clapping of the crowd.

The girl next to me stands on the truck bed and shrieks as the cars jolt into a slippery start.

I hold onto the truck, my knees too weak to carry me. I know Colton races. I just didn't... fully understand it. And also, I was unprepared for *this*. For seeing him stuck in a metal box, hurtling across slippery ice and snow. The screeching sounds of fighting cars. The smell of burned plastic and fuel and oil. The animal excitement all around me.

My stomach bottoms as the cars reach the first curb, Colton's seeming to be glued to the rear left of the one in front of him, the two leading the pack. They're coming our way now, and it's hard to tell why Colton isn't passing. It seems he could. I want to scream for him to do it, but no sound comes out of my mouth. Just a tiny little wail.

Three cars behind, someone skids and leaves the track, and the cars behind it avoid it by some miracle. One of them tailends, the others swerving again, narrowly avoiding a collision. By the time they're back in the race, they're way behind Colton and the other car. The announcer calls the final round, and I clap for Colton to get ahead, convincing myself that second isn't too bad either.

It's better than in a pile of soft snow, like the other dude back there looking dejectedly at his car. Better than the rest of the pack fighting mercilessly for third, trying to pass each other.

The girl next to me is yelling at the top of her lungs. "Don't let him! Don't let him!"

I'm vaguely confused and maybe even a little threatened by how involved she seems to be in Colton's victory.

"No! No! No!" she yells, and I instantly tense up as Colton detaches himself from the car in front, seeming to lose a foot in the last stretch before the arrival.

The commentator is going nuts on the loudspeaker, but I can't understand a word he's saying. It only adds to my tension. I'm standing by now, on my tiptoes, so I can see better.

Colton springs ahead of the car in front of him, and I swear I can distinguish the roar of his engine from the other racers. "Go!" I scream, jumping up and down.

He crosses the line in a roar of applause from the group around the truck, the commentator's voice an uninterrupted string of yelling where Colton's name pops in at intervals. As the other cars cross the line, my gaze follows Colton's as it disappears behind a thicket of woods, closely followed by the car that came in second, then both reappear next to us. The girl next to me hops off the truck and saunters in their direction.

I feel off balance for a moment. He said to wait here, right? I don't feel like *waiting*.

And then I see Colton march toward me, totally rocking his black leather jacket, eyes on me, the girl behind him clutching another guy. He joins me at the truck, tucking himself between my legs. "You liked it?" he asks.

Did I like it? My cheeks are hurting from smiling, my heart is swelling from pride. But mostly, I'm so relieved he made it out alive.

I jump off and wrap my legs around his waist. Closing my eyes, I pull his head to me, my mouth finding his. Surprised at first, he lets me kiss him, then takes over when my tongue meets his. Grunting, he places one hand under my butt to pull me closer then takes his tongue on an erotic exploration of my mouth. His tongue is demanding, his lips are claiming, a thirst I didn't know we both shared being exchanged.

He gives our lips some breathing room. "That's not how I saw our first real kiss going," he rumbles against my ear, his stubble grating my skin. He strokes my butt, making me wiggle tighter against him.

"Get a room," the guy next to us jokes.

"You win the race, I'll kiss you that way," his girlfriend with the awesome hair says.

Colton smiles slightly. "That why you're so horny, sweets? Cos I won?" He peppers my neck with a trail of kisses. I'd moan, but we're in public.

Instead, I breathe heavily in his ear. "Cos you're alive, Colt. Just please stay alive for me." I knead his strong shoulders, his warm nape, everything under me vibrating with strength, yet so fragile. "I don't think I could survive if anything happened to you."

Colton's breath catches. Pulling us slightly apart, his gaze bores into my eyes, something indescribable passing between us. He leans over to take my mouth, long and slow and tender this time, his hand that's not under my butt messing with my hair. Then, with me still in his arms, he walks us to his car while the next race fills the air with its roar and fumes.

Once he sets me down, he faces me and says, "What you said up there... you really meant that." Before I can answer, he adds, "Just want you to know, I'd never put myself in harm's way. 'Specially with you watching."

"I know... that's not—"

He cups my jaw in his hand. "How long you been feeling that way about me, sweets?"

Funny how just a few weeks ago, the answer to that question would have been some sarcastic refutation. But with my walls finally down, the answer is simple.

Since you knocked on my car window and didn't call me a bum or a whore. Since I could tell you liked me but didn't try to take advantage. Since you gave me what I needed at the time: trust; a place to stay; work.

And respect. So much respect.

CHAPTER THIRTY-TWO

Colton

The way Kiara is looking at me right now, I don't even need to hear her answer. She's raw and vulnerable—all her defenses down. Her eyes are two large pools in which I want to drown over and over again.

Her mouth moves without making a sound, then finally she says, "An awful long time." She blinks, eyes wet, the mask of the tough girl finally down. There's pain there, and longing, the feeling of time that passed us by and we should have known better.

But we needed this. *I* needed this. I needed to get out of my asshole phase and grow up and deserve her.

I think I do, now. I think she taught me enough that I can give back what she needs from me—from anyone, really. The kind of deep caring, of building each other up that is the only valid foundation of a couple.

I pull her to my chest, the sight of her lost gaze too much to bear, and stroke her hair.

"Yo, Colt," someone from the racetrack calls. "Where you staying tonight?"

I narrow my eyes on him, not understanding.

"You're not driving up to Emerald Creek. They're closing the roads there."

Shit. The few times this happened to me, I slept on his couch. There's got to be a hotel nearby. I just hate this for Kiara. For us.

This was not how I saw our first night together going.

"I have an Airbnb," he says, glancing at Kiara who's still nestled in my arms. "Empty this weekend. Lemme send you the address. I'll have the caretaker turn on the heat." He gives me a wave and leaves without giving me a chance to protest. My phone buzzes, and Kiara reaches into my back pocket to pass it to me.

She looks up at me, her eyes dancing on mine. "How many bedrooms?" she asks as I read the text, then wiggles against my erection.

I look down at her. "That's not gonna matter."

Surprisingly, Kiara is silent as I lead her to the car. I open her door and look down at her in the passenger seat. "Unless you changed your mind."

She blinks. "I did." Then she grabs my hand, brings it to her chest, and says, "I don't want you to…" She hesitates. "I don't want you to *pop my cherry,*" she says under her breath. "I want to be yours," she adds, nearly bringing me to my knees.

But I'm sitting in the car, snow piling up in thick flakes, and I just promised Kiara to be safe. To keep her safe. So I keep everything I want to do and say to her under wraps and take her hand, kiss the inside of her wrist, and drive us to safety.

"Are you kidding me?" Kiara says when we pull up to the Airbnb. It's an A-frame on a knoll, trees all around it. We barely made it up the steep driveway, and snow is still falling. On the way, we crossed an SUV—likely the caretaker. Smoke billows from the chimney and twinkling lights frame the windows.

I grab the bag of groceries we bought on the way and take her hand as we walk up the steps. Stopping us on the doorstep, I turn her to face me. "You and me, it means... everything to me, Kiara. You gotta know that about me. And you gotta know, I'd rather keep you as a friend and nothing more than lose you entirely. Just like you said. So before we go any further, I gotta ask you. Are you sure about this? Because once I make you mine, baby, there's no going back. I'm gonna love the pain out of your life. For real."

She blinks as she looks at me and gets on her toes to drop a kiss on the corner of my mouth, gripping my jacket to pull me to her.

"I'm already yours," she breathes in my neck. "Show me what that means to you."

The blood in my brain rushes down to my groin. I open the door for her and try to hold back. Between the roaring fire in the hearth calling for some civilized downtime, the bag of groceries in my hand needing attention, I should probably—

Kiara turns around, brings her face up to mine, and kisses me again. "I want you now," she whispers. "Please." With her foot, she pushes the front door closed and reaches to engage the deadbolt, the sound like a seal to her decision.

I drop the groceries to the floor and pick her up, amazed at how featherlight she is. She wraps herself around me as I take a few steps and sit her on the bar top.

Her eyes are two gray pools of water, a fucking storm brewing under the surface. She bites her lip and adds, "I-I don't know what to do. I feel so—"

I shut her up with a kiss, feeling her body relax into mine as she meets each of my tongue strokes with a moan. Lowering my mouth to her neck—I love the way she throws her head back as I aim for her tender skin—I say, "All you need to do is be in my arms, sweetness. That's all the work right there. Nothin' more." I'm not just saying that to make her feel better. Having Kiara melting in my arms is all I need to make me feel on top of the world, in charge of the both of us. I'll bring her to where she needs to be. I spread her legs wider to fit myself against her center, then pull off her sweater and let it fall to the floor. She's wearing a zipped-up thermal that hugs her breasts.

"Colt," she moans as I slowly pull on the zipper.

A flash of black lace draws a stark contrast against her porcelain skin, and I stop the unzipping, frustrating my dick. "Last chance to change your mind, sweetness," I growl, looking up to her eyes.

She looks back at me, and fuck if I don't see begging in her gaze. She does the lip licking thing again, totally unaware of what a tell it is and how it drives me so totally wild I could come in my jeans right now.

I drop my gaze to her chest and drag the zipper all the way down. She shakes the thermal off, her nipples pointing through a see-through black top with a lace border and just two thin straps over her delicate shoulders. "Where the fuck d'you get that top, sweets," I growl, zooming in on her wide areolas.

"You-you don't like it?"

A semi-maniacal laugh threatens to take over. "I wanna buy the whole store."

She exhales, bringing my mouth toward her breasts, breathing heavy. "Colt," she whines, squirming on the counter.

"Where'd you get that?" I repeat.

"Ca-Cassandra's. Wh—?"

I kiss her breasts through the thing, then slowly peel it off her skin, suddenly conscious of the roughness of my fingers on her as I trace her shapes with my thumbs. She's thinner than last time I saw her beautiful body. I could tell from her face, but now that I'm seeing it on her body, I'm concerned. She's working too much. Worrying too much. Hurting too much.

I want to wipe all this out for her. Take care of her, even if she's the strongest of us. Kissing my way down to her waistband, I hoist and carry her to the main bedroom, upstairs.

CHAPTER THIRTY-THREE

Kiara

Colton still has his jacket on when he carries me up to the bedroom, and I can't say I mind my nipples rubbing against the soft, strong leather. Being half naked in his arms while he's still in his racing gear might make me want him even more, if such a thing was possible.

"Are you on birth control?" When I nod, he adds, "You want me to wear a condom? I haven't been with anyone in... over a year."

Over a year? "No," I whisper back, suddenly feeling shy.

He hisses and stops on the steps, looking at me. "Never gone skin-to-skin with anyone, Kiara. I need you to know that. You'll be my first. I want that with you."

My belly clenches with desire. The way he talks to me, soft and strong and controlling yet respectful—what was I thinking all this time, telling him no?

The fact he hasn't been with anyone in over a year.

The fact he wants me differently... skin-to-skin.

The way he looks at me—with so much constrained desire, reverence, want, lust—makes me feel eminently more sexy that I am. It gives me the confidence I lack.

Suddenly, I believe everything he says. To my core, I know that he'll always be in my life. Suddenly, all my hold-ups vanish. I can truly be *me* with him.

Because he *likes* me. All of me. My tiny breasts, my poking bones, my awkward hair.

"God you're so beautiful, Kiara," he says, peeling my pants off. "I don't even know where to start." He inhales deeply into my center and groans. "Missed your smell, babe. Missed it so fucking much." He toes his boots off and straddles me, running his hands up and down my body. "This from Cassandra too?" he asks, and before I can answer, he *rips my panties off my hips*, the tearing sound so fucking arousing I buck my hips and dig my fingers in his shoulders.

"Take that thing off," I say, trying to push his leather jacket off him.

"You don't like it?" he teases.

"It's the sexiest thing you own, but I want you naked. Now," I add in a breath. How long have I fantasized over Colton Harper? And without much to go by, I might add. The man always wears jeans and flannels. Lucky in the summer if you get a glimpse of forearms—last time I checked, very corded and nicely veined.

"Sexiest thing I own, huh?" He drops his jacket to the floor and pulls off his sweater and layers in one smooth behind-the-head grab. "Are you saying this whole racing thing turned you on?" His bare torso is heaving as his gaze roams over my naked body. The barely-there drizzle of chest hair, and the wide expanse of muscles give my heart a mini seizure.

I reach for his jeans. "Like you didn't know it would." I wrangle with the belt for a bit. "Though that really wasn't necessary." The zipper is tight, my fingers fumbling against the stubborn metal.

"Babe," he growls, taking over. "Lemme."

I move my hands along his arms, and my mouth goes dry as he frees his cock, then gets rid of the rest of his clothing.

He takes a deep breath. "You keep looking at me like that, I'm gonna come all over you." He caresses my stomach, up to my breast, while my gaze stays glued to the drop pearling on the tip of his bobbing cock.

I just can't not look. I feel my eyes widening. Swallowing hard, I reach for him and stroke him. Another pearl beads, then rolls off, reaching my thumb. My hips roll of their own accord toward him, but... "Colt," I whisper.

"I know, babe." He seems in pain.

Oh shit. What are we going to do? I state the obvious: "It's never gonna fit."

He drops his head to my chest and laughs softly. Then he reaches between my legs and goes straight for my clit. "Fuck you're so wet."

"But, Colt—"

He takes my mouth in his, kisses me while stroking my center, then frees my lips to whisper, "It'll fit."

"But how?"

He chuckles again. "Inch by inch."

"It's not funny," I say, mildly offended, but reassured that his joke didn't in any way affect his erection. Feeling him in my hand, knowing I'm the one doing this to him is... so empowering. I run the pad of my thumb over his wide tip, loving the feel of it.

He hisses. "Kiara..." then lowers his face between my legs, and I have nothing to hold onto except his hair as he...

"Colt!" I cry out as his tongue strokes me right where it's supposed to—no more licking in circles like last time.

He hoists himself back up, kissing my neck.

I could come just by the way Colton kisses my neck.

He adds a stroke of his thumb on my nipple.

I could come from that, too. Totally could. The thumb is just the right amount of rough from working all day. Now he adds a finger and rolls my nipple slightly.

Then he dips his head lower and licks my other nipple.

My hips meet his cock. "I want you," I whisper. "Please."

He places himself at my entrance. "I've wanted this for so long, Kiara," he says as his cock strokes my clit. "You have no idea."

I wrap one leg around his waist. "Babe," I whine, the want between my legs unbearable, "oh please." I feel the orgasm building inside me, ready to roll out. Colton's scent envelops me, his arms encapsulate me, and this, this is what I want right now: to lose myself inside this man.

I dig my nails in his butt, drawing him closer. With a grunt, he enters me slowly, a sharp pain tearing me deliciously as he slides two fingers between our joined bodies to stroke my clit. He pulses inside me, then stops breathing. "You okay?" he asks me.

I nod and pull him deeper inside me with my heel. "You?"

"Fuck, sweets, you have no idea how good you feel." His dick twitches inside me again, making me moan. The pain is still there, sharp.

But so is the pleasure. Deep.

And my desire of him. Deeper still.

And seeing his hooded eyelids, the way he wants me, the pleasure he's having simply with the two of us almost still, sends me overboard. I orgasm on Colton's desire, and as my hips buck and pull him deeper inside me, the pain deepening then subsiding, the pleasure taking over, and more importantly, seeing, feeling, how much I mean to Colton, how nothing is fake or temporary, how we're connected in our bodies and down to our souls, I let myself go, almost sobbing in relief.

How could I ever imagine doing this with anyone else than Colton? My best friend, my rock, the man who pulled me out of the abyss I thought was a refuge. I stroke his back, wanting him to stay here forever.

"You okay?" he asks.

I blink my eyes open. "You're still hard."

He pulsates inside me and takes a slow breath. "Didn't want to hurt you more."

"I need you to come inside me," I say, almost begging.

Another pulse inside me, and he groans. Then he dips his face to my neck and suckles on the tender skin, making me arch my back. "Mmm," I moan.

He kneads my nipple between two fingers and trails kisses up to my ear. My hips start rocking on their own, and Colton begins to move inside me. "Tell me how this feels," he says.

"It feels awesome," I whisper.

"Any pain?"

"No," I lie.

He stops moving. "Kiara."

"M-hm?"

"I don't want you to ever fake an orgasm."

"I didn't fake—"

"I also don't want you to ever tell me you're okay when you're not."

"I'm okay," I say, and do the heel-in-his-butt thing to get him back on track.

He starts moving again. *Thank god.* "You said you didn't have pain and that's not just not true." I'm about to say *How can you tell?* when he adds, "Your pain line right there is showing," he says, tracing some place between my eyebrows.

"I didn't fake the orgasm," I say, changing the topic.

"Oh, I know." He starts moving inside me in a way that's absolutely glorious. Deep, slow strokes. The pain is now a pinching, pleasure taking over. He looks down at our joined sexes, then groans and cups my whole body in his arms, bringing us closer still, burrowing his face in my neck.

His body vibrates with constrained energy, then he lifts his head off me to look me in the eye while his warmth fills me. Whispering my name, he cups my face. "Are you alright?" he asks, like he's worried about something.

"Colt, I'm not gonna break," I tell him. I might, but the feeling of inadequacy is seeping back inside. He hasn't been with anyone in a year, and now he needs to be careful because I'm—was—a virgin. I might lack experience, but I'm well read. I know how these things are supposed to go, the first time. A man like Colt, he would probably have—

"Get out of your head, sweetness. Swear to god, best sex ever."

I huff. "I didn't do anything, and you're afraid you'll hurt me."

He pushes himself up on his forearms, his body hovering over mine, his cock slowly sliding out. His gaze roams my face. "I got to taste your entire body for the first time, feel you shake under me for the first time, lick your neck for the first time, hear you say my name in a tone I've never heard before, feel your nails dig into my shoulders for the first time, find out there's a good chance that for the rest of our lives you're gonna be using your heels to bring me into you. So yeah, best fucking sex ever, sweetness." He leans over, kissing me softly while I fight the tears of happiness that threaten to spill over.

These are the sweetest, deepest words he could tell me right now, but it isn't going to do. "Colt?"

His lazy gaze roams my face, two fingers pushing my hair off my forehead. "Yeah?"

I narrow my eyes on him. "I'm still a virgin."

Confusion spreads on his face. He frowns, and smirks, waiting for more.

I run my nails on his shoulders. "I'm a virgin until you come inside me and that's it." Locking my heels on his butt (I've been paying attention to what he said), I yank him in. "No discussion," I whisper.

He groans and bucks his hips slightly. "Fuck but I love your bossiness, sweets." He enters me in one stroke, making me flinch, pleasure and soreness deliciously mixed.

"You asked for it," he grunts as he picks up the pace only slightly.

"That's all you got?" I tease him, tugging him deeper inside me. He was right. He *does* fit. And being full with his heavy length is the best feeling ever.

"Saving you for later," he whispers with hooded eyelids.

I slide my nails down his back, to his ass, and back up.

"Fuck it, babe, you feel so good," he says as his back bucks under my hands.

My breathing hitches. "Ohmygod, Colt. Yes. Just let go with me. Please."

With a groan he lifts himself slightly off me and makes eye contact, his gaze never leaving mine as his strokes become more and more powerful. He stills and throws his head back with a groan as heat fills me and I buckle under my own orgasm, gripping his shoulders.

Tremors seize his body, his forearms holding him right above me. "You okay?" he whispers.

I clutch his nape to bring him down on me. "Never been better," I whisper back.

His heartbeat resonates through my whole body while he gently strokes my hair. He drops a kiss on my temple. "Don't move," he says, pushing himself off me. He disappears into the bathroom, the water runs for half a minute, then he comes back with a warm washcloth and runs it inside my thighs. "Does it still hurt?" he asks as he gently runs the soft side of the cloth over my folds.

I smile so big my cheeks hurt. "No," I whisper, drawing him closer.

He drops the cloth on the floor and pulls me against his chest. "You know what I love the most about you?" he asks, his voice a low rumble.

"Mm?" I ask back, stroking his hair.

He cups my hip with one hand. "You're such a bad liar."

I chuckle softly against him. I've got nothing to say to that.

We stay quiet for a while, until he breaks the soft silence. "Can I ask you a question?" he says, stroking my hair.

I brace myself. "M-hm?"

"Why did you bake me cupcakes for my dates?"

I lift my shoulder and continue to trail his chest hair with my finger. "To be nice."

His face tilts down toward me. "You wanted to be nice to my dates?"

"I wanted to show them that..." The vision of Colton showing up at a date with a box of cupcakes pops into my brain and I chuckle. "What would they say?"

"You did it on purpose, didn't you? To scare them off?"

I swat his chest. "No!" *Maybe, to be honest. But not in a conscious way.*

"What would they say?" I repeat, now curious as hell.

"Babe, I didn't bring them your cupcakes."

"No?!" I push myself up, pretending to be offended.

He brings me back against him with one effortless contraction of his bicep. "Not gonna waste pure perfection on some random chick I'll never see again," he mutters.

What?! My mouth stretches in a smile despite myself, and my center warms at the confirmation that none of these dates meant anything to him. "Colton Harper, did you eat them all by yourself?"

He tilts his head down at me. "Sure did. Each one of your cupcakes. Thinking about you first thing in the morning isn't all that bad, let me tell you. Last thing at night, either."

Is he saying he thought about me after his dates? My mouth dries up, and so does my brain. I have no follow-up question to this, not even something to confirm whether I heard him right or just made something up.

He groans, shifts to the side, and runs his calloused hand alongside my torso, the pad of his thumb barely grazing the curve of my breast. When he reaches my waist, he dips down to cup my hipbone and gives it a squeeze. "But the best goddamn cupcake is right here between your legs," he mutters, moving down the length of the bed to place his mouth at my entrance.

"You did not!" I half giggle, half moan as he nuzzles my labia.

"Did not what?" The vibration of his voice against my intimate parts is almost untenable.

"Compare my vajayjay to a cupcake."

He lifts his head, looking at me with amusement. "Vajayjay?" he repeats mockingly. Lowering his gaze, he adds, "*This* is the ultimate cupcake. Don't care what silly name you want to call it. This here is my cupcake."

His lazy tongue strokes kindle my arousal, but then he seems to have a different idea and licks his way up to my neck, then cups my whole body in one arm and pulls my back against his front. "You okay being the little spoon?" he asks as he wraps a leg over my hips and strokes my arm.

What is he talking about? "The what?"

His stroking halts a beat before resuming, but he doesn't answer my question. "I'm not too heavy, am I?" he asks instead.

"No, I'm good," I answer, wiggling my ass to be deeper inside his hold.

"God you feel so good," he says, propping his head on one hand, the other caressing my shoulder, my breasts, my hip, then back up all the way to my head. I feel him harden a little against me, and it makes me want him again.

But without transition, he says, "Dude has a nice place here."

We're both looking in the same direction. The bedroom area on the mezzanine opens on the vast living area below, all natural wood and exposed beams. A comfortable sectional is an invitation to cuddle and read all day near the wood-burning fireplace, looking outside to the evergreens heavy with fresh snow. I'm just now noticing the bedroom—deep white duvet, fluffy white faux fur area rugs on blond hardwood floors, soft pastels of deer, wolves, and bears on the walls. "The best."

He drops a kiss on the edge of my ear. "You like?"

"Love it. Don't you?" I ask, twisting my neck to look at him.

He has a dreamy smile on his face. "Yeah."

"I don't ever want to leave," I whisper.

He cups my hip. It seems to be his favorite place to rest his hand. "Pretty sure we can stay as long as we need to."

"It's not like we can go anywhere," I add. The race car is barely visible under the snow now, and you can't tell the access road from the rest of the forest floor.

"What kind of birth control are you on?" he asks out of the blue.

I flop on my back to look at him "The Pill. Why?"

His gaze roams my face. "Bad periods?" he asks.

It's just like Colton to know about these things. "The worst."

He pushes a lock of hair behind my ear. "Does the Pill help?"

I shrug. "Kinda."

He stays silent for a little bit, caressing my belly. "You hungry?" he asks.

"Starving."

Chapter Thirty-Four

Colton

While Kiara takes a quick shower, I open a can of soup and heat it on the stovetop, setting crackers and cheese on a plate. We also have sliced roast beef and a chicken jambalaya the woman at the deli insisted we try, but I'll let Kiara decide if and when she wants that.

I'm not real hungry right now, especially not when I see her come out of the bathroom wrapped in a plush white robe that's big enough to cover her feet, the sleeves rolled so much they look like floaters. "It's all yours," she says.

I kiss her lips, wanting her again. I was dying to shower with her, but I know better than to ask for too much, too soon. Kiara's virginity is—was—not so much about anatomy as it is about trust. She knew where all her relevant parts were. She knew what to expect when I made love to her.

But she's still a virgin when it comes to intimacy.

My body hums at the thought of everything I want to do to her, with her—that I will do. Starting with taking a bath together. And showering together.

This place has a Jacuzzi bath, and I'm not letting it go to waste.

I quickly towel off, wear the other robe, and join Kiara downstairs.

She turns her back to the window to look at me. "You look like a boxer," she says, smiling at the way the robe barely covers my knees and constricts my shoulders. She blows on a cup of tea. "I made a whole pot. Want some? It's really good. Dude has good taste."

I wrap my arms around her as she turns around to resume her observation of the outdoors. "What were you looking at?" I set my chin on the top of her head. "Is that what I think it is?" I say, eyeing a square-like shape under a pile of snow.

"Hot tub, yeah. There's instructions over there. Too bad it's under three feet of snow and we don't have swimsuits."

I kiss the top of her head. "Swimsuits?" Damn if I'm wearing anything when I'm alone with Kiara near a hot tub. "Lemme find a shovel."

She looks at me with a glint in her eye. "I guess the soup can wait. I'll grab a couple of towels."

By the time we're in the water, it's totally night. We turned all the lights off in the A-frame. The snow stopped falling, the sky cleared up, and despite a bright moon we have a spectacular view of the stars. Kiara drops her head back to look up.

"Colt, look!" she says, glancing at me.

"Your neck is a way better view than the stars to me."

She straightens her head. "Awww," she says, her foot reaching mine to give me a stroke. Her smile is soft. I've never seen Kiara soft or heard her say "*awww*." It's new to me. I knew she'd be soft inside. I didn't know how good it would make me feel when I finally found out.

"Why are you so far away?" I clutch her thighs between my feet and draw her to me.

She slides off the seat and dips under water for a beat, reappearing with a squeal. Instead of sitting next to me, she straddles me and looks me in the eye. Her nipples are right at the surface of the bubbling water, her naked shoulders glistening. She slides her arms around my neck and dips her face down to kiss me. "D'you think it'd be okay to have sex in here?"

Sweet Kiara. My dick was already paying attention. He answers for me. "I think it's required."

She laughs softly. "I didn't see that in the Airbnb rule book."

"It's an unwritten rule, Kiara. I find myself naked with you, anywhere, I have to take you. That's rule number one. Rule number two, I find myself in a hot tub with you, I have to take you."

"Isn't that the same thing?" she asks, lifting herself on her knees so she can place her entrance right where it needs to be.

"There's a distinct—aaaah, fuck."

She throws her head back and takes a deep breath. "I'm never forgetting this moment. You inside me and the stars above us." She moves slowly up and down my shaft.

"You okay?" I ask. It's been only what—two hours? She has to still be sore.

She moans softly as she lifts herself up, then comes down, setting her own rhythm. I hold onto her waist, feeling the hum build inside her, licking her perky nipples as they inch closer to my mouth, making my way up to her delicate neck. "Can I tell you something?" she whispers, leaning against my ear so I can hear her over the sound of the bubbles. "You're better than in my fantasies. Like, *way* better." Then she licks the side of my ear and moans so close to me I almost lose it.

"Fantasies?" I croak, nudging her face so I can look at her. Reaching to the side, I turn the hot tub controls off so I can hear her better—and see us in the water.

"Yeah, fantasies," she repeats as she settles on me, my dick inside her to the hilt, and sways her hips.

Kiara. Kiara had fantasies. About me. I throw my head back and hiss.

"You like that?" she asks, increasing her movement.

"Cupcake, I like everything you do," I answer. "Now, about those fantasies..." I cup her hips with my hands, my thumbs in the crease of her thighs, my fingers splayed on her tight butt.

She clenches around me. "Yeah?"

"Wanna tell me what they were?"

She bites her bottom lip, then chuckles. "Um... no."

She's killing me. "Come on! Please?" What could she possibly be fantasizing about, that she won't repeat to me?

She stays silent, and I can tell she's focusing on our joined sexes, and the feeling between her legs and inside her. Her bottom tenses a bit and she grips my shoulders in a more mechanical way.

It's time to take her out of her head. "Was it that dirty? I can handle dirty, you know." I caress her back, then lean over for a quick suckle on her offered tit.

She snaps out of her mind. "It was nothing dirty... it was nothing that you would do. I was just trying to imagine how you looked and how... how..." Her insides clench around me.

"How it would feel if I licked your body inch by inch? Rubbed your feet after a long day of work? Got into a bubble bath with you and gave you a scalp massage?"

She gives me a shy grin that morphs into full-on smile. "I was really wondering how you looked naked. I'd remember the little I saw and made up the missing parts."

"And?"

She pretends she doesn't understand my question. "And what?" she asks, lifting herself almost off my dick and lowering herself back down, doing her ass wiggle at the end. The now still water splashes softly around us, filling the silent night.

"And you did what with that?"

She swallows. "I made myself come." She goes up and down again, her breasts sloshing in and out of the water.

"Sweets."

"Yeah?" she whispers.

"*I* made you come. The thought of me. And guess what?"

"What?"

"There's a good chance I was doing the same, one floor up, thinkin' 'bout you." I want to plow into her right now, but I let her keep the lead.

Reading my thoughts, she says, "You okay?"

I have to chuckle at that. "Whadda ya mean? I'm in heaven."

"Can I go faster?"

"Babe, I don't know what those books you read taught you about sex, but yes, fuck yes, you can go faster and harder. Just let go, sweets, and have your way with me."

Her eyes turn as dark as ink as her gaze goes from my eyes to my lips to my torso to our midsection. "Colt..." Whatever she was going to say morphs into a full-on moan. The way her eyebrows narrow and her moan pitches when my cock hits her deepest spot is such a turn-on, I have to focus to keep it together.

"Fuck you're hot, Kiara. Always thought you were hot, but this... this..." My gaze zooms back down to her breasts bouncing in front of me.

"Suck on me," she says, leaning against my face. An owl toots, and then it's only the water sloshing around us, faster and faster as she increases her speed, and her little cries of pleasure.

"Colt..." she moans as I feel her clench around me. I let go of her breast to cup her back and bring her to me as she comes undone, the long tremor of her orgasm filling me with something like pride.

Then she folds down onto my chest, aftershocks rocking her and teasing my dick in an unbearable manner.

"How 'bout you?" she asks in a small voice, moving her hips around my enraged cock.

"Not gonna come in here and then hafta ask my buddy how and why I should drain the damn thing."

She chuckles, the movement another torture to my dick. "Good thinking," she murmurs. "Let's go inside. I wanna finish you off with my mouth."

Holy mother. I hoist us off the tub, wrap us in the towels, and get us inside, in front of the roaring fireplace. I'll take care of the trail of water later. "Don't you ever tell me that the books you read at Millie's are sweet little romances. No virgin talks dirty like that. Holy shit, sweets."

"You don't like it?"

"I fucking love it. Tell me again what you're gonna do with your mouth?" I say as she sets herself on her knees in front of the fireplace.

She licks the tip of my cock and locks eyes with me. "I can't talk with my mouth full, Colt. So what will it be? Dirty talk or..." She runs her hands up the back of my thighs and cups my ass.

The only answer I can manage is a hiss.

She takes the tip into her mouth and swirls her tongue around it, then takes my cock deeper in her mouth, giving it a few sucks with barely there teeth, then lets go and looks up at me, holding my cock. "It tastes good," she says in a raw voice, her gaze back on my cock. She runs her thumb on the tip, smearing a pearl of cum. A string stays attached to her thumb as she brings it to her carmine lips to lick it dry. "And it's just so soft, I could suck on it all day."

I groan. God, she's so fucking perfect. And she was there all along. *My friend.*

With a deep, contented breath, she brings her mouth back to my purple cock and sucks me dry. She doesn't let me pull her off when I warn her I can't hold it anymore, and I come in long spurts, the orgasm she gives me so powerful that my knees buckle.

I collapse to the floor with her in a tangle of limbs and cover us with the thick towel as we catch our breaths. She arranges herself so her back is to my front and we both watch the dancing flames. "Sweets?"

"Yeah?"

"Can I just say, I love a lot of things about you. And fucking you is way up there." My dick twitches and she wiggles her ass against me.

"You're making me horny again," she says.

I drop a kiss in the curve on her neck. "For real?"

"Yup. Let's keep it for later," she says, right as my hand falls on her breast, the nipple hardening.

"Or I could just take care of it."

I feel her smile under my lips. "Or you could just take care of it."

CHAPTER THIRTY-FIVE

Kiara

An hour later the hot tub has been covered, the floor swept, and we're back in our robes, having a dinner of canned soup, crackers, and cheese on the couch in front of the fire. I ask Colton a question about the race, and let his voice simply turn me on.

If I'd known sex was so great, I'd have had it sooner.

But something's telling me sex was great because it was with Colton. He was only giving, not trying to get anything from me. His generosity with me almost brought tears to my eyes.

And the way I had to beg him to let me take care of him? Looking at the fire, I'm brought back to me on my knees, taking him in my mouth, and how until then I'd thought it must be weird at best, but it wasn't.

It was phenomenal.

He was reluctant at first, because he wanted everything to be about me today. I know that's why. But pleasuring him might be way up there on my list of favorite things to do. There's something about the way he fell apart for me that was...

He reaches his hand up my back and into my hair. "Where'd your mind go, sweets?" he says when I don't chime into whatever he's saying.

"Just wondering how you got into racing," I say. It is, partially, the truth. I've been meaning to ask him—but not right now

"That's not where your mind was," he says, tugging at my hair.

Busted. "Just thinking how I can totally relate to the sex slave thing now." I slurp my soup, waiting for his reaction. I'm half hoping he'll throw me on the floor and have his way, but my vajayjay reminds me we should take a break.

His hand leaves my hair but his mouth twitches at my words. "I got into racing like others get into drugs or petty theft. For the thrill. Basically, because of stuff going on at home at the time."

I almost challenge him on avoiding the sex slave discussion, but my throat tightens. I set my bowl on the floor and sit cross-legged, facing him.

"Your dad?"

He nods. "I wasn't too good at handling... whatever was wrong with him. I had so much anger. I needed the escape. And a community where there was little crossover with Emerald Creek."

"Hard to believe no one in Emerald Creek went to those races."

He plays with a strand of my hair that keeps falling in my eyes. Funny how I don't even care how I look right now. "Those who did... just kept it to themselves. It never got to my dad's ears."

I frown, wondering how that's even possible. "How old were you when you started?"

His eyes dance. "Sixteen."

"Wow. Was that even legal to do that without your parents' authorization?"

A log rolls in the hearth, prompting Colton to jump off the couch and rearrange the fire. "Course not," he says as he adds a fresh log to the stack. "The race itself wasn't legal at the time."

The couch dips as he sits back, and we both turn our gaze to the crackling fire. "Who got you into it?"

He drags my legs onto his lap and strokes my knees. "You should have been a detective."

"You didn't answer the question."

"You could *still* be a detective. You'd get benefits."

I'll let this go. It doesn't matter now, does it? "What made your dad go sober?" I ask instead. That's a more important side of Colton's story.

He takes a deep breath. "I think it was when Grace left for Texas. We were worried about her for a while, and when she came back, I think that's when it hit him. That alcohol was keeping him away from the family. That he could still turn things around. Nothing lasts forever. Not even when you mess up. You can still pick yourself up and make things right."

The Dennis I know is a good guy—I think. But what do we know of what goes on behind closed doors? "At the end of the day, he was a good person," I offer, taking his hand between mine. I want to tell him he was luckier than me as far as parents go, but this isn't a contest.

Colton gives my bare legs a soft squeeze. "Every person makes their own decisions in life. It's nothing someone else says or does. What your dad did... It was never about you, Kiara. It was about him all along."

"I know."

"He didn't need to shut you off. He could have faced the music and still have his daughters in his life."

My heart clenches. This is not the discussion I wanted to have. I wanted to talk about Colton, get to know him better. But that's who he is. He thinks about others before himself. Particularly, it seems, when it comes to me. It's his love language to try and fix things. In cars as in people. "That's the thing, though. *She* told me it was my fault. For a seventeen-year-old, it's near impossible to not believe it."

He gives my thighs a squeeze. "It's totally impossible. You know that, right?"

I nod. I don't answer that the hardest part for me was losing my twin that day. What she did with David would have been hard to come back from, but to top it off she turned against me after what Dad did to us, and I didn't get it. There was a theme there—I just didn't want to see it. But I don't want to talk about this right now. Right now is for happiness.

For the night and day that we stay stuck here, I focus on our own little bubble. There's so much to discover. Eating berries out of each other's lips. Showering together. Staying tangled all night and waking to a steamy cup of coffee brought by a totally naked Colton.

We sip it looking out the cathedral window of the A-frame. Then we put the robes on and take a second cup snuggled on the sectional. The storm is over, and the snow glistens as if millions of diamonds were spread on it.

Colton pulls me against him. "Seems like we don't have a reason to stay here anymore." His hand moves up and down my arm and we stay like that for a moment, taking in the peace, until he stretches out and stands. "I'm gonna go clear the car."

"I'll help."

He takes our cups to the kitchen. "I only saw one shovel."

I follow him. "I'm sure there's another."

"Sweets." He swivels and grabs my shoulders. "I know you're a strong, independent woman. I'm not gonna question that."

I raise my eyebrows.

"Okay," he concedes. "Lemme get the bulk of it out, and you can help with scraping the windows and shit."

I get on my toes and kiss the tip of his nose. "Much better. Meanwhile I'll sit here and watch you flex your muscles while I do my nails."

He chuckles. "You do that."

Once he's outside, I rummage through the cupboards and the stuff we bought at the deli and get started on an apple pie. While it's in the oven, I join Colton and help him finish clearing the car of snow.

Glancing up at the A-frame with its fairy lights twinkling against the backdrop of snow and evergreens, my thoughts drift to the barn I visited, and my conversation with Emma. Baking the pie earlier, I was thinking how cool it would be to work each day in that type of environment—something between a home and a shop. A place where everyone would want to stop by to pick up dessert or order a birthday cake with pop-up clowns. With the setup the way it is, I'd have ample space to continue making pastries for Chris and Chloe—and even Millie. It would be perfect.

"Where's your mind at, sweets?" Colton says, bringing me against him with one arm as we walk back to the house.

I clear my throat. "Well, I could use some advice on something."

"Yeah?" We ditch our shoes and coats as we enter the house. "Damn it smells good in here."

"It's for your friend, or the housekeeper." I'm trying to find the right words to ask him my question.

He grunts.

"I only had enough apples for one pie."

He chuckles. "What's the advice you need?" He moves to the living room area to straighten the throw pillows, then moves to the chimney and starts sweeping the ashes.

I set my hands flat on the kitchen counter. "So... I've been looking for a place for my business?"

He glances at me. "Uh-huh."

"And I saw the cutest place. Perfection."

He straightens, his attention all on me, excitement showing on his features as I describe the Dewey's barn to him.

"The only problem," I say once he's sitting on a barstool right next to me, "is that it needs a..."—what's the name again?—"a variance."

He grunts and makes a face.

"I'm not asking you to pull any strings or anything, I'm just asking if you think it's doable. Like, what are my chances? How hard is it to get a variance? Anything I should be aware of?"

He rubs his face. "Didn't it use to be a farm stand?"

Yes! Yes it did. Emma was right. Colton is exactly the person to talk to. He knows about these things. "Maddie—that's the realtor—said something about using the owner's Agricultural... Use?" I'm not sure about the verbiage anymore.

"Yeah, you're not a farmer. That won't stand. You said Maddie, right?"

I nod. "Maddie Parker."

Something passes on his face. "Uh-huh. And the place is cute inside?" He draws me between his legs, his hands resting on my hips.

"Adorable."

He brushes a strand of hair off my forehead. "Fit for a pastry shop?"

"More than enough."

"Price is right?" The rough pad of his thumb grazes my earlobe.

"Price is too good to be true. That's why I wonder about the whole permitting thing."

He frowns. "You're right. Let me look into it."

The finality in his tone worries me a bit. "Colt, I'm not asking you to do anything about it, right? Just asking for advice. Your *opinion*."

His gaze lights up, joy dancing in his eyes. "Sure."

"I heard Justin loud and clear when you were appointed. No favors, okay?"

His eyebrows shoot up, mock disbelief painted on his face. "You heard that? Seemed to me you were very preoccupied with your dating app that day."

Busted. "Yes I was. There was someone whose profile was... calling to me. Are you saying I shouldn't have hearted on *Nigel*?"

He boops my nose. "You're cute, you know that?"

I give his biceps a squeeze. "I'm serious. Don't make me regret asking you for advice."

His features turn serious. "Sweets, it's a board of five people. Our meetings and votes are public. No one is doing anyone a favor. You asked me for advice. I just need to look into it to give you the best possible *advice*." He cups my face in his big hand. "Nothin' more than looking into it."

Our lips touch lightly. "Okay," I whisper against his mouth.

The scent of caramel and apples calls me back to reality. "I think the pie is ready. We should get ready to go."

We clean the place up together, and it feels good and even fun wiping the shower and sink while the sheets and towels are in the wash, giving the place a quick vacuum, bringing fresh logs inside.

Making the bed together.

My heart does pinch a bit there, I have to admit. After I fluff the last pillow against the headboard, Colton wraps his arms around me and holds me tight, rocking me to the sound of his heartbeat. "This is where we begin, Kiara. I don't want you to be sad about that."

I lift my eyes to him. "I'm not sad. I'm... emotional."

His head jerks back imperceptibly. "Emotional's good," he declares before taking my mouth with his. After he pulls away, he says, "Let's go home now," and holds my hand as we leave the bedroom.

CHAPTER THIRTY-SIX

Colton

I tear myself from the smell of the A-frame, leaving the apple pie behind. Kiara wrapped it in beeswax paper, left a thank-you note, and made sure I texted my friend so that either he or the housekeeper got the pie.

"You're gonna have a lifetime of pies, and cupcakes, and napoleons. I'm gonna make you grow a belly." She snorts in the most adorable way as we triple-check that we left everything in shipshape.

I swat her ass and look at her in the A-frame. I want to give her something like that, someday. A house we'd call our own.

But this isn't for now, and as I hit I-91, the stuff I got waiting for me in Emerald Creek starts creeping back into my consciousness, quickly chased by what Kiara asked me concerning the variance application.

I'll have to look at previous applications and their outcomes and also make sure Kiara's application has all its i's dotted and t's crossed. "You should probably apply for your variance sooner than later," I say while we're coasting north. Kiara is quiet, and I'll bet her thoughts are on work as well. "There's a whole process of notifying neighbors and a wait period, as well as putting it on the agenda ahead of time." That much I remember from all the legal material Ms. Angela gave me. "But I'll look into it tonight."

"Thank you," she says softly. "I don't want special treatment, right? Just advice."

I grunt. I'll give her advice, and if there's something I can do to help, I'll do it. Damn right I will.

"How do you like being on the board so far?"

I shrug. "It's alright. Someone's gotta do it. I like seeing people come in and discussing our problems." I smirk and add, "But the cakes are the best part." A lot of people bring food to share at the meetings, setting it in the back of the room. Kiara never fails to bring a cake or two.

"I draw the line at Louise bitching about Shy Rabit or asking that the noise ordinance be amended to start at eight p.m. The minute she goes to the mic, I'm outta there," Kiara says.

"She should be on a temporary ban," I joke.

She laughs at my suggestion. "See? No one ever thought of that. You're adding value already."

"What's your favorite part of the meetings?" If she's going to be in the audience, I'll want to know what makes her tick, what annoys her. Not that I'm treating it like a performance, but I'm realizing we won't be sitting next to each other, commenting on what's going on. That's the fun part of these meetings.

"Ah... where do I start? Declan's reports on—"

Oh those. Priceless. I finish her sentence "Daisy's whereabouts and another 911 call about the food at the Silver House."

"Now what's up with that place? I read about that on Echoes last summer but, honest to god, there was so much going on at the time I never thought to ask."

I keep forgetting that Kiara didn't grow up with all of Emerald Creek's history. "The retirement house is funded by a trust left by some wealthy recluse, decades ago."

"Wealthy recluse seems to be a theme here," she says, referring to Louise, who funds the library and is on a personal crusade against romance books as well as anything remotely fun.

"Yeah well, this one's hobby was old people, not books. She left a building to the town and an endowment for them to run it as a retirement home. The town has an oversight on how things are run there, so obviously when the potatoes aren't cooked right, we hear all about it."

"On the other hand, they don't have much to think about, over there."

She's wrong about that. "They got plenty to keep'em busy other'n potatoes. They got yoga and music and tarot and petting zoo and knitting and crocheting (there's a difference), and carriage rides and shows—we take 'em to shows!"

"How d'you know all that?"

"Mom's on the board. She keeps us updated every Sunday. And she and Lynn hold a mini council about the Silver House on the Sundays that we go to the farm for dinner."

"That's sweet," she whispers, her fingers trailing up my wrist.

"Yeah well—how well we treat our old folk is a matter of pride here. And those in need."

"That too," she murmurs almost too low for me to hear. Louder, she adds, "I can talk to Shannon and Lynn about doing some consulting for the Silver House. I'll ask Chloe to send her chef. I remember her mentioning something about that last summer."

What is she talking about? "Consulting?"

"Yeah, pretty much, you go into a restaurant, look at their menus, the way they prepare the food, and you propose changes. It's fun." She lets go of my hand and starts making motions in the air. "Depending on what the objective is, the proposal is going to wildly vary. Let's say you want to cut costs, you look at both what's on the menu and where it's sourced. Next, you observe the kitchen to see if you can reorganize the work to have less payroll—"

I look at her sideways. Who is this cutthroat person and what did she do with Kiara? "You *fire* people?"

She shrugs. "If your business is losing money, and the choice is between losing one or two employees or folding three months from now... Then yes, you *downsize*."

I suppose if anyone is able to make decisions based on reason and not emotion, it'd be Kiara. And I'm not saying this is a bad thing. She's had to fight for her survival and cut people out of her life who should have been supporting her and were just dragging her down.

"There's other ways to save money without losing workforce," she continues, "like extending your open hours and offering light fare before and after regular service. Again, those costs need to be calculated against the sales you can project."

With the way her brain is wired, I'm glad she's finally taking the steps to own her business. She'll be crazy successful, and I'll do everything in my power to make it happen.

"Anyway, back to the Silver House," she's saying, "that'd be easy peasy. Just fix up the recipes. Could be a good project for the apprentices around town. Talk to your mom about it."

Her energy and rationale make me so goddamn proud of her. I can't believe I get to call this woman my own. "I will," I answer, my voice catching. I clear my throat.

"What?"

Emotion overcomes me as I brace to ask the simplest question. "Would you-would you want to come?" I feel myself blushing like a fucking teenager. "To Mom and Dad's. With me, I mean. I-I know you go there often and obviously you're one of their favorite people and you don't need an invitation from me to come, but I meant as my... as my... as my... I mean I'll tell Mom and Dad we're together. Obviously. That's what I meant." I clear my throat again, squinting and focusing back on the road.

She stares at me, barely containing her laughter at the way I'm fumbling my words. She doesn't need an invitation from me to eat at Mom and Dad's. She's had dinner there often, spur of the moment things when she was bringing a cake for one of Mom's groups and ended up staying for dinner, or more planned-out evenings with Chris, Skye, Grace, and me. From the beginning, Mom has brought her into the fold of our family.

It's going to be interesting to see their reaction at the fact that we're *together*.

"As your what?" she teases me.

"Hm?"

"You asked if I wanted to come as your...?"

My mouth twitches. Kiara wants to hear me call her my girl-friend. That's cute and shit, but I don't really care about that stage, since my goal is to call her my wife. But I feel like having a little fun with everyone. "I got an idea."

"Yeah?"

"Next Saturday, I'm gonna call Mom and tell her I'm bringing my girlfriend." She squeezes my hand. Who knew it would take so little to make her happy? I shouldn't have discarded that so quickly. Then I lay out my plan. "Mom's gonna be pissed. It's gonna be epic."

She pulls her hand away. "What's so funny about that?"

"I'll let her stew a little, make her believe it's someone she doesn't know."

Kiara snorts and twines our hands back together. "Yeah, like she's gonna buy that. Did you forget where we live?"

I bring her knuckles to my lips, a smile pulling my cheeks to the point where they start to hurt. "Shit, you're right." There's a good chance everyone in Emerald Creek already knows we've disappeared together for twenty-four hours. One more week and the whole town will ask when we're tying the knot.

CHAPTER THIRTY-SEVEN

Kiara

We've reached the fork to Emerald Creek, where the only place the road can now take us is back home. In any journey, this is the point where I feel a sense of peace. Today, that feeling is tinged with a little bitterness: we're each going back to our own apartment. The party's over.

It would have meant the beginning of the end, however slowly it may come, if Colton's words at the A-frame weren't still ringing in my ears: "*This is where we begin*." And somehow, I believe him.

Giving myself entirely to Colton unlocked something inside me. I feel loved. Supported. Invincible.

"You ever talk to Alex about your business?" Colton asks me, taking me out of my thoughts.

Alex inherited a fortune from her grandmother—in the baking business, no less. She's transforming the company to help independent bakeries get started. She could solve my problems with one stroke of a pen on a checkbook, and it would make no difference to her life.

Colton shakes his head. "You're too proud."

"I didn't say anything!"

"I can hear you thinking, sweets. Can't say I don't understand where you're coming from, though. But if she's the solution to your problems, what are you waiting for? She's helping people she doesn't even know. Why not you?"

Because I want to prove myself, and I don't think I've done that yet. I don't think I've given it my all, tried everything I could to make it on my own. There are still things I should be doing. Like training in Paris, or taking a chance on my own shop.

He pushes. "D'you hear what Annabel said?"

I shuffle in my seat. "She went through all the normal channels. The schools, the internships, the right jobs at the right places. It's easy for her to say it was all useless. No offense, but I'm not sure it's true."

He grunts. "I didn't look at it that way."

He's right, though. "I'm talking with Emma about setting up my business at the barn, see if the numbers work out."

He smiles wide but doesn't say anything.

We've arrived at Sunrise Farms, and he pulls up to the front door. "Dropping you off, then I'm going straight to the garage. I'll see you at Lazy's?" he says as he leans over to kiss me.

Lazy's goes without saying. It's a given when you've spent any time outside of Emerald Creek that you'll go there for a beer. It's the part after Lazy's I want to figure out. *I don't want to sleep alone tonight.* It feels too brutal. How do I bring it up? "I wish we could have stayed another night," I whisper against his mouth.

He puts a little space between us, and I dip my gaze to his leather jacket. "Yeah... about that..." He tugs me back against him, his jaw caressing the crown of my head. "Not sleeping without you if I can help it. Wanna wake up with you tomorrow. You choose the place. Yeah?"

And just like that, another weight lifts from my chest. "Yeah." I twine my fingers tighter around his neck as I kiss him, relishing the coarseness of his stubble.

I spend the rest of the day with his taste on my lips, running numbers, and texting Emma. Basically, filling my day until I can be with Colton again. Despite my actions, my mind isn't on my work. All I'm doing is thinking about Colton, about everything he said to me, everything he did to me, and everything he means to me now.

Colton texts me out of the blue. I tease him a little, then I decide it's time to text Willow.

> So

> Something happened

Willow

> No shit. Get your ass here.

I laugh. The evening is closing in on us anyway; I might as well go to Lazy's now and get all the gossip fodder out of the way.

I hit the remote starter of my car and quickly change into a bottle-green turtleneck that brings out the color of my eyes, fix my hair, and put makeup on.

Then I'm on my way, low-key excitement coursing through my veins. Now that I'm with Colton, everything looks different to me.

CHAPTER THIRTY-EIGHT

Colton

"Hey, boss, where you been?" Orson asks when I show up mid-day at the garage in the Subaru. "Got us worried."

"Huh?" Kiara's scent was still floating in the car, and it's like I can feel her all around me while I make my way to my office.

I hook my leather jacket behind my door and walk straight inside the bay, out of habit. Then, forgetting what I came here for, I back out again into the reception area. Maybe if I check the computer I'll get some sense of what I should be doing today.

"Colt?" Orson asks.

"Yup?" I scroll through the calendar without really seeing anything. God I wish that snowstorm had lasted a whole week, kept us holed up for days.

"What you been up to? How was the race?"

I lift my eyes to my oldest employee and squint. *The race. Right.* "Um... went great, placed first."

"Uh-huh."

I sense something, so I add, "Got stuck down there, buddy put me up. You guys did okay without me this morning?"

Orson shuffles. "Not really. Kiara didn't bring her muffins. Think she's alright? Should we call her?" I draw a blank, and it must show, because he continues. "We can't assume she's gonna bring muffins every Monday, but she has for years, so... I think we should check on her."

"Oh... um..." I straighten from the computer. "No, she... she's fine. She's totally fine... just uh..."

He frowns. "She sick? Those migraines again?"

"Yes! Yes. Migraines. That's it." I focus back on the computer screen. *Let's see... oil change. There. I'm gonna do that right now, get my head back in the game.*

"Shame she doesn't have a boyfriend."

I lift my eyebrows but know better than to answer.

"Who doesn't have a boyfriend?" Patrick asks as he walks in.

"Kiara. She got one of her migraines again."

"Oh yeah. She needs a man," Patrick drops.

I stare them down. "What the fuck you guys talking about?"

"It's a known fact," Orson says, picking at his nails. "There's a direct correlation between orgasms and migraines. The more orgasms, the less migraines."

"She must have had a shit weekend," Patrick concludes as he grabs an order from the printer and examines it closely.

I feel myself heat up, but I clench my jaw. I don't need to engage in this conversation. They're clearly trying to rile me up. Fishing for information they already have.

"I'll be doing Craig's oil change." Before I even reach the first bay, I hear them laughing uncontrollably.

I should probably rough them a little for daring to bring up orgasms in the context of Kiara, but I know they didn't mean disrespect. They just wanted to talk to me about it. Deep down, they're happy for me, and why wouldn't they be? She's the best woman there is, and they do like their boss.

I grab the socket wrench and get to work. Once the drain plug is loosened, the familiar scent of oil and metal fills the air as the catch pan fills. It's a good thing I could do this in my sleep, because while I unscrew the filter, replace the drain plug, pour new oil, check the dipstick, and go through all the routine tasks I've done a million times, my mind is on Kiara's breasts, Kiara's smile, Kiara's heels in my butt, Kiara scent, and the sounds she makes when I take care of her.

After I'm done, I can't stand it anymore. I get back behind the computer in the reception area and pull out my phone.

> Hey beautiful

Sweets

> Hi handsome. How's your day going?

> Can't wait til tonight

> ...

> ...

> Same <3

> I've been a good girl

My dick stretches painfully, and I ignore the calls coming from the bay. Something about a socket wrench.

Yeah? Tell me

I worked on my business

...

That better be dirty talk.

Hahahaha! It's not.

We're gonna have to work on your sexting skills.

...

...

...

What's wrong?

I don't know how to do that.

Me neither. Never done that before. So let's set some rules. Rule #1 is, you don't call yourself a good girl or a bad girl and—

"Hey boss!"

"Just a sec."

not follow up with something real dirty

Oh okay

I been a real good girl

Yeah?

I read a real dirty romance and didn't finish myself.

"Boss!" Orson is standing in front of me, so I tuck my phone in my shirt pocket and hope to god he doesn't notice my erection. Jesus Christ! I'm a fucking teenager.

Patrick comes right behind Orson. "Colton, man! Where's the socket wrench?"

"The what now?"

They both look at me like I'm crazy, and maybe I am, because right now I just want to get back to my phone.

Yup, fucking teenager.

"I found it!" Linwood calls from the bay. "Jesus Christ, dude," he yells, his voice coming stronger as he gets closer. "It was in the metal recycling bin!" he says, holding the tool up.

They all look at me like I have three heads.

I lift my hands in apology. "Dunno what happened."

Orson rolls his eyes, Patrick and Linwood mumble incomprehensibly, and they all return to work.

But then Patrick yells "Fuuuck!" and when I run into the bay, I stop in my tracks. There's a huge oil spill under Craig's car.

"I guess someone forgot to tighten the drain plug before refilling," Orson says. Turning to me, he adds, "Don't you have somewhere you need to be?"

"Shit. Let me deal with this."

He shakes his head. "The silly phase will do that to ya."

I frown at him. "Dunno what you're talking about." The ribbing about Kiara's migraines was one thing, but I don't want to talk about *phases* with Orson.

He arches a bushy eyebrow. "You met my wife? She makes sure I know everything I need to know. Get outta here, we'll take care of that. And get your head on straight, will ya? You made enough of a mess to last us a whole year."

Grunting, he adds, "I'll keep an eye out for you at the garage." He punctuates this with a back slap. "Just don't mess up with her. They broke the mold."

I might be in the silly phase, but I still have it together enough to stop at Town Hall before heading to Lazy's. I spend an hour in the offices looking up the variances the town has approved over the past two years, and I leave rather unsettled. It's not looking good.

But when I walk into Lazy's, the sight of Kiara sitting at the bar next to Willow brightens my mood. *We'll figure it out.*

I slide up to her, barely noticing Justin and Haley behind the bar, and Chris, Alex, Grace, Ethan, and Noah at the nearest booth.

She whips around, her cheeks get some color, and her hand goes up to my chest. "Hey," she says. I don't know how Kiara feels about PDA, and I don't want to make her do something she's not comfortable doing in front of our friends. I want to kiss the daylights out of her, and if it was just me, I'd carry her to my truck and we'd go home to fuck the night away.

Granted, we have our whole life for this. I can exercise some restraint for an hour or so—but not much more.

She swivels on her stool and places her knees on each side of me, tugging on my jacket to bring me closer. "I missed you." Her other hand plays with my hair. "Aren't you gonna say hi?"

I did not see that coming. After all the running around in circles she had me do, she's totally liberated and upfront about what's going on between us.

No complaints.

The sound of Justin setting a foaming pint in front of me—"On the house," he says as he sets the beer down rather loudly—doesn't break the magnetic field that is Kiara's silver gaze on me. I lean down and kiss her softly on the mouth. Damn I missed her. And damn I want her again, so bad.

She returns my kiss, the tip of her tongue briefly wetting my lips. I grip the bar with one hand so I don't bring her deeper against me.

Justin might be my friend, but he has standards for his bar.

I pull away from her. My gaze slides to Willow, who's looking at us with an unconcealed look of victory. "You're welcome," she mouths.

Chris straightens and semi-shouts, "Can we talk about how Kiara is glued to Colt like a naked hand on an ice-cold mailbox?"

"Nice metaphor, babe," Alex says.

Willow pushes her stool back and runs around the bar with her hands in the air, shouting, "Whoot! Whoot!"

Noah shakes his head and wipes his glasses, Grace comes around to give Kiara a hug, then leans over to me and whispers for my ears only, "You hurt her, you answer to me."

How and why the fuck would I hurt Kiara? I frown at my sister, my fuck-off look on my face. She shrugs, winks, and says, "It's a Bitch Brigade thing. Just thought you should know."

Justin comes back with three bottles of hard cider. "Best I have, until Haley gets off her ass and makes her own." His sister gives him a friendly shove and helps him fill our glasses.

After they've all toasted to us, we've polished off three more bottles, and we've helped Justin clear the tables, Chris takes Kiara and me aside. I bring Kiara against me, loving the way she fits perfectly under my arm, loving the way her face tilts up to mine, the way her hand grabs my shirt around my waist like she needs something to tether herself to. Feeling her so vulnerable undoes me. I know how she's feeling right now. Like she jumped off a cliff and isn't sure about her parachute. "We're gonna be okay, sweets," I whisper. "I promise." I lean over to kiss her temple.

Chris looks between the two of us. "You're two of my favorite people. I didn't see it coming, but it doesn't mean I don't like it. I fucking love it for you guys, and for me." He ruffles Kiara's hair, and she swats his hand away, leaving my side to sit back with the group of women.

Then he takes me in a bear hug. "I kinda thought there was something going on between you two when you first brought her to me for a job. What happened?" he asks once he releases me.

"She uh…" Laughter takes a hold of me at the memory seared in my brain. "She said she'd chop my balls off if I ever looked at her that way again."

He chuckles. "Sounds like something she'd say. She gonna be okay?"

"What do you mean?" Does he think her being with me is a problem?

Chris looks down at his feet, then over my shoulder. "Alex's been wondering why she's not applying for a grant with her. We all know she could be doing so much better. Not sure how to help her if she won't let us."

"She's trying to make it on her own, but I'm working on getting her to ask for help. Right now, she's looking for a place to open her own business, but it's not easy to find." From my research at Town Hall, getting the variance will be a tall order. "At the same time, she applied to this training in France. She thinks it'll help her—"

"Help her with what? She could probably teach them."

"She's self-taught. Self-conscious about it."

"That's bullshit and you know it. They have nothing on her."

"She doesn't see it that way. She thinks with a stamp of approval..." I hesitate and speak my fears, "hell, with a high position somewhere international for a while... she thinks it would make a difference in her career."

"Dude—"

"Women have it harder than we do," I say, suddenly seeing the world through Kiara's eyes. "It sucks, and hopefully that bullshit will be over when your kid is all grown up, but it's true. They have to fight harder to get to the same place. And if Kiara thinks going to that school can help her, I'm not gonna stand in her way and try and convince her otherwise. Because what do I know? I'd just be trying to keep her here for myself. I'd be part of the problem. And I wanna be part of the solution, even if that school doesn't end up being the solution for her. End of the day, what she needs is confidence, and if Paris gives her that, and hell, Tokyo, Dubai, or wherever the fuck she might end up, then... I'll support that."

"But—"

"Look, Annabel wasn't against it, so..."

"Annabel?"

"Yeah, Annabel Plum, the—"

"I know who Annabel Fucking Plum is! How do they know each other?"

I tell him the story of how I met Annabel's husband, how Annabel was introduced to Kiara's baking (he laughs so hard at the part where

I suggested she take inspiration from Kiara's pie that his eyes well up), and the date I arranged for Kiara.

"What did Annabel say about going to that training in France?" he asks, sobering up.

My gaze zeros in on Kiara at the other side of the room, currently gushing over Grace's nails. "You know, she didn't say. But she's who made me realize the whole part about women seeking recognition more than men do."

Chris grunts. "She didn't try to talk her out of it?"

"Nope."

"Thing is, with people like Annabel who come full circle and end up where they started, they don't always realize the journey is what made their destination," he says.

The fuck does he mean? "You're gonna have to spell that out for me."

"Annabel doesn't seek fame and accolades because... she's had those. She came back down from her high and settled in her home state, but it took her twenty years."

"Thirty," I snap, seeing where he's going. "I love Kiara. And if that's what she wants, if that's what she thinks she needs, I want her to have it."

"Even if that means losing her?"

My heart shatters at his words. I know it's unrealistic to believe that we could have a long-distance relationship that would span decades and still survive. "One thing at a time," I answer, more for my sake than his.

If I want to be there for Kiara, be the man she needs, there are certain things I'm not ready to fully face yet. Hell, I have a heart too, and it needs protecting like any other.

CHAPTER THIRTY-NINE

Kiara

Nervous excitement courses through me as we take an early leave from our friends and drive to Sunrise Farms in separate cars. Colt opens the building door for me, cupping my waist as I brush past him. My breathing hitches, and he takes me in a kiss. Our tongues intertwine, the faint taste of beer on his lips barely hiding the unique taste of him. He hitches me on his hips and carries me up the stairs as I trail my mouth on his neck, relishing the saltiness of his skin.

"Keys," he grunts, setting me down so I can search my bag. He wraps himself around my back, breathing heavily, hard against me.

The stupid keys are in my bag. I can hear them. They just seem to evade my grasp.

"Come on, babe," he says gently as he trails one hand down between my legs.

I throw my head back. *God this feels good.* "Not helping, Colt."

He moves his hand up, but the way he holds my hip is even sexier with the warmth of his palm penetrating through my clothes, and his fingers kneading with impatience. "Might need to take you right here, cupcake. Been a long day," he growls against my neck.

My center clenches at his words, and finally I feel metal. "Got 'em, got 'em."

With trembling fingers, I unlock my door, then Colton shuts it behind us and turns me to face him, his hands roaming my body up and down. I throw my jacket toward the couch, the faint glow of the side lamp I've left on enough to go by.

Colton hoists me on the kitchen counter, pulls my sweater off, and narrows his gaze on my breasts. "Let's get rid of this," he says, swiftly unclasping my bra. I shake it off, letting it land on the floor next to the sweater, then Colton flicks his tongue on my nipple—an agonizing tease. "Ah fucking hell, missed this all day. Jesus, Kiara—I'm obsessed with you, you know that?" He drags his mouth over the swell of my breast, suckling it so expertly I cry out in pleasure and clutch his hair. Laying me softly flat on my back against the cold kitchen counter, he licks his way to the other breast, cupping it for better access. His warm, rugged hands on my skin, his cold leather jacket molding his shoulders, and the pull of his mouth take me to the edge.

"If you keep doing this, I might come." My voice is barely a breath. "You should... We should..."

He deepens his clamp on my breast, pleasure zinging from my nipple down to my center. My moans increase, mingling with the hum of the refrigerator and the creaking of his leather jacket. "Fuck," he says in ragged breath.

I writhe under him. "I want you inside me, Colt." He suckles harder on my nipple, making me arch under him. "Please, now."

And in this moment, looking at him fully clothed losing his mind over me, I want to be naked under him. I snake my hands to my waist and unzip my jeans. "Take me now, Colt."

"Ah, but you taste so good," he says as he lifts slightly off me. "Come here," he says, pulling me to him.

I try to resist, to stay right here, the sudden fantasy of having the daylights fucked out of me by Colton Harper on my very own kitchen counter the only goal at the moment. "Take out that big cock of yours and give it to me, baby. Take me."

He peels the jeans off my hips, my panties with them. I lift my head to watch him free his cock, his metal belt buckle jingling lose. Then he tugs under my knees to bring my center against him, making me cry out in surprise. The warmth of his erect cock contrasts sharply with the cold surface under my back. I buck from the feeling of being at his mercy, totally exposed.

Leaning on his elbows, he cages me in, playing with my hair, his leather and laundry scent mixing faintly with oil and beer. *All man.* "Do you know how sexy you look, entirely naked for me?" he grunts.

I lick my lips. "Just about as sexy as you do in your hot leather jacket, ready to have your way with me."

He dips lower and kisses my throat, smiling. "Oh, I see. It's the leather jacket. Got it."

My fingers in his hair, I arch my back. "Don't tease me more, Colt. I'm gonna come and you won't be inside me and that'll be a waste of an orgasm." I rub against him.

He reaches between us to flick my clit and grunts. "Soaking wet for me—and I only had the appetizer." He dips a finger inside me, and I cry out in pleasure, then he brings his finger to his mouth, making a show of sucking my juices off. "Ah fuck, you taste so good."

The scent of sex sets me off deeper. "Babe, please, I'm begging you..." I rub against the hard ridge of his cock, its softness and hardness a stark contrast to his jeans chafing my inner thighs.

"Show me," he says, lifting my leg so it rests on his hip. "Show me how much you want me."

I dig my heels in his butt.

"Atta girl, you ride that. Take your man." I pull my legs in, and with a glorious grunt he thrusts inside me in one shot, filling me. "Fuck but you're so tight. So tight."

"Fuck me harder, Colt."

"You sure?" he rasps.

I bring his face closer to me. "Listen to me cos I'm not gonna say it twice. I want you to fuck me like you just came out of twenty years in prison and you won me at an auction."

He jerks his head back, surprise painted on his face, and for a fleeting moment I think he's going to laugh—I even feel his dick hesitating—but thankfully that moment passes, a dark shadow passes through his gaze, his jaw clenches, and he realizes I'm serious.

"Twenty years, huh?" His thrusts accelerate.

"Yeah, babe," I say, sliding my hands under his jacket and pulling his Henley up so I can rake his back. "Twenty years without pussy. And you get me. All to yourself."

Sweat forms on his back with each of his thrusts. "Fucking hell. At an auction?"

"Yeah, babe. You won me at an auction."

For a beat the only sound we make is the squelching of our joined sexes, the creaking of his jacket. I can almost hear him think. Then he says, "Tell me how that went."

I swallow hard, the pleasure he's giving me making it hard to speak. "I was on a stage... wearing almost nothing..." His powerful thrusts pin me against the hard countertop in rhythmic thuds, the absolute best. "And all these men were raising their paddles... but you... you... you wanted me the most so... you... you bid the highest."

He locks eyes with me and stops moving inside me. "I did, huh. You bet I did." He pulls out. "How much?" He pushes himself back in, and I moan, but he barely moves.

"More, Colt. More. In and out. More."

He stops moving entirely. "How much did I bid on you?" His cock is twitching inside me, frustrating and pleasing me at the same time.

"Huh?"

He rolls my nipple, pulling on it slightly, his other hand holding his head like we're having a casual conversation. "How much did I bid on you after twenty fucking years in prison?" He inches out of me, his tip at my entrance, an unbearable tease.

"Oh... A-a-a million dollars."

"You bet I did." And then he disappears and I'm left cold and alone, wondering what I did wrong, until he anchors his strong hands to my thighs and licks my clit.

No-no-no. I want him inside me. "Colt, please. Take me."

"I been twenty fucking years without pussy, I spent a million dollars on this cupcake, I'm gonna do what I'm gonna do, sweets," he growls while rubbing his nose against my clit.

Then he feasts on me until he brings me to the edge, his tongue teasing and circling, his fingers digging in my hips, his growls resonating inside me. When I'm about to come he lifts me as he stands and turns us so I'm against the fridge. "Slide that million-dollar pussy around my cock, you dirty little virgin," he says as he pushes inside me.

He's bigger and thicker than before, or maybe it's the position, I don't know, but I know he's feeling it too because he's losing it. In two quick movements his jacket is gone, the Henley is gone, and his glistening skin is against mine, our bodies tense and slick and demanding. "Come here, you little tease," he says as he places one hand under my ass, touching my butthole. I squeeze in surprise. He slams a fist on the fridge as he powers in and out of me. "Atta girl. Show me what a million bucks gets me."

I want to come and at the same time I don't want the pleasure to stop. "Colt," I say, deciding conversation is the way to extend this. "Colt. Babe."

He throws his head back, his neck tense and dripping with sweat. I'm not sure he heard me.

"Babe, you know..." I start as he increases his thrusts.

But he brings his face back down, his eyes boring into mine, then he dips to my neck and suckles on it. This gets me crying out, "Colt!"

"That's right, babe. My name on your lips when you come. I bought you at auction, 'member?" It's his deep voice that sets me off. I think. Or the fact he's playing the role of winner of the auction to a T. I bite his shoulder when I come, because the fridge is right next to the front door, and I discovered a few hours ago that I'm a screamer.

He grunts and shakes and grunts some more, then with a loud exhale, he grips me tighter and carries me to the bedroom, drops us both sideways, and cradles me while we catch our breaths. "Best auction ever," he whispers.

My heart still beats like crazy from my orgasm. But more so from the way he wants me. It's in the way he looks at me, the way he holds me, takes me, breathes me in.

"You know you can have this for free? All your life. Right?" I say, panting.

"Don't cheapen yourself, sweets. Million bucks sex right there. Guaranteed. And the night is just beginning."

Then he laughs and lifts me against his chest and moves us so our heads are on the pillows. He leans over to turn a side lamp on, and I instinctively bring the duvet to cover myself. "Are you cold?" he asks, lifting the duvet off me. His finger trails a path from the corner of my mouth to my neck, down between my breasts, then his palm flattens on my side and pulls me against him. "Mmm? Let me crank the heat up."

"I'm good, Colt. Not cold." Just a little self-conscious.

His gaze darkens. "You're mine, sweets. I get to look at what's mine. I get to savor it. Caress it. Possess it."

He's now cupping my hip, like he's pondering what to do next. "Open up," he says, and my legs part, giving him access. "Mmm... all wet again, aren't you." He gets on his knees and grabs his bobbing cock in one hand. "Turn around. On your knees."

His commanding tone should fire up my resistance, but it does the opposite. I'm putty, and obey him with anticipation. I glance at him over my shoulder. The smoldering look on his face confirms it: This man wants me like I never thought possible, and doing his bidding is my only concern right now.

"Come here," he says, lifting my hips so I align with his cock. "Hold onto the headboard, sweets. Just like that. Sweet Jesus," he grunts as he enters me.

The feeling is different. Fuller. I don't see him, only feel his powerful thrusts, the sensation all-encompassing. My whole body is on fire, taut, ready to snap. His growls and swears only increase my pleasure.

He rolls my nipple in his fingers. "Fucking hell, sweets, losing it here," he murmurs against my neck.

My center is ready to explode. "Babe, lose it. Please lose it with me."

He leaves my nipple and wraps his arm around me, the other hand next to mine on the headboard. "Is it as good for you as it is for me?" he asks raggedly.

My orgasm tears through me, lightning fire that ripples from my hair to my toes, and a feral scream escapes me as I feel him empty himself inside me. Violent tremors shake my body, Colt's strong arm holding us together through his own orgasm.

"How was it for you?" Colt asks once we're flat on our backs again, a sheen of sweat covering our bodies, the scent of sex pungent in the room.

"I don't have the words," I answer. Turning my head to him, I say, "To be honest, half the pleasure comes from seeing you take your pleasure with me."

"That so?" he says with an adorable smile.

"I feel like I'm really yours." My confession makes my body feel weak, but in the best possible way. And weirdly, it makes me feel... content. At peace with myself.

He swipes a stray hair from my face, looking dreamy all of a sudden. "Time for a shower," he declares.

I'm a little disappointed the after-sex doesn't last longer, but if Colt feels like he needs a shower, then so be it. "You go first."

"Nuh-uh. We're showering together."

That sounds both awesome and very... exposed.

He must read my conflict because he frowns. "I won you at auction. A million bucks. That gets me a shower. Or ten."

I laugh at that and follow him. He pours a generous amount of shower gel in his palms and runs them all over me. I tense when he gets to my private parts but he just slides as if it's no big deal. It's both highly erotic and sweet.

"You really got into that auction thing, didn't you?" I tease once we're both covered in suds. Did he think it was weird?

"You know," he says as he massages shampoo in my hair, "in hindsight, I think you were a part of me, one way or another, from the day I saw you in your car, hiding in that thicket. I just didn't know it." The memory is distant, something I've tried to forget, really. I need to sit with what he said for a minute, and the fact he's tilting my head back to rinse it under the shower is a perfect excuse to say nothing.

After that, I focus on lathering his pecs, his back, taking my time to admire his strong physique. When I get on my knees to soap his legs, his cock bobs. I lick my lips and look up at him, his body shielding me from the shower for the most part.

"Keep some for later, sweets," he says with a smile.

We towel off, I use the hairdryer to get most of the humidity off my head, then we find ourselves in my bed again, me curled up inside his arm, one leg over his midsection. I trace question marks on his chest with my finger.

Since he's brought up the circumstances under which we met, I can't let it go. I'm not sure if I hate or love what he said. I need more, at the risk of learning something I don't like.

Maybe this will be how we end.

I *have* to ask

"What did you mean earlier... about being yours from the very beginning?"

CHAPTER FORTY

Colton

Her fingers keep mindlessly playing with my chest hair, but her body tenses in my arms as she asks her question. "What did you mean earlier... about being yours from the very beginning?"

I don't think those were my words, but I let it slide. If it's how she feels now, I'm more than okay with it.

I smile, remembering that day vividly.

I'd been to New Hampshire on a call for a 1967 Ford Mustang Fastback stranded on the side of the road—turned out it was just a loose belt. On my way back, off a township road, I noticed fresh tire marks that continued straight into a thicket where the road angled sharply left. Slowing down, the glimmer in the trees indicated a car was there, tucked deep in the underbrush.

I pulled over. My immediate thought was that the driver might have fallen asleep at the wheel and hit a tree. Prepared for the worst, I had my phone out to call EMS when I saw the most angelic face. She had reclined the driver's seat. The window was cracked open an inch or so. "You okay in there?" I asked.

She started, momentarily confused, large eyes widening, then her face closed off and she said, "I'm leaving, I'm leaving." She went to start the engine and muttered, "Can't fucking sleep in peace."

"Hey, miss," I said, hands up in the universal sign of someone who doesn't want to cause trouble. "I was just checking. Just making sure you're okay."

"Yeah right," she answered, avoiding my gaze. She backed up into a clearing and made a swift three-point turn.

My truck was blocking her access to the road. She stared at it, straight ahead. That gave me time to admire her small, pointed nose. Her clear, porcelain-like skin. To notice how thin she was. And that her fingernails were bitten to the quick.

The back of her car seemed packed with bags. I knocked on her window, signaling her to open it.

"What?" she snapped but did as I asked.

I bent down so that my face was closer to the opening. It didn't smell like booze or weed. At least there was that.

"You traveling?" I asked, glancing at her bags obviously again.

"What's it to you?"

"Maybe this is my land."

This got me a once-over. "I don't think so." She was young, I could tell, and yet her eyes were weary. Something in me wanted to protect her from whatever she was running from. She'd seen shit, and she didn't want to deal with more of that. "Besides, I'm leaving. What do you care?"

Good question. I didn't know why at the time, but I did care.

I wished I had her spunk to deal with my own shit, and her comebacks when people got in my way. I was instantly attracted to her energy.

At the same time, she got me riled up—concerned. I didn't know what to do with her, but one thing was clear: I wasn't leaving her. So I went back to my truck, grabbed my emergency box of cookies, and waited.

She got out of her car and stomped to me. "Hey. Move."

"My mom says you don't catch flies with vinegar."

"You calling me a fly?"

"I'm saying you're the vinegar. You want me out of your way, ask me nicely." I popped a whole cookie in my mouth, relishing what was to come.

Whatever it was, the way her eyes danced was my reward. "Can you pretty please get your fucking truck out of my fucking way?"

"You talk to your mom with that mouth?"

Her face closed tighter than it already was. "No." Then she clarified, defiance in her tone, "I don't talk to my mother."

Her eyes had a shine that I instantly loved, although later I'd find out it meant pain. But at the time, it intrigued me. *She* intrigued me. Pulled me in.

I wanted some of that strength.

"Okay," I said, shrugging like I didn't care. I took another cookie and offered her the box. "Hungry?"

She looked starved. "Not enough to eat your industrial shit."

I swallowed. "I have a cousin," I started.

She rolled her eyes. "You gonna go through the whole family? The mama, the cousin... Fuck." She set her fists on her hips and stared up at me. She was short, and I was sitting in my truck.

I chuckled. This was getting entertaining. "My cousin is a baker," I continued, noticing her features soften and her interest pique. "And he's constantly on our case about the food we eat."

"And?" she said, and something in my chest fluttered. *I had her hooked.*

I shrugged. "That's it. You made me think of him."

"Is he hiring?"

That thing in my chest blossomed, the heat of hope and never-ending tomorrows filling me. "Who?"

"Who?! The pope! Is the pope hiring? 'Cos I'm a qualified cardinal."

The fight in this girl was like nothing I'd ever seen. I hid my smile. "When was the last time you ate? Are you thirsty?"

She licked her lips, my gaze flicking there for a beat. "Are you saying I'm a bum?"

"Your word, not mine. Your getup suggests something's going on."

She stood taller, shoulders back. "What's it to you?"

Her answer made it clear that she was living out of her car. And yet, she oozed pride and confidence.

Coming back to the present, I stroke her shoulder. "I didn't feel like you were mine. More like, I tried to make you a part of me." It's really hard to explain. "You were everything I wasn't. You looked fragile but you were strong. You looked lost but it seemed like you knew where you were going. I was the opposite, on all fronts—or that's how I felt. I wanted to be more like you."

She lifts herself off my shoulder. "You're kidding, right?"

I shake my head. "I wanted to be able to say fuck you to people who got in my way—the way you did to me. I wanted to have a sense of purpose that was other than just... following."

"Really," she says, clearly perplexed.

"Course, it didn't hurt that you were a stunner. But you shut that down pretty quick."

She laughs. "Yeah, I was that way, back then." She tucks her head deeper in the crook of my arm, and splays her hand flat on my chest, her memories maybe taking her where mine are. To how she got to Emerald Creek.

"Why don't we go ask him?" I'd answered to her question about Chris.

"Ask who what?"

"My cousin. He might be hiring. Only one way to know."

"'Kay. Where is he and what's his name? I'll check him out. Are you gonna get out of my way now?"

"No." I wasn't letting her out of my sight so easily.

She rolled her eyes so far back she could have played in an exorcist movie. "Ugh!" she cried out.

"I'll take you to him. You follow me."

That day, after meeting with Chris, she slept in the spare bedroom at Mom and Dad's (the one that had been Chris's not so long ago), and once she had her first pay stub from the bakery, she moved into Sunrise Farms.

"You kind of were my knight in shining armor," she murmurs. "I don't think I ever thanked you for that."

"No need to. I did what anyone would have."

She snorts her disagreement. "I was so scared at that time, you have no idea. I didn't know where the next blow was going to come from. I couldn't trust anything or anyone."

I hate that she went through that. Someday I'll have to find out absolutely everything that happened to her, but now there's something I need to know. "What made you trust me?"

She thinks on that, her fingers playing on my chest again. "It seemed like you were... Like you cared enough to have an opinion on what I should be doing. But at the same time, you respected me enough not to judge me if I acted differently. And it felt like, for the first time in a long time, I had a choice in how I lived my life. A real choice." Her gaze lifts to me as I look at her.

I sear this moment in my memory forever.

Always give her the choice—a real choice.

We fall asleep tangled together and I wake up with her to the sound of chirping birds. "What the fuck?" I grunt as I roll off her.

"What?" Kiara says, stretching her limbs like a lazy cat.

"Birds. It's winter."

A thump sounds, the chirping stops, and a soft glow lights Kiara's naked body. "That's my alarm." She turns her face toward me. "Just makes facing the world easier. Coffee?"

"Come here," I say, and hold her tight against me.

"What's wrong?" she asks, her breath tickling my chest.

"Nothing's wrong, baby. Everything's..." Overcome with emotion, I hug her tighter, unable to express myself with words. "What else am I going to find out, huh?"

"What do you mean?"

"Sweets, yesterday I found out you were scared shitless when I thought you were so strong that I wanted to *be* you. Now I find out you wake up to the sound of chirping birds in order to face the world. I did *not* see that coming. A swearing parrot is the only kind of bird I thought you'd tolerate in the morning."

She giggles. "Now that's an idea."

CHAPTER FORTY-ONE

Kiara

After Colt makes fun of my alarm, he orders me to stay under the covers so he can bring me coffee in bed—which he manages to do with surprising speed. I usually need an hour to be halfway functional, but he's all business the minute he's up.

He ends up waking me with way more than just coffee. "Careful, I might get used to that," I tell him when I'm down from my orgasm.

"You might as well, sweets," he grunts as he pecks my lips goodbye. I bring the duvet up to my chin as he walks out of the room, but as soon as the front door shuts on him, I'm restless.

Grace

Don't forget to come to Town Hall tonight

Sure. Something important?

Laskin. Final preparation

Oops. Almost forgot about Emerald Creek's largest festival.

Right. I remembered

I'm sure you did

It's not like you had anything else on your mind recently

...

I switch to Colton's contact.

Don't forget Town Hall meeting tonight

Colton

Hey

I want your cupcake

I laugh despite me.

I'll definitely bring cupcakes. Can you share?

Someone's asking for trouble

Someone already found trouble

Damn girl, you're making me hard

I didn't do anything

...

...

I spend my day off baking for the meeting tonight, daydreaming about Colton. I hear his footsteps run up the stairs an hour before the meeting is set to start and decide to leave early so we're not arriving together.

Town Hall is on Old Farmway Road, right off The Green. It's a simple building with white clapboard siding, a central front door, symmetrical windows, a gabled roof and a belfry. Inside, there are two offices, and a large meeting room with exposed beams. The wooden floors, high ceilings, and simple architecture all contribute to a welcoming atmosphere. Rows of foldable chairs face a podium with a long wooden table where six people are already seated, shuffling papers, whispering among each other. By the time I have my baked goods set at the back of the room, the five selectpersons are facing us, shuffling through papers and whispering to each other, while Ms. Angela, sits at the top, a laptop open in front of her.

I slide in next to Chloe, who's sitting next to Emma, leaving the chair to my right empty for latecomers.

Cassandra taps her microphone to bring silence to the room and calls the meeting open. "First order of business is to appoint our chairperson, since Stan, who left recently, filled that function. I'd like to make a motion to appoint Colton Harper."

My heartbeat picks up. Colton stepped in to be on the board out of a sense of duty. I can't see him happy to be in the limelight. Surely Owen wants to be the chair. It fits his personality to a T.

Colton's head snaps up from his papers. Like I thought, he was not expecting that.

"I'll second that," Owen says.

Now here's a surprise. I thought there was history between these two, and I didn't think either of them was over it.

Looks like I'm wrong.

"All those in favor?"

Four ayes sound, and Angela types as fast as she can with two fingers on the laptop.

Colton won't be happy to be on the forefront, having to lead discussions. But I'm happy. This will be great for him. And he'll be great for the town. I'm so proud of him it hurts.

He scans the room and his gaze locks with mine. I give him a small thumbs up. One of his eyebrows shoots up while the corners of his mouth dip down in mock deprecation. *This.* This moment of silent complicity, of knowing I'm going home with him later. That I'll be snuggling with him. That I'll be telling him how proud of him I am, even if it annoys him—especially if it annoys him. These little things make the scariness of a relationship worthwhile.

"Next time you sit in the middle!" Nathaniel, an old man who does everything that needs to be done around town, bellows from his front-row seat. Colton's gaze turns to him and he gives him a small smile.

Ms. Angela nods. "I was going to say just that."

Chloe elbows me. "Look at that, your man is head honcho now," she whispers, making me chuckle.

Colton clears his throat and reads from the paper he's been toying with since he got here. "A'right, I guess I'm taking over."

"Yeah!" someone behind me shouts.

Colton continues. "Next on the agenda is Declan—*Officer Campbell*'s report on recent incidents."

A woman squeezes by and sits on the empty chair to my right. A discreet waft of jasmine and citrus emanates from her, making me instantly relax. "I want to hear that," she says. "It's not good for business, this vandalism." I turn my head and realize it's Maddie.

She smiles at me, then her mouth rounds in an O. "You were there, right? You saw it happen?" she asks in a whisper as Declan starts recounting the events, reading from his spiral notebook.

I nod.

"Were you scared?" she asks, her eyes on Declan as she listens to him as well.

"More like stunned," I whisper.

She looks at me and silently mouths, *I know!*

Once Declan is done, Nathaniel stands up. "Could it be the Prattsville folk? They usedta do a lotta that sorta..." His hand shakes as if to fill in for the word he's looking for. "Shenanigans," he finally says. "Not so long ago. Been a few years. I always said, 'It's too quiet, somethin's up.'"

Maddie shakes her head, disapproving.

"We looked into it," Declan answers, tapping his notebook nervously. "But uh... this is a personal assault on someone's private property."

"They usedta do stuff like that," Nathaniel retorts.

Declan tilts his head. "Not really. They toilet-papered the North Bridge, put a... a gigantic..." He blushes.

Maddie leans over and says, "a gigantic blow-up penis on The Green," while someone in the audience helps out Declan. "An inflatable appendage!"

"Thank you," Declan says.

Nathaniel spreads his hands out. "What else do you need?"

Declan is torturing his notebook now. "What I'm trying to say, is that this seems more personal to the bookstore. It's not even remotely funny—"

"You saying the rest was funny?" someone hollers. Half the audience laughs out loud while the other half murmurs in disapproval.

Cassandra gently taps her mic, then Colton leans over his. "Guys, please. Let Dec—Officer Campbell complete his report."

Ms. Angela lifts her head from her note-taking, looking pleased at Colton's take-charge approach.

Declan is crimson. "It was an ill-advised attempt at making fun of all of us. Hurtling eggs at a window is a lone gesture that signifies aggression. Very little planning. It's the sign of an angry person looking for revenge. Or to get even. To inflict harm on a particular individual, or... corporation. The other... events required several organized individuals, planning, and overall, as unpleasant as it was, it didn't carry the same meaning."

"I still think we should look at'em," Nathaniel says, then sits down.

"And we are. I met with their chief of police. Bottom line is, if this was... Let's say we find Daisy painted purple or-or-or Moose dressed in a tutu or a bunch of rubber ducks floating on the Emerald lake? Then yes. Chances are, it would be Prattsville. But in this particular case, I'm leaning toward something more... sinister."

The room is eerily silent, then a low murmur spreads.

"And private," he adds, his hands extended to calm everyone down. "No need to panic."

"Thank you?" Colton says. "And keep us informed."

Owen leans over his mic. "Sorry, another question."

Colton lets out an audible grunt, which may be construed as encouragement for Owen to talk.

Maddie leans toward me until our shoulders touch. "You're together now, right?" she whispers, her gaze clearly on Colton.

Heat flushes my face. "Um... yes. It's-it's very new. But we've been friends a while," I add for no reason.

She nods. "I thought so," she says. We both go back to looking at the Select Board.

Owen rounds his mouth like he's looking for his words. No sound comes out for a couple seconds, and I feel like I should fill this awkward silence with more explanations. *It took us a while. It took* me *a while. I don't know why it didn't happen sooner. There's a reason it didn't happen sooner. He's too good to be true. It's bound to fall apart sooner than later. That's how great things always end up.*

Owen finally speaks. "Should we be concerned about the stop signs?"

Declan squints. "Pardon?"

"I'm thinking of the potential for graffiti." His hands start making rolling motions. "What I'm getting at is, should we budget for... whatever product is used to remove graffiti?"

Declan shrugs. "We own a total of three stop signs. The other two are state property—they're on a state route. So... I don't know." He turns to Nathaniel.

All eyes turn to Nathaniel, who shrugs. "Coupla magic erasers should do."

Next to me, Maddie huffs. "This isn't good."

"A'right, next on the agenda is Laskin. Lynn?" Colton says.

A collective sigh and the buzz of muffled conversations take over as we move onto a happier topic. "Laskin?" Chloe asks, leaning over. "Is that the Christmas fair?"

"Lynn, why don't you take this," Colton says in the mic as I nod to Chloe. We both listen up, as this is when the logistics will be finalized.

I'm tasked with staffing the hot chocolate hut, Chloe gets to coordinate the food tent with Justin, while Alex will be in charge of social media for the whole event. Other people will be baking goods and selling them to profit Emerald Creek's various sports teams.

The horse parade will be coordinated by Craig, Lynn's husband. Various other events are discussed, but I'm not paying attention to the content anymore.

The delivery is so much more… palatable. Colton speeds people kindly to move the meeting forward, has a nice word to make them feel awesome, shuts down Owen's nonsense with a "who moves to table this?" He even shuts down the usual bickering over the ribbon's shade of red on Town Hall's six-foot wreath with a "whatever you guys decide will be awesome" and a gavel tap to end all gavel taps.

Grace taps my shoulder from her seat behind me and leans forward. "Who is this man and what have you done with my brother?" she whispers.

Willow turns back to answer her. "She's demonstrated to him the power of patience and persistence."

My heart flutters at this, and while I feel a physical pull toward Colton at her words, I lean over to Willow to whisper, "By the way, you and I never sorted out your role in that dating app scheme."

"Nothing to sort out, hun. Look." She tilts her chin toward Colton. The way his shoulders roll under his flannel as he fidgets with a sheet of paper and the intensity of his dark gaze scanning the audience bring all kinds of inappropriate thoughts to my mind as he asks the most innocent questions.

"A'right, who's taking over the hearthsong this year?" he asks.

I pretend to be fascinated by the question, not the man. "Who usually does that?" I ask Willow, which gets me a snort and a shoulder-bump *Nice try.*

Several voices murmur, until Louise stands up. "I will, if no one else volunteers," she almost screeches. It's hard to picture her singing or coordinating people. Colton visibly winces and pretends to look everywhere but in her direction. "Anyone?" he asks.

"I can do that," a very familiar voice sounds a few rows behind me. I feel my eyes widen as my gaze latches onto Colton. *Nigel?* I mouth. He glances at me and with a smirk says, "Luke, you're it. Check in with Ms. Angela after the meeting."

Maddie audibly sighs. "I don't know who this Luke is, but it can't be worse than Louise."

I go to turn around and check out my mystery voice on the phone, and just as I do, I catch Emma turning around in her chair, all flushed. "What's up with her?" I ask Chloe.

She shrugs. "No idea."

I lean over Chloe and tap on Emma's arm. "Who's this guy?" I ask her.

"No idea. Why?"

"I thought he lived in Prattsville."

"No, he..." she starts, then catches herself. "If he volunteered, he must live here. Why don't you ask Colton? And what makes you think he lives in Prattsville?"

I'm saved from answering her questions by the arrival of Willow, who asks Maddie to "slide down so I can sit with my peeps."

"We need someone to make waffles," Lynn is saying. "Alex, are you and Chris up for that?"

Alex nods. "Sure, we can do that. Happy to coordinate with others."

Millie stands. "Let's have a hot chocolate/waffle/coffee hut!" she exclaims from the back of the room.

"And grass!" Nathaniel says, lifting his fist in the air.

The room laughs, but Colton taps on the mic sternly. "Just a reminder, weed sales are regulated and I don't think there's a license for sale outside of 420."

Declan stands and nods, but the whole room is laughing.

Colton rolls his eyes. "You guys are worse than a bunch of teenagers," he says, laughing too. "Right, Ms. Angela?"

She smiles, holding her laughter in.

"A'right, meeting adjourned. Stick around for Kiara's awesome cup-um... cookies."

He jumps off stage and reaches me in three swift strides.

"You have ruined cupcakes for yourself, haven't you?" I ask him after he's pecked my lips. I'm still laughing from his private embarrassment.

"Nah. I've elevated them," he says. "Hey, Mom," he adds, looking beyond me.

My reflex is to jump out of his grasp, but he tightens his hold on me, turns me around, wraps his arm around my middle and plops a kiss on the top of my head.

Chapter Forty-Two

Colton

Mom wraps us both in a quick hug, like I knew she would. Her eyes twinkle a little more than usual, but she doesn't say anything. Mom could always read me like an open book, and treating this—us—like it's the most natural thing is exactly what I want.

"Hey, kiddos," she says. "We're celebrating tonight. Lasagna is in the oven. See you at home?"

Of course Mom wants us for dinner. And although the only thing I want right now is to take Kiara home—wherever that may be—I'm not really given an option.

"We'd love to!" Kiara answers Mom's question. That *we* nearly undoes me. In my mind, it states that we're a couple, even if that may not hold the same meaning for her. No matter—I'm like a puppy now. I know it. And I fucking love it.

Kiara slides from the front of me to my side and latches herself tightly to me by fisting the side of my flannel shirt, to loosely grazing my back, and finally hooking her thumb in my jeans belt loop.

Our intimacy in front of the whole town and in front of my mom doesn't bother me. It feels right and natural.

"Okay then," Mom says with a chin tilt. "I'd better get going."

Kiara twists to look me in the eye. "You okay?"

"It's not like she gave us a choice," I say. I'm torn between the soft happiness of seeing my life fall into place, and the raw need of making Kiara mine again right this fucking minute.

"I mean, about your mom seeing us together..." She looks down to her feet, seeming conscious of the people surrounding us.

"Give me a second." I hop back to the stage, grab a folder from Ms. Angela, then pull Kiara from her group of friends and walk her to her car. "I'm following you to Sunrise Farms, then we're driving together to Mom and Dad's."

She looks a little panicky. "I need to bring something."

I take her chin in my fingers. "No you don't. You're family."

"That doesn't mean—"

I should have known this was coming. Imagining Kiara fussing over what dessert she should make to bring to my parents', projecting how happy Mom will be that Kiara is now family and bakes truly just for us, is the icing on a cake I did not see coming. "This time it does. You had minus thirty seconds' notice. Mom's not expecting you to bring anything. She'd probably be embarrassed if she knew you're worried about that right now. Now let's get going. It's late already."

I hold her hand when we walk up the steps to my parents and damn it if I don't see her eyes glistening in the dark of the front porch. "What's up, sweets?"

Her mouth pinches. "Nothing."

I squeeze her hand. "Come on, it's cold. Tell me what's eating at you before we go in."

"This is imp—this *means* something to me, Colt. Going to your parents' house for dinner with you. With *us* being together."

"It means somethin' to me too." I go to pull her in my arms to give her kiss, but she stands back.

"You don't understand. It means I could lose *this* too. Them."

She means if we break up, which I suppose she assumes there's a risk that I will. Although that's laughably out of touch with my reality, I can't really dismiss her fears with a chuckle. So I tell her the truth. "Pretty sure if we broke up—which we won't, not on my account—they'd choose you over me."

She lets me pull her in for a kiss. "You're just being nice."

"No I'm not. Just saying the truth." I lean over to kiss her nice and full before the next couple of hours force us to keep the PDA to a minimum, when the door opens wide, casting light on our embrace.

"Last one before dinner at the old folks'?" my dad bellows. "Honey! The kids are here. Told you I heard the truck."

Once inside with the door shut behind us, he adds, still loudly enough for Mom to hear, "You were right! Looks like she didn't bring dessert."

Kiara turns a deep shade of red. "I didn't—" she starts.

I shut her up by placing my hand on her mouth, pulling her side flush against mine, and saying, both for Dad and for her, "Now you know how they really treat family in this house."

Dad makes a face at me and adds, "Your mother made fruit salad."

I mock clench my heart. "How brutal. Mom looking out for your health."

"Yeah-yeah-yeah," he says, then drags Kiara away from me and places his hands on her shoulders. "I'd say welcome to the family, kid, but you've always been ours, in a way. It's just this dimwit here that took his sweet time figuring it out."

Kiara's shade of red isn't showing any sign of improvement. "Um... thanks. I-I'm probably as much to blame—"

"No... nope," Dad says.

"Dad. Why don't you leave her alone, yeah, 'fore she changes her mind 'bout me."

Mom pokes her head out of the kitchen door. "Kiara dear, come over here and help me, will you?" she says, giving Kiara an excuse to leave. "I have no idea what I'm doing here," she mumbles, and we all know it's a little white lie to pull her deeper into our fold. No speeches. No teary-eyed declarations. Just what Kiara needed.

At some point during dinner, the conversation rolls to our visit with Annabel Plum. "Oh, I've heard of her," Mom says. "She has her own TV show."

Dad shakes his fork in the direction of Kiara. "See, that's what I don't get. She thinks you're better'n her. Why don't ya take her with you to go see the bank? Heck, why doesn't she finance you?"

"Now that's an idea," Kiara jokes. "Seriously though, she said she'd try and help me get into that program in France. Put in a good word for me."

I wipe my mouth and take a sip of water. "She said that?"

Kiara nods. "Couple days after we left, she emailed me." She glances my way and shrugs. "It's a long shot."

"Well that sounds very exciting," Mom says. "How long is this training for?"

"Three months."

Mom glances my way. "Oh, that's not too bad."

"I'm also looking at renting space somewhere," Kiara says, taking a long sip of water as if she'd said something stressful.

"Oh that's wonderful," Mom gushes. "Any place in particular?"

"Nothing set yet. But I'm looking at the Dewey's barn."

"Oh," Mom says. "Isn't that a little out of the way?"

Kiara's face lights up. "It outside the village, but it's so dreamy. When you're inside, all you see is nature. I just love it!" Her enthusiasm quickly dies off. "That's also a long shot, to be honest."

"Well, we'd love it if you stayed here, honey," Mom says. "Maybe once you come back from France, things will clear up." She gives Kiara an encouraging smile.

"I don't think France can teach you anything," Dad grumbles.

I place my hand on Kiara's knee. "I hope you get in," I say to encourage her. I don't want her to feel any pressure to stay here, and I know Mom and Dad are bound to do that. They just love having their family around. The short time my sister was across the country, years ago, was hard on them. "I really do," I add when Kiara looks at me quizzically. "If Annabel says it's a good idea, then it's a good idea."

After Dad and I clear the table, the two of us get started on dishes. We work in silence, as we always do. Dad rinses and scrubs, and I load the dishwasher. It's been years since I've argued against his method, but today he's spending an inordinate amount of time on the scrubbing.

"Dad?" I say, extending my hand.

He gives me a near-clean plate. "I stopped being an asshole the day I realized I was losing your mom, and she'd always been the best part of me. I fixed myself for her," he declares.

I don't want to talk about those days. They're behind me, as far as I'm concerned.

"What I'm trying to say," Dad says, completely losing track of where we are in the dishwashing process, "is that I'm happy you have Kiara in your life. You're different already, I can tell."

"Different how?" I'm feeling both defensive about this, as if there was some hidden criticism there, and agreeing with him. After all, it was Kiara who convinced me to join the board, and tonight's session went nothing like I expected.

"It's like you're coming into yourself," he says. "I can't explain it."

He's right. I can't explain it either, but there's a sense of inner peace growing inside me recently that makes me look at life differently.

Later, back in my truck, I take her hand in mine and kiss her knuckles. "This was nice, but I just wanna be… be with you." I almost said *home* with you, and I'm glad I caught myself. I know where I want this to go, but I need to give Kiara breathing space. She's figuring out her life, and I don't want to put pressure on her, one way or the other.

CHAPTER FORTY-THREE

Colton

I was not prepared for the number of details that need tended to for Laskin, but here we are three weeks later and everything is in place.

Cassandra oversees the timing of the various events, Nathaniel is directing people to where they need to be, and Owen reviewed all the participants' insurance and permits. That's thirty-five groups for the horse parade alone, forty-some merchants on the Christmas market, two a cappella groups, and three theater groups.

The King brothers helped the fire department hang the lights all around The Green and on the streets under the supervision of a decorator in town, and all the shops are decked out in their holiday best.

But best of all? Kiara is off hot chocolate stand duty, and we get to stroll around and mingle without a care.

"How did you manage to get Willow to take your place?" I ask her as we leave the waffle and hot chocolate hut, decorated like a gingerbread house.

Kiara shrugs. "Good ol'fashion way. I paid her." Then she sniffs nervously. "She's going through stuff right now, and she needs the money. It made me sad to see how happy she was to have that extra little coming in."

I frown, wondering what's up with Willow, but right now I just want to enjoy some carefree fun with my woman.

"Autumn!" she says, gushing over one of our friends. "The decor is awesome. That gingerbread house? And the tunnel of lights all around The Green? It's so dreamy. You're a real artist."

"Wait until you see the tree!" Autumn says as she takes her phone out. "Oops! Gotta go fix an angel's wing at the church. Have fun!"

The Christmas market occupies one side of The Green, with the other side being the ice-skating rink, the gingerbread house sitting in the middle.

"Where d'you want to go?"

"Let's walk through the market," Kiara answers. "The parade is starting soon, I don't want to miss it."

Kiara buys stuff at several booths, and it's amazing to me how that makes her happy. Then she gets restless and we haul it to Chris's bakery. "They have the best view on The Green," Kiara informs me as if I didn't already know. She pulls my hand up their steps. "See?" she says, turning around on their porch.

"Sweets, I'm not freezing my ass out here. We're gonna go inside."

"No we're not. I want to hear the bells and the '*Merry Christmases*' and even smell the poop. It's part of the experience."

"Alright, well, lemme go back and get us some hot chocolate. I'll be just a minute."

When I come back with a whole tray of steaming mugs, Kiara is surrounded by Alex, Chris, Skye, Isaac—an apprentice whose mom works at my sister's spa—and a couple of other people who work at the bakery. I hand out the hot chocolates, noticing that Kiara looks uneasy. "What's wrong?" I ask her.

"I'll tell you later," she answers right as Cassandra announces on the loudspeaker that the King Knoll Farm is opening the parade. We all turn our heads to the left, Chris hoists Skye on his shoulders, and we clap and holler as Craig and Lynn appear all decked in red and black plaid, Sunshine and three other horses pulling a long carriage full of people.

"Graaaaace!" Skye shrieks, making us all jump. My sister waves frantically at us from the carriage, her happiness so contagious my heart swells. Seeing her on her fiancé's family's carriage makes me so fucking happy for her. Next to her, Chloe grasps her husband's hand. Justin and Ethan are the first two of the five King siblings to be engaged or married. Hunter, Logan, and Haley are on the carriage as well, huddled among the farm employees.

"How long do you think until that carriage is full of spouses and kids?" Chris asks to no one in particular.

"Daddy, we should get our own carriage!" Skye exclaims.

"Sure, sweetheart. Soon as you can take care of the horses."

"Watch out, she might take you up on that," Alex says.

"How will you see the parade if you're in it?" Kiara asks.

Skye stays silent, then says, "I think I'd rather watch the parade."

Chris pokes me. "She's got the kid thing all figured out, in case you were wondering."

"Oh my god," Kiara says with true horror laced with laughter in her voice right as Louise appears in the horse line up, mounting a black horse, and wearing a long black dress. She looks straight ahead, her mouth a thin line.

"Daddy, she's scary."

"I think she got the wrong holiday," Kiara says.

"We should totally do a Halloween parade," Chris says.

"Just her would be enough. Walking around town all night," Alex adds.

Thankfully, the Hendersons come next. Their ponies are all decked in glittering red and white with a bunch of bells, and the Henderson family is dressed as elves, waving and cheering to the crowd. Right after them comes the high school band playing Christmas music, then several other equally festive groups.

Our hot chocolates are long finished by the time the parade wraps up. Chris and Alex invite us inside to warm up with some wassail until night sets in and it's time for the Christmas tree lighting, then hearthsong in front of the church.

It seems the whole town is gathered there. Kiara nudges herself against me, and I wrap her under my arm as we start singing under the guidance of Luke, holding up little lanterns and swaying softly to the familiar tunes. Sophie hands out lyric sheets, and Kiara holds one for the two of us.

Between "Silent Night" and "Jingle Bells," my gaze is pulled toward two people I did not expect to see here, and don't want ruining the day.

Kiara is reading the lyrics, and she doesn't budge when I kiss her temple. "Be right back," I say.

I intercept Maya and David right as they spot Kiara and are making a beeline for her. "What's up?" I say, positioning myself squarely in front of them.

"I need to talk to my sister," Maya snaps, trying to circle around me.

The crowd makes it easy for me to block her. "'Bout what?"

"None of your business."

"Kiara's business is my business," I say, looking between Maya and David.

"Something happened," David says. "She should know about it."

I shrug. "Why don't you call her?"

"She won't pick up."

I grunt and look back where Kiara is, catching glimpses of her in between the other carolers. Happiness radiates from her as she joins in "Holy Night."

It's traditionally one of the last carols, if I remember correctly. After that, we'll light the massive bonfire and drink spiked wassail. It's my first time being with Kiara like this for Laskin, and I want her by my side when I look through the dancing flames and reflect on the past year. Heck, will she even be here next year? While she'll always be in my heart, I'm lucid enough to know she might be living across the globe next December, if that's what she wants. This moment is for us, and I won't let anything ruin it.

"Meet us at Lazy's in an hour. It's the pub right there," I say, pointing down and across the Green.

CHAPTER FORTY-FOUR

Kiara

Colton wraps me back under his arm and squeezes me tight, then kisses the top of my hat. "You okay?" I ask him. He was pulled out from the hearthsong a few minutes ago, but thankfully he's here for the bonfire.

"I'm good," he says, but I can tell he's tense.

The youngest firefighter volunteer lights up the fire, and soon we're stepping back a few feet under the heat. Faces glow in the warm light and shadows stretch on the church's white facade. This might be my favorite part of Laskin, when the daylight festivities definitely come to a close, people fighting the cold and darkness with fire and community. This year, I won't be going alone to my cold apartment after all this is over.

I nestle deeper in Colton's strong embrace.

"Beer at Lazy's?" I ask him. "Or soup. Or both."

He takes a deep breath. "In a bit, sweets. No rush."

"'Course," I answer him.

He looks a little worried, or maybe just pensive. "You okay there?" I ask him.

He squeezes my shoulder. "You heard from your family lately?"

I shrug. "Nope." Though Maya tried to call me at the most inconvenient times. Once when I was reading a book, and the other when I was staring into nothingness, trying to visualize my future after working on my business plan.

"Your sister wants to see you."

I look up to ask him how he knows, but instead say, "She's gonna have to wait. I'm not in the mood."

He kisses me again and turns us toward Lazy's. "Well, she's waiting for you at Lazy's, so why don't we get this out of the way, uh?"

My feet stop working. "She *what*?"

He prompts me forward. "It's not a big deal. Hear what she has to say and then move on from it."

I take a deep breath.

I should have answered that fucking phone.

They're both there, Maya and David, next to each other in a booth. We slide in front of them. They don't bother with hello.

"Hey," I say, vaguely worried that she felt the need to come all the way here. It can't be that something happened to Nana—Uncle Bill would have called. Or Mom, for that matter. What could she possibly want with me? "What's up?"

"He died last week," she says, her eyes brimming, reproach clearly on the tip of her tongue.

I lift my eyebrows at her. "Okay." I'm going to assume we're talking about our father.

She turns to David and with a smirk, says, "I told you."

He rounds her shoulders with his arm and gives her a quick squeeze.

"Are you happy?" she asks me, defiance and incredulity in her voice. Back then, it was "Are you *happy now*?" Like I'd been the one to betray my whole family. Now, she's looking at me like she doesn't know me at all. At least we're on the same page.

"Are you?" she repeats when I don't answer.

The past hits me with full force and I feel my eyes tingling. Not at the fact that my father is dead. No. But at the way he could turn his back on us and never see us again. Ever. A wife, two children. Nothing. We meant nothing to him then. We meant nothing to him our whole lives.

"We were nothing to him, Maya." I return her stare, my jaw hurting from clenching it so hard. I barely register the warmth on my side as Colton slides closer to me, then wraps his arm around my shoulders.

Maya's cold rage drips with contempt. She turns to David. "See? I told you. Effing heart of stone."

I shiver.

"Hey," Colton's deep voice interrupts her. "Tone it down, will ya."

"I'm not talking to you," she snaps back loud enough for the din of the pub to go down several notches as people take notice.

I feel Colt rear back, but he stays quiet. I've never seen him get into an argument. He won't start one here, at Lazy's. He just growls softly while rubbing my shoulder, tugging me closer into him. "You're talking to your sister, and that's no way to talk to her," he answers softly. "If I'm not mistaken, she's the only one you got. Whole lotta sweet you're missin' out on, too. Whatever's going on between you two—"

"I said, I'm not talking to you," she yells, her eyes still locked on mine.

Our booth is darkened by Justin leaning over. "Ma'am," he says under his breath, then turns his gaze to David. "Outta here. Now."

David hesitates for a beat. Then he tugs on Maya.

Justin moves just enough to let them come through, his gaze following them until they exit Lazy's, then looks at us, frowning. With a sigh, he sits in front of us, occupying the whole booth with his arms spread across on both sides.

Then he clicks his tongue and picks at a slip of paper on the table. "Looks like they stuck you with their tab." He smiles real big and looks at Colton. "In-laws, man. Get used to it."

I snap the tab from him and push on Colton to let me go through. "What d'you think you're doing, sweetness?" he says, not budging an inch.

"Teaching her a lesson," I answer in gritted teeth.

"She's not worth it."

"I was kidding, Kiara," Justin says. "Tab's on me. What are you guys having?"

"You wanna stay here?" Colton asks with so much softness I wonder if I look sick or something. I don't *feel* sick. "Or you wanna go home. You wanna call Eloise?" *Why is he...?*

Then the realization of why he's being so careful around me hits me, and so does the piece of news. My chin wobbles, my eyes sting.

The definiteness of it all. There's no fixing things now. No mending bridges. No breaking walls. No one to forgive.

My father's dead, and my hatred for him doesn't even protect me from the immense pain I feel. Feeling my face contort in an awful grimace, I bury it in Colton's chest.

"Let it out," he murmurs softly, rubbing my back as silent sobs shake me. "Let it out," he repeats. I keep my sobs quiet, and from the shield of his hug, overhear him saying, "Her dad just passed away," and some muffled explanations. Then, "There... there. That's it... better?" he whispers as my breathing evens and my soul calms down.

"You have a tissue?" he asks, and a feminine voice answers, "here."

I lift my face from Colton's protective shield and grab the tissue Willow is handing me, blow my nose, grab the second tissue she's holding out, dab my eyes, and put my brave little face on while I tuck the rolled tissues in my pocket. "Okay," I breathe. "Sorry 'bout that."

"Sorry?!" Colton, Willow, and Justin say.

"Pff, honey," Willow says, taking my hand, "you just lost—"

I raise a hand between us. "I don't want to talk about it. Guys, sorry, really. I need-I need..." I don't know what I need right now. I know for sure I don't want my friends' pity. I feel a million feelings—guilt, and anger, and the feeling that life is way too short.

Coming out of nowhere, Shane, Justin's chef, sets a charcuterie board in the middle of the table. "Here," he says. "Eat."

"I'm really not hungry right now, but thanks. You guys go ahead."

Shane puts his hands on his hips, tilts his head like a puppy, and says, "The cuts are from the Henderson farm, the cheddar and butter from the King's farm, and the baguette is obviously from Chris's bakery, but it's also this afternoon's bake, still warm from the oven. It's guaranteed to feed your soul. You know it will."

While he was talking, Colton buttered the bread and topped it with prosciutto. The way he hands it to me now, mimicking the puppy look, I can't say no. Lifting my gaze, I take in Willow on the other side of the booth. She ducks under the table to sit next to me, silently pressing her head against my shoulder in support as I chew the food, fighting the feeling of cardboard in my mouth. I swallow with difficulty.

Grace slides in front of me, followed by Ethan. "Get her something to drink, please, honey," she asks Haley who's standing at the top of the table, looking helpless. "Wine." Then, to me, she says, "We're so sorry. We came as soon as we heard."

Alex appears, her hair dotted with white flakes.

"Is it snowing?" I ask her. I need to talk, to make things normal again, but my voice comes out funny.

She sits quietly next to Ethan and throws her coat over the partition, then reaches across the table to take my hand. "It's snowing, and it's beautiful out. Just like you like it."

Dad hated the snow and the cold, yet one of my best memories with him was a snowball fight in the backyard of our split ranch when I was a kid. Colton takes my coat off, then his, and passes them to Ethan to throw overboard to the next booth. Everyone's else's coat follows, and while we slide closer to each other to make space for more people joining us (all of Grace's team at the salon, Sophie, Ms. Angela, Cassandra, Lynn and Craig, Dennis and Shannon), Chris and Noah drag another table next to ours.

We pass down glasses, plates, and cutlery while bottles of wine appear on the table, followed by more food.

"Let's share a soup," Colton says, plopping two spoons in a small bowl between us.

"Is that the potato-cheddar-ale soup?" Willow asks.

"It sure tastes like it," Colton answers. "Here," he says, sliding a bowl her way.

"Hand me the little thingys there, will ya," Ethan says.

"They're bacon-wrapped figs stuffed with chèvre," Haley informs her brother.

"That works, although I was talking about that," he says, pointing further.

Chris reaches over Alex to place a whole serving platter of meatballs in front of him. I watch as he doesn't realize this is the shareable portion and digs directly in it.

Grace looks at me with amusement, her eyebrow going up, then lifts one shoulder. We share a brief moment when that instant is infinitely more important than my overarching grief. Then Colton thanks Ethan for overseeing all the ice-skating activities during the day and the kid competition, and *that* instant then becomes the most important. Conversations grow and laughter ripples through the table, then someone seems to remember why we're here and silence falls again, gazes turning to me.

I don't want this, for them or for me. I take my glass and lift it toward the end of the table. "Special toast to Autumn, who did a magnificent job with the decor this year. You really turned this place into a Christmas wonderland. Thank you."

She places her hand on her heart to thank me in return, her smile tentative.

I feel the need to say something to all of them. To acknowledge why they came and thank them for it—yet that's not how I feel exactly, or what I want to say. "You guys are my life, and you make life here magical." I blink the tears away. "Life is made of a succession of tiny little moments. How and with who you spend these tiny moments is what matters." I shut up for a second, trying to gather my thoughts, to say something thoughtful that encapsulates what I'm feeling. "Shit, guys, I don't know how to say this. I'm feeling really big things right now that should come out as, like, this grand speech, but that's all I got. I love you." My chin wobbles as I say the last words, and as a chorus of "we love you too" sounds through the bar, Colton rocks me in his arms, kissing the top of my head.

As the evening progresses, more friends join, more food appears, more wine is poured. Even Annabel Plum, who was here to enjoy Laskin, finds her way to our table.

Before long, someone takes out the karaoke machine, and questionable songs are sung by tone deaf people.

It turns into one of the best evenings of my life.

CHAPTER FORTY-FIVE

Kiara

When we leave, most everyone is still there, singing the night away. But we've been up since dawn, and honestly? I need to be naked in Colton's arms to make the world go round again.

He catches my shiver as he starts his truck and takes his coat off to wrap me in it. Won't listen to my feeble protests. "You're exhausted," is his answer. He cranks the heat up. "Shoulda started the truck earlier," he mumbles.

I close my eyes and let the rocking of the engine lull me. Taking a deep breath, I try to talk myself out of rehashing the confusing feelings of my father's death by reliving the day's events. It was, by all accounts, one of the best Laskins we've had. Clear skies, no snafus that I could notice. A beautiful parade. Something I've been meaning to tell Colton but never found the right time for resurfaces. "I think I know who the egg bomber is."

He glances at me. "Really?"

I nod. "While we were at the bakery, looking from their front steps, I saw Isaac's sister leave through the delivery entrance."

"Chris's apprentice? The one whose father got in trouble last spring?"

"Yeah, I think his father's in jail now. I'm sure it was his sister. I recognized her coat—it has a tear on the back. That and how she walks."

"That's not a lot to go by."

I know it was her. She recognized me too. The way she looked at me when our eyes locked? There was fear in her gaze. "Doesn't matter. It's not like I'm going to turn her in."

"I guess," he grunts. "Dec might wanna know, though. He seemed—What the..." he interrupts himself, taking his foot off the gas.

Ahead of us, slowly crossing the road, is a cow. A big cow. The size of Daisy. Except this one is...

Purple.

Colton brings his truck to a slow stop so we don't skid.

"Oh—fuck. Is that *Daisy*?"

The truck merely six feet from Daisy, Colton takes his phone out and snaps a picture. "Sure looks like it," he mutters. His phone wooshes with the sound of a text going out.

Daisy is staring at us, nostrils billowing with plumes of her angry exhales. "Isn't it kinda cold for her?" I ask.

Colton's phone rings. "It's Dec. Can you call the farm?"

He means King Knoll Farm, where Daisy lives. Where she constantly escapes from. Where she's driving the whole King family crazy since, apparently, she found out she was not a Jersey like their other cows, and that her breed—Angus—was raised for meat. "Hey, Lynn," I say, talking over Colton's discussion with Declan.

"Honey, what's wrong? Did you need to talk more? I'm sorry we left already, we were bone tired—"

"Thank you, Lynn, but that's not why I'm calling. I-we came upon Daisy—"

"Again?" Lynn interrupts me, sighing. Clearly she's gotten used to her now-pet cow's escapes, if this is no longer a topic of panic like it used to be. Granted, there aren't many flowers to graze on in December.

"Y-yeah. She's on Spruce, you know where it dips before the big oak tree?"

"Oh dear," she sighs. "Boys!" Her holler is muffled by her hand on the phone, but loud enough that I can hear it. Then her voice comes back clearer as she has me confirm the location, relaying it, I assume, to her two younger sons, Hunter and Logan. "They're on their way. Are you with Colton? Shannon just heard from Ms. Angela that he called it in. You're with him, right?"

"Yeah, he was-we were driving home."

"Oh good, good. Welp, the boys are out, should be down there in a little bit. Call me if you need anything!"

We spend the next ten or fifteen minutes daunted by the vision of Daisy, eerily detached against the white backdrop, her purple paint turning dirty as the falling snow melts it away, her eyes glinting in our headlights.

Headlights come from behind us, right as a snowmobile and a horse come down the hill. The car behind us stops, and so does the snowmobile, shutting its engine off. Only the horse and her rider walk toward Daisy.

A knock on Colton's window startles us. Declan is scowling at us. Colton opens his window. "Hey, Dec."

Declan clears his throat. "How did this happen?"

"She's been here the whole time. Staring at us."

"Tell me you didn't do this."

"Do what?"

"Paint her purple."

"Seriously?"

"I have to ask."

"Do you really?"

"The two of you are always where trouble happens. Always the only ones to see it hap—"

Leaning over Colton, I try to interrupt Declan. "We didn't see it happen."

Declan ignores me. "—and the ones to report it. No one there to corroborate the facts."

Colton waves between us. "We corroborate each other."

Declan leans on Colton's door to look inside the car. "Is that what they call it now?" he jokes, then squints. "Sorry, guys, that was out of line." He unfolds out of our space, straightens, and takes long strides toward Daisy, his voice coming to us in a low, even tone.

"What is he doing?" I whisper.

"He's talking to her." Colton chuckles. "Fuck. The life of a small-town cop."

By then Lynn's two sons are with Daisy, and the one on the horse (I can't tell who is who) has her roped in. Declan seems to be stroking her.

"Is he..." Colton says.

"...collecting evidence?"

Declan turns around, fussing with a ziplock as he gets back to us while Daisy follows the horse without an issue.

"I might have you come by the station for questioning," Declan tells us sternly, then continues onto his patrol car.

"Seriously," Colton mutters as he drives us back to Sunrise Farms.

"Can we sleep at your place tonight?"

He folds my hand in his. "Sweets, you don't need to ask. That's what you want, that's what we do."

He pulls me up the staircase to his apartment, unlocks his door, and throws his keys on his kitchen counter. I'm a little numb from tonight's events, but being in Colton's apartment stirs something primal inside me. A few dried coffee grounds on the kitchen counter, a rumpled throw on the couch, the TV remote on the floor—all this always felt familiar to me. Now it feels more. It feels like home.

Later, after he's made gentle love to me in his bed, his fingers roaming up and down my bare back, he says, "I got two random questions and you don't need to answer either. How long we gonna keep two apartments, and should I just pretend you never told me anything about Isaac's sister?"

I snuggle deeper in his embrace. "I never told you anything about Isaac's sister," I say, and fall asleep.

CHAPTER FORTY-SIX

Kiara

W e're having coffee at his kitchen counter the next morning, and his question still haunts me. But if he's still thinking about it, he doesn't show it.

I can't quite articulate why the idea of moving in with Colton terrorizes me. I'm torn between wanting this so bad it hurts, and feeling like the day we share a set of keys will set in motion the beginning of the end. Nothing can possibly be better than the state we're in right now. If we mesh our lives deeper together, the untangling might hurt too much to bear.

I'm lost in these thoughts when my phone rings. *Mom*. Any other day, I would let it go to voicemail. But not this time.

Her voice has lost the bite that's always been there since I exposed Dad. "Now that he's gone, I feel I can tell you," she says, after I ask her how she's doing. I know she never got over him, her resentment over what I did proof of that.

"Tell me what?" *Isn't it bad enough that we were his second family?*

Colton stops fussing over eggs to sit next to me.

"As long as you keep it to yourself," she adds.

Really? This family has an obsession with secrets. I'm not promising to keep anything to myself. For one, I'm sharing everything with Colton. That thought fills me with more confidence than I've had in a long time. I don't even feel rattled that there's more that's been kept from me. There's a sort of distance between me and my blood family that doesn't pain me anymore.

"The reason your dad disappeared from our lives," Mom says when I stay silent.

"Okay?"

"He... he was married to... he had married into..." She's so quiet I wonder if the call dropped.

"Hello?"

"Into a family that dealt in organized crime."

I look at Colton. "Dad was in the *Mafia*?!"

"Shhh. Kiara!" Mom says.

"Was he?"

"His *wife*," she says with spite, "she was what you would call..." she whispers, "a *Mafia princess*." She breathes audibly. "Her father had financed your daddy's car dealership, and he was tied to them in ways he couldn't tell. Ours was supposed to be just an affair—I for sure didn't know he was married. When I was pregnant, he came clean to me. He loved me, I know he loved me. He cried. But he stayed with me as best he could, helped raise you two. He managed to keep this hidden from them. But there was no way he could ever leave her. That would have been our death sentence, you understand? Literal death."

My father's two-timing suddenly takes another dimension. "Did he... was I the reason he disappeared? After..." *After I exposed him.*

It's almost like I can feel the weight of the silence between us.

"Daddy was scared it might... it might get out. We were pretty private, obviously. Careful never to be seen in public. You never know. But he said you were hysterical, in Burlington. Yelling all sorts of things. Last thing he needed was the police involved, or anybody who might recognize him. He felt it was safer to just disappear."

Was it safer, or was it the easy way out? Somehow this version of my father, this supposed explanation, doesn't make it better for me. "How did he die?"

"Honey, I... we... there's no way we can know or should dig into that." Her voice is stranded—no—*scared*. She's totally telling the truth, and a small shiver runs down my spine.

I'm not sure what to say, or even think—or feel, for that matter. It's a lot to process when I'm still coming to terms with his death. Colton covers my free hand with his and strokes it. "Okay," I say softly.

"Okay," she whispers. "I'll let you go."

Colton gives my hand a soft squeeze.

"Mom? Thanks for calling."

We hang up without saying goodbye, much less *I love you*. It's too early for that, and frankly, it might never come. And that's okay.

"You alright, sweets?" Colton asks. His facial expression tells me he heard the whole conversion.

I shake my head in disbelief. "I guess?" My voice is strained, my throat constricted.

He stands, starts on the eggs again, and pours me a hot coffee. "This calls for breakfast."

"Does it?"

"Absolutely. Need to take care of you."

Emotion overcomes me, and I round the kitchen island to wrap my arms around him. "Thank you," I whisper.

He turns the range off to return my hug. "For what, sweets?" he whispers.

"For being you."

"Mm," he grunts.

Our mouths find each other, he reaches under my tee, and somehow, I find my legs wrapped around his hips.

"I love you," I say from the depth of my soul. It's never been so clear.

He tightens his embrace and answers, "I love you too."

I smile against his mouth. "No but I think I love you more."

"That's impossible," he growls, nibbling on my lower lip.

I wiggle against his midsection, trying to satisfy the fire in my center. "Not for me it's not."

He takes us to the couch, sets me flat on my back, gets us naked, then flips us so I'm on top of him. "Show me how you love me, sweets." He tightens his grasp on my hips and his breathing becomes labored. There's a mix of possessiveness and expectation in his gaze that's easy to get addicted to. I suspect he's doing this to get my mind off the shit I just heard, and he's spot on. I'd do anything he asks, just so he looks at me this way. He's all that counts right now, and the more that happens, the more my perspective on life in general shifts.

I dip my face to his neck, kiss his stubble, lick my way down his chest, kiss his happy trail, then take his cock in my mouth, settling between his legs. He groans, his hands on my head featherweight. "Like that?" I ask him. Colt has made me feel so comfortable about what I don't know that I have zero inhibitions and no self-consciousness about asking how I'm doing.

He growls and hisses. I guess I'm doing well. If I'm being honest, the ridges of his cock against my tongue, the saltiness of his tip, the strength and softness of it all, is making me so wet and needy I start moaning with my mouth full.

He hisses again, fisting my hair. "Hell, baby, ride me. *Ride me.*" He pulls me up and I take him inside me, lifting up and down, his hooded eyelids as much a turn-on as the length that fills me. He strokes my breasts. "You're just so perfect, you know that?" he whispers. I set a rhythm for us, getting worked up, but then he holds me still. "Reverse cowgirl now. Show me that ass."

I turn around and take him back in, the position doing all sorts of new things to me. As I look over my shoulder to watch him watching me, it's the absolute best. He's coming into his orgasm, and I get to watch it for a second or two, until I give into my own pleasure and come, gripping the side of the couch.

"You're so fucking beautiful, babe," he says once I'm settled on his chest, spent. "I'm gonna put mirrors everywhere in our bedroom so you can watch yourself come on my cock. I promise you it's the best."

I stay silent for a bit, waiting for him to ask me again about moving in together, but he doesn't.

"I know you got a lot on your mind right now, sweets," he says, stroking my hair. "I shouldn't have asked about moving in together last night. It wasn't the right time, and it doesn't really matter."

Another stretch of silence and he adds, "I'll love you wherever you are." I know he's not only talking about the apartment situation here in Emerald Creek. He's thinking about me going to Paris, even if, as days go by, I'm more and more hopeful I can make it work here in Emerald Creek.

The reality is that in the days that follow, I come to understand why I never felt like I belonged anywhere. Dad's betrayal cut deep, and I'm still trying to come to terms with it. I'm trying to not feel as if my whole life was built on a lie.

I see now why Colton was upset when I told him Emerald Creek was holding me back.

It wasn't.

I was the one holding myself back, for reasons that are fast dissolving. After growing up all but idolizing him, believing the only reason he was "traveling" so much was to "make a better life for us" (Mom's favorite lie), I thought he'd coldly turned his back on us.

The truth, as always, is way more complex. He had to leave to protect us. Even some of the horrible things my mother said to me at the time are beginning to make sense. When it comes down to it, my exposing my father was what ruined the fragile family life we had. I don't regret what I did, but I can see where she was coming from. One day maybe, I'll think through the sacrifice she had to make and begin to forgive her.

But now, I'm focusing on building the life I want for me. The life that's so totally within my reach I can taste it. Starting with my business, in the cute little barn. Surely, I'll get the variance. Surely, my business will thrive once I'm there.

Surely, once that's secured, I'll feel more comfortable moving in with Colton. There's something about my own permanence that I need to figure out for myself first.

CHAPTER FORTY-SEVEN

Kiara

The hearing for the variance is tonight. Colton made sure my application was airtight. Maddie said it would be a simple formality.

Tonight, a new chapter opens for me. I'm so happy I can hardly wait.

Even the email I received informing me I was accepted into the Parisian school doesn't faze me. Funny how weeks ago, I believed this to be my lifeline and low-key obsessed over it. Now I hardly care—it's just a nice ego-boost. The barn is the solution to all my problems.

Late that afternoon, Emma and I meet at Easy Monday's. "I need a little positive reinforcement before the hearing," I'd said as an emotional bribe to meet me for tea. We each order a chai and get comfortable in the upholstered chairs around a large cherry table, watching the place empty as the sun sets.

"You guys are on your own," Millie says, turning the main lights off and leaving only our corner of the café lit.

"This feels very conspiratorial," Emma says, licking foam off her upper lip.

"Thanks, Millie!" we both say as our friend leaves.

"I brought this for you," Emma says, shifting through a stack of paper. "Thought it might cheer you up to have it all in print." She points a manicured finger down a column of numbers.

I lean over and literally squint at the nice fat figures she's pointing at. "We're sure, right?"

She crosses her arms and looks at me with a satisfied smile. "If your numbers are accurate, yes. And they are."

They *are*. We've been through this over and over and over. I know how to calculate cost and profit. I just didn't trust myself. I thought something had to be off. There was no way I was so close to making it. No way. And yet here it is. Proof.

If I were that kind of person, I would kiss Emma right now for giving me the validation.

Uncrossing her arms, she stacks her papers. "How is Colton feeling about the variance?" she asks, then takes a sip of her chai.

"I'm not sure," I admit. "He insisted on checking it before I filed it, but he hasn't said anything."

"That's the place down Dewey's Hollow, right?" she asks, her gaze roaming back to the rows of numbers in front of her.

I nod. "A little before. Walking distance from town, except there's no sidewalk."

Her turn to nod, but with doubt in her expression. I'm not too crazy about the no-sidewalk situation either. "There's space for parking. Easy for picking up orders."

"What's the variance you're applying for again?"

"Maddie said something about accessory to agriculture."

Emma frowns. "Really? Even though you're not the farmer?"

I pick at my fingernails. "Maddie said it was just a formality."

Emma's gaze bores into mine. "I'm sure she did. D'you sign the lease yet?"

I raise my index finger, proud of myself. "Nope. I did not. I added obtaining the variance as a condition. No variance, no lease."

Emma seems to breathe out a bit. But only a bit.

Shit. "You're scaring me, Ems."

Her eyebrows do a funny thing. One up, one down. "I mean, the board pushed back on everything this year."

"What do you mean, everything?"

"They're pretty protective of their zoning. They're saying that there's enough commercial and mixed-use space for businesses to do what businesses must do where they're supposed to do it. The rest should stay the way it is. Agricultural stays farmland. Residential stays houses. No businesses." She nods, like she needs to let it sink in.

Fuck. *Fuckfuckfuck! And barely a few weeks into his role, Colton's girlfriend comes and asks for a variance.* Shit.

"Look, they probably won't make a decision tonight. You'll present your case. Make sure you tell them you do not plan on serving on-site. Listen to their objections—there will be many. Just play nice. Owen will probably argue in your favor—he's always pro variances, he would turn this whole town into a strip mall if he could. Colton will stay quiet—he doesn't like to make waves. Lynn will ask a couple of questions. And Cassandra will move to deciding on this at the next meeting."

I take a deep breath. "I hate this. Maddie said it was a formality, but I should have known better." I hate myself right now. "I'm sure Colton just didn't want to freak me out."

"I'll come with you," Emma says, shoving her spreadsheets in her briefcase. "Worst case, I'll just hold your hand. Or we can eat, seeing as we'll be early."

We throw our cups in the recycling bin, turn off the lights, and are about to lock ourselves out of Easy Monday's when a female voice sounds, coming from outside.

"Were you about to leave?" Willow is on snowshoes, taking long strides on top of the thick snow.

"Hey!" I greet her. "What are you doing?"

"I needed to think shit through, but now I just need to chill and be with friends." As she gets closer to us, her face falls. "You were leaving."

"Actually, we were going back in, making ourselves another tea," Emma says, opening the door wider for her.

"What's going on?" Willow asks as she steps out of her snowshoes and leaves her boots at the entrance.

Less than ten minutes later, we're back at our table in the corner, huddled around our teas, filling Willow in on my latest source of anxiety. "Who knows, Colt might fix it," she says. "He worships the ground you walk on, for real. You should have seen him sweating bullets when I told him you were on a dating app!"

Emma's laughter is interrupted by a grimace.

"Everything okay?"

Emma sits up, stretching, and her hand goes to her lower back. "Yeah, just back pain."

"You need a painkiller?" I ask, going for my small backpack.

"It doesn't do anything."

"CBD?" Willow suggests.

"Tried that too."

Willow pushes her chair out. "Ooooh. I know what you need. Gimme a twenty," she says, wiggling her fingers at Emma.

"What for? I'm not giving you twenty bucks."

Willow rolls her eyes but still leaves the table. "You'll pay me back when you feel better!" she says, her voice dimming as she disappears behind Millie's counter. After a minute or so, she comes back, holding...

"Is that a joint?" Emma shrieks. "Are you—did you steal that from 420?"

"Jesus, Ems. You really need to relax. Hence..." she trails, putting the rolled weed joint under Emma's nose.

Emma makes a face. "What are you—fifteen?" she asks Willow, scooting her chair away from her.

Willow makes an appreciative face. "Fifteen, huh? That's the memory this brings? Who would have known prim and proper Emma was a stoner back in the day." She laughs loudly at her observation.

"Anybody have a light?" she asks, looking at us. "C'mon. Let's go outside and get high. You comin'?" she asks me.

I shake my head. "I don't think the Select Board would see my request favorably if I showed up high, to be honest."

Emma raises her eyebrows so high again, it makes me wonder what facial expression she'll have at her disposal if she ever decides to do Botox. "You'd be surprised," she says.

"You hear that, boss?" Willow says. "Come on."

Yeah, no. "Next time," I say.

"You're no fun," Willow says. "Did she tell you about Sexy Voice?" she asks Emma.

"Nope. Who's that?"

Willow fills Emma in on her scheming to get me to date Colton, and how Colton had to find someone whose voice I wouldn't recognize for our phone call.

"You guys are too much," Emma laughs.

"Apparently he's some celebrity," I say. "Did you know?" I ask Willow.

"Tracy might have said something, but we're not supposed to tell."

"Why not?" Emma asks.

"Colt says the guy came here to get away from some shit. We should leave him be. The last thing he needs is the press finding out where he's hiding."

Emma rolls her eyes. "Great, we have someone in the witness protection program now. Just what we needed."

"Who said he was a criminal?" Willow exclaims.

"Where's the criminal?" a loud whisper sounds from the confines of the café. We all jump and shriek. "Sshhh," the voice says.

"Who the hell is it?" I growl, stomping toward where the voice is.

"Holy hell, Kiara, I'm trying to catch a criminal here!" Millie says out loud, coming out of the shadows.

"What criminal?" Emma, Willow, and I ask together.

Millie rolls her eyes. "You were just talking about him. He broke into 420! Must be the egg bomber." Holding a baseball bat, she crouches and goes toward the door separating her café from her weed store.

"Wait! Were you there all along?" Willow asks.

"Got an alarm on my phone. I was on my way to the Select Board meeting. Few minutes ago, someone was inside 420."

"Oh no—that was me. I broke in—well, didn't break anything. I just let myself into the weed store because we had an emergency. Emma had a physical emergency and I had a mental emergency. I left you twenty dollars in ones stuck under the register."

"Oh good." Millie sighs. "I was on edge. I could use a smoke too." She laughs.

"Why were you going to the meeting tonight?" I ask her.

"No particular reason. Just being a good citizen."

I shrug. "Why don't you just stay with these two, then?"

"Excellent idea. Except I'm getting us gummies, so we can stay inside. You'll drive us home, grasshopper?" Millie asks. "Or should I say, sweets?"

I smile at her. "I'll come back to drive you guys home. Wish me luck."

"What's up with her?" I hear Millie ask as I get to the door.

"Eh, it's about to get real for her," I hear Emma reply as the door shuts softly behind me, leaving me alone in the dark, lit by the moon reflecting on the snow.

Walking to my car, I have only the sound of my feet crunching the snow to drown my thoughts.

The meeting room fills up as residents file into Town Hall. Cassandra, Lynn, Noah, and Colton are already seated, talking in low voices among themselves. The high school media team has their camera set up, ready to stream the meeting into the homes of residents who are too old or sick to take the short drive into town.

In the back, next to the macarons I dropped off earlier, there is pizza, pies, juice, and hot cider attracting a sizable crowd and giving the whole thing a festive air. Too nervous to eat anything, I take a seat in the front row, next to Maddie, and pick at my cuticles.

A ruffling sounds at the back of the room, voices rise before falling as people take their seats. I don't need to look back to see who just came in. Walking right by me in through the center aisle, Owen takes hurried steps toward the long table where the board sits, clutching a thick file under his arm.

The board members straighten their chairs, and Colton calls the meeting open. As he sweeps his gaze over the audience, his eyes latch onto mine for a beat. A small smile, quickly suppressed, floats on his lips, then he turns his gaze away to remind those in attendance that they should address the board, not each other, when expressing their opinion on any topic.

He does a quick read of the agenda, then Cassandra says, "Why don't we deal with the two variances, so the applicants are free to go if they want to?" She looks at me, and at Georgie Richardson, who's sitting three chairs down from me.

Colton frowns. Looks at Georgie, then at Owen. Looks at me. He brushes his eyebrow with the back of his thumb.

"That'd be the right thing to do," Owen says, looking at Colton.

CHAPTER FORTY-EIGHT

Colton

Owen says under his breath so only I can hear him, "No way in hell is her case going before Georgie's. I don't trust you yet, Harper." In case I was too slow to realize what this is, the asshole clarified it for me. All along, that was his plan. When he came to see me in my office, booking a fake service for his car—I mean, is this guy for real? Where does he think he is? Backroom deals central?—assuring me the town needed a guy like me on the Select Board, someone who'd know when to *do the right thing*?

"I can't believe this shit," I mutter.

Owen can go to hell. I don't need a deal. I'm done trying to keep the peace for some bullshit, petty zoning rules that only make sense to the handful of people who passed them without anyone questioning it.

My beliefs are only valid in a vacuum. I never tried shoving them down someone's throat.

And what's more, I have no problem playing favorites with Kiara.

She *is* my favorite.

My everything.

And she deserves everything.

I'll vote in favor of Kiara's project, and I'll oppose Owen's. And what's more, I'll argue in favor of Kiara's.

"I'd like to make a motion that Colton Harper should recuse himself from the vote," Owen says in his sickly unctuous voice.

Cassandra turns reddish, Lynn finds a spot on her sweater that needs scrubbing, and Noah wipes his glasses.

One of them has to second that, but none speaks up.

I clear my throat. "On what grounds?"

Owen scoffs. "Conflict of interest, obviously."

Kiara stands to speak up, but Owen interrupts her. "Motion has been made, no public comments please."

Seriously.

Looking me straight in the eye, Cassandra says, loud and clear, "I'll second that. There is a conflict of interest," she adds.

Ms. Angela clears her throat, her gaze fixed on the screen on her laptop. "All in favor?"

Three ayes sound.

"Opposed?"

"Nay," Noah says.

I raise my hand. "I'll abstain from the vote, but I'm not gonna abstain from the discussion. Are we gonna have that discussion now?"

"I'll just record that Colton won't be voting," Ms. Angela whispers, careful not to look at anyone in particular.

"Please," Owen says, sitting back in his chair and gesturing to me like he's in charge of the order of things.

"You can go ahead, dear," Ms. Angela says to me as if Owen hadn't said anything.

Kiara stands again. "Can I speak now?" she asks.

"No!" we all answer her.

She gapes at us and sits back down, her gaze drilling into mine. Maddie rolls her eyes. There's a slight gasp in the audience.

"We'll let you know when you can talk," Ms. Angela says kindly to her, and I want to hug her right now for soothing the hurt I see in Kiara's eyes. "For now, it's just the board."

"Colton?" Lynn says softly, prompting me to talk.

"Kiara has been a part of our community for about seven years now. Part of the Emerald Creek family. During these seven years, she's worked tirelessly at various establishments, helping them grow their businesses. She could have left for more prestigious jobs, but she stayed here, putting our community before her own ambitions. She donates most of the desserts for the community dinners. She's volunteering to train the kitchen staff at the Silver House, selflessly giving away her time and knowledge so that the elderly in our town can enjoy the quality meals they deserve. Everyone in this town knows she's also a volunteer club counselor at the high school. And most of you had a cup of hot chocolate poured by Kiara during our Christmas fair. Kiara donated all the proceeds of the hot chocolate—not just her profits, all the money—to the homeless shelter in Prattsville. She may not have been born in Emerald Creek, but she's one of us in spirit. One of the best of us. What you may not know, is that Kiara has gone through a lot of hardships during her life, and that these hardships brought her here. We adopted her and she adopted us. We have a debt to her. We owe it to her, because of the trust she put into us, to lend a hand now that she needs it. To give back what she so selflessly gave to our community.

"Is it too much to ask to make an exception to a rule so that an exceptional young woman, who sets such a great example to our youth, can finally find the success she deserves by operating out of her own space?"

I fucking hate to talk, and there's a reason to that. I'm not good at it. I can barely say what I really mean.

Ms. Angela finishes typing on her laptop, a thin smile playing on her face. She lifts her gaze to me and winks, then looks around the table to see if anyone else has something to add.

Owen clears his throat. "Yeah, that's not really grounds for a variance, Colton. I mean that was moving and all—goes to show you were right to recuse yourself from the vote—but, what's in it for the community?"

I shake my head. Did he even listen to me? "Doing the right thing," I answer him. "Keeping a gem in town."

"A gem?" He snorts.

I swear, this guy always makes me want to punch him. It's like he's asking for it.

"Alright, alright, boys," Lynn cuts in before I can answer. "I think we got it. Cassandra? Did you want to add something?"

Cassandra looks at each one of us in turn. "As much as I love Kiara, her confections, her ethics, her creativity... there has to be a better way for her to find her place than by asking us to bend the rules. The zoning is here to protect the natural beauty of our environment. The purpose of the land. I'm not opposed to revisiting our zoning in an organized manner. I'm afraid I can't support variances, except in extremely rare cases."

Lynn addresses Kiara directly. "Have you looked at the Potters' cottage?"

"That's for young families," Owen cuts in.

"And?" I ask him before Kiara has a chance to say anything.

He spreads his hands. "Is there something you forgot to tell us, Harper?"

"Ohmyfuckinggod!"

We all turn to the audience, stunned. We're not prudes, and this isn't church. But an F-bomb during a Select Board meeting? I don't think we've heard one of those since the Airbnb debates.

Kiara is standing, flushed, fists clenched down her sides. "I'm withdrawing my application. No need to get angry or waste everybody's time. I get it. I should look for another place." She stomps to Ms. Angela and extends her hand.

"What, dear?" Ms. Angela asks her.

"I'd like my application back."

"Uh, sure." She shrugs, giving her a file. "That's not really how it works, but... sure."

"Just making sure he doesn't change you guys's minds," Kiara says, pointing at me. "He has a way with words."

Lynn smiles at Kiara. "He does, doesn't he? Never heard him talk for so long, and I was quite impressed."

"Ditto," Cassandra says.

"I have it all written down." Ms. Angela beams. "On the record," she adds with a contented sigh.

"Are we done here?" Owen grunts.

But my eyes are on Kiara as she struts out, her shoulders square, her spine straight, the file tucked under her arm.

Everyone thinks this was cute and shit, but I can almost feel the tears she's holding in choking my own throat.

Fucking hell.

When I see Owen's sister Maddie follow Kiara out, my initial instinct is confirmed.

There's no way Owen didn't set this up, or at least heavily influence his sister into convincing Kiara she could operate a pastry shop in an agricultural zone. What pisses me off, is that he and his sister manipulated Kiara, hoping to get my vote for another project, and I didn't see it coming.

Between the vote on George Richardson's request for a variance (denied), Declan's report on the egg bombing and the painting of Daisy (none of which have any resolution), the events' committee's request for an emergency approval of two hundred dollars' worth of pink balloons for Valentine's Day Festival, it's another hour before I can run out of the meeting and make it to Sunrise Farms.

But Kiara isn't there.

Chapter Forty-Nine

Kiara

I get into my car and slam the door. I need a few minutes to calm down, but when I see Maddie come out of Town Hall, I start the engine and pull from the curb. I don't need to hear her bullshit. I'm not going to blame it on her, although she did tell me getting a variance was just a formality.

Clearly, it's not.

And clearly, being a realtor, she should have known. *She knew.*

I don't care what her reasons are. As upset as I am, I'm not forgetting about my friends, getting high at Mollie's.

Maybe that's what I should have done, I think as I round The Green and come back down toward the river, making a left toward Easy Monday. Let them debate my application without me. At least it would have saved me the public humiliation of Colton singing my praises.

I mean, it was really, really nice. The things he said. I'm ashamed he felt that he needed to support me in such a way. He doesn't need to do all these things for me.

As I pull into Easy Monday, I flash my lights and give it thirty seconds, but no one comes out. The faint light seeping from the sides of the blinds calls to me. I need some girl time.

"Boo!" Willow says as I open the door. She springs from her seat with surprising energy for someone who's had a gummy, and lunges into my arms. "The things he said! That man is so into youuuuu!"

"How d'you know that?" Ms. Angela is still at the meeting. Who else would tell them so quickly?

Willow produces her phone. Since the pandemic, the meetings are live-streamed. With decent wi-fi, you can watch them in real time from home. Although now we're back to needing to come in person to interact.

"I think you need some Bitch Brigade intervention," Emma says, her words a little slurred. "Come here," she adds, tapping the place next to her on the couch.

For the next thirty minutes the girls reenact the scene, what everyone said, how Owen's a dick, how Colton is hot for me, and how badass I was.

Millie thrusts a small pouch of weed gummies my way. "Here, you look like you could use one."

"I'm here to drive you home," I say. "Ohmygod, guys, I feel so... humiliated," I finally confess.

"Um... excuse me?" Willow says.

"One of the hottest bachelors in Emerald Creek pretty much publicly declares how he adores you... and you're humiliated?" Emma croaks. "Fuck that. Hand me another," she tells Millie.

"Dude, you've had enough," I tell her.

She drops her proffered hand with drama. "You're right." Then she straightens in her seat. "Hey, I told you so, right?"

"Told me so what?" I ask her.

"That you wouldn't get the variance. No one ever listens to me in this town," she adds.

"Not in so many words, but yes, you did. Sorta."

"Well, listen to me. Willow is right. That man is into you. Don't let him go."

What happened to putting myself first, and no woman needing a man?

"Forget what I said earlier," she adds, reading my face.

Millie's fanning herself, quiet. "That was hot, girl," she simply says.

"All right, bitches, time to go to bed," I say, standing.

Willow grunts but stands. "Lemme get my snowshoes." *Not that high after all.*

"Yeah, time to get outta here," Millie says, going outside with Willow.

Emma follows her in uncertain steps and shuts off the lights while I bleep the car open. "Code?" she asks Millie. If there's one person who's going to keep her focus on our businesses, it's always Emma. Even high.

"Ah," Millie says, waving away her request like it doesn't matter. "Relax, Ems."

"Come on, Millie. Gotta lock up."

"'Kay-'kay-'kay." She comes back inside and taps in a code. "You know what they say, though. What happens in Emerald Creek stays in Emerald Creek." Then she lifts a finger. "But nothing ever happens in Emerald Creek," she adds, giggling. "I just have this thingy for the insurance... and also," she says, frowning comically at Willow, "to know when my friends are getting high without me."

Easy Monday properly shut down, she turns toward me. "The harder the fight, the greater the reward, sista." Then she throws herself in my arms and adds, "You should just move in together, save some money. And bake your cakes out of his garage! Now there's an idea."

"Yeah, yeah, right." I push her softly from me and take her arm. "Come on, let's get you guys home."

They all pile into my Corolla, and I start doing the rounds, promising to pick them up in the morning so they can get their cars. After I drop off Millie, Willow decides Emma lives too far up in the hills, and she should just sleep at her place. "Caroline is at a sleepover. It's unfair to Kiara to drive you that far, after all she's been through," she declares, and that settles it for Emma.

"You know, Millie might be onto something," Emma says as we take the turn to Willow's.

"About what?"

"Selling your cakes out of Colton's garage. Or next to it." Her speech is clear, but her thoughts? I'm going to discard everything she says. "It's a great idea," she continues. "You should tell Colton about it."

"She's right," Willow says as I ease into her driveway. "I mean, you already bring loads of muffins and cupcakes to the garage. There's a reason people book their services on Mondays and Wednesdays. Might as well start selling them."

"What she said," Emma says, before stepping out and blowing me a kiss.

As I drive away, I wish again I'd stayed with them tonight instead of going to the board meeting and making a fool of myself. I really need to unwind now.

Not wanting to go home, I head back into town and end up at Lazy's. I make my way to the bar, crowded with regulars at the moment.

Before I can perch myself on a stool, Justin points to a booth in the back. "He's over there."

A sinking feeling overtakes me. There can be only one *him* that Justin would tell me about. Shit. I never even stopped to think about how Colton would feel about what happened.

I quickly make it to his table. He's lost deep in contemplation of what's left of an amber liquid in his glass. Considering his family history, that's not good.

"Hey," I say softly, and go to slide on the seat across him.

He lifts his gaze to me, relief washing over his features. "Fuck, sweetness, where were you?" he says, standing and wrapping me in his arms. "I got so worried."

"I had to drive the girls home..." My words get lost in his chest. I check my phone out of habit and see all his missed calls. I've been on silent mode since the meeting. "I'm so sorry."

"Sorry 'bout what?" he says, sitting back down and gathering me onto his lap.

"That... that you felt you had to say all those things..." *That no matter what I try, I always end up on the loser end of things.*

"I'm sorry I couldn't help you, sweets. I'm angry at myself. But we'll figure it out. We'll find a way." He gives me a squeeze and one of his fabulous kisses right behind my ear that make the world go right again. I almost give in, want to believe him. But I can't.

And I have to say this before he gets too deep in shit because of me. I don't want to be a burden to him, or anyone. "I'm going to France," I blurt.

His body tightens underneath mine, the vibration nearly undoing me.

I try to turn to look him in the eye as I speak, but his grip on me is too tight. It's like he doesn't want me to say it.

"We already been through that, sweets, and you know I support you. I just don't want you going for the wrong reasons. This seems like running away to me, not following your dream. But sure." He takes a deep breath, his body releasing some of its tension. "What you gotta understand, is that you're not alone. No one ever does it alone. You meet people along the way, and they help you, and that's part of being human. Accepting help from those who are on your path, those you meet on your journey. This was me helping you, earlier. But you ran away. You gotta stop doing that. You have something to prove, sweetness, I get it. But know this: it's only to yourself. And I'll support that. If you need to show the French you know as much as they do, and that'll make you feel better about yourself, go for it."

That's the exact moment Justin chooses to set my IPA in front of me. "What's that about?"

I feel Colton's glare above my head, or maybe I see it in the way Justin receives it. He raises his hands. "Never mind," he says and leaves.

Colton takes a deep breath. "Three, four, five," he mumbles. I'd laugh if I weren't so uptight. "Seven... Nine—"

"What the heck?" Chloe, Justin's wife, says as she slides in the booth, followed by Willow and Emma.

I narrow my eyes on them. "I thought I dropped you off."

Willow nods. "You did."

"We were just too uptight," Emma says.

"Tell me Justin heard wrong," Chloe says. "I mean," she continues without letting me speak, "I was at the Select Board meeting, and by the way," she turns to Colton, "nice speech, but *France*? As in Europe? What—*why*? You're giving up on us?"

Willow's gaze actually gets misty. "Boo," she says, trying to take my hand. "Who's gonna boss me around if you leave?"

"She'll only be gone three months," Colton growls.

"They all say that," Noah says, pulling a chair and sitting at the head of the table.

We all look at him uneasily. There's a family history there that's a little unclear to me. Sometimes I wish I paid more attention to gossip.

Willow glances at him for a beat but directs her focus back on Colton. "No offense, Colt, but Paris, man? Paris? Do something!" Willow's eyes are downright wet right now.

"*No offense*, Willow," Emma cuts in, "but I agree with Kiara. Training in a French institute, maybe a write-up in food magazines, some endorsements from a celebrity chef... That'll go a long way in solving Kiara's cash flow issues. People love to lend money to successful people. Banks don't tend to help people in need."

"That's cold," the man whose voice is *very* familiar says, pulling a chair next to Noah to join the conversation. *Nigel*. Or rather, Luke. Our local celebrity. There's too much happening right now.

"And you are?" Emma says icily, confirming his assessment. Emma is not warm to outsiders.

"No one you need to know, love," Nigel-slash-Luke says.

Emma rolls her eyes.

"Bathroom break," Willow calls, forcing all the men to stand and let us through.

We crowd the bathroom once again. "That guy is hot," Grace says, looking at Willow. "Who is he anyway?"

"He's some rock star in hiding, according to Tracy," Willow says, adding a touch of mascara.

Emma frowns. "You mean *he's* Sexy Voice? Sounds like a jerk to me."

"Guys, fingertips out," Grace says, and plops a bead of cream on each of our fingers. "You need to hydrate those lips, ladies."

"Ready to go back?"

"I'll catch up with you," I say. "I actually need to pee."

While they're gone and I'm in a stall, someone comes in, then rummages through something. "No. No! No! No! Please..." they whisper.

I flush and come out, going straight to the sinks. While I lather, I glance at the woman—no, the girl—and startle. It's Isaac's sister, I'm sure of it. The egg bomber! She looks guilty and without a glance my way, darts into a stall.

I wipe my hands, open the door to the hallway, and let it bang back closed, staying inside.

Sure enough, she comes out and freezes when she sees me.

"Hey," I say with a smile. "You're Isaac's sister, right?"

She's nervously playing with the hem of her hoodie. It's too small for her, the sleeves showing her thin wrists. She averts my gaze and goes to the sink, running her hands under hot water. She nods. "Evie."

There's no point making her more uncomfortable than she already is. "The community chest is stocked only on community dinner nights." During the community dinners that Justin organizes at Lazy's, not only is food free, but there's a box in each bathroom where people can either leave cash or take cash anonymously.

She looks defensively up at me. "What?"

"Pretty sure next one is in on New Year's Day."

She shrugs. "Whatever."

"I could use some help with the baking, meanwhile. Could tie you over."

Her hungry look reminds me of myself, a while back. But I was older than her. This is so unfair. I reach inside my wallet and hand her the three twenties I have. It's not much, but in her situation, I bet it's a lot. "Consider this a hiring bonus." She goes to snatch it from me, but I pull my hand back. "I just wanna know one thing."

Her smirk and forlorn gaze hit me in the gut. This is a look that says, *there's always a catch*. I hate that I'm the one who brought it about.

"Just tell me why you threw eggs at Shy Rabit."

She forces a laugh. "That old witch promised me a hundred bucks."

"A hundred bucks to throw two eggs at a window?"

"Nah. I was supposed to get all twelve eggs. You guys kept me from it. She wouldn't pay me."

I shut my eyes briefly. "That's Louise we're talking about?"

She nods, her gaze fleeting to the sixty dollars in my hand. I give it to her, but I stay between her and the door. "You need help, you go to good people. There's enough of us around here."

"Isaac says we need to figure things out on our own."

Isaac came to work at the bakery with signs of physical abuse last spring. Chris started handling it, so there was no reason for me to step in. Then Isaac's dad was sent away for a long time in an unrelated matter, which in effect suppressed the source of the problem. As always though, the scars ran deeper. Shame and a sense of isolation are still plaguing this family.

"Isaac is a great guy. I see him at work. But he's wrong about that. You need something, you ask any of us." I realize she's unclear who this *us* is. "The Bitch Brigade."

Her eyes brighten. "Mom talks about you. What you did for the spa last summer." She giggles.

"Come on, I have a soup that's getting cold and I'm pretty sure there's one for you too. You prefer potato-cheddar or cheddar-pota-to?"

She stays glued to me the rest of the evening and eats way more than just soup—thank god. No one asks questions, and when Colton grabs his wallet to settle our bill, Grace puts her hand on Evie's shoulder and says, "We'll give you a ride home, hun."

"If I wasn't already totally in love with you, I'd fall again, sweets," Colton says while he peels my clothes off me. He wanted us at his place, and from the look on him, I didn't ask why.

"What'd I do now?" I made a fool of him and am ready to leave Emerald Creek. What is there to love?

"The way you took Evie under your wing. She's who threw the eggs, right? She worships the floor you walk on. I don't know what you told her, but I'm on her side. You're the best there is." He gets to my panties and stretches them to the side, sliding a finger on my clit.

"I didn't say anything... special."

"Shut up and enjoy," he says.

He ends up making love to me like this is goodbye, and it nearly kills me. Two minutes into his caresses and I've forgotten the whole Select Board debacle. Everything about Evie. If I didn't know him better, I'd think the way he kisses every inch of my skin, the sound of his voice when he tells me how beautiful I am, his touch attuned to my every reaction—I'd think all this was to convince me to stay.

But it's not. Colton's not that way. He wants what's best for me, and he trusts me to know what it is.

In the middle of the night, after he's made me come twice despite my low spirits, and he loses himself inside me with a gravity that's downright concerning, he whispers, "Even if it takes you thirty years to come back, I'll be waiting for you."

My heart nearly explodes from the emotion his words carry. "Colt, don't say that," I beg him. Because what if he's right?

I'll hate myself if something happens and I don't come back right away.

But I'd hate myself even more if I stayed here now and gave up on Paris.

"Sweets, don't beat yourself up," Colton says. "You couldn't live with yourself if you said no to that training. I know it. You know it. I wouldn't want it any differently. Hell, if you said you weren't going, I'd put you on the plane myself."

My eyes well up, and clamping my jaw is all I can do not to bawl in his arms.

He runs his fingers in my hair, cupping my head in his hands. "Told you I'd wait thirty years if I had to. Now go and show them."

CHAPTER FIFTY

Kiara

Two weeks later

He hugged me and congratulated me, but I could tell something was... off.

"Colt, you know it's just three months, right? I'll get an international calling plan. We can text. Maybe you could visit?" Colton hates the city. He almost dry-heaved when he had to take Chris to Boston last summer and stay overnight. "Never mind—that was a joke."

He smiles. "We'll figure it out, sweets. Please promise me that if you get an offer that's your dream job, you'll accept it. Wherever it takes you. I don't want you to feel stuck here in Emerald Creek."

"I don't feel stuck—"

He silences me with a finger on my lips. "Just promise me."

"I promise." I can promise him that. After all, he said *dream job*, and that's highly subjective.

Colton drives me to Montreal so I can catch a direct flight to Paris. He hugs me tight, kissing me lightly on the lips among the crowd of passengers hurrying to their flights. "Go show'em, sweets. I love you."

"I love you too."

He lets go of me, but my body is having trouble moving.

"Three months'll go real fast, right?" I say, more for my own benefit than for his.

His gaze scans around my face, as if to memorize contours he won't be seeing for way too long. "We've been through that, sweets. If it ends up being more, then so be it." Colton spent all of last night trying to convince me this was my calling, and that I'd been right all along to seek success out of Emerald Creek.

Coming from someone who only weeks ago had hurt painted all over his face when I brought this exact thing up, I'm having difficulty believing it.

But since then, we've been to Annabel's. I saw them talk together in hushed tones and I know it was about me even if I couldn't hear what they were saying. Though Annabel did encourage me to go that day, and I think it was then that Colton finally understood that being a pastry chef isn't exactly the same as baking cupcakes in your kitchen for the county fair—even if that's when it starts for most of us.

Something switched that day. Another scary part of my life was set in motion—like climbing up the ladder at the deep end of the pool, and now I have to take the plunge.

"Take whatever time you need," he says. He doesn't add that he'll be there waiting for me, and I know why. He wants me to feel free to follow whatever path opens up for me.

"Three months, Colt."

"Sweets. Three months. Three years. You'll just be a flight away. Don't worry about me."

I tug on his jacket, wrapping myself into him one last time. *Don't say that*, I want to say, but I can't. I'm scared I'm not strong enough. For him. For us. I'm scared my life of running away from pain, of trying to prove myself, made me too self-centered. Unable to really love the way Colton does—without restraint. Selflessly.

I want to tell him three months is way too fucking long. I want to tell him I want to worry about him. But I'm so fucking used to being tough, that I don't know how that works. I don't know how to say the words without being weak.

In the end, I kiss him, holding in my tears, then I hurry toward the gate, not looking back.

In the end, as always, I kind of hate myself for being... me.

Until I hear a loud whistle through the airport. A very familiar whistle. Turning around, I see Colton perched on a chair. "Best cupcake in the whole world, sweetness!" he shouts, smiling wide at me.

Tears threaten to choke me, but I manage a smile.

I hope I fake it well enough for him to believe I'm truly happy.

CHAPTER FIFTY-ONE

Kiara

*P*aris, *two months later*

Sunday, 1:00 p.m.

> Are you up?

Incoming call: Colton

Excitement courses through my veins.

"Hiiii."

"Hey sweets." His voice has a pre-coffee rasp that says morning sex and lazy Sunday in. "Send me a picture. I wanna know where you're at right now."

I switch screens and capture the marble table where my espresso sits, with the boulevard in the background shining under the rain. I apply a filter to make it look cozy and vibrant, then hit send.

"Shit, you're living the life," he drawls.

I don't tell him that the bistro chair I'm sitting on pokes my shoulder blades, that the table is cold and hard under my elbows, and that the closed-in part of the sidewalk café is drafty. You don't get to complain about anything when you're getting an all-expenses-paid training in Paris.

"How was your week?" he asks me, and I tell him.

We text every day throughout the day, but with the time difference, it's complicated. The disconnect adds to the actual miles separating us, and these Sunday calls are the most precious of our times together.

"Your turn," I say, and I close my eyes, listen to his voice, and visualize him, his apartment, the garage, and all of Emerald Creek as he talks to me. "Tell your mom and dad I said hi," I say when he tells me he needs to shower and get ready. Grace, Ethan, and Colt are taking Shannon and Dennis out for brunch for his dad's birthday.

The sound of his voice tells me he's stretching when he answers, and for a beat that distracts me. "Gonna see if I can squeeze in another race before it's over for the season."

For some reason I can't explain, that makes me sad. Or maybe it's because he needs to go shower, and we have to say goodbye, and until next week we won't be spending an hour on the phone.

2:13 p.m.

To: Willow

Don't forget the muffins tomorrow. Colt mentioned Cass is dropping off her car—she likes the raspberry muffins.

4:02 p.m.

Willow:

Pretty sure we're out of raspberries.

Really?

I thought there were several pounds frozen at the bakery.

4:03 p.m.

Ask Chloe

4:04 p.m.

Or Corine

4:10 p.m.

Sorry if I'm coming across as a little controlling

But this is Cassandra. She deserves us going above and beyond

6:19 p.m.

To: Chloe, Corine

Any chance you guys would have frozen raspberries?

6:25 p.m.

It's for muffins for the garage. I can Venmo you

6:47 p.m.

Willow may or may not ask you

10:15 p.m.

To: Willow

Everything okay?

10:16 p.m.

To: Colton

How was brunch?

Monday, 1:00 a.m.

Willow

Heeey sorry! Was out of service. Omg Colt took us to one of his races and you were right!!! So much fun!! You should have seen his dad. He was so proud of his son!

3:00 a.m.

Chloe

We got you

3:10 a.m.

Willow

Found raspberries.

6:00 a.m.

...

...

<heart emoji>

The café au lait feels heavier than usual this morning, and the croissant I'm dipping in it tastes bitter. I run my thumb on the surface of my phone.

"Ça va?" my roommate asks as she sits across from me.

"Oui oui. Ça va," I lie. I'm not okay. I thought mastering the art of the soufflé would make me feel on top of the world. It doesn't. It reduces me to a pastry chef, and that's not who I want to be. I still want to do this as a living, because like my friends say, it brings me joy, but I don't want this to be the essence of me.

1:00 p.m.

To: Colton

> Heard you took your dad to the race! I'm so happy for you. How did he like it?

Colton

Hey sweets. Morning. Miss you.

Yeah, bunch of people came. It was okay.

3:00 p.m.

> Just okay?

> I'm so happy you did this.

> Did Willow bring muffins?

5:00 p.m.

Yeah she did.

5:30 p.m.

> What car did you race?

> Did your mom go?

> Who else was there?

9 p.m.

> Sorry, was in the middle of something. Mom drove up with Dad. Grace and Ethan and other people from Emerald Creek came. No idea why or how.

10:10 p.m.

> It was last minute

> Shit, just saw the time. Sorry, love you.

Tuesday, 5:30 a.m.

> Are you awake?

> I'm awake

I click the phone symbol under Colt's name.

"Hey, sweets." His voice sends a ripple of pleasure down my spine, and a pang of want in my sternum. The way I miss him hurts me physically. "You okay?" he asks. There's the telltale sound of ruffling sheets in the silence that follows, and I picture him in his bed.

"Better now." It's only half a lie. I am better now that we've bridged the time difference. Added to the distance, it makes communication so difficult.

But it's also a reminder of how far away he is. Of how it would take us hours to be together. Closing my eyes, I can almost smell him. Almost feel his rugged hands on my nipples. "Are you in bed?" I whisper, stretching my feet on my own bed.

I share a room at the Institut, and privacy is hard to come by. But my roommate went to take a shower, and that buys me ten minutes of alone time on the phone with Colt.

"Yeah," he breathes in the phone. "You alone?"

I sigh my answer and slide a hand in my panties.

He growls. "I read the book, sweets. *Shit*."

I take it he liked the shapeshifter romance. "So... you wanna be the wolf or the bear?" I whisper.

"Imma be the snake that eats your cupcake."

I'm not big into reptiles, but Colton's voice does the trick. "I'm so wet, careful not to slip."

He hisses. "Sliding right into your tight cunt, babe. Ah fuck, sweets."

I haven't read a snake shifter romance yet, and I vaguely wonder how I missed it at Millie's, but I'm not letting that distract me. "Come in deeper." I arch my back.

But a truck passes in the street, and voices sound down the hall, and my fingers are not what I need. "Talk to me, Colt. Please."

"Come on my dick, sweets. I can hear the need in your voice. You're just so ready for me, aren't you? Atta girl. My little French whore, you." His breathing labors. "Take it. Let go for me. Dripping tight cunt just for me." The ruffling sounds on his end of the line accelerate, and I orgasm on my fingers, a pitiful release that doesn't come close to what I've gotten addicted to with Colton.

Still, I whine in the phone, knowing he needs to hear that. It's not a fake whine either, more like something I had to think about adding to our sad phone sex.

We stay quiet for a while, and I get situated on my bed, both hands on top of the covers for when my roommate comes back in.

I feel more than hear Colton's yawn. "I should go to breakfast," I lie. "Another big day today." That's not a lie.

He grunts. "Then I'm gonna sleep," he says. "Love you, sweets. Talk to you tomorrow."

"Love you more."

We disconnect the call right when my roommate comes in. "You look sad!" she says. She's practicing her English for whatever international job she hopes to land. "You should telephone your boyfriend."

"I just did."

"Ah. I see. Let's go out tonight after courses, for a glass."

"After class, for a drink," I automatically correct her.

She nods. "For a drink."

I put on a brave little smile. "Maybe tomorrow. There are emails I need to take care of tonight. And I want to practice some more with the isomalt."

"More practice? You're already the best of us."

"I messed up the beads, and I'm still iffy on the shading with the airbrush."

"Iffy?"

"Not so sure about myself."

That evening, after a full day of class and a quick chat with Colton during his lunch break, I go to the labs that the school lets us use for after-hours practice. After heating the nibs of isomalt, I don heat-resistant gloves, spray them with vegetable shortening, then lose myself in the complex task of spreading, turning, shaping the molten, translucent isomalt into ethereal beads. It irritates me, tests my patience, tests my willpower, and that's why I want to master it.

I'll tame the beast. I'll be the best at this thing that drives me crazy.

It keeps my mind off everything else I can't control in my life.

It's past midnight when I get back to my room on my bed, open my laptop, and start with the email I sent to Annabel last night, and her response.

FROM: KIARA SMITH

To: Annabel Plum
Subject: Tarte aux pommes
Hi Annabel

Hope all is well! Thanks for the tips on talking to the luxury cruise line. I'll let you know how it goes.

Can you please help me craft a pretentious description for my new take on apple pie that needs to pass as poetry? It's a thinly sliced apple tart. The apples are deglaced in chestnut honey, baked with cinnamon, pear liqueur, and caramel. I serve it with heavy cream.

From: Annabel Plum
To: Kiara Smith
Subject: Tarte aux pommes
Are they still doing that poetry shit?

Here you go: Fruit défendu déglacé au miel de châtaigner, présenté en éventail coquin, épices du Levant, soupçon de liqueur de péché brûlant, désir de caramel inassouvi, petit pichet de crème fermière.

Before signing with the cruise line, get a lawyer to look at it or they'll screw you on which labor laws apply.

Stay cool

A.

I smile at her answer about the pie, which is a convoluted, ambitious description with more sexual innuendo than I ever thought was possible in an apple tart, and make note of the legal advice.

Then I move onto the next item on my to-do list: Alex's wedding cake.

FROM: KIARA SMITH

TO: ALEXANDRA PIERCE

SUBJECT: WEDDING CAKE

Okay girl, no rush but here are some things they are doing now in France. Just wanted to throw options for you to think about.

Super long cakes in a rectangle that go the whole length of the table. You can vary the decor and/or the flavors throughout. It makes it less spectacular, but more fun, more convivial. It serves as both centerpiece decor and family-style service but in cake form. We'd make as many as the number of tables you have. Of course that's for long tables, not round.

Another idea, if you're going for a vertical piece, we can make tiny replicas, cupcake size for each of the guests so they can enjoy them while you're doing whatever you need to do with your big ass cake. Photos, cutting, smearing on each other's nose, etc.

For flavors, it's really up to you. I'm partial to maple, doesn't mean I can't pull off the classics, or we can go more creative

and think basil, lavender, thyme, chamomile…
what are you thinking?

Your bitch Kiara

I start browsing through Echoes when Alex's answer comes in.

From: Alexandra Pierce

To: Kiara Smith

Subject: Wedding cake

Isn't that a little much for Emerald Creek?
You're going all Parisian on me. Thanks so
much, though. I have thoughts, but I gotta
run.

Your girl Alex

2:46 a.m.

From: Kiara Smith

To: Alexandra Pierce

Subject: or…

You know what would be super fun? A dessert
food truck. Cotton candy. Pop cakes. Smores.

2:49 a.m.

From: Alexandra Pierce

To: Kiara Smith

Subject: or…

Shouldn't you be sleeping?

2:52 a.m.

From: Kiara Smith
To: Alexandra Pierce
Subject: or....
I don't know, should I? :)
You're such a mamma.

From: Alexandra Pierce
To: Kiara Smith
Subject: or...
:)

2:59 a.m.

Colton

Sweets. Get some sleep

3:00 a.m.

You just woke me up

3:02 a.m.

No I didn't. You been talking to Alex

How do you know?

She's sitting next to me

...

It's community dinner at Justin's

A pang of want like I didn't think I'd feel again hits me. Fuck 3 a.m. It's the worst part of the night. I should have remembered about community dinner. It was on Echoes, and I'm all over that shit 24/7 now. I guess I forgot about it.

3:08 a.m.

Tell everyone I say hi

3:10 a.m.

Is Evie there?

3:14 a.m.

Make sure she takes what she needs

3:17 a.m.

Have Grace talk to her. She'll know what to say

3:25 a.m.

Did Grace say what kind of wedding cake she wants?

3:28 a.m.

Can you ask Grace how many people she's thinking of having over?

5:05 a.m.

Hey babe I'm sorry. Justin made me do his karaoke thing and I couldn't find my fucking

phone after that. Going to bed now. Hope
this doesn't wake you up. Love you.

CHAPTER FIFTY-TWO

Colton

I t's coffee break time at the garage, and the reception area is packed. Since Kiara's been gone, croissants baked by Chris turn up on Monday and Wednesday mornings, brought by a rotation of residents. Sometimes—like today—Emma brings a basket of baked goods when she's due to work on my books. Often, I know Kiara has been working her magic from overseas when it's her recipes for muffins or cupcakes that appear in my shop, their smell as familiar as a sad country song. "You guys realize there's a coffee shop in town, right? Easy Monday?" I half joke as I elbow my way to the coffee machine.

"We just came from there, hun," Ms. Angela answers, her knitting needles clickety-clacking. "Wanted to check on the crocuses I planted last fall, and what you have going in there," she adds, pointing her chin to the garage.

"Impressive," Luke comments before taking a huge bite off one of Emma's cookies. "Damn these are good," he mumbles.

I raise my mug of coffee to the assembly and head back into the bay, Emma following me so we can go over a few pending items for the garage. "None of my business, but... the logo redesign? Was that really necessary?" she asks.

"Yup."

"And-and-and... new sign, new t-shirts, mugs... That's adding up. Just want to—"

"It's abso-fucking-lutely necessary," I bark. Over my dead body is Kiara coming back to something that makes her feel insecure.

"Colton. It wasn't." She crosses her arms. "I'm worried about you."

There's nothing to be worried about.

"Since Kiara's been in Paris—"

"Lemme know what you think," I interrupt her, pointing to the third bay. She falls in step behind me as I walk her to the project I'm currently working on.

Everyone seems worried about me, but I'm fine.

I'm just fine.

Keeping busy until Kiara returns.

If she returns.

I'm not a fool. I know the appeal of the world will be hard to resist for Kiara. And she deserves a huge, beautiful life. Celebrity. Anything she wants.

Me, I can offer her something. So I'm working on that while she's gone. And if she returns, she'll have... something I hope she likes.

"You haven't told her anything?" Emma asks, surprised, as we round Luke's Mustang in the second bay. Since the exhaust scare, he brings it in constantly to have us check for shit. Makes Merritt's day every time.

My gut clenches. At the beginning, Kiara and I would speak several times a week. Now, Sunday's the only day I'm certain to hear her voice.

She says she's tired, and I can tell she is. She says the workload is brutal, and I believe that too. So much so that she hasn't really visited Paris.

But she says she's learning a lot, and she loves it. And that too, I believe.

There's nothing I can do. It's the way it was going to be. The way it should be.

"Nope, and no one better tell her anything."

"She's gonna love it," she says, then peeks inside. "Oh, Colton—that looks *awesome* too." She clasps her hand in front of her mouth to keep herself from shrieking.

I wish I could tell Kiara what I'm working on, but I don't want to ruin the surprise. Or seem like all I'm doing is trying to influence her while she's still in Paris. But fuck do I wish I could make her feel all the love I have for her, from the other side of the ocean.

And I'm not trying to influence her. I'm just being me. This is what she gets with me.

Fuck but I want her.

"When is she coming back?" Emma asks, as if it was a done deal.

I shrug. "End of the month, unless she gets a job offer right away."

She frowns. "She's not gonna do that."

"She might. That's the whole point."

"I thought the whole point was for her to beef up her pedigree, so to speak, so she would get the backing of a bank. That's all she and I have been talking about, before she left."

"I don't want to force her hand. If she gets a job offer that's too good to pass on, I don't want her to not take it on account of…" I'd wave toward my project, but what I really mean is "me." And yet I don't know how I'll live without her if she does.

"How long will you be in Paris?" she asks, confusing me, then adds, "Ohmygod you're going to propose in Paris, right? Please say that's your plan. I can help you strategize. And Willow can help."

"I'm not going to Paris," I groan.

"What?" Emma exclaims as I turn around to get to work.

I can picture it. Me in my walking boots and leather jacket, on the streets of Paris. Rain falling down my face. Her in spiky heels, wearing some pretty dress she would have bought recently, smiling sadly at me under a cute umbrella, telling me she has other plans.

No thank you.

The whole point of Kiara going to Paris is for her to find herself. Explore other options—better options.

"She needs to know that you want her," she states.

I chuckle. "I think I've made that clear." If phones could blush, mine would be perpetually crimson.

"It's not just about *sex*, you know," Emma spits, looking at me like I'm the one who started this weird conversation. "She needs to know you want to make plans with her. For the future. You sure you don't want to tell her what you're doing?"

"Certain." Last thing I want to do is bribe her emotionally. Kiara needs to feel free to live her life the way she wants.

"You should propose," Emma states, crossing her arms.

"I'm with her!" Luke shouts from the second bay, where he accompanied Orson to look at the undercarriage of his Mustang.

"I will propose. Eventually."

Emma rolls her eyes. "See, that's what I'm talking about. Women want to be wanted. Feel wanted. No matter what they say, they want a ring that says someone's..." She huffs. "That kind of thing *means* something to women. Kiara included."

It would mean something to me too. When Kiara comes back, I'm asking her to marry me. I've missed her too damn much. It doesn't make sense to spend another minute with her as just my girlfriend.

Emma stomps away, mumbling something about having work to do. I start working too, my thoughts staying on Kiara.

From the outside, it looks like I changed her life. Supposedly rescued her from living in her car. Found her a job. Helped her with other things.

But she's who rescued me. From being removed. From trying not to care about the people I should care the most about. Behind her tough attitude, she's all sweetness and wanting to make the world a soft, kind place, when it's been so hard on her. She made me see how wrong I was to avoid conflict. "I'm not gonna propose when she's across an ocean," I say, mainly for myself.

"And why not?" Luke asks, suddenly materializing where Emma was. "I could write you a song for her."

I smile at that idea. Luke's become a good friend. But when I'm proposing, it'll be in my words, and in my voice. It won't be Hollywood-worthy. But it'll be me. One hundred percent me. Simple.

"Yo, Colt. You got a minute?" Chris calls from the reception area. "Holy shit! That looks awesome," he says, getting on his tiptoes. He rubs his three-day scruff. "She's gonna love it."

"Be right there," I say, wiping my hands.

"So, listen," he says when I join him, "remember when you guys brought a bunch of local ingredients to me for the baking competition in Boston?"

"Uh-huh?"

He rocks back on his heels like he's super happy with himself. "I'm thinking we should do the same for Kiara."

"Really?"

"That's a great idea," Ms. Angela pipes up from her corner.

"It was actually Annabel's idea. She called me," Chris says.

At that moment, Willow comes in to drop off her mom whose car we've been working on.

"What was Annabel's idea?" she says, handing her mother a cookie and taking one for herself.

"Annabel thinks we should send some local ingredients to Kiara for her capstone project," Chris says.

She makes a face. "Are you sure that's allowed?"

"Annabel suggested it."

I trust Annabel. If she thinks it's a good idea, I'm all for it. "I wouldn't know where to start," I confess, crossing my arms.

"I'll handle it," Chris says. "I started talking to local farms, and I'm brainstorming with Annabel what to bring her."

"She's partial to maple syrup," I answer right away. "Wait—*bring her*?" I ask right as Alex comes in and wraps herself under my cousin's arm. She's really showing now, and the vision of them derails my thoughts for a beat. *I want this with Kiara.*

Chris squints. "We think you should bring the stuff to her."

How did I not see that coming? I rub my cheek. "I dunno, man." I don't want to impose on her. Break her routine, her concentration. There's also a small part of me that's not a big fan of being the bull in a china shop, but I can deal with a little humiliation.

"Colton," Alex says, "you need to show her she means something to you."

"Uh-huh," Ms. Angela says.

I blink. Is she for real? "She knows that!"

"I'm with them on this one, Colt," Willow says. "You've come this far, what's a little plane ride?"

"Yeah, boss, what's some contraband for the love of your life?" Orson chimes in, coming out of nowhere.

"Told you you got to show her!" Emma yells from my office.

"What if I don't bring the right stuff?"

"You leave that part to me," Chris says, tapping my shoulder.

"I'll start a collection for the plane ticket!" Willow says. "Echoes first."

Ms. Angela sets her knitting needles down to get on her phone. "On it!"

"Great!" Willow says, then empties a box of tissues, writes *Help Colton Bring Kiara Home* on it, and sets the improvised collection box on the counter.

"Wow-wow-wow. Why're you writing that? I thought this was to help her make whatever she needs to do for her final exam with her favorite stuff."

Willow tilts her head. "Aww. Is that what you thought?" She glances at Emma who's coming out of my office. "Isn't that cute?"

Emma shakes her head. "Men are so naive, it's borderline sad," my accountant drops as she takes a cookie before returning to work.

Willow takes a deep breath and stares at me like I'm a little slow. "This is not to help her ace an exam that's gonna take her away from us. This is to show her that we love her, and miss her, and she better get her ass back here or she'll regret it for the rest of her life."

I cross my arms. "Not sure about this, guys." If this is the intention, Kiara is going to see right through it. But I look out the window, and Chris is on the phone, no doubt talking to Annabel. Ms. Angela is already fielding questions on Echoes, and Luke folds and slips a bill in the collection box.

This is no longer in my hands—I'm just a willing puppet. I spend the next couple of days fine-tuning the project in my garage.

CHAPTER FIFTY-THREE

Colton

Noah honks outside Lazy's and jumps off his truck, lowering the tailgate. He has business in Montreal and offered to give me a ride to the airport. I step outside, rolling a purple hardcase suitcase—courtesy of Alex—and shouldering Ethan's camo backpack. Grace rushes to attach a smaller bag to it. "There." She smiles. "Now you're all set."

Half the town follows us outside. The other half is already on the sidewalk.

"Did ya weigh the suitcase?"

"Did you make sure you put dirty socks on top of the maple sugar to keeps customs control away?"

"Did you re-wrap the honey? You can't bring honey."

"The maple butter won't do well in cargo. Did you put it in your backpack?"

"Did you put Dad's prescription with the maple beads? They won't see the difference."

Emma's voice snaps in the cold air and shuts everyone up. "Did you take the ring?"

I hoist the suitcase in the back of the cabin and turn around, facing what seems to be all of Emerald Creek. "I'm not proposing in Paris."

A collective gasp takes hold of the group.

"Shannon, what did you teach your son?" Ms. Angela says. "Of course you're proposing in Paris! Do you know how many women dream of a Paris proposal?" she says, a big swipe of her hand maybe suggesting the Paris skyline or the Eiffel Tower.

I'm reaching the end of my rope here. Just because I've needed more than a little help in getting Kiara to where we are now, doesn't mean I'm clueless about women. Kiara doesn't want a Paris proposal. "Enlighten me, Ms. Angela. How many?"

Her mouth hangs open in disbelief. "All of them!" she finally cries, then looks around for support, which she gets from... everyone. The women are nodding, the men are shaking their heads like I'm the village idiot.

I drop the backpack next to the suitcase. "Well, Kiara is unique. She's not like all of them."

Ms. Angela rolls her eyes while the other women *aww* and the men chuckle and say, "Nice save."

But it's not a save. Okay, in different circumstances, I'll admit a proposal in Paris is pretty cool. *Maybe.* But not now. Kiara's in Paris to propel her career. Me showing up with a ring would be an offer to tie her down when she's just spreading her wings. We've talked about this. I encouraged her to go. I told her I'd wait for her—thirty years if needed.

I'm not going to propose just because I can't sleep without her at night. Or I can't focus on work during the day. Or I don't even want to go to the races anymore, if she's not jumping in my arms the moment I come out of the car.

My life is tasteless, boring, and meaningless without her. That doesn't mean she should give up on her dreams for me.

I give Mom a quick hug and jump in the truck next to Noah.

He pulls away and honks again, like we're leaving port or something.

Looking in the rearview mirror, I see most people actually waving goodbye. "Jesus H. Christ, can you believe this shit? You'd think I'm Frodo leaving the Shire."

He laughs. "Eh, they're living through you. Not everyone gets to go to Paris."

A little twist of guilt hits me. I shouldn't have been so grumpy earlier. They all chipped in to send me to Europe, and I couldn't give them the time of day. I guess I do need Kiara in my life to cheer me up. I'll make a point to post pictures on Echoes several times a day to make up for my not-so-stellar attitude.

"And not everyone has a Kiara to bring back home," he adds. The dip of his mouth has turned bitter.

"What's up with you, man?" I really don't know how to talk deep with my guy friends, but this seems to be one of these moments where it's required. I've talked about tough shit with my sister, and each of my parents, maybe once or twice in my life. It's simple. You ask an open question and you just wait for them to answer. Then you ask them how it makes them feel.

"What do you mean?"

"Well, you know—women. What was her name again? What happened with her?"

He's saved by our approaching border control. The US side waves us through, the Canadian sides asks where we're going. "I'm driving him to Trudeau," Noah says as we hand our passports.

"Anything to declare?"

"Nope."

Once we're on the other side, Noah says, "She couldn't handle the whole... family thing."

I nod, not sure what he's referring to. Noah is the eldest of several, and his parents travel quite a bit, leaving him in charge most of the time. But he never made it sound like it was a problem. "She didn't want kids?" I venture.

He looks at me sideways. "N-no. That's not..."

I stick to my tactic of being quiet, but it doesn't seem to work. Maybe Noah just doesn't want to talk. I try one more thing. "Anyone else you're interested in?" Shit, I'm sounding like my mom or Ms. Angela. I'm embarrassing myself.

"Women aren't interested in men who come with my kind of baggage, Colt. But thanks for asking."

Okay, that's a polite fuck off if I know one. But—holy shit. *Baggage?* What baggage does Noah have? His family founded the town; they're wealthy. He volunteers in various capacities and always looks happy to be there. I swallow with difficulty, but I don't ask more questions, and we spend most of the drive in silence, apart from the occasional muttered swear at other drivers.

Then, once we're at the drop-off area, he helps me take the luggage out and takes me in a bear hug. "Hope you bring her back, man."

CHAPTER FIFTY-FOUR

Emerald Creek

H^{*ours later*}
Emerald Creek is buzzing with its low-grade customary activity. Right outside town, the garage overlooking the valley is operating at a slower pace, with its owner away. Easy Monday is where the gossip has returned for now.

In the heart of the village, Ms. Angela trots from Shy Rabit to the general store, where Noah is shoveling snow off the sidewalk. Alex leaves the bakery to go pick up Skye from school.

Moments later, a car parks alongside the curb, and a woman in a pink bandana climbs the steps to the bakery and asks for Chris.

Willow is helping at the register today, although since Kiara left, she's who makes most of the pastries for Chris—and she's grateful for the extra money. She pokes her head into the bakehouse and catches Chris's attention. "There's someone here for you." The woman in a pink bandana looks vaguely familiar to her, she asked for Chris by name… and she's right there, behind her, making herself at home in the employee-only section of the bakery.

The vision of Annabel in his shop fills Chris with pride. Save for a brief encounter during Laskin, so far they've only talked on the phone, and there hasn't been time to make the promises of meeting on each other's turf come true. "Annabel! It's an honor."

"Yes, well…" she says as they shake hands.

"What brings you here? Would you like something to drink? Tea? Coffee?"

Annabel waves the offer away. "I'm good, thank you."

Chris leans against a prep table and crosses his arms, examining the celebrity chef, savoring the vision of her in his inner sanctum. If he wasn't so in awe, he'd ask for a selfie.

"So you should know…" Annabel starts, then twirls around his bakehouse. "Nice little outfit you got here."

"Thank you." He looks down at his feet, her unease creeping into him. "I should know?"

She takes a quick inhale. "Actually, the capstone project at the Institut Pierre de Varanges is a pastry production challenge."

Chris frowns, trying to shake off the unpleasant feeling of doom. "What do you mean?"

She clasps her hands in front of herself and blows raspberries. "It's a black box. A market basket."

Thin, cold sweat forms on his back. Surely she's talking about something else, right? Because why would they have gone through the trouble of sending Colton to Paris with a shitload of local foods if Kiara wasn't allowed to use any in her capstone project?

"Spell that out for me," he says.

Annabel scratches her head, then repositions her pink bandana. "Feel like we're gonna need a drink for this conversation."

Chris stands still for a moment. Is she for fucking real? He feels like telling her off, but this is Annabel Plum. There are limits. "I'll see you at Lazy's," he says. He storms out without a coat or even a hat and climbs over the pile of snow Nathaniel plowed alongside their sidewalk, not bothering to see if Annabel is following. He has two hundred feet to work out his frustration; he better make each one count.

"Hey, dude, what's up?" Justin asks him as he storms into Lazy's.

"I'm gonna need a double for this one. And you might too."

Justin raises an eyebrow. "Let's tackle the Whistle Pig Twelve Year, then. Try and make it last, yeah?" He grabs the heavy bottle and two rocks glasses. His gaze fleets back to the door.

"Thank you, honey," a woman in a pink bandana says to Willow as they both come through the door. "Aww who's a gooddog? Who's a gooddog?" the woman coos at Moose, then lowers herself until she disappears, hidden by the bar, and her voice comes out muffled. "Who needs a belly rub? Yesh. Yesh you do. Aww."

Willow's eyes are like saucers, but her lips are pinched like someone trying not to laugh. "You need a drink too?" Justin asks her.

Willow shakes her head. "Just water. This is gonna be plenty fun enough. Thanks, though."

Justin pours Chris his drink, then leans over the bar. "Afternoon, ma'am."

The woman stands up. "Thank you, you too." Then, turning to Chris who's halfway down his whiskey, she adds, "You ready for the talk?"

"Why don't I move you to a booth," Justin says. In his ten years owning Lazy's, his policy has always been no drama. The last thing he wants is an argument at the bar, right as people walk in.

"Nah, I think this conversation needs to happen right here, where everyone coming in can participate."

Justin shakes his head. "Dude, not happening."

"Why don't you hear what *Ms. Plum* has to say, and then you decide," Chris answers, solidly anchoring his forearms on the bar.

Justin beams. "You're Annabel Plum?" He extends his hand. "So happy to meet you. Welcome. I keep missing you every time you're in town. And thanks so much for everything you did for Kiara." He almost wants to ask for a selfie with her, one he could print and frame in a place of honor, but something tells him this isn't the time. "So uh..." His gaze fleets between her and Chris. *Might as well get this over with now*. "What brings you here?" On instinct, he grabs another rocks glass and pours a Whistle Pig for her as well.

She takes the glass, swirls the liquid, tilts her head, mutters, "What the hell, let's do this," then downs the whole thing. Slaps the glass on the counter and says, "I thought I had a genius idea, but this guy here seems to think differently." Her thumb points sideways at Chris. Their gazes do not meet. They're taking Justin as their referee. *Not good*. Luckily, Chloe slides next to him behind the bar, wraps her arm around his hips, pecks his jaw, then taking the atmosphere in, she asks, "What's up?"

Chris opens his mouth to answer, but is interrupted by Alex and Skye barging in. "There you are!" Alex exclaims. "The bakery's empty, you're not answering your phone, and—" Registering the expressions on both sides of the bar, she interrupts herself. "What's going on?"

"Shit's hitting the fan," Willow chimes in. "We just don't know which way the wind is blowing yet."

"What shit?" Chloe asks.

"Honey, why don't you take Moose for a walk?" Alex says to Skye.

Skye perches herself on a stool on the other side of Willow. "Maybe later."

Alex blinks, seems to have an internal conflict about which battle to fight, then looks at her fiancé. "Honey? What's going on?"

Skye tucks herself against Willow. "This is gonna be good," Willow whispers in her ear.

"You know how we got the whole town to convince Colton to bring food and shit to Kiara?" Chris answers Alex, looking at Annabel.

The door swings open on Grace and Ethan clutching at each other, followed by Cassandra and Noah. All four were having a lively conversation that stops as they soak up the somber atmosphere at the bar.

"What's going on?" Noah asks, his eyebrows furrowing.

"We don't know yet, you inter-rupted Daddy!" Skye pipes in from the other end of the bar.

All eyes converge on Chris. "And you know how we put up a collection to pay for his flight to bring all this shit to Paris, right?"

Alex, sensing her fiancé's anger, places herself to his side so she can rub his back.

Justin nods to encourage him to keep talking. "What happened? Did Kiara drop out? Hell, s'long as she comes back here, we don't care, do we?"

"What happened is that Ms. Plum, all along, knew that the cap-stone project was a black box."

"What's 'at mean?" Willow asks. At some point Skye climbed on her lap to hear better, and Willow is now twirling the child's hair in her finger.

Annabel clears her throat. "It means she's not allowed to use any outside ingredients. They all get the same assignment, and they all get the same ingredients."

Willow slams her fist on the bar. "I knew it!" she hisses. "But no one would listen to me!"

"Why would you let us do that?" Noah asks. "This makes no sense."

Annabel pulls her bandana off, unruly strawberry blond and silver curls springing free as she scratches her head. "You guys were just so... so loving and caring. I never had that." Her eyes moisten a bit. "*I* know how much you mean to Kiara. I don't know that *she* knows how much she means *to you*. The idea of doing that was just so... loving... and generous." Her chin wobbles a bit, and she takes a deep breath to center herself. "I wanted her to feel how loved she was. And I thought Colton bringing all this to her would... *solidify* this."

The room is silent, everyone dealing with their own reaction to this revelation.

Annabel breaks the silence. "I feel guilty for pushing her to go to Paris. I was thinking how it was for me, back then. But she has something good here, and I don't want her to miss out on a life in Emerald Creek, with all of you, and Colton. I... I didn't know how to tell her. She's been emailing me from Paris, asking me for professional advice. She's treating me like a mentor, and while I'm honored to be that for her life as a pastry chef, I can't possibly let that be her whole life. I wanted her to *see*, to *feel*, to *touch*, what she was going to miss out on if she takes on an international career."

Chris exhales loudly, takes Alex in a closer embrace, and grunts. Justin mindlessly rubs Chloe's back. Cassandra slides behind the bar, makes a Shirley Temple for Skye, then starts pouring everyone a shot of Whistle Pig.

Skye stifles a burp, then breaks the silence, expressing the general opinion. "He's gonna feel so weiiiiird."

The visual of Colton in a flannel shirt and muddy boots showing up in a hoity-toity Parisian building with a suitcase full of smuggled cheddar cheese and maple syrup is on everyone's mind.

"Aaaah fuck," Willow says, then, "sorry for the language, kid."

"Best-case scenario, he's held up at customs," Noah says.

Willow turns around to face him. "*That's* your best-case scenario? You got some serious shit to figure out."

"I made him pack Dad's cowboy hat," Grace whispers in horror. "He promised to wear it. For good luck."

A collective grunt erupts from the group. "Why the fuck would you make him wear a cowboy hat?" Chris asks.

"It looked more... *American*. That's what we were going for."

"Honey," Cassandra says, "Texas isn't known for their maple syrup and we sure don't wear cowboy hats over here." She's looking at Grace like she's a little soft in the head.

"It's... the French... they don't know the difference," Grace explains. "Ms. Angela... Ms. Angela had a French guest at the bed-and-breakfast who asked to see 'the Indians!' So I figured—"

Chloe grunts, "Wow. That's wild."

"Right?" Grace says.

"And Colton went for that?" Chris asks in disbelief.

"It took some convincing on her part," Ethan says.

Grace elbows him.

"Ouch, man, did you just throw your fiancée under the bus?" Justin laughs, but it's nervous. They all need a little relief. They're just not there yet.

"I think Col-ton will be okay because Kiara will de-fend him if anyone makes fun of him. She's badass," Skye declares.

"Skye, language," Chris says, dad mode on automatic.

"I think she gets a pass for today," Alex whispers.

Annabel spreads her hands out wide. "What do you want me to do? How can I fix this?"

"I think Skye is right," Cassandra says. "There's nothing to fix. Kiara will see this for what it is."

"What about Colton?" Noah asks. "It's okay to make a fool out of him as long as Kiara is happy?"

"Yeah, looks like that's how it's gonna go," Willow says over her shoulder.

Ethan steps next to Noah. "He'll be fine. You'll understand someday, dude."

"Are you saying you made a fool of yourself for me?" Grace asks.

"No, but I happily would, honey. Every day. Worth it." Leaning toward Noah, he adds, "That's how it's done. You need to learn these things."

Willow turns to Ethan. "You lie to your fiancée?" she hisses.

"It's not a lie," he answers. "It's the honest truth. I totally would make a fool of myself every single day if that made her stay mine."

"You agree with this?" she asks Noah.

He shrugs. "I wouldn't know."

"Guys, Colton's calling," Justin says, loudly enough for everyone to stop talking.

CHAPTER FIFTY-FIVE

Colton

The Uber driver risks both of our lives, but I keep telling myself it's worth it, even if it's unnecessary. The drive from the airport is marred with traffic jams, despite the slalom and the profuse swearing. I don't need to understand French to tell the guy is trying to get the cars to move by the power of his words.

Once inside Paris we get to the most gigantic roundabout I've ever seen, with a monument in the middle, influencers standing in line in the middle of traffic to get their shot, and scooters zigzagging on the wet cobblestones as if their life insurance was about to expire.

I'd take ice racing over that any day.

Then we take a side avenue, and he slows down in front of a stately building with a brass plaque. *Institut Culinaire Pierre de Varanges.* This is it.

Then he makes a right and drops me off in front of the hotel I booked.

Twenty minutes later, I'm back outside, the ingredients now all stuffed in the backpack, taking fast strides toward Kiara's baking school.

Once in front of the building, I take out my phone and call Lazy's, hoping the international plan works. Justin picks up.

"Hey," I say, words escaping me. "Just made it there, and before I go in, I wanted to say thank you."

Justin is weirdly quiet. I examine myself in the glass door. The cowboy hat Grace made me wear adds a couple inches to my stature, which is already out of norm here. I decided to add the cowboy boots she got me a long time ago, and of course I'm wearing the leather jacket that does unspeakable things to Kiara. Under that, a plaid flannel shirt from Noah's shop. People do look at me as they pass me on the street, and I'm thinking that's a good sign. Right? Personally, I think I look pretty fucking great, and that's saying something. "You guys are the best, and I guess... I just wanted to say I love you guys. Thanks for everything. Keep your fingers crossed for Kiara."

Justin clears his throat. "We love you too, dude," he says, then the line goes dead.

I push the door open, and a receptionist materializes in front of me. He looks me up and down and smirks, then picks up a phone. "On a Indiana Jones à la réception. Ouais. Ça marche."

"Mademoiselle Smeess will be here momentarily," he says in a French accent, a fake smile on his face.

I nod my thanks. "How'd you know that's who I'm here to see?"

"She talks about you all ze time," he says. "Colt zis and Colt zat." He mimics a cowboy twirling revolvers in both hands, and suddenly I feel like a side character in a B-movie. The cowboy boots are constricting my feet, I'm too warm under the hat, and I'm wondering if the stickiness seeping from the backpack is maple syrup or honey.

I look up at the grand marble staircase, then down the hallway. All is quiet—no sign of Kiara. I clear my throat. Check my watch. Check my phone. Look at the guy. He's too busy doing nothing on his computer to worry about me.

Half an hour goes by, and I'm finally rewarded by hurried footsteps I'd recognize anywhere.

The footsteps stop.

Way down the hallway, Kiara gasps.

CHAPTER FIFTY-SIX

Kiara

I take a deep breath to steady my hand. Natalie and I have been paired to create molecular gastronomy eclairs today. The empty eclairs (really just pate a choux) are cooling. That was the easy part. The yuzu custard is made. Now we're tackling creating liquid pearls for the garnish, and that's where the rubber meets the road. Neither of us have ever done this, so the pressure is high to succeed. These elaborate ways of surprising the palate are what the institute prides itself on, and students who can't master these techniques won't be selected by the prime employers.

Right now, I'm the dropper and Natalie is the monitor. Using a culinary syringe, I drop the mixture of orange blossom-flavored water and sodium alginate into a bath of calcium chloride, making sure they're all the same size. Tomorrow, we'll use a tool called caviar maker to make it easier, but they like to torture us a little here and make us do everything by hand first before moving onto time-saving techniques.

Meanwhile, Natalie keeps track of the time and pulls out the pearls as they are ready.

I'm on a roll, bead after bead pearling perfectly into the liquid below. At this cadence, we'll be done before most, if not all, the other teams.

That's another staple of this place: competition. It's ruthless. Our grades are partially based on velocity, along with taste and presentation.

The phone trills on the wall, making me jump. I refocus on my task.

"Smeess! Un visiteur." Today's instructor hangs up the phone, visibly irritated by the interruption.

Bead, bead, bead, bead. I really got that rhythm going now. "You wanna go?" Natalie asks.

I shake my head. "It's probably a trick to make us place last," I say. "Wouldn't put it past Draco and Malfoy," I add, referring to two guys who think they'll get to the top by playing tricks on others.

Natalie giggles, then frowns as she looks down at the syringe. "Oh, merde, what's going on?"

My beads are pitiful droplets, and the liquid starts backing into the syringe. I press harder. "It's clogged. Fuck," I mutter. I had a nice cadence going, but now we're losing precious minutes. She helps me load another syringe. "You're keeping an eye on the time, yeah?" I ask her, worried the other beads will stay too long in the bath.

"Oui oui," she says.

After another fifteen minutes, my shoulders are stiff. "Why don't you take over," I say. "I feel I might cramp."

"I think we have enough," she says. "Let me start on the filling." She loads the nitrous oxide siphon with sous-vide yuzu cream, and we work together to perfect our eclairs, garnishing them with the translucent beads and an edible gold leaf each.

"I think you were right," Natalie says when all our eclairs are filled and decorated. "It's too pale."

I nervously eye the other teams. They're almost done too, but we have a chance of nailing this. "Do you trust me with the fiddleheads?" I ask her. I've been telling her about this delicacy we commonly eat in Vermont in the spring. She's never had it, but the school ordered some—anything remotely exotic, they have on hand.

Natalie smiles. "A little homesick?" she teases.

I start a simple syrup in a pan, then grab a handful of the green twirls. Minutes later, the subtle fragrance hits me, making my heart beat faster. I drain the caramelized fiddleheads. "That's gorgeous!" Natalie exclaims. "Like little trees or something." We take our culinary tweezers and complete the decor of our eclairs, the gold, pale orange, and deep green looking like Vermont at the beginning of fall. "Next time let's do pine-flavored pearls and—"

"—and maple cream, I know." Natalie laughs.

"I better go check on this fake visitor," I say once we're entirely done. "It'll give me a reason to ream into these two idiots." I check in with the instructor on my way out to make sure he's okay with me leaving.

I'm a little pissed at the interruption, which only adds to my low-key annoyance at the assignment. Every day now, I think about how Chris approaches his baking, and food in general, and I miss it. I also think about how Annabel worked in all these fancy places then came back to her roots, growing herbs and fruits and berries in her garden, using eggs from her hens, and talking about having a cow or two for her own cream and butter. Her creations have a soul, and there's a reason. They're as close as possible to the earth.

Nothing she uses has an unpronounceable name or sounds like a chemical.

What she makes comes from love. It's unpretentious, like a home-cooked meal—the best there can be.

Still, the competitive part of me wants to know what today's instructor has to say about our eclairs. So I charge down the elevator, through the side hallway, and to the grand entrance, hoping I can clear the misunderstanding, then rush back upstairs.

The sight I'm faced with hits me like a tidal wave, my suppressed want hitting me full force. I lose my breath, my eyes blur, and the undertow of need sucks me in, pulls me across the long hallway, my feet flying, my legs propelling me, the wave of my emotion lifting me up, up, up—into Colton's arms.

He lifts me effortlessly, twirls me around to cushion the force of my jump, his arms clasping around me while my ankles lock behind his back. "Sweets," he whispers in my neck.

I inhale his scent—leather jacket, coconut shampoo, and something uniquely him—then dart my tongue to taste his skin, right under his ear.

He growls and moves to capture my mouth in his. Our tongues twirl softly at first, a timid re-acquainting I hate. Since when are we shy with each other? Tears spring to my eyes. This has been too long. *Never, never again do I want to be away from Colton.*

I run my fingers up his nape, knocking off the hat he's wearing, and tug at his hair. His cheeks have a slight hollow that didn't use to be there. His fingers dig deeper in my upper thighs, our teeth clash, and our kiss deepens to a level of erotic. We breathe through it, never breaking it, and all the while Colton is slowly twirling me in the middle of the grand foyer, under a crystal chandelier.

Finally we break the connection, staying an inch apart, drinking each other in. Colton's eyes are shiny, his smile the biggest I've ever seen. "Hey there," he says.

"Hi."

A slow clapping erupts, bouncing off the empty walls. Antoine, the receptionist, is standing, watching us, a smirk on his face. "Ah, chapeau," he says. "Bien."

"What'd he say?" Colton murmurs. "He likes my hat?"

I lick his lobe, and this gets me a deeper squeeze of my thighs. "I don't think that's what it means, no."

"Maybe it means 'Get a room'."

"Yeah, I think something along those lines."

"Good, cause guess what?"

I squeeze my legs tighter around his midsection. "Good boy."

He drops me with a slap on the butt and picks up a backpack. The thing seems to weigh a lot and is oddly shaped. "What's going on here?" I say, picking up the cowboy hat on the floor and sticking it on my head—I'll get to the bottom of *that* later.

He rubs a thumb on his eyebrow and a shy smile illuminates his face. "Ah, sweets, you're gonna love that. Hear me out."

I hear him out, and my heart cracks open, my stomach flip-flops, and my mouth gapes.

Meanwhile, my brain is racing to figure a way out of this.

Chapter Fifty-Seven

Colton

Kiara's face goes from red to pale to red again, at least the part I can see under the too-big hat. She bites the inside of her cheeks, then attacks her fingernails.

"You can use whatever you want, sweets. It's just a suggestion. Chris and Annabel put it together, we wanted to make sure you'd have whatever you needed from home to make something... you know... uniquely you."

She tilts her head back, her throat bobbing in an erotic way when she swallows before adding, "How d'you get all this through customs?"

"I lied."

"You *lied*?"

I shrug. "They asked if I had anything to declare, I said *non*. Et voilà."

A small smile lights up her face. "Shit, Colton, you coulda gotten in trouble, like real trouble."

"Well, I didn't. And it woulda been worth it. I know what this capstone project, or whatever they call it, means to you. I—we—wanted you to have the best chance of winning."

She goes pale again, to the point where I'm wondering if she's coming down with something. Maybe it's the emotion—she wasn't prepared to see me. That makes sense. That must be it.

"So the thing is," she says, "the thing is, umm... it's not a capst—it..." Her eyes widen. "Shit, Colton, I'm so sorry." She twirls her hands like she did something wrong.

"Is it over? Did it happen already?" I look around like the answer is somewhere on the walls. Fuck, I hope we didn't mess up the date.

"No, it's-it's-it's..." She looks even tinier under the stupid cowboy hat.

I just want to scoop her in my arms and tell her everything will be alright. I cup her nape in my hand and run the pad of my thumb on her earlobe. "Hey, it's alright."

Her eyes round, two pools of silver I've missed so damn much. "We're not allowed any outside ingredient. Like, *nothing*."

I must have heard wrong. "You what now?" There's no way Chris and Annabel...

She rolls her eyes. "In order to be on equal footing, the school is providing the same ingredients to everyone, with the same prompts or list of pastries we should make."

My stomach bottoms a little from disappointment, but mainly I hate the way she looks: embarrassed, guilty. Like she's the one who did something wrong.

"Oh... uh. That makes sense. That makes total sense. So when is it?" I glance at my watch, calculating what time it is in Emerald Creek. They're going to be so disappointed. How am I going to soften the blow?

"We start tomorrow, and it goes over two days."

And... we *almost* missed the date. I knew I'd look stupid coming here, I just didn't expect it'd be like this. "You uh... you have to stay here at night?" I'm not sure if her lodging at the school is just a matter of savings or if it's required.

She wraps her arms around my middle, making me want to take her right here, right now. "No, I don't." Her gray eyes do that thing where they turn darker when she wants me. "Did you book a hotel already?" she asks, her voice husky.

I tilt the hat back. "You bet I did." The urge to carry her there right now is hard to fight.

She sighs. "When were you going to tell me?"

"When were you going to ask?" I growl.

She gets on her tippy toes and runs her lips on mine. "What does a girl need to do around here to sleep with a hot cowboy?"

I dig my fingers in her back, bringing her flush against me. "Just needs to ask like a good girl."

She lifts a shoulder. "Wear the hat, ride the cowboy."

"That right?"

"M-hm."

Right at that moment, the sound of voices echoes down the hall-way, and a shriek pierces the otherwise stately atmosphere inside the building.

"Ahmagawd!" a girl cries out, and starts running in little steps toward us, followed by others. "You are real!" She reaches us and turns to Kiara. "Tu rigolais pas, hein."

"I was not kidding," Kiara answers as the girl actually pinches my bicep.

"Une photo! Une photo!" she says, taking the hat off Kiara and plopping it on my head. She gives her phone to the receptionist and takes a ridiculous pose next to me, one hand on her jutted hip, the other on my shoulder.

Kiara's laughter is contagious, and I start laughing too. "She thought for sure I'd made you up," she says. Other girls crowd us, handing their phone to the receptionist. We move to the marble staircase, and the guys join, one of them lying at my feet. The hat goes from head to head as photos are snapped.

"Okay ç'est fini!" Kiara declares and breaks the group. "Question! Colton brought... a lot of things to eat from Emerald Creek. On se fait une petite bouffe après l'exam?"

They all cheer, then file out of the building.

"What was that about?" I ask as I take her hand and grab the backpack.

"We're not letting all this go to waste," she answers. "We'll get together and have a little baking party after the exam, just for fun."

She slides her hand under my jacket and tugs at my sweater. I pull her closer to me. Thank god I booked a hotel right around the corner from her school.

Chapter Fifty-Eight

Kiara

Colton rushes us to the hotel, and my feet seem to fly over the sidewalk as we dodge office workers rushing home, school children holding hands, and dogs pulling on leashes.

In the tiny elevator, I get drunk on Colton's scent, inhaling him deeply as I close my eyes and lean against him. He finds my lips with his, and seals us together again, and in this moment, I'm certain of it.

He's my home.

His taste is the only one I need. His smell makes me vibrate, and is one I can't find anywhere else. The deep rumble of his voice calms me, his laughter brings me up. His moods are mine and I know mine are his; we're more than just together. We're one. That's why being apart is so... unnatural.

He lets me inside the hotel room first, drops the backpack in a corner, shucks his jacket off, and rolls the sleeves of his flannel up his forearms. Then, hands on his hips, he says, "Before we tear off each other's clothes…" He runs his palm on his chin, and darkness clouds his gaze. "You got any offers you're accepting?"

My stomach bottoms. We haven't talked about that—ever. I've emailed Annabel about possible jobs, more out of courtesy to her, and also interest on my part. But talking with Colton about moving out of Emerald Creek for good is something I couldn't bring myself to do.

"I just need to know what I'm in for, sweets. Last three months were hell, not saying that to influence you, but you gotta understand. I need to know if this is another goodbye." He reaches for my hand and draws me to his chest, and I'm grateful this hides the tears pooling in my eyes. The last three months were hell for me too, and I felt weak for feeling this way.

I run my hand under his shirt, my fingers catching on ridges that are harder than I remember them, bones where flesh used to be. I dip my face inside his shirt while unbuttoning it, my tongue licking its way down, making him hiss.

His lips skim the top of my head as his voice echoes in my own heart. "Don't get me wrong, this is the sweetest goodbye and one I'm ready to have over and over and over again. Even looking forward to it. I just need to know." He loosely strokes my back, a comforting touch he feels necessary to allow me to open up. "Just need to manage my expectations, yeah? How's the next few years gonna look like for us."

I tilt my head up and our gazes lock. "You're my home, Colt. From the day you knocked on the window of my car. It's been a long time coming, and I resisted pretty much every step, every hand you held out for me."

He kneads the back of my head. "You had every reason to do it. And I understand you want a career. I told you I'd—"

"Stop being so fucking nice to me, baby. What do *you* want?"

His erection pokes my belly as he pulls me against him. His fingers tug my hair, exposing my throat. "I want to drag you back home," he says in a low growl, "put a ring on your finger, and wake up next to you every morning, my mouth eating your cupcake, my babies in your belly, my car in your driveway. That's what I want, and I want it now."

My center clenches. I want to climb him and get us both naked and on top of each other on the small bed, but I can't help myself. I hear myself say, "Is this your way of proposing?" Which, really isn't so nice and why—

Any coherent thought is erased as he rips my top off me, pushes me on the bed, and leans down, suckling on my nipple to the sound of his belt unbuckling. He yanks the rest of my clothes off, his eyes feasting on me. "Not sleeping one more night without you—ever," he growls. He nibbles on my earlobe. "Missed you so much, you have no idea." Then he licks his way down my belly as my legs open for him. "Need to taste you."

I moan at the rasp of his stubble against my inner thighs, then arch my back when he takes an inhale right against my center.

"That's it," he says, his voice caressing my clit. "That's my girl. Greedy for me, are you?"

"Take me, Colt. Please."

He licks my folds, then suckles on my clit as I rake through his hair for purchase. The pleasure is intense, but I want more. "Take me and don't ever let me go again."

He lifts his head up, his irises two dark pools I want to drown in. In one motion his body is covering mine and he's inside me, filling me so completely I almost blabber. My legs wrap around his hips, my heels find his ass.

He sets a punishing rhythm for us, pumping in and out of me, his bulging biceps caging me, his torso shining with fresh sweat. "Fucking love the way you pull me in, Kiara. You missed me?"

My nails rake his back. "I missed you, babe. Missed you *so much*."

He growls, gives two more pushes, then flips me over. "Pretty little ass you got there," he says and gives it a slap.

I tilt my hips up, missing him already. "Colt…"

"Here you go, babe, take it." He pulses inside me, hisses, then pumps in and out, his strong hands setting the movement.

I clutch the bedsheets, abandoned to Colton's whim, letting him control my orgasm with his cock, a flick of his finger against my clit, then a pinch on my nipple. What does me in is when he lowers his front against my back, and I can feel his heat and the faint brush of his chest hair and his breath against my neck. "You've always been mine, Kiara. And I take care of what's mine."

CHAPTER FIFTY-NINE

Colton

The next two days, Kiara has her final exams, so I spend my time visiting vintage car repair shops. At first I'm hesitant, seeing as I speak absolutely no French, but the mechanics I meet seem excited to meet me, and between their knowledge of English and translation apps, we make it work. The vintage car community has this love for making old things work, it's like we're speaking the same language already. I show them photos of repairs I've done at the garage, and I'm surprised how much they know about American cars. "Films. James Dean," someone tells me. I nod. They show me photos of 2CV they've done work on, as well as a Traction Avant. One of them shows me his pride and joy, photos of a Bugatti type 35 that he worked on. One thing leading to another, we start talking about races.

If I wasn't meeting Kiara after her last day at the *Institut*, I could stay all night talking with these guys, but there's not a chance in hell I'm late for her last evening here. She's been on my mind all day, and even though over the hours I've felt more and more at ease with these guys and had interesting conversations with them, she's all that matters to me.

That last night, we gather at someone's apartment with all the food I brought from Emerald Creek. Kiara wasn't kidding when she said she wanted to have a get-together and bake or cook. There are about eight people there, other students she's become friendly with. They speak a combination of French and English, with most sentences being in English but the pastry or cooking terms in French.

I'm really not paying attention to the conversation, just observing how Kiara comes alive as she unwraps the stuff I brought, her eyes lighting up as she explains the different ages of cheddar, the grades of maple syrup, and the process to make it. At some point she rubs her thumb on sage, turns to me and asks, "Is that from Cassandra's windowsill?"

"I think so." I nod as she reverently sets it aside. "We got four feet since you left, so…"

"Just four feet, huh?" She smiles. "Any thawing yet?"

I tilt my head. "It's this year's maple syrup."

"Right. It's already the end of March."

"It ain't mud season yet. We got a few more weeks. I hear Red Mountain is all powder today."

"What are you talking about?" her roommate, Natalie, asks. Kiara explains the six seasons of Vermont. Winter being bookended by stick season at the end of fall, and mud season right before spring. She tells them that yes, one to two meters of snow over the season is what we like to see, and while they will be going to the South of France for a first dip in the Mediterranean after school, we'll be happily snowboarding down a slope called Avalanche. To which one of the guys retorts that the Alps have the best skiing in the world, and Kiara responds with a shoulder shrug.

"What about the job fair?" I ask Kiara when we leave her friends with a promise to stay in touch and maybe even visit.

She shakes her head. "I don't need to go. I told the Institut I'd give them some credit for whatever success I have in Emerald Creek when I go back. They did give me a chance, and a full scholarship, and there's no reason for me not to recognize that. But there was no expectation on my part to do anything in return. Just make the best pastries I can with what I learned. Take on an apprentice or two to pass along the knowledge."

We climb in the ride share car and she tucks herself under my arm. "You know I was coming back to Emerald Creek anyway, right? You didn't have to come get me. But I'm so glad you did."

I squeeze her shoulder. "I want to get better at showing you how much I love you, sweets. It's a fine line between that and letting you be who you want to be."

She turns sideways to look me in the eye, the seriousness in her gaze hitting me below the rib cage. "You made me become who I am. Don't you ever hold back on showing me how much you love me, Colt."

Overcome with emotion, I lean in to kiss her, but she tilts her head back. "Promise me," she says.

Suddenly I get it. It took me months—years—but I get it now. Kiara's fight to be independent, successful on her own? Her resistance to even date me? It's because she didn't think she had anyone other than herself that she could really count on. No one to support her, understand her, dream with her, fight with her. Love her entirely and unconditionally.

I was that person. She just didn't know, and that's on me.

"I promise. I'm gonna show you how much I love you, sweets. It's gonna be a lot, so get ready." I lean over to kiss her properly—we're in France, after all. And as the saying goes, when in France, do as the French do.

Once our tongues are sated and our bodies are asking for more, she breaks the kiss, her lips swollen. "It can never be too much."

I smile against her mouth. "Hold my beer, honey."

Chapter Sixty

Kiara

I t's late but not quite dark yet by the time we approach Emerald Creek. Three months in the city lights, dazzled by the Eiffel Tower at night and confined inside during the day, and I'd almost forgotten how huge the sky is here. I open the window, and the air slaps my face.

I feel alive again. The Vermont cold isn't this insidious humidity that seeps into your bones, but instead it's a healthy slap that resets your energy, activates your blood flow, and wakes you up instead of making you want to stay in bed all day.

My heart skips a beat as we approach the garage, the familiar sight hitting me hard. Just like when I saw Colton in Paris, the feelings I've suppressed are now flooding me. The familiarity of home. Knowing that no matter what, everything is going to be alright.

Instead of continuing onto Sunrise Farms, Colton eases onto the empty parking lot and shuts down the engine. Something looks different about the place. The sign on the garage.

Harper's Body Works is now called Harper's Auto Haven, and a cool, vintage-looking logo replaces the sleek design I'd come to dislike so much.

A nice tingling takes over my belly when I realize he's had it changed. All it took was one involuntary pout telling him I wasn't a fan that Valerie's touch was still on his business, and it's gone. My emotion tinges with a dose of guilt, but the smile is there nonetheless. "You changed it!" I whisper. "Why?"

His mouth twitches in a suppressed smile. "We can talk about that later," he says as he pulls up beyond the garage, coming to a full stop where his land extends and shows Emerald Creek—the river and the village, down below.

I squint into the deepening darkness, unable to make out the lights lining the main streets, The Green, and twinkling from the dozens of houses huddled around it. There's something blocking the view, like another building. Could it be a hangar? Is Colton expanding? Why didn't he mention it? I want to hear more about that.

He cuts off the engine, jumps out of the truck, and opens my door. "What are you doing?" I ask, laughing at his obvious excitement and jumping out into his arms. He sets me down and wraps his arm around my shoulders. "Did you expand your garage?" I look up at him, but he's looking ahead. Suddenly, as he takes a clicker from his pocket, lights illuminate the planes of his face.

I turn to see where it's coming from, and my knees go weak as breath eludes me.

I blink.

Ahead of me, darkness is replaced by thousands of small lights outlining... a house? A barn? "What is it?" I ask, knowing in my heart what the answer will be.

Colton nudges me ahead. Soon our steps find solid ground where a pathway leads to the building. Colton stops us and takes the clicker from his pocket again. Now, floodlights illuminate the scene: a red barn with a sign on top.

Sweetness Delivered.

"I thought of moving the Dewey's barn, but turned out, we were better off building from scratch. Believe it or not, it wasn't as much as it seems—"

"Shut up," I say. "It's-it's-it's... everything."

"Now, before you get all excited, equipment hasn't arrived yet. I asked Annabel to get on that. She and Alex are working on sponsors to give you stuff for free and—"

I slap his chest playfully, but tears are threatening, and my voice falters. "Babe. What is happening?"

"You said to not hold back showing my love. This is me showing my love."

"Colton."

He squeezes my shoulder. "You have no idea, do you?"

I blink back tears again. "No idea what?"

"You have no idea how happy it makes me, being able to do stuff for you. You letting me do this, instead of... you know." His chest heaves and a big grin brightens his features.

"I think I'm beginning to get it."

He nudges me forward, and we get to the barn-type structure. The front is a wall of glass, giving full view to the inside. Strings of fairy lights adorn the post and beams inside, softening the rustic look. Colton slides the front door open, and we step inside. It smells of wood and fresh paint. "I wanted you to choose the furniture," he says, "though Autumn already has a whole list of stuff for you to look at."

Taking my hand, he leads me up a staircase, to a mezzanine. The view from up there is breathtaking, the whole valley at our feet. "You could have your tasting area here," he says like it's no big deal. He points to a wooden door halfway up. "Thalia and Lucas already roughed it in for a dummy," he adds, referring to the couple who moved in town last year and opened an architecture firm and construction company. He leads me back downstairs. "Lemme show you the best part."

The best part? My head is spinning as we get to the back of the main room. How could this get any better? Pushing on a swing door in the back, he reveals a space as big as the front room, with a row of windows offering a unique view on Emerald Creek—the same as the one from upstairs. It's empty, but the outlets for water, electricity, and gas are there. It's ready to become the pastry lab.

"Didn't want you to have to spend your days baking without seeing the outdoors. Doesn't seem right," he says. "It's uh... a blank canvas. That's what Annabel and Autumn said. So you make it how you like it."

Blinking tears of emotion, I raise a shaking hand to my mouth. "I don't know what to say." From his comments, I gather that the whole community contributed. It feels like too much, and I should say so. But I heard Colton loud and clear in Paris: I need to let him love me. And I need to let all of Emerald Creek show me their love as well. They didn't have to do this. No one forced them to. They chose to do it. They chose me. Just like Colton chose me. "I don't know what to say," I repeat.

Colton pulls me against his chest. "I know, sweets. I know. You don't have to say anything. Just keep baking, keep giving us your sweetness and your love. That's all anyone's really hoping for. Nothing you can't do." Then he lifts his chin to me and kisses my lips softly. "Come on, let's go to Lazy's."

He walks us out to the truck, clicking the lights off.

"That's a cool thing," I say.

He hands me the clicker. "It's all yours," he says as he opens the door for me, leaning in for another long, wet kiss once I'm seated.

Once he's behind the wheel, I say, "So... New name for the garage? New logo? When were you going to tell me? What happened?" He starts the truck and creeps to the exit, giving me time to look at my pastry store next to his garage.

"What happened is that my woman had a bad taste every time she saw that thing. Woulda gotten rid of it sooner if I'd known."

My mouth drops. I liked that he changed it, because he's right, it did something to me, if only subconsciously. But I didn't expect him to do it *for me*. "Colt..."

"Tracy's friend from high school designed it. Inn't it cool?"

"It's... awesome. But..."

"But?" He comes to a stop and looks at me. "Lemme be clear. My ex designed it. I should have thought of getting rid of it sooner. It wasn't fair to you. Okay? That's the only but."

CHAPTER SIXTY-ONE

Kiara

I end up nearly falling asleep in the booth at Lazy's from jet lag and emotion. The whole town is there, and they all want to know how I liked the barn. I think some of them were afraid I might not stay after all, and it pains me that I've sometimes been so abrasive that people thought I didn't really like it here.

I love it here. I love the people, I love the place, and more importantly, I love Colton.

"It's more than I could ever wish for," I say. "I just don't know how to thank you." There's also the question of who paid for this, but I'll get to the bottom of it later.

"Just keep baking!" someone hollers.

"Told ya," Colton says, rubbing my shoulder.

He takes me to his apartment. We fall asleep in his bed, after some lazy, sweet, yet much-needed sex.

I jolt awake at three in the morning, Colton sleeping next to me, one arm thrown over his eyes. The sheets are pushed aside, his strong, beautiful body on full display for me. I lick my lips but resist the temptation to kiss my way down from his throat to his flat stomach. I want nothing more than to wake him with my mouth around his cock, but as arousing as it may seem, three in the morning seems unfair. The man can wait. He needs his sleep, after everything he's done for me.

I slip out of bed before I give in to my desire and wake him up, and curl up on the couch in the living room. My apartment is rented out until next week, but I'm wondering if Colton and I shouldn't just move in together. It seems like the reasonable thing to do, and it would continue to bring in some much-needed cash to finance the barn. I'm appreciative of all the efforts everyone has put in to make it happen. Truthfully, I couldn't dream of a better location or look for my business, and I'm beyond grateful for the collective effort that made this happen. But I'm not letting anyone pay for it.

That's a daytime problem, so I pick up my phone to kill time and scroll on social media. My attention catches on missed messages from my sister, wishing me much luck in Paris, then welcoming me back stateside.

That's unlike her. I head over to her social media. She's only posted two photos recently, both black and white. One is of a meadow under the snow. The other one an artistic rendering of her profile. Then I notice her proclaimed status: single.

I stretch my legs and shoot her a quick thank-you for her messages. I don't even feel anything at this point. That chapter of my life is definitely over—the one where I try and fail to gain acceptance from my mother and my sister. It's not that I gave up on them. I did that a long time ago, but it used to hurt so bad thinking about it. It's that it doesn't matter anymore. It's irrelevant. They're irrelevant to me, to my life. They can be a part of my life if they choose to, or they can not be. It doesn't affect me. Strangely, I find that I'm more open to forgiving them, to letting them back into my life if they wanted to, now that I don't seek their approval anymore.

My thoughts inevitably drift to my father, and I let them take me there. It's okay. I've also accepted he's gone, and I've accepted who he was, with all his imperfections. It's still hard for me, at this point, to make peace with the fact that my childhood was a lie. I'm trying to reframe this way of thinking as well. Maybe it wasn't a lie. Maybe it's really what Mom said—that he was trying to protect us. Maybe the snowball fights and the dolls he'd bring back from his "travels" were as real for him as they were for us. I have no reason to believe he didn't love us in his own way.

What's still hard is the way everything went down, and how my family turned against me. It was unjust and cruel of them.

A small part of me is hyperaware that maybe I take after them when I'm stubborn in keeping people at arm's length, even if Colton has helped me become much better at not being that way.

I don't want to be that way. I don't want to be them. I want to be like my found family here in Emerald Creek—open-hearted, welcoming, forgiving, understanding.

"Boy, do you look serious this morning," Colton says, standing in boxer briefs, hair all mussed up, one hand scratching his belly, the other behind his neck as he lets out a lazy yawn.

"Boy, do you look yummy this morning," I answer, heat growing between my legs.

He chuckles and bends over to graze my lips with a kiss. "What're you thinking about, sweets?"

"I think I should change my name. Take my mother's maiden name or something. I dunno." I know Smith is a common name, but I feel icky carrying my father's name. Even if I'm telling myself stories about how he probably loved us in his own way, it still remains he was associated with organized crime and a cheat all his life. "I'd like to put some distance," I say to try and explain to Colton.

"Sure, that makes sense," he answers to my surprise. I was expecting a push back, a question. "I'm gonna make coffee," he says.

I jump off the couch. "Why don't you let me make coffee, and you go back to bed and get rid of the underwear and let me take care of you?" I'm up against him now, and I run my fingernails against his back so there's no possible confusion about what kind of care I have in mind.

He pulls the cami I wear to bed off me, our skins now heating against each other. "Coffee can wait," he says. "Get back to bed, it's barely past four." He leans over to take me in a kiss while I slide a hand under his boxers.

He hisses and I drop to my knees. "Or don't get back to bed," he mumbles while I take his length in my mouth. "Christ, Kiara, you have some mouth on you." I lick his shaft, making eye contact with him, and his cock bobs. "That's it, dirty girl. Lick it."

I give it one more lick then take it as far as I can down my throat, sucking and twirling my tongue, reveling in his growls and hisses, and at the way his hands land on my head to give me direction. "Take it like a big girl."

Wetness pools between my legs as he fucks my mouth, and I moan.

"Christ, Kiara, you're gonna make me come if you keep doing that."

I take him deeper, suck him harder.

"Touch yourself," he orders. "And moan for your man."

One hand latching onto his ass, the other in my panties, I whimper.

"Ah. Atta girl."

I glimpse up at him. His abs are corded, his eyelids hooded, and his mouth twitches as a salty bead hits my tongue. I lower my eyelids and suck him harder. "Are you sure?" he whisper-growls. "Fuck you're so good."

I nod and suck him harder.

"I'll hold it til you come. I wanna come in your mouth when you're falling apart for me."

His words set me off. One more stroke on my clit, focusing my attention on his throbbing cock shoved down my throat, how he's totally fucking my mouth with both his hands on my head, and I'm done. My mouth gapes when my cries of ecstasy take over. Despite my best efforts, I fall on my heels, my fingers in my panties, eyes on him now jerking off to me, going for my face. This is not what I had in mind, but it's hot as hell. His whole body is taut for me, his eyelids hooded, as he aims for my open mouth, then my tits. "Fuck, Kiara." He's shaking too but keeps it together, emptying himself on me. As my orgasm fades, I lift off and take him in my mouth, sucking him dry.

"Oh," he moans, then hisses. "Jesus, woman, you weren't kidding."

After we shower, I insist on making coffee and we cuddle in bed. "There's something I wanna show you before you start your day," Colton says. He reaches inside his nightstand and hands me a folded paper.

"An invoice for... a new transmission?"

He snaps the paper and turns it around. "Wrong side," he grunts.

I frown and sit up. "What—what is this?" There are lines scribbled haphazardly. I can make out the word *reading*.

"Proof. You wanted proof it wasn't really Luke talking during the first phone call, but me through him. Emma found this when doing the books."

I squint, focusing.

I'm ready to meet someone who's not like anyone else. Someone real, honest, no bullshit. That's what your profile said to me between the lines, and your voice between the words, and your answers to my questions.

There's more, but I'm getting too emotional picturing Colton scribbling these words as a last lifeline to our romantic relationship. My heart swells as I fold the paper preciously. I'll read it later. Eyes misty, I curl in Colton's embrace.

"Are you down for going to the garage now?" he asks me. "There's something I need to show you," he says as he gets dressed.

"Yes! I want to see the barn again and start getting organized. Take measurements, make a list of priorities. An open house! I want to schedule an open house. It's the best way to keep everyone motivated and on track. D'you have the list of everyone who worked on that? I need to send thank-you baskets, and coupons, and—"

"Sweets, relax."

Relax? "But, Colton, this is huge! Huge! You have no idea how-how-how *overwhelmed* and ecstatic I am." While I'm talking non-stop, I slip into a pair of jeans and the cami and thermal Cassandra gave me. I pick up my shoes, then drop them to cradle Colton's face and kiss him. "You know what you did for me, but you have no idea how—"

He chuckles. "Okay, sweets, I think I get it. But there's something I need to show you inside the garage, and I want to go now before the workday starts. I need some privacy for that."

"Oooh. You wanna do it in your truck?" I joke.

"Better'n that." He takes my hand, then drives us to the garage.

We enter through the reception area, then Colton grabs a flashlight and guides me through the dark bays. "Watch it," he says as we round a car with its hood open.

"Might wanna think about getting electricity in here," I quip. My eyes are getting accustomed to the dark, the glint of metal tools and the smell of oil feeling oddly familiar. I like being in Colton's workspace.

"Let there be light," he says as we reach the third bay and he turns the overhead lights on. The most adorable pink van, barely bigger than the VW minibus, glimmers in the sudden light, so precious in its dark surroundings. Colton takes my hand and walks me to it, then turns on bright lights that make that little jewel shine even brighter.

Speaking of jewel... The side has a logo that makes me gasp.

It's the cutest cartoonish representation of a wedding cake on legs, wearing heels, with the diamond of a wedding band sparkling at the top.

All around are cutesy cursive letters. The bottom says Sweetness Delivered. That's enough to make me literally sway.

But it's the two words at the top that make my blood thrum.

Kiara *Harper*.

Colton's hand falls on my shoulder, bringing me to him. He says nothing as we both look at the delivery van painted in my colors with legs that are probably supposed to represent me (they do, after all, feature fishnet stockings). The wedding cake is teetering, my legs unstable on high heels, puffs of snow completing the picture. The throwback to the day my car wouldn't start and I hauled my pastries into Colton's car is clear.

Except there's a diamond ring shining bright on top of the cake.

And at the top, my first name and his last name.

My throat tight, I ask, "Is that the day you fell for me?"

He wraps both his arms around me. "No. It's the day I realized I'd loved you all along."

Before I can answer he's on one knee in front of me, the keychain dangling in his fingers.

"Sweets, I was gonna prepare a whole speech, and maybe do something a little more organized around this moment, but then this morning you started talking about changing your name. Meanwhile I'm thinking, Kiara Harper has a nice *ring* to it. Don't ya think?"

Tears start pooling in my eyes. "Yes, it has a very nice ring to it."

He lifts the keychain to me, and I glance toward the van, a smile stretching my mouth. My fantasy vehicle, a ring painted on it, and my new name? "Colt, that's the most awesome proposal," I say, drawing him up to me.

"You like it?"

"I love you."

"Yes, but do you like the van?"

"I love it!"

He slides the side door open, revealing the interior setup, then hands me the keys. "Four-wheel drive, studded tires for now, new suspension, new brakes... new almost everything. Refrigeration. It's got everything."

I shove the keys in my pocket and pull him in for a deep kiss.

"Sweets," he says when we come up for air.

"Mmh?"

"Show me the keys."

I take them out of my pocket and let them dangle off my finger.

"I almost forgot," he says, snatching them from me. The keychain jingles as he arranges it, until a solitaire shows between his fingers.

It's the same ring as the one painted on the van.

My voice is tight, but I let the tears fall freely, just as I let Colton shower me with his love. "Colt, you didn't have to."

"No, I didn't. But I wanted to."

Thank you for reading Friends Don't Kiss! Your support is essential to the success of indie authors starting out. Please remember to post your review on Goodreads as soon as possible, and on Amazon and other platforms as early as April 30.

And if you loved the book, please spread the word on your social media of choice!

Thank you again so much.

Bella Rivers

Epilogue

"**S**weetness, come here." Colton doesn't wait for me to move, probably doesn't expect me to. In a few long strides, he's at my back, his arms encircling me.

"You done with work?" I ask as I place one last silver pearl on the wedding cake.

Our wedding cake.

His cheek caresses my temple and he takes a deep breath. "Done for today, and so are you. Done for the next couple of weeks." Our wedding is tomorrow, and we're flying to Paris the following day for our honeymoon. "I don't think you can make that cake any more beautiful, Sweets."

It stands on the prep table that's under the large window facing the valley. The landscape is lush now, full trees lining the blue ribbon of the river as it meanders lazily through the village.

Colton presses his face into my neck and takes a long inhale, then stops abruptly. "Is that...?" He steps to my side and crouches slightly. With astonishment in his tone, he asks, "Are these race cars?"

I smile. "M-hm." In the intricate details of the white cake, I carved a racetrack lacing around it. It could be mistaken for a vine or a ribbon, but up close, there are race car cutouts I shaped from white modeling chocolate. They are barely there, only for us to see.

"And the A frame!" Colton exclaims, pointing to a shape high up.

I turn the cake around for him to see the other side. He squints. "Avalanche?"

I nod. "Look at the bottom."

"Ah, man, that's me carrying you off Devil's Pass after you fell!" His eyes are misty as he scrutinizes the cake. "And that's the garage, and Sweetness Delivered!" he adds, pointing to the white-on-white shapes hidden amid the piping of simple flowers that cascade down the cake.

He turns and stands to his full height, pulling me into him. His heart beats loud and fast in his chest. "I can't believe my luck. That *you're* marrying me. So fucking talented, Sweets, and kind, and loving."

He kisses me, then steps back to look at the cake. "You sure you're gonna be okay cutting into that masterpiece?"

I lift my face to him. "I can't wait."

Colton turns me in his arms again and draws me in another long kiss. "Did I ever tell you that you give my life meaning?" he says when we come up for air.

My heart stutters. Colton's been expressing his feelings more and more—we both have. We've made the conscious decision to tell each other how we feel, and it now comes naturally to us. "Not in so many words."

"Well, you do. I used to believe my purpose on this earth was to help keep people safe as far as driving around in their cars. And that's still the case. But helping you get the life you want and deserve has topped that now."

"Colt…"

"It's true, sweets. You have something to offer the world, and I was literally put on your path to help you achieve that. End of discussion." He boops my nose right as the front door chimes despite the *Closed* sign.

"That'll be Chris and Skye," I say. "Help me with this?" I ask Colton. He's already opening the walk-in fridge, and I delicately place our wedding cake on the middle shelf.

"Aunt Kiara!" Skye screams happily as she rushes in.

A huge smile splits my face as the little girl encircles my waist in her arms. I twirl her around and pull her slightly off of me. "What did you just call me?" I say, knowing the answer.

"You're marrying Daddy's cousin which s'posedly maybe makes you only a cousin, at least that's what Caroline says, but I already call Uncle Colton uncle and Aunt Grace aunt so I can call you Aunt Kiara, right? Tech-ni-cly I should wait until tomorrow but I can't."

She has no idea how happy she's making me right now. "You absolutely can and should call me Aunt Kiara. I wouldn't want it any other way."

She sighs deeply. "I call Uncle Justin uncle but he's not a real uncle, and same for Uncle Craig and Aunt Lynn. But you're a real aunt."

I tilt my head. Actually, there is a remote connection between the Kings and Alex, but I'm not getting into the family trees right now. I'm just soaking in the happiness of making a connection with this little girl. We were both adopted by Emerald Creek in different ways, and although we've experienced that the love of a found family can run way deeper than that of your blood family, we're always looking at ways to cement these new ties. Calling someone aunt or uncle does that.

Maybe it's why it came so naturally to me to call Shannon and Dennis, Mom and Dad. That's how they feel to me, and now that I'm marrying Colton, I feel... entitled to it.

"I'm honored to call you my niece, Skye. I think it's freaking cool." She high-fives me.

"You know what else is cool?" I ask her.

"What?"

"You're free labor now," I joke.

"Nu-huh. I called dibs on that," Chris chimes in as he drops a pink backpack at our feet.

But Skye claps her hands. "I get to make cakes with you?"

I wink at her father and answer Skye , "Anytime you want, honey."

Chris chuckles. "I should go."

Alex is near her due date, and Chris's concern is clear. "How is Alex doing?"

"Feeling very big, but no contractions yet. Hopefully we make it tomorrow. You sure you're good with Skye?"

"Of course! We're doing a mini bachelorette of sorts at your sister's. It'll be fun. And then Grace will have her over for the night, right?"

Two hours later I step down from the massage table at A Touch Of Grace. All the neck and shoulder tension from working on the cake is gone. Between Colt's attentive love and the pampering, I feel like I'm walking on clouds.

The rest of the Bitch Brigade is there. Haley is pouring bubbly, Skye is admiring her manicure and getting a trim of her locks. All my female friends are there, including Alex who decided to join us for a foot massage, my soon-to-be sister in law Grace, and of course Willow.

I take her in a quick hug. "Boo, you know this wouldn't happen without you, right? I'm so stinking proud and happy to call you my friend. Never stop the crazy, m'kay?"

"Me? Not a chance," she smiles.

Willow

I couldn't have hoped for a better day for Kiara and Colton's wedding. Under baby blue skies, a slight breeze comes up from the river, cooling down the sun's warm embrace.

The wedding is taking place at the park that slopes from The Green down to the Emerald Creek, so the whole town can attend and celebrate. Ethan, Nathaniel, and Autumn directed a team of helpers to erect an arch now covered in flowers. Rows of foldable chairs delineate an aisle. Cassandra walks down it now, greeting everyone by name as she prepares to officiate the wedding.

"Alright, time to line up!" Ms. Angela says to the small group huddled in a tent. Kiara waits in her pink VW van, turned into an airconditioned bridal room by Colton and currently illegally stationed at the top of the park per Declan's orders. She's with her uncle Bill, who will walk her down the aisle, while Colton is with us in the tent, waiting to go last.

"The best man and the maid of honor first," Ms. Angela calls, and I take Chris's arm.

"Alex and Noah next." Alex stands from her chair.

"You gonna be okay, pancakes?" Chris asks her. As we turn around to check on her, my gaze involuntarily crosses Noah's, and a twinge of want pinches me. Days like this, it's hard for me to forget the crush I've held for him, even though I've long come to terms with the fact that he barely registers who I am, and if he does, I'm a hard pass.

After Alex and Noah come Grace and Ethan, followed by Chloe and Justin. The men are wearing dark suits and white shirts, the women dresses in assorted pastel shades. Kiara wanted us to choose whatever we wanted to wear, so we coordinated the colors and picked the shapes that would suit us best. Alex and I went for a mid-length wrap (light green for Alex and light blue for me), Chloe is super classy in her soft yellow A line, and Grace is radiant in a sparkly light pink full-length gown. If I may say so myself, we look spectacular without taking any attention away from Kiara.

We make our way down the grassy expanse, joy filling the air as Luke strums a mellow tune on his electric guitar and croons softly, and I quickly forget my mini heartache. But Cassandra opens the ceremony with some heartfelt words on love and commitment, and before long I'm fighting the urge to look at Noah.

Then I feel more than hear Alex stifling a gasp, and I'm brought back to more important questions. I know she doesn't want Chris to be worried and she really wants to be here. But now *I'm* worried about her. I can feel her struggle to not show her discomfort, and I'm upset at myself for believing her when she said she didn't need a chair for the ceremony.

I dash out of my station as maid of honor, nearly trip in the soft grass, grab an empty chair, and plop it behind Alex before anyone has a chance to realize what's happening.

She lets herself fall into it with a sigh of relief. Chris narrows his eyes on her, worry painted on his face. "I'm fine," she mouths and squeezes my hand as a thank-you.

Next to him, Colton wipes away a tear as Kiara says her vows in an assured voice, and I find myself tearing up too.

On Chris's other side, Noah pushes his glasses up his nose and narrows his eyes on me. I let my gaze fall down to my feet, trying not to register how good he looks in a suit.

Noah looks good in anything, my internal devil whispers, and I shut her up. *We're not doing this anymore.*

I take a deep breath as Colton says, "I do". Kiara's bottom lip trembles as she answers, and it's the most beautifully shattering thing to see—the way these two are brought to their knees for each other. Being the maid of honor is as close to a happily-ever-after as I can get, so I soak it all up as their bliss radiates into me.

Once Cassandra pronounces them husband and wife, Alex holds my hand to stand up and leans over to me. "I'm going to step ahead of you to get to the tent sooner and walk down with Chris."

"Yeah-yeah-yeah, of course," I say, taking a step back to let her in front of me as Kiara and Colton saunter away to the tune of Luke's electric guitar.

Chris wraps an arm around Alex and leans in for a kiss. "I'm fine," she assures him under her breath. "Just need a comfy seat."

"Ready?"

I whip my head around, startled by the voice at my ear. Noah is extending his arm to me. Of course he is. We swapped places in the line. Now I'm paired with him.

"Let's go!" I quip, falling into step, but avoiding his touch.

He takes my arm and laces it with his. As he sets us at a regal pace behind Chris and Alex, I try to forget his touch and focus on my friends' happiness.

Which I manage to do during cocktail hour, until dinner when Luke prompts the wedding party to join Colton and Kiara on the dance floor.

Chris declares he's staying with Alex, Justin dances with Chloe, Ethan with Grace, and I'm left staring across the table at Noah.

He's frowning, looking at his phone, then looks across the room to his siblings, having fun at another table. Something passes through his gaze, and in an instant I feel selfish for only thinking about the silly little feelings I've had for him when he's dealing with a lot at home.

But I'm already up and standing in front of him, so when he looks up at me, I say, "We don't have to do this."

"Do what?" he asks, looking genuinely puzzled. Then he glances beyond me to our friends dancing around the newlyweds. "Oh, sorry." He springs to his feet and once on the dance floor, takes me in a firm hold, his gaze not exactly on my eyes but not exactly off me either.

"Everything okay?" I ask.

Framed by those familiar glasses, his gaze registers surprise as it falls on me, stirring something deeply nostalgic inside me. "You notice everything, don't you?" he asks.

I'm not sure what he means by that, and I sure as hell am not having a conversation with Noah while dancing with him. This would require eye contact and other dangerous things. I need to snap out of the feeling of Noah's arms, his inebriating scent, and the burn of his gaze.

So I just shrug lightly at his question and focus my attention on the married couple looking at each other, then let my gaze drift to the wedding cake while Noah sways us to the music. It's displayed in a corner of the dance floor, on a rotating table that Lucas made especially, as a surprise. I'll have to check it out later, as Kiara insisted on making it entirely on her own.

"Everything good with you?" Noah asks, without having answered my question.

Well, let's see. Mom's cancer is back, the insurance is denying her claims, and I'm considering moving back in with her so she'd accept money disguised as rent. "Everything good," I lie, looking him in the eye, my mouth tight in a fake smile.

He frowns slightly. "That's good to hear."

I try to pull my gaze from his, but I feel tethered to him. Pretty sure there's something he wants to say but doesn't know how to. So I jump in. "Anything I can help with?"

"Maybe," he answers right away.

My stupid heart babooms. "What is it?"

He looks around and leans dangerously close to me. "I can't tell you here."

I giggle. "Is it illegal?"

He tilts his head. "Some people might object to it."

That can't be. Noah is a color-inside-the-lines person. A rule stickler. Hell, he's a rule setter. Now I'm definitely hooked. "Then I'm your girl," I say a little too fast.

He twirls me in an underarm pass. "You should wait until you know what it is," he says as he brings me back into his fold.

"I trust you," I answer. "Besides, how bad can it be?"

Famous last words.

Willow and Noah's story is coming next in How To Fake A Husband!

Didn't get enough of Colton and Kiara? As a thank your for signing up to Bella's newsletter, click here for an extra chapter, type www.bellarivers.com/bsfdk, or scan:

About the author

Bella Rivers writes steamy small town romances with a guaranteed happily ever after, and themes of found family and forgiveness. Expect hot scenes, fierce love, and strong language!

A hopeless romantic, Bella is living her own second chance romance in the rolling hills of Vermont. When she's not telling the stories of the characters populating her dreams, you can find her baking, hiking, skiing, or just hanging around her small town to soak in the happiness.

Her newsletter is where Bella shares progress on her writing as well as sneak peeks into upcoming books, the occasional recipe from her characters, and books from other writers she thinks her readers might like. Subscribe from her website, www.bellarivers.com.

The Emerald Creek series includes:

One Night in Emerald Creek, a novella (Thalia and Lucas)

Never Let You Go, a single dad, small town romance (Alex and Chris)

The Promise Of You, a one night stand, enemies-to-lovers, small town romance (Chloe and Justin)

Return to You, a second chance, small town romance (Grace and Ethan)

Friends Don't Kiss, a fake dating, friends-to-lovers, small town romance (Kiara and Colton)

How To Fake A Husband, a fake marriage, small town romance (Willow and Noah)

Acknowledgements

I have said it for my previous books, and I will say it again here: this book would not be what it is without the skilled guidance of my wonderful editor, Angela James. Thank you for helping me bring this story to life, for seeing its strengths and weaknesses in its early stages, and for cheering me on when I needed it the most.

Teresa Beeman, thank you for your precious time, eagle eye, and thoughtful comments. You take the stress out of the releases!

My heartfelt thanks, as always, to the indie writing community for your friendship and support. You make the writer life much less lonely!

And to my husband, that you for your patience with me as, book after book, you navigate the highs and lows of my inspiration, self-doubt, creativity and never-ending questioning. Extra kudos to you for your commitment to discovering the romance genre and your passion in chasing errors and typos in my work. With you by my side, I don't need a book boyfriend!

Printed in Dunstable, United Kingdom